HEXED

ILONA ANDREWS

YASMINE GALENORN

ALLYSON JAMES

JEANNE C. STEIN

BERKLEY BOOKS, NEW YORK

THE BERKLEY PUBLISHING GROUP
Published by the Penguin Group
Penguin Group (USA) Inc.
375 Hudson Street, New York, New York 10014, USA

Penguin Group (Canada), 90 Eglinton Avenue East, Suite 700, Toronto, Ontario M4P 2Y3, Canada
(a division of Pearson Penguin Canada Inc.)
Penguin Books Ltd., 80 Strand, London WC2R 0RL, England
Penguin Group Ireland, 25 St. Stephen's Green, Dublin 2, Ireland (a division of Penguin Books Ltd.)
Penguin Group (Australia), 250 Camberwell Road, Camberwell, Victoria 3124, Australia
(a division of Pearson Australia Group Pty. Ltd.)
Penguin Books India Pvt. Ltd., 11 Community Centre, Panchsheel Park, New Delhi—110 017, India
Penguin Group (NZ), 67 Apollo Drive, Rosedale, Auckland 0632, New Zealand
(a division of Pearson New Zealand Ltd.)
Penguin Books (South Africa) (Pty.) Ltd., 24 Sturdee Avenue, Rosebank, Johannesburg 2196,
South Africa

Penguin Books Ltd., Registered Offices: 80 Strand, London WC2R 0RL, England

HEXED

A Berkley Book / published by arrangement with the authors

PRINTING HISTORY
Berkley mass-market edition / June 2011

Copyright © 2011 by Penguin Group (USA) Inc.
"Magic Dreams" by Ilona Andrews copyright © 2011 by Andrew Gordon and Ilona Gordon.
"Ice Shards" by Yasmine Galenorn copyright © 2011 by Yasmine Galenorn.
"Double Hexed" by Allyson James copyright © 2011 by Jennifer Ashley.
"Blood Debt" by Jeanne C. Stein copyright © 2011 by Jeanne C. Stein.
Cover art by Tony Mauro. Cover design by George Long.
Interior text design by Kristin del Rosario.

ISBN: 978-0-425-24176-9

BERKLEY®
Berkley Books are published by The Berkley Publishing Group,
a division of Penguin Group (USA) Inc.,
375 Hudson Street, New York, New York 10014.
BERKLEY® is a registered trademark of Penguin Group (USA) Inc.
The "B" design is a trademark of Penguin Group (USA) Inc.

PRINTED IN THE UNITED STATES OF AMERICA

10 9 8 7 6 5 4 3 2 1

CONTENTS

MAGIC DREAMS

Ilona Andrews

1

ICE SHARDS

Yasmine Galenorn

69

DOUBLE HEXED

Allyson James

157

BLOOD DEBT

Jeanne C. Stein

249

MAGIC DREAMS

ILONA ANDREWS

I PEERED THROUGH THE WINDSHIELD OF MY '93 Mustang. The Buzzard Highway stretched before me, a narrow line of crumbling pavement vanishing into the dusk. Below it ran the Scratches, a twisted labyrinth of narrow ravines gouged out of the ground by magic three decades ago, when our world began to end. The old road skimmed the top of the ravines, rolling far into the distance, where the sunset glowed gold, red, and finally turquoise. There was something vaguely wrong with this picture, but I couldn't put my finger on it.

The Buzzard Highway took no prisoners. Step too hard on the accelerator, turn the wheel half an inch too far, and *Boom! Pow!* Fiery crash! To the bottom of the ravine you went. Only Atlanta's best and craziest raced here.

That's why I liked it. When a girl weighs a hundred pounds soaking wet, her glasses are thicker than Sherlock Holmes's loupe, and everybody under the sun makes fun of her because she's a vegetarian and blood makes her vomit, she has to do *something* to prove that she isn't a wimp. The wild, deafening chaos of the Friday night Buzzard race was a strictly no-wimps-allowed kind of fun.

It was so peaceful now. So quiet. Just me and the Mustang. I had named it Rambo. It was a sweet car, built from the ground up for one purpose: to go fast. We understood each other, Rambo and I. Rambo liked to kick ass, and I made sure it had a chance to show off.

My body was so light. It was an odd feeling, almost like I was swimming or floating through some feathery cloud.

A familiar face appeared in the windshield: pale skin, dark eyes, the long tattoo of a dragon wrapped around his neck, snaking its way down under the blue tank top. Kasen. Decent enough guy as wererats went. He operated a tow truck and liked to hang out and watch the races at Buzzard Highway. They were good for his business.

Kasen's lips moved, but no sound came out. He looked kind of funny there, sideways, flapping his lips in silence. What is it you want, silly person?

Kasen was *sideways*.

The sunset behind him was sideways, too, the highway running to the left of the sky.

Oh crap.

Crap, crap, crap.

The phantom cotton clogging my ears vanished and the world rushed at me in an explosion of sound: the distant roar of car engines, the groaning of metal, and Kasen's voice.

"Dali? You okay, baby girl?"

I tried to talk and my mouth worked. "Cool like a cucumber."

He grinned. "You know the drill. Hold on, I'm gonna set you upright."

I clamped the edges of my seat.

Kasen stepped out of my view, and I could hear him grunt as he grabbed hold of the bumper, lifted, and twisted. Rambo screeched. Metal clanged. I winced. Rambo, you poor baby.

The sunset turned and dropped into its rightful place with a shudder. Rambo's tires hit the pavement and bounced once. The left lens of my glasses popped out of the frame and plunked onto my lap. I swiped it off my jeans, squeezed my left eye shut, and climbed out of the car.

"I flipped!"

"You flipped."

Hot damn! Rambo's front end looked like a crushed Coke

can. Water soaked the asphalt, leaking from the hood—the enchanted water tank that let the car run during magic waves had ruptured. I must've taken the turn too fast.

Warm wind fanned me. Technically it was the middle of January, but after two and a half months of severe freezes and snowfall, the weather got confused. For the past week the temperatures held in the eighties, all the snow had melted, and I had traded my thick winter coats for jeans and a T-shirt. You'd think it was May. Magic did odd things to climate. Today it was warm. Tomorrow we could wake up to a foot of snow on the ground.

Kasen peered at me. "Why is your eye closed? Did you hurt yourself?"

"No, it's closed because my glasses are broken, and looking through one lens makes me dizzy."

"Situation normal, all fucked-up." Kasen rubbed the back of his head.

Thank you, Captain Obvious. "It's not that bad!"

"You want Rambo towed to the usual place?"

"Yeah." My races would be canceled for a month. Bummer.

Kasen nodded at the Mustang. "That's your second crash in three weeks."

"Aha."

"Didn't Jim forbid you to race?"

Jim was my alpha. The shapeshifter Pack was segregated into seven clans, by the family of the animal, and Jim headed Felidae with a big Jaguar paw hiding awesome claws. He was smart, and strong, and incredibly hot—and the only time Jim noticed my existence was when I made myself into a pain in the ass or when he needed an expert on the ancient Far East. Otherwise, I might just as well have been invisible.

I raised my head to let Kasen know I meant business. "Jim isn't the boss of me."

"Actually yes, yes he is."

It's good that I wasn't a wereporcupine, or his mouth would be full of quills. "Are you going to snitch on me?"

"That depends. When you die, can I have your car?"

"No."

Kasen sighed. "I'm trying to make a point here. I've been watching this race for six years now and I've never seen anyone crash as much as you. You're my number-one customer. You can barely see, Dali, and you take stupid chances. No offense."

No offense, right. "No offense" stood for "I'm going to insult you, but you can't be mad at me." I bared my teeth at him. When it came down to it, he was a rat and I was a tiger.

Kasen raised his hands up. "Fine. Forget I said anything."

The world blinked. The colors turned slightly brighter, the scents grew sharper, as if someone had dialed the picture's resolution up a notch. A welcome warmth spread through my body—a magic wave had flooded the world. The distant roar of the gasoline engines choked and died. It would take fifteen minutes of chanting to get the enchanted engines to start. The race was dead.

"What if I take you to dinner?" Kasen said. "I know this really nice place down on Manticore . . ."

Wererats always knew this nice place to eat. They munched constantly or they went twitchy, meaning they suffered attacks of hypoglycemia: cold sweat, headaches, and convulsions, accompanied by nervousness and bouts of aggression. Not fun.

I squinted my open eye at Kasen. There was no reason for him to offer me dinner. Most likely, he just wanted to butter me up so he could get a shot at Rambo after my demise. Too bad for him—I might not have been the strongest weretiger or the most bloodthirsty, but my bloodline was pretty damn old. Lyc-V, the shapeshifter virus, and my family were good friends, and the levels of virus in my body ran higher than they did in most shapeshifters. The higher the concentration of the virus, the faster the regeneration. Normally higher levels of Lyc-V also meant a greater risk of losing your mind and turning into a crazed loup killer, but so far I hadn't had to worry about that.

I was hard to kill. Nothing short of a fiery crash complete with a giant explosion at the end would send me into the afterlife, so if Kasen was hoping to inherit my car, he would get a smoking wreck for his trouble.

I wrinkled my nose at Kasen. "Thanks, but no thanks. I need to get home." And get my spare glasses out of Pooki's glove compartment.

He heaved a sigh. "Maybe next time."

"Sure. Maybe next time."

* * *

I DROVE THROUGH the tangled streets of Atlanta with the windows down. The wind swirled with scents: a hint of wood fire, a dog marking his territory, horses, one, two, three, four, something tart and spicy . . . The streets were deserted. Most people hid at night. The dark was when the monsters came out to play. Even nice monsters like me. Rawr.

The magic flowed full force, and Pooki, my Plymouth Prowler, made enough noise to shake the gods in their celestial palace. I'd modified him to run on gasoline when the tech was up and on enchanted water when the magic was running the show. Pooki didn't go very fast during magic waves, and he was so loud he made me wince even with the earplugs, but that was the best I could do.

About three decades ago, Atlanta was the happening place in the South: all skyscrapers, trendy restaurants, and modern conveniences. Tons of money and people moved through the city. And then the first magic wave hit. Magic ripped through the world. For three days it raged, making complicated technological marvels fail. Planes dropped out of the sky. Satellites plummeted to the ground. Guns jammed or misfired. Electricity vanished and the cities went dark. Three days later, technology returned, but the world was never the same.

People said the magic came out of nowhere, but my grandmother told me she felt it building for years. It made total sense, considering the historical pattern of the First Shift, the one that was lost in antiquity. Approximately six thousand years ago, *Homo sapiens* had built a great civilization based solely on magic. It generated so much magic that the balance between technology and magic was permanently disrupted. The world seesawed way over to the technology side to compensate. The ancient civilization suffered an apocalypse, and the human race began rebuilding, this time using technology as its base. Of course, they created a civilization so technologically advanced that the seesaw shifted once again. The magic had to come back and crashed the party. Now it flooded the world in waves, one moment here, eating tall buildings, fueling spells, permitting manifestations, and the next gone. Apocalypse in slow motion.

It just goes to show that no matter how great a nail you give humanity, we'll manage to hammer it into the ground crooked. We suck. It's the nature of our species.

My house sat in a large wooded lot, all by its lonesome. The street to the left led to a ruined apartment building, now little more than a heap of rubble, and the neighbors to the back of me had fled the city a long time ago. I bought their land for a grand before they took off, busted the house up, hired contractors to build me an extra-tall privacy fence, and now I had an awesome backyard. With the trees and the fence, I could even go out in my natural form, roll around in the grass, and nap in the sun without anybody pointing and yelling, "Hey, look, a white tiger!"

I maneuvered Pooki into my driveway, got out, raised the garage door, and carefully eased the vehicle inside. Of all the cars I ever had, the Prowler was my favorite. I loved the Indy-style wheels. That's why I never raced it. As much as I hated to admit it, Kasen was right—I wrecked. A lot.

I lowered the garage door and stepped into my kitchen. A scent floated past me on the draft. I inhaled it and froze. It smelled of sandalwood and amber, spiced with a hint of tangy sweat and male musk. A shiver dashed down my spine, setting every nerve on high alert.

Jim.

The masculine fragrance filled my house, screaming, "Mate!" at me so loudly that I held my breath for a second to get a grip.

Jim was here, waiting for me. In my wildest dreams, I would walk into the room and he would kiss me. The picture was so vivid in my head, I shivered. It would never happen. *Come on, ugly blind girl, snap out of it. Let's try to be less pathetic.* Jim was here because Kasen snitched on me, or because he needed some obscure scroll identified. He wasn't here to make my sad little dreams come true.

I marched into my living room. "Jim?"

No answer.

The scent was hot and alive. He was still here, or he had been here just a second ago.

"Jim? It's not funny."

Nothing.

Fine. I followed the scent, moving softly on my toes. Living room, hallway, bathroom, bedroom. The scent sparked here. He was in my bedroom.

Oh my gods. What if I walked in and he was naked on my bed?

I would lose it. I would lose it right there and never get it back, whatever "it" was.

Get a grip, get a grip, get a grip. I padded into the bedroom.

Jim slumped against the wall on the floor. His eyes were closed. He wore black jeans and a black turtleneck, a couple of shades darker than his skin. His black hair was cut short. His leather jacket lay on the floor in a heap. Asleep.

I tiptoed into the room and crouched by him.

He looked so peaceful here. Usually Jim scowled, just to remind people that he was Serious and Important and would Kick Your Ass if Necessary. But right now, with his head tilted back and his face relaxed, he was beautiful. I wanted to sit on the floor next to him and snuggle up into the crook of his arm. It looked like the perfect spot for me. Instead, I sighed and touched his forehead with my finger. "Hey, you. Wake up."

He didn't move.

Odd. Usually Jim woke up if a pin dropped half a mile away. Most shapeshifters did, but Jim especially. He oversaw security for the Pack and he exhibited paranoid tendencies. The only time he would pass out like this was when he was injured or exhausted from changing too many times and Lyc-V shut his brain down to conserve resources and make repairs. I smelled no blood and Jim's clothes were still on. But if he had passed out after shifting, he'd be on my floor . . . naked. I closed my eyes and gave myself a mental shake.

Something was wrong.

I grabbed his shoulder and shook him. "Jim! Wake up. Wake. Up."

His eyes snapped open. His dark hand grabbed my wrist. "Was I asleep?"

"Yes."

"Fuck."

He surged off the floor, dark eyes pissed off. "You were gone. Dali Harimau, where were you?"

I stood up and crossed my arms over my chest. It wasn't much of a chest, so crossing my arms was easy. "I was out.

You're not my daddy, Jim. I don't have to check in with you before I leave my house."

A green sheen rolled over Jim's eyes. "Dali, where were you?"

He had pulled the alpha card. You didn't argue when his eyes lit up. "I was racing on Buzzard. There. Happy now?"

He exhaled. "Good."

Good? Since when was my racing good? "You're not making any sense."

"You didn't check your messages?"

"No, I just got home."

"So you didn't go to the house?"

"What house? I told you I just got home."

Jim's eyes dimmed. He rubbed his face with his hand, as if trying to wipe something off. "I need your help."

JIM SAT IN my kitchen, staring at a cup of hot ginseng tea like a demon was hiding inside.

"Drink it. It's good for you."

Jim gulped it down. "It tastes awful."

If I were a guest and turned up my nose like that at the tea my hostess served me, my mother would tell me I had shamed the family. "It's as though you have no manners. I offer you a gift of tea and you make funny faces at it."

"Do you want me to lie and tell you it tastes great?"

"No, I want you to say 'thank you' and tell me what's going on."

"I'm not sure." Jim's face was grim. "The northeastern office on Dunwoody Road didn't report in on Tuesday. I was out doing other things, so Johanna waited twenty-four hours and sent a scout in to check on them. He came back disturbed. I talked to him this morning. He claimed 'something bad' was in the building and he wasn't going near it."

"Who was it?"

"Garrett."

Garrett was lazy, but he wasn't a coward. Maybe there was something bad in the house. "You went there yourself, didn't you?"

Jim shrugged. "I had to go that way for an errand anyway."

I rolled my eyes. "You didn't take anybody with you?"

He looked at me like I had insulted him. Mr. Badass didn't need anybody to go with him, oh no.

"What happened?"

"I went to the office. The place looked empty. The windows were covered with dirt, like nobody had been there for years."

Jim and I looked at each other. The Pack had seven offices in Atlanta and the surrounding area and every single one of those would have clean windows. Normal people looked at us like we were filthy animals. The animal part was true, but most of us were sensitive about the filthy part. If you wanted to insult a shapeshifter, you told him he stank. We kept ourselves and our offices clean. Besides, you can't see angry mobs with pitchforks and torches coming at you through a dirty window.

"I went up to the door." Jim looked at his cup. "The place smelled wrong. A weird scent, dusty, pungent, and bitter, not something I've ever come across before."

"Like herb dust?"

"No, that wasn't it. Not anything I recognized. And it was too quiet. There should've been four people at the office. Not a damn whisper, no sigh, no sound, nothing."

Roger worked at that office. And Michelle. I liked Michelle; she was nice.

"I opened the door and smelled blood. The place was empty. There was a symbol on the floor in magic marker."

"What kind of a symbol?"

He shook his head. His eyes turned distant. If I didn't know better, I'd say he was confused, except Jim didn't get confused.

"A Chinese symbol," he said slowly.

"Like a sinograph? Hanzi?"

Jim gave me a blank look.

"Did it look like Chinese writing, Jim?"

"Yes."

I got up and brought him a piece of paper and a pen. "Draw it for me."

He picked up the pen and looked at it.

"Jim?"

He growled under his breath. "I can't remember."

The hair on the back of my neck rose. Jim didn't have perfect recall, but he was very close. He practiced, because remembering details was a useful skill for the chief of security. I once watched him draw a complicated tribal tattoo he saw for two seconds completely from memory. He got it nearly perfect. A hanzi character on the floor in the middle of an office smelling of blood—he should've remembered it. The symbols weren't that complicated. Something had fried his memory.

"What was next?"

"I called you."

We both looked at my answering machine. The screen was dead—the magic had taken down the electricity. No way to tell if Jim had called me.

A green glow sparked in his irises and vanished. Frustration rolled off Jim in a hot wave. He was acting like a person with a concussion, but Lyc-V cracked concussions like nuts. I ought to know, I had gotten enough of them. Thirty seconds, and your brain was like new. Still . . .

"Do you think someone might have whacked you on the back of the head?"

Jim looked at me for a long moment.

"Sometimes trauma to the head results in short-term memory loss."

"Nobody traumatized my head. Nobody quiet enough to sneak up on me would be strong enough to knock me out. I wasn't knocked out, I passed out."

Huh. "Passed out?"

"Yes."

"What do you remember before passing out?"

"The magic wave hit. I saw a woman."

"A woman?" Great, now I've turned into a manga character who repeated everything everyone said.

"I saw her in the house."

"What did she look like?"

"She was very beautiful."

It stung like a slap. "Jim!"

"What?"

Yes, what, Dali? What exactly? "When did you see her? What was she wearing? Concentrate."

He shook his head. "I was in the doorway. I looked up and

she was standing at the back of the room. She was wearing some sort of a long robe or gown. The fabric was almost transparent, like a negligee."

And he probably took a second to look at her boobies. Awesome.

"She had long dark hair. I told her to come outside. She said, 'Help me.'"

"In English?"

He nodded. "She started backing up into the house and I went after her."

"Four shapeshifters are missing, the office smells like blood, you see some weird woman in a transparent gown who clearly shouldn't be in the building, and you run after her?"

"It's my job to run after her."

"Without backup?"

"I *am* the backup."

I waved my arms. "Fine, what happened next?"

"I remember my legs getting heavy and thinking that something was wrong. Then I woke up in the middle of the floor."

"How long did you sleep?"

"Eighteen minutes. I woke up tired as hell. I knew I'd pass out again if I didn't leave, so I got up, locked the door, and got the hell out of there. I knew I'd called you and I thought you might go to the house. The magic was up, so I ran over here, got inside with my key, but you were gone. I went to the bedroom to see if your calligraphy kit was still here, because I knew you would've taken it, and then I don't remember."

And then he'd fallen asleep on my bedroom floor. "Do you feel any different?"

"I feel tired."

"Right now? Even after sleeping?"

He nodded.

Jim could go forty-eight hours without sleep and still be as sharp as his claws. That was one of the fun gifts of Lyc-V: improved stamina, immunity to diseases—and crazy homicidal rage, just to spice things up. Something was seriously wrong. If it had been a typical curse, my magic would've purged it by now. He had to go to the medic. "We need to see Doolittle."

"No. No Doolittle."

"Jim, you keep falling asleep."

"Doolittle is a surgeon." Jim bared the edges of his teeth. "If he can't cut it out or stitch it back together, he doesn't know what to do with it. I have no symptoms. Pulse rate is normal, temperature is normal. I just fall asleep. You're Doolittle. I come to you with this story. What's your first move?"

"Lock you up for observation."

"Exactly. I don't need to be locked up."

"How do you know something isn't interfering with your regeneration?"

Jim pulled a knife from his waist sheath so fast I barely saw it. The bluish metal flashed, slicing across his forearm. Blood swelled. The scent hit my nostrils, sending goose bumps over my arms. As I watched, the cut knitted itself back together, the skin and muscle flowing to repair the damage. Jim wiped the blood from his skin and showed me his forearm. The thin line of the scar was already fading.

"I'm not sick and my virus is working. Whatever this is, it's magic. Four of our people are missing, and you're the only magic user I have. I can't just leave them in there."

"They might be dead."

"If they're dead, we need to know." He leaned forward, his brown eyes looking straight into mine. "Help me, Dali."

He had no idea, but when he looked at me like that, I would've done anything for him. Anything at all.

I got up. "Let me get my kit. We need to go see that house."

THE NORTHEASTERN OFFICE of the Pack sat on Chamblee Dunwoody Road, well back from the road behind a carefully cut lawn. Tall pines framed it on three sides, with four picturesque trees shading its parking lot. To the right, another copse of pines bordered a large open field converted into pasture. To the left, behind the buffer of greenery and a chain-link fence topped with coils of razor wire, rose short stubby apartments. The guard at the gate gave us a nasty look as we thundered on by and clutched at his crossbow just in case. Silly man.

I steered the Prowler up the curving drive to the office's lot, parked, and shut off the vehicle. The enchanted water engine took at least fifteen minutes to warm up, but leaving it running made no sense. The engine made so much noise I had trouble thinking. Besides, Pooki's top speed during magic barely scraped fifty miles per hour, and if we had to bail, both Jim and I could run much faster than that.

We stepped out into the night. Painted an ugly olive color, the office looked like two separate buildings had been jammed together: The left half resembled a ranch house while the right was a two-story Queen Anne with green shutters.

The wind brought with it a salty metallic scent that burned my tongue. Blood. Jim bared his teeth at the building.

I closed my eyes and concentrated, trying to sense the magic. In my head, the house turned dark. Long translucent tentacles of magic slivered from inside it, sliding back and forth over the walls, out the windows, over the roof, clutching at the siding and tiles.

I pushed a tiny step farther. The closest tentacle rose, hovered above the roof for a long moment, and snaked over to us. Magic lashed at me in an icy wave, fetid, terrible magic. I didn't know what it was, but every cell in my body shrank from it. My eyes snapped open and I jerked back.

Jim caught me from behind. "What is it?"

The house looked mundane again, just a drab olive building. I swallowed. "We're going to need protection. Lots of protection."

I set my wooden box on Pooki's hood and flipped it open. Jim peered at the calligraphy set inside. Most shapeshifters didn't do magic, because we were magic enough as it was, and most didn't trust magic. I totally understood why. Magic was iffy, but claws and fangs produced the same result every time. However, I was born to a long line of magic users, so concerned with tradition that they passed on their knowledge and rituals even when technology was at its strongest and almost no evidence of magic remained. My family took my education very seriously.

Half of the time my magic didn't even work, but Jim had seen me pull it off once or twice. It's not that he was impressed—he was far too cool for that—but Jim treated my talent with respect. He was in trouble and he trusted me to get him out of it. I had to step it up.

Jim nodded at the house. A pale yellow light appeared in one of the upper-floor windows, as if someone held a candle up to the glass.

"Isn't it cute," I murmured. "It's saying hello."

Jim smiled at the light. The only time a jaguar showed you his teeth was when he was about to sink them into you.

I pulled two thin strips of *hanshi* paper out, dipped my brush into the ink, and wrote the string of characters for general protection on each piece.

The ink shimmered a little in the moonlight. I held my breath.

Please work. Please, please, please work.

The magic snapped, sparking through the paper. I exhaled and tossed one strip at Jim. The paper sliced through the air, stiff like a blade, and stuck to his chest. He stared at it.

"Don't mess with it. It's a defensive spell." I tossed the other piece of paper in the air, stepped toward it, and it adhered to me, over my left breast. "Let's go."

Jim pondered the little piece of paper. "You want me to go back into that house protected by a magic sticky note?"

"Don't even start," I told him. "It's working. If it weren't working, you couldn't drag me into that place."

"What did you write on here? 'Don't die'?"

"No, I wrote, 'Don't be an a-hole!' " I headed for the house.

"On yours or mine?"

"On yours."

"Well, in that case, your magic isn't working. I'm still an asshole."

Grr, grr, grr.

Twenty feet to the house. A shiver shook me and I clenched my teeth. You can do it, White Tiger. Don't be a wuss.

Fifteen feet. I could see it now, the translucent mess of sliding tendrils, ready to grab us, like a nest of colossal dark snakes about to strike. The bad magic would hit us any second.

Ten feet. The tentacles rose as one.

Screw it. I reached over and grabbed Jim's hand. His fingers closed on mine, warm and strong.

The magic shot toward us. I clenched Jim's hand. The paper on my chest sparked with pale blue and the tentacles fell away, as if singed by fire.

Oh gods. Oh phew. My heart pounded in my chest at about a million beats per minute. Pheeeww. Okay, alive. Alive is good.

I realized I was still clutching Jim's hand like a moron and let go. He was looking at me. "Is everything cool?"

"Mhm." I nodded, my voice a little too high. "Everything is great. Let's go."

We walked between the tendrils of magic to the door. A long scrape marked the dark green paint, exposing steel underneath. I could tell by Jim's face that he didn't remember it. We both leaned close and sniffed.

Smelled like paint.

Jim tried the handle. It clicked under the pressure of his thumb. The door swung open slowly, revealing a gloomy large room, as if the house had yawned and we were staring straight into its maw.

He said he had left the door locked and I knew he would have.

Jim stepped through the doorway and I followed him.

The inside of the house smelled wrong: hot and sharp with an undercoating of dust, like rusty iron scrap left to bake in the sun. Through it floated the stench of burned coffee and a faint scent of blood, fouled with a hint of decomposition. The blood was old, at least twelve hours, probably more.

The front of the room lay empty. Ahead, a large counter cut the room nearly in a half. To the right, a small stove supported a teakettle and a coffeepot. Gloom pooled in the corners, and if I squinted just right, I could see the faint tentacles of magic snaking their way in and out of the walls.

Jim skewed his face in a silent growl, stalked over to the counter, and leapt on it, landing with easy grace. He did it in absolute silence.

Wow.

I would've given anything to be able to match him, to be

sleek and elegant, like a supple phantom. But no, even in my
animal form, I was a klutz. The change dazed me and it took
me about two minutes to figure out where I was or why. It took
Jim about two seconds to kill something. If we both shifted in
the middle of a room full of ninjas, by the time I could see
straight, they would all be dead and Jim would be wiping
blood from his hands.

All my life I was told I was special, the mystical white
tiger. Guardian of the West, King of Beasts, Lord of Mountains, Slayer of Demons. Majestic of bearing and fierce in
battle. The irony was thick enough to swim through.

Jim pointed at the floor. I looked down. Gashes scored the
wood, digging deep into the floorboards. Something had
clawed the floor, something large and powerful. Here and there
small sections of black marker lines peeked from under the
scratches, but no force on earth could decipher what had been
written there.

I glanced at Jim and shook my head. He jumped down and
I followed him deeper into the house. We passed a small file
room on the right, separated from the counter by a partition. If
people had died here, something must've taken their bodies.

The doorway to the stairs waited, a darker rectangle in the
dark wall. I took a step forward. Magic washed over me, bad,
terrible magic, smelling of death and blood and corpses, as if
someone had taken a piece of ice and dragged it from the base
of my neck all the way down my spine. The paper on my chest
shivered. I froze, trying to catch every tiny noise, every hint of
movement.

Jim was looking at me.

"Bad," I mouthed, letting him read my lips. "Bad magic."

Above us the ceiling creaked. We looked at it.

Another creak. Something heavy moved across the floor
over our heads.

Jim pushed ahead of me and we padded up the wooden
steps upstairs.

THE STAIRCASE WAS narrow and Jim's muscular back
took up most of it. I gave him a couple of feet to make sure he
had room to strike if we ran into something unpleasant.

Magic saturated the staircase. It dripped from the rail in long viscous droplets, it slimed the steps, it boiled in long coils along the wall so thick and potent I wished I'd brought a rain slicker. Now, that was a totally irrational thought. It seemed insane Jim couldn't see it, but I knew he couldn't.

We reached the landing. A hallway ran perpendicular to the staircase, and right across it, a doorway was lit by a pale yellowish glow. I smelled lamp oil.

Jim paused for one long second on the upstairs landing and strode on, through the hallway into the room. I padded after him.

A lone lamp burned on the floor at the far wall, illuminating a naked woman, who sat cross-legged on the grimy boards. Her dark honey hair hung in ragged strands down her back. I inhaled, sampling her scent. Michelle. But the scent was wrong. A living scent is hot, vibrant. This was a cold odor, laced with traces of toxic stenches: feces, a touch of urine, and a revolting patina of putrescence, like a meat broth left out for too long. Degrading amino acids. I've smelled this nauseating cocktail before: cadaverine, putrescine, and a dose of indole for good measure. My eyes told me Michelle was alive and sitting in front of me. My nose told me she was dead and had been so for at least two days. I trusted my nose. It never lied.

Jim pulled a knife from his sheath. It was his giant G.I. Joe knife, dark gray with a wicked curved tip and a serrated edge near the handle.

Michelle turned and looked at us. Her eyes were empty. Dead eyes, like two dark holes in her head. And I had really liked her, too.

Behind Michelle, another body lay in the corner on its side, long dark hair fanned out on the filthy floor like a black veil. Roger, a werelynx. Dead as well.

Michelle's left arm jerked up and forward, resting on the floor. Her right followed, like she was a puppet on a string.

"What do you want?" Jim's voice was a low snarl. That's why Jim was in charge. I didn't have to explain that something was controlling the dead. He figured it out all on his own and wasted no time on being weirded out by it.

Michelle's body turned, flipping her into a crouch.

Many things controlled the dead. I had to figure out who pulled the strings, before I could try a curse. Think, Dali, think.

"Any advice?" Jim asked, his voice casual.

"Keep her busy, so I can figure this out."

Michelle's mouth gaped open, showing dark nasty teeth.

"And try not to get bit."

Michelle launched from her crouch, hands outstretched, fingers like claws. Jim lunged at her. He grabbed her arm, the knife sliced in a furious arch, and Jim hurled Michelle across the room into the wall.

I clenched my calligraphy brush. This thing could've sent Michelle at us the moment we stepped through the door. But no, it taunted us from the window with the light. It made the ceiling above us creak on purpose.

Michelle rebounded from the wall, flipping in midair, kicking at Jim. He sidestepped, but she was fast. Her nails raked his chest with unnatural strength, ripping through clothes. Blood swelled through the tears. Jim grabbed her arm and twisted, his knife biting deep into Michelle's shoulder. Something crunched and Michelle's arm came away in Jim's hand— he'd cleaved the ball joint from the socket. Like cutting a wing from a chicken.

Michelle spun around. No blood spilled from the cut. She bared her teeth and lunged at Jim again, swiping at him with her remaining hand. Michelle was a jackal. They didn't claw, they bit.

He'd have to mince her into tiny pieces before she'd stop.

Something chuckled in the corner, where the magic knotted into a dark bramble. It was laughing at us. Playing a game, a cruel game.

Michelle clawed at Jim.

Just like a cat.

I began drawing my *kanji*. "Kill her now, please."

Jim jerked Michelle down. He cut in a vicious swipe and her head plunked down on the floor.

A dark shape coalesced from the knotted magic in a blink and leapt over Roger's corpse. I hurled my curse at it. The rigid white strip hit it between the eyes. Magic pulsed and I saw yellow cat eyes glowing like two moons at me from a round fur face.

Roger rammed into Jim.

The cat beast leapt in a blur, straight at me. The huge body knocked me off my feet. I flew and the back of my head bounced off the boards.

The cat clamped me down, its weight crushing my chest. A dark feline mouth gaped at me, exhaling fetid breath into my face. Pain punctured my shoulders like red-hot needles. I tried to snarl, but I had no air and only a small squeak came out.

The black mouth bit down. The *kanji* on the white piece of paper flared with green.

The paper burst into a dozen strips. They shot outward, jerking the cat off of me.

I blinked, trying to suck in a breath. Jim leaned over and thrust his hand down to me. I grabbed it and he pulled me up. Roger's corpse, broken and twisted, crumpled on the floor. Above it, a long feline body hung about two feet off the ground, wrapped in long strips of paper. It was six feet long and shaggy with orange and white fur, a house cat that had somehow grown to a leopard size. The strips adhered to the walls and ceiling, clutching the cat like the wrappings of a mummy.

The beast wasn't moving. Two paper strips had caught its throat in a makeshift noose. Its head hung limp, mouth open, a long tongue sticking out of the corner of its mouth. The yellow eyes, once glowing with bloodlust, were dull now.

I swallowed. My mouth tasted bitter. The cat monster was dead. My hands trembled from adrenaline. I had screwed up.

"WHAT THE HELL is that?" Jim asked. His voice was calm. His hands didn't shake. Cool as ice. Why couldn't I be more like that?

I sniffed, trying to hide the trembling. "Two tails or one?"

Jim took a step to the cat and lifted two long furry tails.

"It's a *nekomata*," I said. "A *yōkai*."

Jim gave me a blank look.

"The *yōkai* are Japanese demons." I rubbed my face. "Legends say that if a cat's tail isn't cropped and some other conditions are met, it has a chance to become a *bakeneko*, a demon ghost cat. *Bakeneko* cats grow to a huge size and get supernatural powers. Sometimes their tails fork and they become *nekomata*, demon monster cats. They have the power to control the dead, take on human form, and can do some nasty things."

"Do they have the power to put people to sleep?"

I knew he'd get around to that sooner or later. "No. It's possible that the woman you saw was a *nekomata* in disguise, but it's not likely. She had you and she let you go. The *nekomata* is a cat, Jim. It's cruel and mean, and it likes to play games, but you know yourself, the prey never gets away. This"—I waved my arms around—"is complicated. Too complicated for a demon cat. They mostly set fires, steal corpses, and walk around in human clothes, pretending to be your elderly mother so they can get free grub. There is magic here, really bad magic. It kind of scares me. The *nekomata* is dead, but the magic is still here. Something else is going on. This isn't over."

Jim tapped one of the paper strips with his knife. The strip didn't give. "And this?"

"This is the curse of twenty-seven binding scrolls."

Jim slashed at the paper strip. The paper held. Jim scowled. "How the hell . . ."

Kate, one of my friends, always said that the best defense is a good offense. "Before you say anything, yes, I know that the curse didn't function as expected and I know that it would've been better to have the *nekomata* restrained so we could question it, and I was trying to do that, but it's not like it's an exact science, and how was I supposed to know that the binding scrolls would choke the stupid demon to death? So you don't have to tell me—I know! You try guessing some weird creature's identity and writing calligraphy while it's trying to bite your nose off and then don't come crying to me."

And that didn't make even a tiny bit of sense. I was an exceptionally smart woman. Why did Jim always reduce me to some sort of ditzy bimbo idiot?

"I was going to say, how the hell did you pull that off," Jim said. "You made paper with the tensile strength of steel out of nothing. The physics of this makes my brain hurt."

"Oh."

"And I would've said it and some other nice things, except that you jumped in my face and started sputtering and waving your tiny fists around."

"Tiny fists?"

"That's the root of your problem right there. You always rush into things looking for a fight. You're like one of those

First Responder magic cops: Ride in, kill everything, and then sort bodies into two piles: criminals and civilians."

My face turned hot. My body was pumping out all sorts of angry, upset hormones. He was chewing me out like I was a child. I was this close to going furry, except it wouldn't do me any good.

"If you take a tenth of a second to check if the fight you're charging into isn't there, it would save you a lot of grief."

He didn't get it and he would never get it. "Are you finished?"

"Yes."

"Good." I turned away from him and crouched by Roger's body. Roger's head hung in a weird angle, and both of his arms bent in places where no joints existed. Jim had broken him like a twig.

"What is it?"

You're so special, why don't you tell me, Mister Always Look Before You Leap. I dragged my finger against Roger's skin. It came away with a powdery gray residue. I showed my finger to Jim. "I'm pretty sure normal corpses don't do that."

"I saw that," Jim said. "Michelle was slippery, too."

I rose. "We need to search the house."

We combed the house. We found no sign of the two other shapeshifters: Neither Mina nor August had been in the house for at least thirty-six hours. Their scents were old. I swiped the log from the front office and we escaped.

Outside the cold night air swept along my skin, washing away the nasty magic. I headed straight for Pooki and opened the log on the hood. Four different types of handwriting filled the pages. The last entry was three days old. I flipped back a month and scanned the entries.

"Are you actually reading this or just flipping pages?"

"Jim? Shush. I need to concentrate." Shift changes, notes on shapeshifters caught in the city for one reason or another crashing at the house, routine, routine, routine . . . Mina's entries identified different types of herbal tea she drank during her shift. Roger documented the patrol routes of three neighborhood cats, complete with battles for territory and places where they chose to mark it.

I kept turning the pages, and when I finally saw it, I almost

didn't realize it. Thursday before last, August failed to come
in for the shift change. The log showed him signing in four-
teen hours later. His *p*s, *g*s, and *y*s showed longer vertical strokes
than usual. I ran my fingers on the other side of the page and
felt the outlines of the letters. August had pressed too hard on
the paper. He was excited when he signed in, confident, angry,
maybe determined. His reason for the failure to show up read
"overslept," which made no sense considering the amount
of pressure he put on the page. There was something grim
about the way he wrote, as if he'd etched each letter into the
paper.

I tapped the page, thinking. A *nekomata* was a Japanese
monster. August was half Japanese, half white by birth, but
American culturally. He couldn't read *kanji*, and his Japanese
was terrible. Atlanta had a large Japanese population, with its
own school and stores, a place where American customs
didn't apply. August visited his family there, but he never
quite got the Us and Them mentality, and being a halfer, he
was looked down on. A few months ago he told me that one of
his cousins was gay. August had gone to pick up the thirteen-
year-old kid at Japanese school to take him to a family gathering and he'd seen the boy sit on his friend's lap after recess. I
had to explain that it was a cultural thing that didn't indicate
anything about his cousin's sexuality, but it just didn't com-
pute from his Southern guy point of view. He didn't completely believe me either and told me that if anyone ever
picked on his cousin, he'd break their legs.

Magic tended to stick to nationality and region. People generated magic, and their superstitions and beliefs channeled it.
If enough people believed that a certain creature existed and,
worse, took precautions against it, eventually the magic birthed
it into being. If you had an area densely settled by Irish, you
got banshees. If you had Vietnamese settlers, sooner or later
ma doi, the hungry spirits, would be haunting the streets. And
if you had a Japanese community, you would get *yōkai*, demonic
creatures.

The residue on Roger's skin really bothered me. Either the
top layer of his skin had turned to dust, or he'd been liberally
powdered with something. No creature I could think of could
do that to a body.

Of the four people in the office, August would be the most likely to come into contact with a Japanese legend. We had to retrace his steps.

I flipped the pages. The entries were becoming shorter, more erratic. On Saturday some of them looked unfinished, as if the writer had simply stopped in the middle of a sentence. Sunday had no entries. There should've been some. On Monday, a single entry written in Michelle's neat handwriting read, *Can't stay awake. Help. m.*

Oh shit. Oh shit, oh shit, oh shit.

"We need to go to August's place. We need to figure out why he was out on Thursday." I looked up.

Jim was asleep leaning against the car.

"Jim!"

No response. I grabbed him and shook his shoulder. "Wake up! Wake up!" He slid to the ground, still asleep. I slapped his face. He didn't move.

I pulled Pooki's door open, popped the trunk, jerked the extra gallon can of enchanted water out, and dumped it on his face.

The water poured. Come on, come on . . .

Jim coughed and shook himself.

I dropped the can and grabbed his shoulders. "Wake up!"

Dark eyes looked at me. "I'm awake."

"Don't fall asleep! Don't fall asleep, you hear?"

He growled and pushed off the ground. "I'm okay."

No, he wasn't okay. We were in trouble. We were really, really in trouble. I paced back and forth. My heart was beating so fast it felt about to explode. Something was wrong with my Jim and if I didn't fix it now, he would end up like Roger, a dry cadaver full of nasty magic.

"Calm down," Jim said.

"I am calm! Get in the car." Emergencies called for desperate measures.

He got in. I flopped into the driver's seat and chanted the engine into life, watching him like a hawk. He stayed awake. I dropped the parking brake and gunned it out of the parking lot. "Roll the window down," I yelled over the roar of the engine. "You need wind on your face."

"Where are we going?" he roared back.

"To see my mother!"

* * *

MY MOTHER LIVED in a small cluster of apartment buildings in Riverdale. It took me more than an hour to drive over there through the crumbling city, and the entire time I watched Jim out of the corner of my eye. I punched him in the arm a few times to make sure he stayed awake. After the first eight times he told me to quit it.

I maneuvered down the smallish road and into the horseshoe formed by the squat two-story townhomes and parked in front of my mother's house. The pale blue light of her fey lantern filtered through the window. I climbed out. Jim already waited by the door, surveying the houses.

"Why are those three buildings facing to the left?"

"Because this is an Indonesian community, mostly older people who practice magic. They're more superstitious than usual. It's bad luck to build a house facing north. Some people believe it will make you poor. The subdivision street was already laid out when people moved in, so those three families chose to build their houses facing east."

"Aha."

"It's bad luck to build a house facing a field, it's bad luck to have the kitchen face the front door, and it's bad luck to build a fence taller than six feet. This is just the way things are, Jim. Just go along with it."

"Your fence is taller than six feet."

I turned to him as I walked. "I didn't say they were my superstitions. But they're important to my mother."

We headed to the door. The familiar scents washed over me: rice, onion, chili peppers, cumin, coriander. Mom was cooking *nasi goreng*, fried rice. I was home.

Help me.

Jim sampled the wind. "It's past one. Does your mother usually cook after midnight?"

"No, it's special for me. She sensed us coming."

I raised my hand to knock on the door. Before my knuckles touched the wood, it flew open and my mother clamped me in a hug. Looking at her you could tell exactly how I would look in thirty years or so: tiny, skinny, dark, quick to move.

"Why are you so dirty?" My mother pulled a cobweb out of my hair. "What is happened? Come inside. Who is this man?"

Here we go. I took a deep breath and walked in. "This is Jim."

Jim stepped inside.

My mother shut the door and peered at him. "He is dark. Very, very dark."

Jim grinned, showing a tiny edge of his teeth.

I felt like slapping myself. "Mother!"

"What is it you do?" She leaned over to Jim. Her accent was getting thicker. "Do you have money?"

"He is my alpha. He's in charge of the whole Cat clan. Very important."

My mother's eyes sparked. Oh no.

She leaned over and patted Jim's hand. "That is so nice. My daughter is so smart. Always respectful and well behaved. Never any trouble and she does as she is told."

"You don't say," Jim murmured.

"Doesn't spend a lot of money. Two doctor degrees. Little problem with her eyes, but that's her father's side of the family. Very rare magic, a white tiger. One in seven generation. Very special. She can cure evil eye with a touch. And if you had your house cursed, she can purify it for you. Everyone respects my daughter. All our people know her."

Jim nodded to her with a solemn look. My stomach lurched. I felt like throwing up. "Mother . . ."

She nodded to Jim, as if sharing a grave secret. "And she's a good cook, too."

Jim leaned a little toward her, his face deadly serious. "I'm sure she is."

My mother smiled, as if he'd given her a diamond. "Best match. Of all the girls, mine is best match."

Aaaaa! "Mother! There is something wrong with him. He's magic-sick."

My mother stood up on her toes and peered at Jim's eyes. For a long moment they were eye to eye, my short mother and tall, muscular Jim, and then she switched to Indonesian.

"Let him go."

"No." I shook my head.

"He is strong. Very good in the body. But you must find another one."

"I don't want another one! I want him."

"He's dying."

"I have to save him. Please help me. Please."

My mother bit her lip and pointed at the chair. "Sit."

Jim sat. She leaned over and pulled his right eye open with her fingers, examining the iris. *"Something is eating his soul."*

"I figured that out. But I can't see it."

Mother sighed. *"I can't see it either. Until we see it, we can't do anything about it. We need Keong Emas."*

The Golden Snail. My heart dropped. My legs gave out and I landed on the couch. The only place we could get a golden snail would be in Underground Atlanta. It used to be a shopping district in Five Points, where all the big buildings stood before the Shift. The Underground started out as a big train depot in the mid-1800s with shops, banks, and even saloons, but eventually the city had to build viaducts over the railroad tracks for the car traffic. The viaducts ran together until a good portion of the train tracks, the shops, and the depot were underground. Before the Shift, it used to be full of little bars and shops. Once the magic hit, the shop owners fled and the black market moved in. The mob-sponsored traders had burrowed deep, cutting tunnels running from their shops right into the ruined Five Points and Unicorn Lane, where the magic ran wild and no sane cop would follow them. Now the Underground was a place where you could buy anything if you were desperate enough.

"Is there any other way?"

My mother shook her head. *"Don't even think about it. You can't go to the Underground."*

I exhaled, blinking. *"We don't have any choice."*

My mother made a short cutting motion with her hand. *"No!"*

"Yes. We need to buy the snail."

My mother drew herself to her full height. I stood up and did the same.

"No, and that's final."

"You can't keep me from doing it."

"I am your mother!"

Jim opened his mouth. *"Mengapa?"*

Oh my gods.

He spoke Indonesian.

My mother's eyes went wide and for a second she looked like a furious cat. *"He speaks Indonesian!"*

"I know!"

"Why didn't you tell me he speaks Indonesian? This is a thing I need to know!"

I waved my arms. *"I didn't know!"*

"What do you mean, you didn't know? You just said you knew."

"I meant I didn't know that he did and then he did and I went 'I know!' because I was surprised."

"Ladies!" Jim barked, standing up.

We both looked at him.

"You're speaking so fast, I can't understand," he said. "Why does Dali need to go to the Underground?"

"You explain it to him," my mother said. "I will make tea." She went into the kitchen.

I pointed at the chair. "Sit."

He sat and lowered his voice. "What happened to your mother's accent?"

"We're past that now," I whispered to him. "Her little Asian lady act is just for show. She has a master's in chemistry from Princeton."

Jim blinked.

"Well, where did you think I got my brains?"

Jim shook his head. "Explain the Underground thing."

I sighed. "How much did you understand? And since when do you speak Indonesian?"

"I've got the idea that something is seriously fucked up and it seemed like an interesting language."

"Interesting language? Really? So what, you got up one day and said, 'Hmm, I think I will learn Bahasa Indonesia today'?" He was up to something.

A green sheen rolled over Jim's eyes. "Dali, the Underground?"

There was no easy way to say it. "Something is feeding on your soul."

"Explain."

I leaned closer. "All people generate magic. Some can use it, some can't; some generate more than others, but all of us are magic engines: We absorb it from the environment and emit it back out. That's why we can shift during technology: We store enough magic in our bodies to allow us to change shape. Let's take Kate."

Jim's voice betrayed a quiet warning. "What about Kate?"

Kate used to work with Jim in the Mercenary Guild. Kate was gorgeous, funny, and she could kill anything. I hated her. She could say anything to Jim and he would just needle her back. I was so jealous of her I used to have to leave the room, until I realized that Kate crushed on Curran. She was now mated to him, and since he was the Beast Lord, that made her the Beast Lady and not interested in Jim. Kate and Curran had some seriously rough time with an ancient goddess who blew into town, and now Kate walked with a cane and Curran was barely three weeks out of a coma.

"Ever notice how when Kate gets stressed out the phones stop working?"

"The phones are unreliable as a rule," Jim said.

I shook my head. "No, it's Kate. She generates so much magic, she short-circuits tech if she isn't careful. I do the same thing, except I control mine better. She can't shoot a gun either. I've watched her practice and it either goes wide or doesn't fire at all. And she has no clue. Watch her sometime: She will stomp in, grab the phone, make that growly noise, and walk away. Ten minutes later you can order takeout on the same phone. It's the funniest thing."

"What does that have to do with my soul being drained?"

"You're magic, Jim. You absorb and consume magic, emanating it into the environment. By doing so, you modify the environment to be more suitable to your existence. It's like the evolutionary loop: A species is shaped by its environment, because those with the mutations most suitable to the environment survive and reproduce, but a species also modifies its environment to make it more suitable to its survival."

Jim sighed. "Give me the short version."

"Something is interfering with your ability to emanate magic. You absorb and convert it, but then something or someone is siphoning it off. That's why you feel tired and sleepy."

"So it's feeding off of me?"

My mother walked in carrying a platter with a teapot and three cups. "Yes."

Jim frowned. "Makes sense. That's why it didn't kill me—the more magic I make, the more it eats."

"You do realize that you're going to die?" My mother shook her head.

"Yeah, I've got the dying part."

"You found some sort of zombie instead of a man." My mother pointed at Jim. "Look, he isn't even concerned."

I poured the tea. "He's concerned, Mother. He just doesn't panic, because he's in charge and if he panics, everybody else will panic."

"I can jog around the room pretending to scream if you would like," Jim offered.

My mother raised an eyebrow. "You're working so hard to dig your own grave, you might work yourself to death. Simmer down."

Jim drew back as if she'd smacked his hand with a ruler.

"We have to sever the connection between you and whoever is doing this," I said before they started slapping each other. "But we can't see it. To make it visible we need Keong Emas. It's a magic snail. There is a legend in Indonesia that talks about a beautiful princess, who was cursed and turned into a snail. The legend is figurative and the snail doesn't turn into an actual princess, but with the right magic, it will reveal hidden things. The only way to get the snail is to buy it at the Underground. It's rare and expensive."

"Money isn't an issue," Jim said.

"It's not about the money, you stupid boy." Mother set the teacup down. "She can't go there because of the *yisheng*."

Jim looked at me.

"*Yisheng* is the Chinese word for a medicine man," I said. "The dealers at the Underground call themselves that, but they aren't medicine men. They're animal-parts dealers. Do you remember that big shapeshifter case in Asheville three years ago?"

Jim frowned. "Vaguely. I was in Florida, dealing with Kaja's loup pack. I remember there was a fifteen-year-old kid, Jarod, I think. He was a black bear. He said he was walking in the woods, encountered a group of hunters, waved to indicate that he was a shapeshifter, and when he turned away, the hunters shot him in the back and he had to defend himself. By the time the game wardens showed up, Jarod had the shooter pinned and everyone else had cleared out. The medic pulled sixteen bullets out of the kid. The hunter claimed he was attacked without provocation. They had a hard time proving Jarod's story because his wounds had closed, so there was no way to determine how he'd been shot. The prosecution argued that Jarod was so huge in his beast form that if he was walking away from a hunter, no sane man would have shot him, so the hunters must've fired in self-defense. Curran sent the entire legal division down there."

Clearly, Jim wasn't sure what the word *vaguely* meant.

"My uncle Aditya testified in that trial," I told him. "He is a federal park ranger for the Smoky Mountains National Park. The hunter's name was Williams. Chad Williams, MD. Uncle Aditya testified that Williams has been detained several times on suspicion of poaching with intent to sell animal parts. He had friends in the right places and he was let go every time."

"Stupid people believe that bear cures everything," Mother put in. "Diabetes, stomach pain, weak heart, limp penis . . ."

"A black bear gallbladder goes for about forty-five thousand dollars on the black market," I said.

Jim repeated, "Forty-five grand?"

I nodded. "When your family is sick or your equipment stops working, people get desperate. Especially ignorant white people—they think mystical 'Oriental' medicine will cure all their ills."

I refilled our cups. "A black bear's gallbladder is expensive. A bear shapeshifter's gallbladder is worth even more. Williams shot Jarod on purpose. He wanted his organs. They found silver bullets hidden in his campsite."

"Poachers think that if the bear dies in pain, his gallbladder will get bigger." My mother grimaced.

Jim's eyes sparked with green. "They shot the boy with regular bullets to torture him before they killed him."

"Yes. Once all this stuff came out on the stand, everybody got involved." I waved my arms. "The marshals, the FBI, the GBI. Williams even got in trouble with the post office because the idiot used the mail to ship some animal parts down to Atlanta. He went down in flames."

"And our family got blacklisted with the poachers forever and ever and ever," my mother said. "That's why Dali can't go into the Underground. A black bear is a valuable animal, but you know what's better?"

My mother got up, went to the cabinet, and pulled a folded paper out. Oh no. Not again.

"A tiger!" My mother slapped the paper in front of Jim. On it a stylized tiger curved his back in a garishly bright water-color. Arrows pointed to different parts of the tiger's body, each marked with a label: brain to cure laziness and acne, blood to cure weak constitution and gain power, teeth for breathing problems and venereal diseases, whiskers to help with the toothache . . .

Jim stared at it. His eyes went completely green, glowing with barely restrained violence.

"They will kill her," he growled.

"If she's lucky, they will kill her." Mother crossed her arms.

Jim looked at her.

"White tiger, powerful magic. She heals very fast. They'll put her in a cage and harvest her parts over and over. She'll be their organ factory. We've heard of such things happening. She can't go."

Jim's face was terrible. When Curran was angry, he roared. Jim never roared. Jim did this . . . this horrible stone-faced thing, where the only indication of life on his face were his eyes. They were hard and furious and full of icy calculation. He scared me when he looked like that. My throat closed up, and I just wanted to sit in the corner and be small.

Today I didn't have that luxury. The anxiety sat in my chest. I swallowed. Come on, blind girl. You can do it. "We need the snail, Mother. He will die without it."

"There has to be another way," Jim said.

I shook my head.

"Then I'll get it myself," Jim said.

"Ha! Keong Emas is not some black bear. It's very rare. They won't sell it to you," Mother said.

I met Jim's eyes. "I know what you're thinking. You can't show up there with an entourage of shapeshifters and force them to sell you the snail. You can't buy the snail yourself, because they won't sell to you."

Jim opened his mouth.

"No, you can't get a different shapeshifter to go get it, because the snail looks ordinary, until someone with enough magic touches it, and I'm the only one I can think of with that much magic, besides Kate, and Kate is hobbling around with a cane at the moment, so she can't go either. And no, you have no choice, Jim, because there is no other way."

Jim's eyes sparked.

"That won't work either. Even if you put me under guard, I will still get out," I told him. "It doesn't matter how many people you attach to me, I will curse my way out if I have to. I won't sit here and watch you die."

He snarled. I showed him my teeth.

A rolled-up newspaper landed on my head and then on Jim's. "None of that in my house!"

Oh my gods. The alpha of Clan Cat just got smacked with a rolled-up newspaper. "Mom!"

She pointed at me with the newspaper. "Do not shame me."

I clamped my mouth shut. When she pulled out the shame card, it was all over.

My mother stared at Jim. "You will go with her tomorrow, when the market opens. You will bring my daughter back to me, unharmed, do you hear? And you better be worth it."

Jim held her gaze.

If he struck at my mother, I'd strike him back.

Jim opened his mouth.

I tensed until it hurt.

"Yes, ma'am."

Oh phew. Dodged the bullet. Not that I thought he would *really* strike at my mother, but you just never know.

"Take him outside, to the tree," my mother said. "And keep him awake until morning. He falls asleep, he dies."

THE TREE GREW in the inner yard formed by the backs of two houses on one side and a sturdy stone wall on the others. A long twisty pond took up half of the yard. Pink lotus blossoms and yellow lilies thrust from the dark water, flanked by the round leaves. In the middle of the pound, a statue of Lak-shmi rose, surrounded by shrinking violets in orange glazed pots and linked to the shore by dark stepping-stones. Philo-dendrons bordered the pond, fighting for space with bamboo and ferns. Gold bird of paradise plants bloomed here and there. To the left a bunut tree rose with a small teak bench beside it. A bucket and ladle waited by the trunk.

I led Jim to the bench. "Sit here."

He sat.

I dipped the bucket into the pond, set it between us, and sat on the low stone wall of a flower bed.

He looked around. "It's a nice garden."

I nodded. "I like it. It quiet and beautiful. Most Indonesians are Muslim, but we're Hindu. A place for meditation is impor-tant to us. The tree you're sitting under came from the seed of a very special holy tree in Bali, the Bunut Bolog tree. It's a type of fig. The Bunut Bolog tree is so large and so powerful that it is like a forest by itself. It has a hole at its base, and the hole is so wide, there is a two-lane road running through it."

"Why did they build a road through the sacred tree?" Jim asked.

"It was too dangerous to go around it because of the cliffs. They thought about cutting the tree down, but the spirits of the tree's guardians refused to allow it, so they just had to make the best of it. It's not wise to piss off the tree's guardians. They are ferocious."

"What sort of guardians?"

I gave him a little smile. "Tigers."

Jim grinned. "Tigers, huh."

"Mhm."

He leaned forward. His face was calm and I wanted to kiss him. I couldn't help it.

"You looked worried after that newspaper thing," he said. "I'm sorry for that. I didn't mean to make you—"

If he said "scared," I would make him wear this damn bucket on his head. Vegetarian and half blind, I was still a shapeshifter, a predator. I had my pride.

"—upset."

Hmm, upset I could probably live with. He didn't need to know that. "I wasn't upset."

"My point is, I would never hurt you or your family."

I raised my chin at him. "If you tried to hurt my mother, I would totally kick your ass."

"Aha."

"Yes. You would be lying on the ground, crying, 'No more, no more,' and I would be kicking you in the stomach, wham, wham, wham!"

He laughed softly. He was so terribly handsome. Here we were sitting two feet from each other, and we might as well be on opposite sides of the Pacific Ocean.

"I don't want you to do this," Jim said. "I don't want you to go there, I don't want you to get hurt trying to help me. It's not your job to save me."

"Yes, it is."

"Says who?"

"Says me."

"Look, tomorrow I'll go in there myself, and if I choke somebody long enough, they will bring the snail."

"Aha. And how do you plan on determining if they've brought a garden snail or a golden one?"

"I'll spray somebody's magic blood around until the snail lights up."

"Good plan." I dipped my ladle into the bucket and tossed the water at him.

He recoiled. "What the hell?"

"You're delirious from lack of sleep."

"Dali!"

"The poachers are smart and a lot of them have magic. Some of them can tell what kind of a shapeshifter you are from a hundred yards just by looking at you. If you go to the Underground tomorrow, you will fall asleep there, alone and helpless, and then the poachers will kill you and cut you into tiny pieces, and then your precious werejaguar bones will be sliced into thin wafers and put into wine, so some sicko can have magic powers in bed."

He let out a frustrated snarl.

"It's just like with the tea—somebody offers you a gift, and you turn up your nose at it."

"You're taking chances again. I won't let you do it."

"It's cute of you to think you can stop me, Jim. Usually you order me around and I do what you say. I might gripe and I might make a fuss, but I will do it, because you are my alpha and I respect you. On this, you get no respect. You know nothing about this world. Your rules don't apply here, but mine do. You will follow my lead and you will let me save you, Jim." *Because thinking about you dying makes me hurt.*

He opened his mouth.

"If it was the other way around, we wouldn't be having this conversation," I told him.

"I'm your alpha. It's my job to keep you safe."

"It goes both ways," I said.

He rubbed his hands over his eyes. I tossed another ladleful of water at him.

"Quit it!"

"You looked sleepy."

"I'm not sleepy, I'm at the end of my patience with this stupid hocus-pocus shit."

"Whatever."

Fine. He could be dense and pissed off all he wanted, it didn't matter.

We sat in silence. Off to the side night insects chirped and seesawed sad little songs. Tomorrow would suck. It would suck so much, and we didn't even know what was wrong with him. I wished the markets would be open already so we could get it done before he fell asleep again.

"Do you at least have a plan?" Jim asked.

"Yes. Most likely we'll have to get down to Kenny's Alley in the Underground. That's where the most expensive animal parts are sold. I will go inside the shop. You will wait outside. I will offer them a lot of money for the snail. If I get in trouble, I'll scream and you will get me out."

"A hell of a plan."

I wrinkled my nose at him.

"And if I fail to bring you back unharmed, your mother will skin me alive."

"She might just turn you inside out."

Jim had this funny long-suffering look on his face, and then his eyes sparked. "So does she grill every guy you bring home?"

I don't bring guys home, you stupid, stupid man. "Ignore it. She's just worried. I'm almost thirty and still unmarried. It's a big deal in my culture." Not that he would understand.

"I like it how wealthy trumped black."

"Jim, ignore it, okay?"

"Okay." He raised his hands up.

Gah. "She's desperate, all right? She just wants me to be happy, and she's afraid I'll never make a good match."

"Why?"

Oh my gods. "What do you mean, why? Jim, look at me."

He did. "Yes?"

What, now I had to spell it out? Talk about humiliating. "My mother tried to describe me in a glowing light: She went through all my virtues."

"I've got that," he said. "Especially the part about obedient and respectful . . ."

"Never mind that. She went through the whole list. If I could do origami, she would've mentioned it, too."

"Okay, and?"

"Did she tell you I was pretty?"

He gave me a blank look.

"Did the word *pretty* come out of her mouth? At all?"

"No," Jim said.

"There you go." Happy now?

"So this is it? This is your big hang-up? You're pissed off because your mother doesn't think you're pretty? Don't let it bother you. It's not important."

Oh, you idiot. It's not my mother I'm worried about. It's you. I waved my arms. "Jim, what's the first thing you said to me when I asked you to describe the strange woman? Let me help you remember: You said she was beautiful."

"And?"

"I bet you didn't notice what she was wearing on her feet, but you noticed how hot she was."

"She was barefoot and her feet were dirty."

Him and his stupid memory. "That's how it goes: Men are supposed to be strong, women are supposed to be beautiful. Well, I'm not beautiful. You can put me into a room of a hundred women my age, and I'll be smarter than most of them put together, but it won't make a damn bit of difference, because if you let a man into that same room and let him pick, I would be the last one left. If I were a normal woman, I could use my brain to earn money and then I would get plastic surgery. I would fix my nose, and then I would work some more until I could afford to fix my jaw and so on and so on, until I was pretty. But I'm not a normal woman. Lyc-V won't fix my eyes, but it will undo any surgery. I know, I've tried. I'm stuck this way and there's not a damn thing I can do about it. And you say, 'Don't let it bother you,' as if that's supposed to make everything go away!"

"And if the surgery did work, when would you stop having it?" he asked.

"When I walked into the room, and men turned their heads to look at me. I want to be beautiful. I want to be a knockout. I would trade all of my intelligence and all of my mystic tiger magic for that."

The green glow backlit his irises. "And be what? A pretty idiot?"

"Yes!"

"That's the stupidest thing I've ever heard."

I glared at him.

"Nadene is pretty," he growled. "Beautiful woman. Dumb as a board. She can't keep a guy longer than a couple of months. Phillip left her and she wanted me to intervene so I went to talk to him. He told me that she was fun to fuck for a while, but being with her made him feel like he was getting dumber. They couldn't have a normal conversation. He couldn't handle it. And you want to be that? Are you crazy?"

"You don't even notice the fact that I am female, Jim! I'm just a brain with a pair of glasses that you occasionally have to put under guard so it's not damaged trying to have a little bit of fun. Did you ever ask yourself why I race?"

"I know why you race," he snarled.

"Tell me!"

"You race because you have a chip on your shoulder the size of a two-by-four. You think that because it takes you two minutes to come to when you shift and because you're not the best fighter we've got, you have something to prove. And you do this by making metal cages with four wheels go really fast without any point. You don't win anything, you don't accomplish anything, and you hurt yourself all the time. You're right—that will show everyone how hard-core you are."

"Aargh!"

"The only thing you're proving is that the smartest woman I know has zero common sense. You have powerful magic, you're smart, you're competent, but none of that matters. I have a dozen Nadenes, I only have one you. What good would Nadene do me right now? And I know you're female. I've noticed. This hysterical thing you're doing right now, that's female. If you were a man, I would've put your ass to haul rocks for the Keep a long time ago."

I heaved up the bucket.

"Don't do it," he warned.

I hurled it at him, water and all. Water splashed, and then a completely drenched, pissed-off Jim grabbed the bucket, scooped water from the pond, and tossed it at me. Water hit me in a cold rush.

I turned around and stomped off.

"Where are you going?" he called.

"Away from you!" I sat on the bench at the far end of the pond.

"You're supposed to keep me awake."

"I can keep you awake from here. If I see you falling asleep, I'll curse you with something really painful."

"You do that. You're still wrong."

"Whatever."

THE MORNING CAME way too slow. Jim had almost dozed off four times and I ended up moving next to him, with my bucket. At some point he asked me if my girly emotional outbursts were over, and I swore at him for a while in Indonesian. And then he ruined it by asking me what some of the words meant, and of course I had to teach him how to pronounce them properly.

It's good that my mother stayed inside, or I would have gotten another lecture on how to behave as a proper daughter.

It was seven o'clock now and we were standing on Pryor Street, in front of a grimy white arch marking the entrance to

Kenny's Alley. Set apart from the main Underground, Kenny's Alley had no roof, and entering through the narrow ramp off of Pryor Street was the quickest way to get there. It was also the most dangerous—to get down, I'd have to walk up the narrow ramp that squeezed between two brick buildings, enter the old train depot, and then walk along the balcony and down two floors, all filled with people who'd kill me for a dollar. Sometimes people who entered the Underground through Pryor Street didn't come out.

The wind swirled, rushing down the narrow gap between the buildings, and flung the Underground's scents into my face: odors of a dozen of animal species mixed with the bitter stink of stale urine, human and otherwise, old manure, fish from a giant fishmonger tank, pungent incense, and salty blood. The revolting amalgam washed over me and I had to fight not to retch.

At least the magic had vanished during the night. Usually the miasma rising from the Underground made my head hurt.

"You don't have to do this," Jim said.

"Yes, I do."

He reached over and put his arm around me. I froze. There was so much strength in that muscular arm that suddenly I felt safe. The scent of him, the comforting, strong Jim scent, touched me, blocking out other smells. I would know that scent anywhere. Here he was hugging me. I had wished for it and now I just wanted to cry, because no matter what I did, no matter how much I raced or how belligerent I got, he would never want me. Not in that way.

I stepped away from him, before I lost it. "I'm going inside. If I go inside a shop, give me about five minutes. If I don't come out . . ."

"I'll come in," he promised.

"Don't fall asleep."

"I won't."

I looked into his brown eyes and believed him.

"Okay," I murmured. "I'm going now."

I turned and headed down the narrow alley, into the dark belly of the Underground. Panhandlers and street people lined the ramp and the balcony, swaddled in filthy clothes, hats and tins in front of them. This early in the morning they didn't even bother begging. They just stared at me as I passed by, all except an old black man, who was doing a wobbly moonwalk across a covered walkway, gyrating to the beat of some melody only he could hear. His eyes were wide-open; he looked straight at me but didn't see me.

The ramp led me up to the top floor, to a wide balcony. Kenny's Alley stretched below: a dank narrow space, filled with stalls and vicious-eyed people, its brick floor barely visible beneath cages and refuse. I kept walking. The balcony ended and I took the stairs down to the lower floor, where vendors hawked their wares. Dull electric lamps were strung out between old Christmas lights, marking the little shops. Despite the hour, customers already flooded the market, men, women, and children of every color and race looking for the magic cure to their problems. They were what allowed the poachers to exist. They'd stop poaching if people stopped buying.

What I needed wouldn't be sold here. I had to get to Kenny's Alley.

The electric lamps blinked and died. Darkness clenched the Underground in its mouth and spat it out with the hiss and crackle of magic. Fey lanterns ignited with a pale blue glow, their thin glass tubes twisted into *kanji* and familiar shapes: phoenix, tiger, dragon. Magic flowed and twisted around me. Here and there, wards shielded the storefronts, strong, solid. To the left a wavering miasma of something foul and wrong leaked from behind a closed door. Straight ahead, a stall of small coin charms radiated something pleasant, almost warm.

Another magic wave. There shouldn't have been one. Nobody could predict when magic came and went, but it rarely flooded the city twice in twenty-four hours. Just my luck.

I kept moving, winding my way between the stalls. If Jim was following me, I couldn't see him. I hoped he stayed awake. I hoped he would with all my might, because if he fell asleep, there was no hope for either of us.

The entrance to Kenny's Alley loomed ahead, a rectangle of weak sunrise light. The smell hit me first, that unforgettable stench of too many animals kept too close together. Then came the noise: the braying, the mewing, the snarls. I stepped out into the open. Three-story houses rose on both sides of me, boxing in a narrow alley. Stalls and tables lined the front of the shops, offering dried ox penises, tanks containing geoduck mollusks, deer antlers, bundles of dried herbs. To the left a man dipped steel tongs into a box and plucked out a black poisonous centipede. The insect writhed, trying to break free. The man took the lid off a pot on the kerosene burner and tossed the centipede inside.

Small-time. I kept walking. I needed a rare-goods dealer.

People were looking at me. From the shop front on the right a middle-aged white woman in camo fabric stared at my legs, then at my head, as if she wanted to shoot me. Magic probed me, teasing, testing. A couple of younger men, probably Chinese, leaned to each other, whispering. I caught bits and pieces. A word stood out: *hu*. Tiger. Didn't take them long to see through my human form.

I felt like a cow being led past a row of butcher shops. I raised my chin. Show no fear, or they will swoop like vultures.

A stall to the left looked richer than the rest: The table was sturdy and the cloth on it was red silk, the real thing, not a cheap imitation. An old wizened woman, Korean by her dress, sat guarding the wares, looking bored. I stopped and looked at the dried-out parts displayed on the silk.

I bowed. *"An-nyung-ha-se-yo."* Hello.

The woman bowed her head back. "Hello."

English. Great. My Korean was rusty.

I paused by a small white sack that lay half open. Inside lay minced leather strips.

"Bear gallbladder," the woman said.

I picked up a small slice and sniffed it. "Pig." If it had been a real bear gallbladder, she wouldn't have let me pick it up. "Do you have bear?"

The woman reached under the table, pulled out a small wooden box, and opened it. Dried leathery strips. Could be bear gallbladder.

The woman snapped the box closed. "When were you born? What is your sign? You have nice pale skin, but the eyes are not so good, yes? We have snake glands for the eyes. Dried cicadas, make it into soup, it will make your eyes stronger. Or does your man need help in bed? I have something very special for that. Not like all those dried-out dog parts over there." She grimaced at the stall across the street. "I have a sure thing. Want to see?"

I nodded.

Another box appeared as if by magic. I looked inside. Rhino horn. The genuine article, too.

"I'm looking for a rare thing."

The woman pondered me. "How rare?"

"Very rare. Keong Emas."

"The Golden Snail."

"I will pay well." I reached into my hoodie and showed her the money, just a hint, but it was enough.

"Keong Emas is powerful magic." The old woman stared at me. Her eyes were cold like two pieces of coal.

"Makes it easy to recognize a fake," I told her.

She let out a short little grunt and called out something in Korean, too fast to follow. "You go inside now."

I stepped over a small crate containing a pair of frightened rabbits, and went inside. Cages lined the walls. Monkeys, dogs, birds. Big frightened eyes. They screamed and shied away from the bars at my approach. I clenched my teeth. I just had to get the snail. Just get the snail.

An adolescent boy came through the curtained doorway and waved to me. "Come this way."

I didn't want to go that way.

The boy waved at me. "Come! Come!"

Crap. I followed him through the curtain. A long dark room smelling of blood. Great. We kept going, farther from the street, deeper into the house. I was probably walking into a trap, but I had to get the snail. This was the only way. As long as Jim stayed awake, he would get me out. He would. Of course he would.

Another set of curtains and I stepped into a large room lined with tables, supporting a medicine man's smorgasbord, as if a dozen street vendor carts had vomited their contents into the room. Boxes, wicker, wood, and plastic. Bloated glass bottles, skinny glass vials, jars containing powders and liquids. Dried herbs, in bundles and packets. And bones. So many bones: bear bones, wolf bones, tiger bones. Bastards.

An Asian man sat at the table, wizened and old, dressed in dark clothes. Behind him a white man leaned against the wall. He was tall and beefy, and his fatigue jacket made him look rectangular, like he was made out of bricks. A short reddish beard hugged his chin. A red NC State baseball cap covered his hair.

In the right corner a large cage sat covered by a tarp. A blond woman stood by it, leaning on a baseball bat. She wore jeans and a huge man's T-shirt with an oversized blood drop and the words DONATE BLOOD on it. The T-shirt was threadbare and patched in a couple of places.

Something moved in the cage. I could hear it breathing in long, labored gasps. People moved in the outer rooms, too, to the right of us and behind, making small noises. A lot of people. At least eight, maybe more.

I just had to get the snail. That's all. Just get the snail and save Jim.

The old man regarded me. I wouldn't bow to this asshole. My back would break.

"You want to buy Keong Emas."

"Yes."

The boy who brought me here walked over to the far table and brought a wicker box to the old man. The man opened the box and removed a glass tank with five snails inside. Each had a dull brown shell.

The old man offered me the tank. "Choose one."

This was it.

I reached into the tank and passed my hand over the snails. The smallest one tugged on me, tiny needles of magic prickling my skin. Gently, I plucked it from its leaf and held it in the palm of my hand.

A faint glow lit the snail from within. It lingered for a second and burst, painting the snail's shell with brilliant gold.

"Only powerful magic can see Keong Emas," the old man said. "White tiger magic."

Oh shit. I clamped the snail in my hand and felt it slide into its shell. "How much?"

"Take her." The old man nodded to the guy in the red hat.

Red Hat peeled himself from the wall. Behind me a man and a woman moved from behind the curtain, cutting off my exit.

"You shouldn't have come here," the old man said.

"Jim!" I yelled.

"He won't help," the old man said. "Nobody will help."

I dashed left, but Red Hat's hand gripped my shoulder and he jerked me off my feet with superhuman strength. I kicked at him, but he batted my legs aside and carried me back to the corner, where a woman pulled the tarp off the cage. A man knelt in the cage on all fours, filthy, wearing rags smeared with old blood. Plastic ties forced his wrists together, and above them a ragged cloth with a holding spell scrawled in ink bound his forearms. A leather muzzle clamped his whole face, leaving only the narrow strip of space around his eyes visible. Bandages hid his head and all I saw was one eye, mad, furious, and brilliant turquoise.

There was a second cage next to him. An empty cage.

Panic squirmed through me. I kicked and thrashed, but the cage kept coming closer and closer. If I went tiger, he couldn't carry me, but I'd be too dazed to fight and I would drop the snail. I couldn't drop the snail, or Jim would die.

Jim would come for me. He wouldn't fall asleep. He wouldn't let them kill him.

I kicked and jerked with all the shapeshifter strength I had.

"Don't make this harder on yourself," Red Hat told me.

We were almost to the cage. "How can you do this?"

"Your uncle kept a lot of people from feeding their families." Red Hat shoved me the final five feet. "We have mouths to feed. I don't have a problem doing this."

I thrust my legs at the cage and braced myself. "Jim! Come get me!"

The man in the other cage moaned a wordless scream and rammed the bars.

Red Hat jerked me down. "Nobody's coming for you."

No! No, I will not be put into a fucking cage. I kicked against the cage, pitching myself backward. My head smashed into Red Hat's face. He dropped me. My feet touched the ground. Yes! I scrambled left.

Something smashed against my temple. Pain exploded between my ears. I spun. The woman behind me swung again and the bat took me straight in the face. The world shivered and I tasted blood on my lips.

Red Hat clamped me and muscled me forward. The man in the other cage let out a long desperate wail.

It was over. Jim fell asleep. Nobody was coming for me.

* * *

RED HAT WAS dragging me to the cage. The blond woman leaned over and swung open the door.

A man flew through the curtain and slid across the floor, knocking the tables and benches out of the way until he hit the wall. I caught a glimpse of long dark hair. He clenched his hands to his throat. A thin red spray shot from between his fingers. He gurgled, his eyes huge with sharp fear.

The curtain fell, revealing Jim, drenched in blood. His eyes glowed green and his face was terrible.

He came! Oh my gods, he came for me. It was going to be okay. Everything was going to be okay.

A stocky man lunged at Jim from the left, swinging a machete. Jim grabbed him. His knife flashed, and the man crumpled down, his machete slick with his own blood.

Red Hat threw me aside. I crashed into the cage and thrust the snail into the pocket of my jeans.

The blond woman by the cage screamed and swung her baseball bat at me. I ripped it out of her hands and bashed her with it. The bat snapped with a sharp wooden crunch. The blow knocked the woman across the room. That's right, fuck you!

A man fired a crossbow at Jim. Jim swayed out of the way, leapt, clearing the tables, and struck. The crossbowman fell like a lifeless doll. More people streamed from the back doorway.

Jim looked at me and smiled.

Red Hat shrugged his jacket off. A dark pattern swirled along his skin, like the whorls of wood grain. He headed toward Jim. A table got in his way, and he knocked it out of the way. The table splintered. Oh shit.

In the corner the old man waved his arms. Angry magic streaked through the air.

Jim was cutting his way toward me, his knife sending arcs of blood left and right. People screamed, wood crashed, Jim snarled. The scent of blood made me dizzy.

The prisoner moaned at me. The empty cage blocked his door. I pushed it. It didn't move. I wedged myself between the wall and the cage, planting my feet on its base, and pushed, pushed as hard as I could. Wood creaked, and the cage slid out of the way. I dropped to my knees. A long knotted cord bound the door, the knots holding coins. I grabbed it. Magic scorched my fingers and I jerked back, wincing.

The prisoner screamed, hitting the bars.

"It's okay," I told him. "It's okay, it's okay. I can do this. Just hold on one second."

Red Hat smashed into Jim.

Everything slowed down as if we were all underwater.

Jim's knife sliced, across, down, across the other way, still so fast, like lightning. The blade glanced off Red Hat's new wooden skin. Red Hat bared his teeth and swung his giant fist. Jim leaned out of the way, lean and graceful, and thrust. The knife bit deep into Red Hat's left eye. The big man bellowed like a bull.

Jim vaulted over him.

The caged man moaned. I'd need a week to figure how to break the seal without hurting myself. I didn't have a week.

Outside the window people screamed. More poachers coming in.

I grabbed the magic cord and jerked. It broke, leaving dark stripes of burned flesh across my hands. Pain lashed me, but I was too busy. I jerked the door open, grabbed the man by his shoulders, and pulled him out of there. He crashed on his side.

A hand caught my shoulder and pulled me up. "Time to go," Jim breathed.

"No!" I pointed to the prisoner. "I can't leave him. Help me."

Red Hat spun toward us, screaming, the knife still in the socket of his eye.

Jim cut, once, twice, and the prisoner's hands came free. Another cut took the mask from his head, and I stared at the face of the most stunning Asian man I had ever seen. He was like a celestial being from a Chinese watercolor—absolutely flawless.

The eyes of purest turquoise stared at me and within their depth I saw a spiral of fire.

Oh no.

The prisoner surged to his feet. Magic unfurled from him like a mantle in splashes of red and gold, forming the translucent outline of a scaled beast on four sturdy muscled legs.

Jim pushed me behind him and raised his knife.

Transparent claws the size of my hands dug into the wood. The head of a dragon formed upon the massive shoulders. The prisoner stood within the beast, still clearly visible. His hair had broken free of the bandages and it streamed down his back in a long dark wave.

Red Hat froze in midstep.

The old man howled a curse and clawed the air. A serpent of bright crimson launched itself from his fingers and bit at the translucent beast. The prisoner waved his arm, and the serpent sparked and melted into ash.

A Suanmi.

People burst through the door.

The Suanmi looked at them. The magic beast's maw gaped open.

Red Hat turned and started running.

Fire burst from the beast's mouth, roaring like an enraged animal. It caught the old man first, jerked him upright, and swept by, leaving a charred ruin of a body. The smoking corpse took two steps toward us and fell.

Jim clamped me to him, trying to shield me.

The men at the door scrambled to get out, but the fire fanned hot, all-powerful. Screams filled my ears. I shut my eyes and stuck my face into Jim's chest.

The screaming went on forever.

Finally the roar stopped. I pulled my head away from Jim.

The man within the dragon turned and looked at us. Jim growled, and his clothes exploded off his body. His skin ripped, releasing muscle underneath. Bones thrust, growing, muscle formed new powerful limbs, and a new skin sheathed it, showing the coils of black rosettes against a thin golden pelt. A new creature stood in Jim's place: half man, half monster. A werejaguar in the warrior form.

Jim snarled, his black lips framing enormous fangs, and stepped between me and the prisoner.

The Suanmi opened his mouth. Words flowed in English. "There is no need to fear me."

There was every need to fear him. He had dragon blood in his veins. I swallowed. "We mean no harm to you."

"I know." The Suanmi looked at the cage. "I'd come here,

sick and helpless. My family had been slaughtered and I was hurt. I came looking for medicine, but I lost consciousness and I awoke here. Nine months. I spent my eighteenth birthday in this cage while they carved pieces of my body to make themselves stronger. Healing the damage and waiting to be cut again. Nine months. Felt like forever."

"It was a bad dream," I told him. "It's over now."

"For me, yes." The man smiled. The transparent beast stretched his maw, mimicking the smile, baring enormous teeth. "For them, the nightmare is only beginning."

I took a deep breath. "We don't want to be a part of their nightmare. May we go?"

The Suanmi bowed his head, his turquoise eyes fixed on my face. "I owe you a debt, White Tiger."

I bowed back. Just let me and Jim go and we'll call it even.

"When you wish to collect it, come here," the Suanmi said. "It is my place now. I will take it from them by midday and by evening they will be bringing gifts to their new emperor."

He turned and walked away, deeper into the house.

Jim picked me up and took off running. I hugged his neck and then we were out in the courtyard. Around us people ran in panic. Smoke and fire billowed from the buildings.

"What the hell was that?" Jim growled, his words distorted by his huge mouth.

"A Suanmi. In Chinese legends the dragon had nine sons, each with their own powers. Turns out the nine sons gave rise to nine families. He is a descendant of the son who wields fire."

"He's part dragon?"

"Yes!"

"I don't care if he's part dragon. If he looks at you like that again, I'll cut his face off."

"How did he look at me?"

Jim leapt up the stairs and stopped almost in midstep.

"Why did you stop?"

He pointed at the vendor's cart filled with reproductions of old Japanese pornography. "The scroll with the woman in red."

On the fake scroll, the woman lay on the floor, her red kimono falling apart while a man with a huge mutant penis crouched over her. A string of *kanji* characters explained the scene. "Yes?"

"The first two characters in the second column, that's what I saw on the floor in the office."

"Put me down."

He lowered me to the ground. I leaned toward the scroll. The first character, second column: 女郎. *Jorō. Jorō?* Really? "Are you sure?"

"I'm sure."

"Jim, that's a very old word for whore. *Baita* is more common. I've never even seen *jorō* on a sign anywhere, it's that obscure."

"That's what I saw."

I had no idea what that meant. How would August even know that *kanji*? He could barely remember the word for bathroom.

Behind us someone roared and a burning wood beam crashed down, just like in an old movie. Jim took my hand, and we ran up the stairs, out of Underground Atlanta, and we didn't stop running until the door of my mother's house loomed before me.

AS SOON AS we walked through the door, my family mugged us. My mother had called an emergency. Everyone was there: uncles, aunts, cousins, neighbors. They pulled Jim away from me and took him to the garden. I tried to follow, but my mother stopped me.

"Do you have it?"

I dug in my pocket and deposited the snail into her hand. She held up the shell to light. "Alive. Good!" She swept to the corner of the room, where a glass box held the delicate white stars of the jasmine blossoms. She gently deposited the snail onto the snowy petals and shut the box.

"How long?" I asked.

"Six hours, if we're lucky. Ten, if we're not."

People fussed over me and asked me questions, and then I had to explain that the poacher market was no more. Then I was pushed into the kitchen and made to eat. There were so many dishes that the counter had no space. In my family, any emergency was met with an avalanche of food; the more dire the problem, the bigger the spread.

Over an hour later, I finally snuck away to steal a look at the Keong Emas. The snail had fed on jasmine. Its shell lay discarded and the fat body of the insect glowed with weak golden radiance.

"It's going well," my mother said. "So far."

"I'm going out," I told her.

"Where to?"

"To Komatsu Grocery to see August's family. I want to know what we're dealing with."

My mother pursed her lips. I knew what she was thinking. Of all the nationalities I have come across, the Japanese were usually hardest to talk to. They were always polite to a fault, but they didn't speak to police and they didn't speak to foreigners. Family matters were kept private and problems were resolved behind closed doors, so no undue attention would be drawn to the family.

"A waste of time," Mother said.

"I have a plan."

My mother clamped her hand to her chest, pretending to be scared. "Dali, do not make Komatsu Grocery explode. Where will I shop?"

"Mother!"

My mother rolled her eyes to the heavens with a look of uttermost suffering. I growled and went off to find my alpha.

By the time I fought my way through my relatives to the garden, Jim was human again and very naked. He was seated by the tree and the four older women were pouring spelled water over him, trying to purify the body.

His gaze found me, dark eyes pleading for help. I walked over to him, trying not to ogle.

"Help," he said.

I took his hand and held it. "They're trying to keep the evil out, until my mother can get the snail to hatch."

"Snails don't hatch," he said.

"This one does. Stay awake until I come back."

"Where are you going?"

"I have to do something. Nothing dangerous. I'll be back soon, okay? Don't worry, my family will take good care of you."

The hard alpha mask snapped onto Jim's face. "I look worried to you?"

"No. Don't kill any of my relatives while I'm gone either."

"Where are you going?"

I walked away.

If you deny a cat information, it will nag at him. If the cat happens to be a spymaster, it will drive him completely crazy. It would keep him awake. Besides, after his lecture on how I was smart but stupid and had a chip on my shoulder, I was allowed a little payback.

IT WAS ALMOST noon by the time I made it to South Asia. It was a grand name for a small spot in southern Atlanta, where the Asian-themed shops aggregated in a large plaza formed by an old mall. I stopped there a couple of times a month—it was the closest place to buy manga. Also, Komatsu Grocery was hands down the best Asian market in the area. They had a large selection and their seaweed salad was delicious. Whenever I went, I'd buy a two-pound tub of it and then pig out as soon as I got home.

I parked Pooki on a remote street, stepped out of my car, and stripped off my clothes.

There was a thing that August's family would dislike even more than having to speak to outsiders. They would go to great lengths to avoid attracting attention. And I was about to Cause a Scene.

My panties were off. I crouched and scratched a name in the pavement with the car key: Jim. Next I put my glasses on the passenger's seat, locked the car, dropped the keys behind the left wheel, and took a deep breath.

The world dissolved, swirling into a thousand *bokeh*, blurry little lights in every color of the rainbow.

Pretty colors.

Ooooh, so pretty.

Mmm, pretty, pretty.

So many scents. I liked that one, and this one, and this other one was kind of disgusting, and this one made me hungry.

I licked my lips. Mmm. Yummy smell, so good.

The *bokeh* slowly came into focus: I was lying in a street. Hmmm. I knew this street. This was South Asia.

Why was I here?

I looked down. On the pavement in front of me, right between my two paws, was a single word: *Jim*.

Jim. My handsome, awesome, scary Jim. Rawr. I smiled and sniffed the name. It didn't smell like Jim.

A memory popped in my head like a soap bubble bursting: Jim, dying, soul siphoned, Keong Emas, poachers, August. I came here to find out why August had disappeared for twenty-four hours.

I rose and padded around the corner. The magic was still up and when the light caught my fur, every hair gleamed. People stopped and stared. They knew who I was; I had come to South Asia before many times. They knew my magic, too, because it rolled off me with every step.

I walked over to the door of Komatsu Grocery and lay down in the middle of the street, staring at the door.

People looked at me, shocked.

I gave them a nice big smile. That's right, look what big teeth I have. I knew I was a vegetarian, but aside from Jim and a few friends, nobody else did. Besides, just because I didn't eat meat, didn't mean I wouldn't bite.

The few people aiming for the store decided they had better places to be.

After fifteen minutes August's second cousin, who liked to call herself Jackie, stuck her head out the door. I released my claws and stretched, making long scratches on the pavement. She gulped and ducked back in.

I could just imagine the conversation inside: "She's lying in front of our store!" "In front of our store? In the street where everyone can see?" "Yes!" "Oh no."

Minutes passed by. A little blue butterfly landed on my nose. I blinked at it and it fluttered to my ear. A big yellow butterfly gently floated over and landed on my paw. Soon a whole swarm of them floated up and down around me, like a swirl of multicolored petals. It happened in my backyard, too, if the magic was strong enough. Butterflies were small and light, and very magic sensitive. For some reason I made them feel safe and they gravitated to me like iron shavings to a magnet. They ruined my ferocious badass image, but you'd have to be a complete beast to swat butterflies.

If a baby deer frolicked out from between the buildings

trying to cuddle up, I would roar. I wouldn't bite it, but I would roar. I had my limits.

I flicked my tail. Hmm, a half hour had passed and we were getting close to the forty-five-minute mark. The family was trying to save face or having an argument, but if nobody came to say hello in the next few minutes, their behavior would be edging on rude. One can't ignore a mystic white tiger on their doorstep. It just wasn't done.

The door opened and August's auntie bowed and held it open. "Please, come in."

I trotted inside, leaving my Lepidoptera entourage outside. August's auntie led me past the counter to the back room, where August's grandmother, his uncle, and his mother sat. The entire Komatsu family with the exception of the children and August's white father. Their faces looked ashen.

I sat, curling my tail around me.

We looked at one another.

"We know why you are here," August's uncle said. Mr. Komatsu was a solemn-looking man in the best of times; now his expression was so grave, he could've been carved out of stone.

I waited.

"August is dead," he said.

I sighed. August was the first male son in his generation. The one who would be forgiven every wrong and permitted every privilege, because years later, when his father and uncle were old, he would assume the burden of taking care of Komatsu family. It was a terrible loss for the family.

"We have buried his body. It is our affair," Mr. Komatsu said.

I shook my head slowly. August was a shapeshifter and other shapeshifters died because of him. It was our affair now.

Mr. Komatsu stared straight ahead.

The grandmother leaned forward. "It's the woman. Her name is Hiromi. We do not know her family name. It happened seven years ago, just before the flare."

The flare came every seven years. If a normal magic fluctuation was a wave, the flare was a tsunami. Bad magic happened during the flare. It dissipated after three days or so, but those three days were terrible. The flare before last dumped a phoenix onto the city, right over the Asian neighborhoods. We had another flare this year and I made my family go to the Keep to stay safe.

"The bad magic was coming," August's mother said. "People boarded up their houses and flooded the stores to get supplies. Everyone was in a rush. Hiromi came in to buy groceries. I'd seen her before a few times. She looked poor. Her clothes were bad and she was thin. Very skinny. She had her daughter with her, a small little girl. She might be two or three."

"The child liked cookies," Mr. Komatsu said. "We offered some to her every time. Hiromi would only let her have one. Very proud."

August's mother took a deep breath. "Hiromi bought her groceries and went out, carrying her little girl. A street person stabbed them outside the door. We found him later. He was a crazed old man. The flare had made him insane. He didn't even remember doing it. He just stabbed them and walked away. Hiromi slumped against the wall, holding her baby, and people walked by. Everybody was in a terrible rush. Nobody wanted to get involved. Nobody stopped him and nobody helped her."

How terrible. To lie there and bleed out slowly into the street, knowing your child is dead in your arms. How awful.

"We didn't know she was dying outside of our store," Mr. Komatsu said. "When we found her, she had no pulse. She looked dead. We brought her and the little girl inside, in here. They were both cold and neither had a heartbeat."

"The flare had unleashed a phoenix and the city was burning," August's mother said. "We had to go. We left her. Meanwhile, the flare had awakened magic within Hiromi and pulled her back from death, but her little girl didn't survive. When we came back after the flare, she had woven a cocoon within the store. Before she left, she warned us that everyone would pay."

I had this sick cold feeling in the pit of my stomach. I knew exactly how this story would end.

"She remembered everyone who'd passed by her as she lay dying and didn't stop to help," Mr. Komatsu said. "On the one-year anniversary of her child's death, a mark and a note appeared on the door of the first family. Hiromi demanded a sacrifice: One member of the family had to go to her so she could . . . feed. If someone volunteered, the rest of the family would be left alone. They ignored it at first. Three days later she took the family."

"The families put together our money and hired the Mercenary Guild," August's mother murmured. "She killed them. Nobody would help us after that."

If only I could speak. They had let this monster terrorize them. They didn't ask for help. They could've gone to the Order, they could've gone to the cops. They could've gone to the Pack—August was a shapeshifter, after all, and his family was in danger. But they didn't, because everyone was too ashamed to admit that they had let a young woman and her child die alone on the street in plain view. They just took their punishment, paid their blood debt, and lived with guilt. It was the old honorable way and it cost them so many lives.

August's mother kept talking. "She is growing stronger and stronger. She has turned her cat into a *nekomata*, and it serves her with dark magic. Even her blood is no longer human. She bleeds ichor like a spider. She is growing greedy like one, too. People have been disappearing more and more as time goes by. Every year she marks a new door. This year she marked ours."

I'd guessed as much.

"I said I should go." August's grandmother drew herself upright. "I'm old. I've lived long enough."

"We argued about it," August's mother said. "While we argued, August decided that nobody should go. He went to meet Hiromi himself." Her voice broke and she closed her eyes.

August had died for them. For his family. The first son of the new generation, the heir to the family. They had lost their future and they were crushed.

Because August had disobeyed and fought, Hiromi had toyed with him. She must've infected him somehow, and he brought her magic with him to the shapeshifter office. Jim was in the wrong place at the wrong time, and now she wanted him. Well, she couldn't have him. He was mine.

Mr. Komatsu rose and put his arms around his sister. "We don't know what happened between Hiromi and my nephew.

We found August's body on our doorstep. He was drained. His corpse, it was devoid of all liquid. We buried him. The mark has disappeared from our door. We cannot help you. Now leave us in peace so we can grieve."

I rose and walked out, leaving the shards of a broken family behind me. I felt sick, but I finally knew what my enemy was.

I STOOD NEXT to my mother by the kitchen window. Through it, I could see the garden and Jim by the tree. It had taken eight hours for Keong Emas to mature and every hour had added years to Jim's face. His beautiful skin looked dull, as if rubbed with ash. Puffy circles clutched at his eyes. He looked exhausted, drained, like a man who had spent a decade working in some hellish mine. Only the eyes remained the same: sharp, dangerous eyes, backlit from within by a lethal green glow. He had the will to live, but no strength to keep going.

He was dying.

Poor Jim. My poor, poor Jim.

My mother pursed her lips. "It's not too late to let him go."

"It is."

"Your magic will not work on her. She is an insect demon."

Arachnid, actually. "I have a plan, Mother."

My mother turned to me slowly. Her lip trembled.

Oh my gods.

She hugged me, clenching me to her. "My brave baby, you're the only one I have. The only one. My precious one, my sweet daughter. You're my everything. I'm begging you, please, please, let him go."

I smelled tears and I knew she was crying, and then I cried, too. "I can't, Mother. I love him so much. I just can't."

She held on to me so tight, she must've been afraid I'd disappear into thin air. We stood holding each other for a long minute, and then she let me go. "All right. I will help you then."

She picked up the glass jar. Inside it, a single fat pupa hung off the glass wall.

My mother sniffed back her tears. "We go now."

We went out into the garden, my mother leading the way, and me following, carrying my calligraphy kit and old *keris* in my hand. The dagger curved in a wavy pattern from the asymmetrical base to the razor-sharp point, and the dozen metals that formed the blade shimmered as if the weapon was forged out of silvery running water.

Up close, Jim looked even worse. My family had kept him awake, but it had sapped all of his strength. Only the shell of a man was left.

Jim saw the knife. His lips moved. The words came out slowly. "If you needed a good knife, I'd let you borrow one of mine. You can't even cut straight with that thing."

I almost cried again.

My mother looked at me. Last chance to change my mind.

I nodded.

She sighed, opened the jar, and touched the tip of the pupa with her finger. Magic sparked through the tiny cocoon. It cracked and fell apart, breaking into dust. A radiant moth spread its wings in the pupa's place. Magic washed over me, warm beautiful magic, so potent and strong, it made my heart skip a beat. I held my breath.

Golden and glorious, glowing with a soft light, Keong Emas crawled to the lip of the jar. It fluttered its wings, sending tiny sparks of magic into the air, and took to the air, raining golden dust and minuscule bits of magic. It hovered above Jim, circled above him once, twice, fluttered through the garden, and flew away, far into the trees.

The entire garden lay bathed in a golden glow, tiny sparks of magic gleaming on plant leaves like precious jewels. I'd never seen anything so beautiful.

Mother gasped. I spun to Jim. Long strands of spiderweb clenched his neck, stretching upward, growing more transparent with each inch until they finally vanished about three feet above his head.

I glanced at my mother. "Go."

She set the glass jar down, turned, and fled. The rest of my family followed. In a moment, the garden and the house were deserted. Only Jim and I were left.

I came over and knelt by him. He slumped on the bench. He was so weak, he probably couldn't even move.

"How are you?"

Ashen lips moved. "Great. Never better."

"I found out what happened," I told him. "During the last flare, a woman and her daughter were stabbed in South Asia. They bled out into the street and nobody helped. It was horrible. The daughter died, but the woman survived. She turned into a monster and once a year she demands a sacrifice from the people who ignored her dying."

Jim's voice was weak. "How long has that been going on?"

"Seven years."

"And nobody said anything?"

I shook my head. "They felt ashamed. They tried hiring the Guild, but she killed the mercenaries. It became every family for themselves. August's family was the last one targeted. He went to fight the monster."

"With no backup?"

"Yes."

Jim sighed. "People are idiots."

"That theory seems likely, yes."

Jim coughed. "So what now?"

"There are spiderwebs attached to your throat. I'm going to cut them with my pretty magic knife. When I do, you will faint from shock. Then the woman will come back and try to devour you anyway, because her type never lets prey get away."

"Is that why everyone left?"

I nodded.

"Are you going to curse her?"

"Something like that."

Jim stared at me. "Dali?"

How did he always know when I was hiding something? "There is a small problem with that. My curses only work on animals and people. Something with blood. Hiromi has no blood. She has insect slime. Remember the *kanji* character you saw on the floor? *Jorō*, the whore? That was part of her demon name. That's why August knew it. His family had been terrified of her for years. She's *jorōgumo*, the whore spider. So I'll have to be creative." *And if I fail, you will never wake up.*

He tried to rise but managed only a twitch.

"You can't stop me," I told him. "Don't worry. I've got this."

"You should go," he said. "Leave me."

"Having a vegetarian blind girl save your behind really bothers you, doesn't it?"

"I don't want you to get hurt."

I took his hand and squeezed it, trying to keep the tears out of my voice. "I'm about to cut the web, Jim. You have about a minute, so if there is something you really need to tell me, you have to do it now."

His eyes told me he understood. This could be the last time we spoke to each other.

"I'm sorry about our fight."

"I forgive you," I told him, and sliced through the first line. The *keris* severed it in one short cut. It blinked and vanished. "You just don't understand what it's like not to be pretty. It's because you've always been hot."

He coughed. "Hot?"

"Mhm."

"Have you ever looked at me?"

"I have. I look at you all the time, Jim." I severed the second line. It disappeared. A shudder ran through Jim's body. His legs trembled.

"About Indonesian," Jim said. "I learned it so I could talk to you."

Oh, Jim. What the hell, I might never see him again. This was my last chance. I leaned over and kissed his lips.

He kissed me back. It was tender and loving and everything I had dreamed it would be. Tears ran down my face and I couldn't stop them. I loved him. I didn't know if he loved me back. He might have kissed me out of gratitude or for some other strange reason, but it seemed so unimportant now. If someone offered me a choice, his life or his love, I would give him up. Even if it meant he would never remember me and we would never speak again. As long as he lived. That's all I wanted. I just wanted him to be okay.

We broke apart and I looked into his eyes. "You're ready?"

"Kick her ass," he said.

I cut the third line.

His eyes rolled back in his head. He slumped back. I touched my fingers to his neck. Alive. Come on, Lyc-V. Fix him up.

There was nothing left to do but wait. I sat down. If I were Kate, I could pull out my sword and when Hiromi showed up, I'd spit some magic at her and then cut her to pieces. If I were Andrea, I'd shoot it until it died. If I were Jim's cousin, who served as the female cat alpha until Jim found a mate, I'd rip into her with claws. But I wasn't. I was me. All I had was my brain, ink, and some paper.

I opened my kit and began to write.

A small noise made me raise my head. A Japanese woman stood on the edge of the garden. She wore a long, flowing white robe. Her skin was like fine porcelain, her eyes were beautifully shaped, and her hair spilled down her back like glossy black silk.

Twenty minutes. Didn't take her long at all.

"You can drop the disguise," I said. "I know what you are."

"And what would that be?" she asked. Her voice was like a silver bell. Even if she didn't attack Jim, I'd hate her out of pure jealousy.

"You are a *jorōgumo*. The whore spider."

The woman's kimono split at the bottom and ripped apart. Thick chitin legs spilled forth, bristling with stiff dark hairs. A demonic creature rose before me: her bottom half, spider, and her top half, a human torso sheathed in overlapping bands of black exoskeleton. Her spider body was as long as my Prowler and twice as wide. This was bad.

Ice clamped my spine. My throat threatened to close up. I bet Kate never got scared like that. I unclenched my teeth. "I think I just threw up a little bit in my mouth."

"The man is mine." Hiromi pointed her slender arm at Jim.

"No, this man is *mine*."

Hiromi moved forward, one spider leg after another, probing the ground. I watched her come toward me, a dark monster in the glowing garden. In life she had so little, and the only thing she treasured, her daughter, was ripped away from her. If I were Hiromi, I'd see becoming a demon as a great honor. It was my chance to use my powers to punish those who wronged me, to be strong and feared. But the longer she stretched out her revenge, the more selfish she became. Punishing the wicked was no longer enough, I could see it in her eyes. She had given in to greed.

She was almost to the line I'd scratched earlier in the dirt. Step, another step . . .

If the magic fell, both Jim and I would be in serious trouble.

The ugly spider leg touched the line. A gold glow sparked and dashed across the grass and rocks, outlining an octagon with Jim in the center. The demon yowled and recoiled.

"A very complicated ward. Took me an hour to make," I told her. I had made it while still in tiger form, after I had learned at the grocery store what I would be facing.

"I am Hiromi *Jorōgumo*, the Binding Maiden, the Bloody Mother. You will give him to me!"

Wow, now she was bestowing titles on herself. I crossed my arms on my chest. "And I am Dali, the White Tiger, the Guardian of Bunut Bolog. My magic is as strong as yours. You will not pass."

I'd guessed right—Hiromi was hung up on being a *jorōgumo*. She viewed it as an honor and she was arrogant and vain, which meant I had a chance. It was a tiny, tiny chance, but it was better than nothing. I just had to play the game by her rules.

A grimace jerked her face. "I've heard of you, Dali Harimau, White Tiger. You can't guard him all the time. He has to sleep eventually and when he does, I will devour him."

"I'm not arguing with you. That's why I want to offer you a bargain." I held up the piece of paper.

Hiromi leaned forward. "What bargain?"

"A contract. You ask me a riddle. If I answer correctly, you will leave him and me alone."

Riddles were the traditional way to resolve issues. If she truly thought like a demon, it would appeal to her.

Hiromi's eyes narrowed. "And if you don't?"

"Then you get to eat Jim and me."

"You? The magical White Tiger?"

"Yes."

Hiromi's mouth gaped open, releasing a row of sharp fangs. Saliva stretched down from her teeth in thin strands. She was imagining eating me and drooling. Eww.

"Three riddles," she said. "You answer every one."

"Fine."

I corrected the contract.

"What guarantee do I have that you will submit?" she asked.

"The contract is magically binding." I put the paper on the

ground and pushed it across the ward with a stick. "It's signed in my blood. If you sign it in your ichor, we will have a deal."

Hiromi lowered her big spider body to the ground and swiped the piece of paper with her human hand.

Come on, Hiromi. Be as greedy as I hope you to be.

Hiromi struck at her side. Pale translucent liquid spilled out, carrying with it small knots of yellow slime. Ew, ew, ew!

The *jorōgumo* dipped her finger into the liquid and drew it across the contract. Magic snapped, clutching at the paper.

I took a deep breath and touched the ward. It melted into nothing.

"First riddle." Hiromi bared her teeth. "It rises to the heavens but never reaches them; it flies like a bird but has no wings; it makes you weep without a cause; those who see it stop and stare; it served as my black funeral shroud and it was the only one I had. What is it?"

Funeral shroud. What did she see as she lay dying? People walking and the city on fire, because of the phoenix birthed by the flare. And where there was fire, there was . . . "Smoke," I said. "When you died, Atlanta was burning. Next."

Hiromi clamped her mouth shut. Her spider legs kneaded the ground. "Men make it, but gods crave it; its loss weakens, its appearance threatens; fear chills it, war heats it; it binds family together, and I watched mine leave me."

"Blood. You watched yourself bleed out onto the street."

Hiromi rocked back and forth. She had powerful magic, but it didn't make her smart. The blood riddle was almost painfully obvious. What else could fear chill except for your blood?

"Last one."

Hiromi shifted back and forth, left and right, thinking. On the bench Jim opened his eyes. He blinked and saw the *jorōgumo*. His lips drew back, revealing his teeth. Hiromi saw him and hissed, her legs churning the ground.

I pointed at Jim. "Stay where you are! Hiromi, we had a deal. The last riddle."

Hiromi bit the air with her fangs and hissed at me. "It has eyes but cannot see; it has ears but doesn't listen; it has fangs, but it doesn't hunt; it has a womb, but it's shriveled and dry; it has knowledge but can't save itself; it will die alone, regretting everything. What is it?"

Ha! "It's me. Do you think I don't know myself, Hiromi?"
She snarled. Spit flew from her mouth.

That's right, rage away. You know you want a piece of me.
I'm so tasty. Come get me.

Hiromi wailed in helpless fury.

She was almost there. I just had to piss her off enough. "You
are stupid, Hiromi. *Baka, baka* Hiromi. You are dumb like a
worm."

White substance burst from behind her in wet clumps and
flew to the trees and the house, unfurling into webs.

Behind me Jim tried to rise.

"Jim, stay down!" I barked. "Look at him, you had him and
I took him away from you. Even if you weren't a freak, he
would never be with you. There is nothing you can do about it,
Hiromi. Nothing! We will go free. You are weak! Helpless and
we—"

Hiromi let out a screech and charged at me. The huge spider body swept me off my feet. Hiromi's chitin arms grasped
me and dragged me up to her mouth.

Jim pushed himself off the bench and stumbled forward,
like a drunk man on wet cotton legs.

A sweet, slightly woodsy aroma drifted through the air.

Hiromi's mouth gaped at me, the fangs dripping drool and
venom.

A swarm of long yellow petals swirled around us. Wet mist
slicked my skin and Hiromi's chitin.

Jim conquered the last two feet and clamped onto Hiromi's
spider leg, trying to rip it apart.

Hiromi's arms shook. "What is this?"

"Punishment for eating people."

Her fingers lost their strength. I slipped through them and
fell clumsily on my butt.

Hiromi reared above me on her hind limbs, the six remaining spider legs waving in the air. Her back arched, farther and
farther, and for a second I thought she would crush me. The
jorogumo screamed, a desperate shriek of pain and sheer terror.

Jim threw himself over me.

Hiromi twisted left, her legs jerking back and forth, rocked
by spasms. She dashed into the water and smashed into the
statue of Lakshmi, leaving a yellowish splatter on her side,

veered left, banged into a tree, trampled through the oleander bushes, rammed herself into the fence, and spun in place, screaming. The yellow petals chased her, clinging to her skin.

I pulled Jim up into a sitting position and hugged him in case he fell. He wouldn't remember it later anyway—far more exciting things were happening.

Hiromi's legs churned the ground. She sprinted to the house, ran up the wall partway, until she was almost vertical, and crashed back down. Her human arms flailed. She plunged them into her body and ripped chunks of skin out.

Her front left leg snapped like a toothpick. She screeched and hammered herself into the house. A yellow stain spread on the wall. She rammed the house again and again. The brick walls shook. Tiny cracks crisscrossed Hiromi's body. She charged the house again and her body burst. Ichor drenched the wall. The remains of the *jorōgumo* slid down and lay still.

A sickly salty smell hit us.

"That's a hell of a thing," Jim said.

He came for me again. He could barely move, but he dragged himself up and threw himself at an enraged demon for my sake. It was enough to make a girl cry. Except that now the danger had passed and my head was clear. I knew I was reading too much into it.

"What did you do to her?" he asked.

"I couldn't curse her directly, so I wrote a contract with a curse in it. She signed it with her ichor," I said. "She gave it power over herself, and when she broke the agreement, it tore her apart."

"And the petals?"

"Chrysanthemums." I smiled and rested my cheek on his shoulder. "The punishment curse written into the contract. They produce pyrethrum oil. It's deadly to insects and arachnids: It attacks their central nervous system, drives them mad, and then kills them."

We looked at the yellow mess on the side of the house.

"My mother is going to kill me," I said.

I TOOK THE metal teakettle off the stove and poured boiling water into the smaller ceramic one. The delicate jasmine fragrance spread through my kitchen. Around me my house was quiet.

It had taken two days to clean up my mother's house. For two days I did nothing but scrub nasty demonic spider insides off the walls, the benches, and the rocks while Jim got to eat great food and be fussed over by my mother. Last night he got better and left. I spent the night at my mother's and then came back to my place. The mail had piled up. Pooki probably missed me, although he didn't say anything when I came to check on him in the garage.

It was evening now. I poured the tea and sat on my short couch.

I'd made a total fool of myself. I had kissed Jim and then I hugged him. So embarrassing. Hopefully he wouldn't remember.

That's what happened when you let your emotions get the better of you—you lost the ability to think clearly. Sooner or later we would have to work together. It would be so awkward. I put my hand over my face. I was by myself in the house and I was still embarrassed.

Sad, pathetic blind girl drinking her tea and hiding her face. I took a deep breath and let it out slowly. I needed another race. It would make me feel better. Somewhere in that stack of paper was the estimate from the repair shop. The sooner I gave them the okay, the faster I'd get Rambo back.

A familiar male scent tugged on me.

Oh my gods. No. No, no, no, no.

I took my hand from my eyes.

He was inside the room, leaning on the wall next to my patio door. He looked great. Like nothing ever happened.

What do I do now?

Jim raised a small wicker basket.

"What's that?"

"That's a steak for me and mushroom pasta for you. The pasta is made with tofu and palm oil instead of eggs. I cooked it myself. My steak is wrapped in several layers of foil. It's not touching the container with your food, so no worries."

Um . . . He made me dinner. He cooked for me. In shape-shifter terms that was like delivering three dozen red roses with a tag that read I LOVE YOU. What in the world was he doing?

"I thought you might want a change from your mother's

cooking." Jim grinned. He looked almost unbearably handsome. "Not that it isn't great, but three days of rice is a little much."

"Jim . . ."

"The problem with being an alpha is that you can never make the first move. Makes you feel like you're taking advantage of your position. You have to wait until the other person decides they want in."

Jim set the basket on the coffee table and crouched by me.

"And sometimes it seems like that person likes you, and you try to test the waters, so you try to tell her how you feel, that she matters and that you want to be with her and you're concerned about her safety. And every time you do that, she waves her arms around and accuses you of being a controlling alpha asshole. So you back off and hope you didn't completely fuck it up."

He was close, too close. I just stared at him. What was happening . . . "Why are you telling me this?"

His voice was low and smooth. "That time when I told you it didn't matter what your mother thought about your looks . . ."

"Aha . . ."

"I meant it," he said. "Because I think you're beautiful."

This was actually really, really happening.

He kissed me.

Oh my gods.

ICE SHARDS

AN OTHERWORLD NOVELLA

YASMINE GALENORN

Dedicated to

My Lady Mielikki

I seemed to vow to myself that some day I would go to the region of ice and snow and go on and on till I came to one of the poles of the earth, the end of the axis upon which this great round ball turns.

—ERNEST SHACKLETON

Though lovers be lost love shall not;
And death shall have no dominion.

—DYLAN THOMAS

ONE

I STARED AT THE PORTAL, WONDERING IF I
really wanted to do this. I'd been running from this moment
for almost six centuries. I'd been running from my memories
for just as long. Now, even though I wasn't sure how, I had to
return to the place where my downfall had taken place—and
right what went wrong.

*If I can. If I am truly innocent. But what happens if I find out
that I did it? What happens if I find out that I really did kill Vikkommin and forever lock his soul within a shadow, to roam the
northern lands, crazed like a wild, magical beast? What . . .
what if I am the monster the temple Elders thought I might be?*

Camille, Smoky, and Rozurial stood behind me, Camille's
hand on my shoulder. "All you have to do is say the word and
we go through. Or turn back. It's up to you, Iris. We'll support
whatever decision you make."

I glanced up at the raven-haired beauty who made up one-
third of the half-human, half-Fae D'Artigo sisters. She had
dressed for the journey, eschewing her usual bustiers and chif-
fon skirts and stilettos for a warm, black split skirt and turtleneck, and a heavy cape slung around her shoulders. The cape

was thick and resonated with magic, having been cut from the hide of the Black Unicorn himself. Camille carried a staff with her that I'd never before seen.

"Where did you get that?" I pointed to the intricately carved stave. The wood resonated as yew. The head was a polished knob of intricately wrought silver surrounding a crystal orb the size of my fist.

She smiled and ran her hand over the burled surface of the wood. "A gift. From Aeval. I still don't know how to use it, but I thought I'd bring it along. It will make hiking easier, in any matter."

"Enough said." I didn't have to ask any more. The Queen of Darkness was to be Camille's new mistress, and it seemed she intended for her new acolyte to return in one piece.

Two men stood beside Camille—Smoky, one of Camille's three husbands, and Rozurial, an incubus. Smoky's hair coiled with a life of its own, surrounding him like a cloud of spun silver, and he stood more than two feet taller than me. Smoky was a dragon—half silver, half white, and pale as milk on a snowy morning. He'd come down from the Dragon Reaches high above the Northlands untold years ago, leaving his homeland to reside Earthside. Rozurial had dark curly hair, and he'd searched the Northlands from one side to the other, looking for the crazed vampire who had destroyed his family, the same one who had turned Camille's sister Menolly. Rozurial knew the land like the back of his hand.

Smoky knelt beside me and took my hand, bringing it up to press gently to his forehead. "Lady Iris," he said, his eyes whirling, a glacial pool of hoarfrost and ice. "We will do whatever we can to protect you on your journey. The Northlands are a dangerous place but you know this better than anyone. You are part of my wife's extended family; therefore you are my sister. Whatever I can do to help, if it is within my power, I will do."

My hand seemed so small in his—we Talon-haltijas were, like all types of sprites, tiny. I was barely a smidge over four feet tall, petite though sturdy. I gazed at his hand and then curled my fingers around his, squeezing them tight.

Rozurial joined him. "The only thing that can drag me back to the Northlands is to help a good friend. You're one of the best. Even if you won't date me." He gave me a twinkling smile, but concern lurked behind the mask of humor.

I grinned at him. Roz would never change, and for that I loved him. "I won't date you because I'm already dating Bruce. And you . . . you're a heartbreaker."

"Not my fault, just my nature," he pleaded.

I turned to Camille, whose lips bowed in a gentle smile. She let out a long sigh. "If we're going, we'd better get a move on. It will be freezing in Otherworld, and we need to portal jump to the Northlands before nightfall."

I steeled myself.

You know it is time . . . The words tickled my thoughts, sliding over my doubts and fears like cool comfort on a hot summer night.

Yes, my Lady, I know . . . I cannot avoid this any longer. But please, guard over us, and whatever happens to me, watch that the others return to fight against the demons. I am taking them into danger.

But Undutar's voice was soothing, and for the thousandth time I was grateful she hadn't forsaken me when the temple Elders had.

They go with you willingly, my Priestess. Come now. Return to the lands of your power. Return to me. Free Vikkommin's spirit, break the curse upon you, and clear your name so you will be able to marry and have children.

I stared at Grandmother Coyote's portal. We were standing in the middle of a snow-shrouded wood, in the Belles-Faire district of Seattle, a few miles from home. But we were about to travel through the veil, to Otherworld, the land of Camille's birth. From there we would journey to the Northlands, the world I'd left behind so long ago, when I'd been branded a murderer, stripped of my strongest powers, and cast out of the order of Undutar, the Goddess of the Mist and Snow.

I sucked in a deep breath and turned to the three of them. "I'm ready." As we stepped through the portal, the world shifted. There was no turning back.

WE EMERGED FROM the portal near the mounds surrounding the Elfin city of Elqaneve. Great, snow-covered grass barrows served as the ancient tombs of elfin lords and heroes, the site where horrific battles had been waged and won or lost, long past in the mists of time.

We arrived in the midst of a snowstorm—the seasons in Otherworld matched those back home. By the looks of things, the snow had already fallen thick and fast. On a positive note, Otherworld had escaped the global warming that was affecting Earthside. The air over here was also cleaner than the air back home, and a soft flow of magic replaced the constant hum of electricity.

Nearby, a family of elves readied themselves for a jump somewhere—Dahnsburg, according to the sign they were standing next to—and I stared at them, thinking that it was no different from a family holiday vacation back in Seattle, except they were traveling via portal rather than airplane.

"What do we do first?" Camille asked.

"We meet up with the Great Winter Wolf Spirit. He's agreed to help me."

Actually, Howl and I had struck a bargain, is what we'd done. He would help me, if I worked to help his Earthside wolfen children. I'd joined Wolf Whistle—a new organization in Seattle dedicated to spreading the return of the wolves across the United States and protecting them from slaughter—and I was pouring time and energy into the group. That seemed enough to satisfy him.

"I'm glad I caught you."

Turning, I was surprised to see Trenyth standing there. Queen Asteria's adviser, the elf was kind and regal and fair. It seemed that trouble always followed close on his heels.

"Trenyth—what are you doing here? We didn't tell anybody we were coming."

He gave a genteel bow. "I've come to escort you to your meeting."

Camille glanced at me, a question in her eyes. I shook my head slightly. I hadn't let him know we were on the way, so he must have found out through some other means. We waited until we were in the carriage headed toward the inn on the other side of the Elfin city, before Camille turned to the adviser.

"How did you know we were coming?"

I knew she wanted to ask how her father was—they were on the outs—but she didn't, and I decided not to broach the subject. Trenyth seemed startled. He paused, then gave a sideways glance at Rozurial, who cleared his throat.

I turned to Roz. "What did you do?"

He hemmed and hawed for a moment, then gave a little shrug. "Well, I figured the elves should know what we're doing. Just in case . . ." With a sideways glance back at me, he smiled and I realized he thought I'd be mad at him. Which wasn't far off.

"Rozurial is right on one thing." I sighed, then looked over at Trenyth. "We're heading into danger. Some of the creatures in the Northlands could rip us to shreds without the least exertion. And my end goal . . . is dangerous as well. I suppose somebody had to know over here. Just in case we don't check back in, would you let them know back home?"

Trenyth tried to keep his voice light, but his eyes were somber. "Of course, Lady Iris. But you *must* come through this alive and in one piece. The war against the demons is too dangerous for *any* of you to die."

Smoky punched Roz in the arm, and not all that gently. "Good thinking, though I hate to admit it. But next time, I'll take care of the worrying."

"Easy, Dragon-Boy. I am not after your woman. She has three husbands, and there's no room for me." Roz arched one eyebrow, but now he was teasing and the tension slipped away. Though they had actually gone tooth and claw at one point, they were friends now. For the most part.

Camille shook her head. "No use arguing. They'd gang up on us."

Feeling outnumbered—and loved—I laughed. "Not a problem, as long as we don't miss our appointment with Howl. I'm not upset he spilled the beans."

But inside, I was pissed at Roz for sticking his nose in where I hadn't asked him to. I didn't *want* anybody else knowing about this. The last thing I needed was for Asteria, the Elfin Queen, to look at me with a question in her heart. I had enough of those myself.

Trenyth seemed to sense my mood. He leaned toward me. "Lady Iris, Ar'jant d'tel—the Queen knows only that you are planning a 'vacation' to the Northlands. I did not tell her the reason and, unless it threatens security, I will not tell her. I give you my word."

Relieved, I forced a smile to my lips. "You're all right, Trenyth. I owe you one."

"Just do what you need to do, and reclaim what is rightfully yours." He lifted my fingers to his lips, gently kissing the top of my hand. A shiver ran through me and I gazed up at him, wondering just how much he knew.

Ar'jant d'tel. In the language of my childhood—the language of the Talon-haltija—it meant Chosen of the Gods, bound for great hope and responsibility. But the title had been stripped away with my honor and every hope I'd ever had. I opened my lips to protest, but one glance at his eyes—at his caring gaze—stopped my tongue. *Trenyth* believed in me. Could I do any less?

I let out a long sigh and nodded. "Thank you. And we gratefully accept your help. I'm afraid . . . but I have to do this."

"I know," he said. "I know."

MY NAME IS Iris Kuusi, and I'm one of the Talon-haltija, a Finnish house sprite. I was born for greater things. Chosen by the Temple of Undutar when I was very young, I was carried away, much like the young Dalai Lama, and raised to be a priestess. My destiny was to become High Priestess—to rule over ice and mist and fog as the handmaiden of a goddess.

My consort was chosen in much the same way. We were raised together, never questioning our destinies, accepting that we would rule over the Order until we were old, if our goddess willed it.

But shortly before we ascended to our posts—before the elderly Priestess let go and fell into her final, mist-shrouded sleep—something happened, and I left the temple under a cloud of suspicion, never to return.

For six hundred years, when winter sweeps into the land, I feel the chill of the snow in my heart, and in every shadow I see Vikkommin's accusing face. And I wonder—did I commit the crime of which they accused me? The Elders never ascertained whether I was actually guilty. And in my heart, I do not know the truth. I don't know if I'm a murderer, or whether I was framed . . .

* * *

"WHAT ARE YOU thinking about?" Roz tapped me on the shoulder. I gave him a slow smile, thinking that he, too, had seen a life of pain and torture. The gods were cruel in their play and fate unmerciful in her choices.

"I'm wondering what I'll find. Whether I'll be able to find the answers."

Trenyth glanced over at me from his seat opposite mine. "I have every faith in you, Iris. I trust you are innocent. But you need to prove it, once and for all, to lift the curse and to move on with your life."

I nodded. There was no going back, no turning around and ignoring it. I wanted to marry Bruce O'Shea, my leprechaun lover, and have children—a whole passel of them. I was still young, young enough to have the large family for which I longed. But until I could answer the questions as to what happened that night, the temple Elders had cursed me to forever be barren.

But what if I'm guilty? How will I live with that?

With these thoughts running through my head, I stared out the window as we passed through the city streets. The houses in Elqaneve all had a mossy, leafy feel, even though they were made of stone and wood just like back Earthside. But their yards and lawns—they were brilliant works of art, living gardens that sparkled and popped with energy. Even in the winter, under a thick blanket of snow, they were filled with ice sculptures and the crystalline look of snow on conifers.

Camille leaned her head against Smoky's chest, and he wrapped his arm around her. She was five seven, and next to his six four, she was positively diminutive. "Where are we headed?"

I let out a low sigh. "We meet Howl at the Wounded Warrior. It's an inn."

"How will we know him? I assume you know what he looks like?"

I nodded, quietly. I knew what Howl looked like all too well. "We've talked several times over the years. The last, near the fall equinox when I came to Otherworld with Camille. Howl and I met then, and I asked for his help." And then I told them what I'd asked.

* * *

SEVERAL MONTHS BEFORE, near the autumn equinox, I'd journeyed back to Otherworld with Camille and Morio— her second husband. While Camille reunited with her alpha lover Trillian, Morio and I'd prowled the streets of Dahnsburg. I'd left Morio outside in the streets telling him I'd be out later. Howl had instructed me to come alone and I didn't want him to think I was cheating on our deal, so I entered the tavern by myself. The Crystal Bridge, a sister bar to the Wounded Warrior in Elqaneve, primarily serviced veterans of the Y'Elestrial civil war. Elfin vets, that is. Too many had been killed or captured by Lethesanar, the Opium Eater drug-crazed queen who had been taken down by her sister. A number had retreated to Dahnsburg, on the shores of the Wyvern Ocean, hoping for rejuvenation.

The bar was dark, gloomy, and filled with smoke from a dozen different herbal smoking mixtures. I coughed, glancing around. Amid the shadows that flickered in the dim lights, I saw a variety of elves mingling with Fae and even a few Svartans. But these elves didn't have the easy look of most of their kin. They were weathered, some missing limbs or limping, and had a look in their eyes that reminded me of myself six hundred years ago. They'd been through hell, and returned.

One wandered up to me and leaned down, his fingers reaching for my hair. "Beauty. You are such a little beauty—"

"I can cut your privates off with a whisper to the wind," I said, smiling sweetly. "Do you *really* want to chance it?"

Most people thought I was a pushover, an easy mark, since I was so short and petite. Some assumed I was mild and delicate; others thought I was a cozy maid. But I'd seen too much to ever be mild or cozy or an easy mark. I hid my memories well, but they were always there to fuel the need to fight.

He looked at me, looked deep in my eyes, and backed off. "No, I don't think I do. Mistress, be safe on your way." As he turned to leave, a small gleam of clarity peeked out through his fog-shrouded gaze.

I continued through the bar unaccosted, the cacophony of noise crowding my thoughts. The smells of ale and wine were thick, and I motioned to the bartender. "Brandy, please."

Tossing a coin on the counter, I took the proffered glass and turned to let my gaze flicker through the crowd.

There . . . in the corner . . . a man who was staring directly at me. He was tall, at least to me, probably about five nine and rough looking. Five-o'clock razor stubble shadowed his chin. I knew those features.

Howl.

He was wearing leather buckskin pants, and his chest was bare, with a cape of wolf pelts draped around his shoulder and a headdress of teeth and bones and cedar rising from his head. His eyes were dark, so dark you could fall in and lose yourself for days. He looked to be in his early forties, and I noticed everyone had given him wide berth.

When he caught me staring at him, he raised his glass silently to me and I headed over in his direction.

"Howl. It's good to see you again."

"As it is you, Lady Iris." He motioned to the opposite seat. "Please, sit."

I slid into the booth and carefully placed my brandy on the table in front of me. "Thank you for meeting me. I did bring a companion but left him outside." I wanted to be straight up in case he somehow knew I'd come with backup.

"Not a problem," he said, attending to his own drink. He paused, sipping the golden liquor in his glass. "So, tell me, how can I help you?"

"I'm seeking information and help and it has to do with something in the Northlands. You are one of the Elemental Lords, ruling over the plane of ice and snow. I thought perhaps you might be willing or able to help me."

"You ask, knowing there is always a price to pay. I sense no fear. Desperation, perhaps? You are able. Willing? We shall see." He raised one eyebrow. *"Ar'jant d'tel.* Chosen of the Gods. You wear the cloak in your aura but not on your back. Why?"

I let out a soft sigh. "I was accused of murder, of misusing my powers. I have no memory of whether this is true. That is what I seek to find out: What really happened so many centuries ago. Whether I destroyed the man I loved or whether I was framed. That's why I need your help."

"How would I be able to help you with that?"

I paled. "They say I ripped away his spirit and embedded it

in a moving shadow, then destroyed his body. I certainly had the power to do so, but . . ."

"And again, I ask, how would I be able to help you with this?"

I gazed into his eyes, direct, opening up my fears that I would be forever cursed. "His spirit roams in shadow form through the Northlands, through the lands you rule over, and that is where I must go to seek the truth. Vikkommin is forever trapped within the shadow and he's gone mad over the years. I need to set him free and hope to learn the truth of my past if I'm ever to break a curse placed on my head."

Howl finished his drink and signaled for another. He leaned forward, across the table. "Mistress Sprite, you have been living in sorrow for centuries now. Are you sure you want to chance deepening that pain? What if you find out that you were responsible?"

I swallowed the rest of my drink, and when the waitress came I motioned for another.

"If I did do it, then I'll turn myself in to the temple and await their punishment. They set me free the first time because we couldn't find the truth. If I *am* culpable, then I will accept their decree, whatever it is."

The thought of what the Elder Council could—and would— do to me should I be proven guilty terrified me. But if I had done it . . . if I'd trapped Vikkommin for centuries in shadow form and tortured his body, then I deserved whatever they offered me. I hung my head, waiting.

Howl reached across the table and took my hand in his. His touch sparked the wild, feral side of me and I gazed into those brilliant eyes.

"You truly deserve your title, stripped or not. Few are so brave as to willingly walk into the fire. But my dear Iris, I cannot help you. Not now. This is not my season and the Northlands are in the throes of autumn. Return to me near midwinter. Return to me when the snows are high and the winds howl around the eaves. And then I will help you. You may bring with you three friends. That is all I will allow when it comes to mortals."

I caught his fingers in mine. "Thank you. I did not expect you to agree."

"Beware, Iris Kuusi—I have offered my help in uncovering your past. It may not be the help you want. It may be the door to your own destruction."

"Understood." I polished off my brandy and nodded to him, turning to leave.

"Iris?"

Turning back, I saw he was leaning forward, watching me. "Yes?"

"You are caught between worlds, you are caught between paths, between destinies. If you do this thing, it may alter your life forever. Make very certain you are willing to pay the cost before returning to me. Only then shall you summon me."

He tossed me a shimmering quartz bead. I caught it, gazing into the fractured surface. I could have sworn snowflakes glimmered from within. "What is this?"

"When you are ready, smash the gem and it will alert me. I'll meet you in Elqaneve, in the Wounded Warrior tavern, two days after you have shattered the crystal. If you do not come to me within that time, then it will be as if we had never spoken."

As I watched, he flickered and began to vanish, and then— he faded out of the booth and it was as if he'd never been there.

I GLANCED UP, shaking off my memories. Everyone was looking at me, including Trenyth. I let out a long sigh. "I broke the crystal yesterday. If I don't meet him before sunrise, I won't ever meet him at all. He'll lead us to the Northlands."

Smoky nodded. "I have spoken with him, long ago. He is as honorable as you can expect one of the Elemental Lords to be."

"I came prepared with some gifts to make your journey easier," Trenyth said. But my mind was far away, returning over and over to the bloody room and what was left of my fiancé. And the dark shadow he had become.

TWO

THE STREETS WERE NEARLY CLEAR BY THE
time we pulled up in front of the Wounded Warrior. Trenyth
had given us climbing rope and food, and delicately light elfin
cloaks that shed snow and water and cold like a duck's down.
As he helped me out of the carriage, he took me aside.

"Mistress Iris, I have something for you and I want you to
promise me you'll carry it with you." He held out a small jew-
elry box.

I frowned, slowly accepting it. "What is this?"

Inside the velvet box sat a ring, a silver ring with a blue
stone. It was beautiful and ornate, the band embellished with
etchings of roses and leaves, but the energy coming from it
was obscured to me.

"This is a ring of Shevah. It captures the spirit of Elqaneve
and draws on the powers of Queen Asteria. It will strengthen
you in the storm and shadow, and guide you when you are not
sure of which direction to go. It won't save you from harm,
nor will it bring you victory, but the gift it bears may help see
you through your task with a little more safety."

His soft smile touched my heart, and I gazed into the eyes

of the royal assistant. He was right-hand man to the Queen, her personal bodyguard. We had seen into his heart and knew something he didn't even know about himself—Trenyth was in love with Queen Asteria. She was his all, and he would die for her. Any gift or help he gave to us had come from the heart of a gentle soul.

I held up the ring. It had been sized for small fingers, and so I slipped it on my right index finger and it fit, perfectly. As I gazed at the soft glow of the gem, a tear slid down my cheek and I found myself crying—just a little.

"Oh, Lady Iris." Trenyth slipped his arms around me and I rested my head on his chest as he patted my back. "You'll come through this. I know you will. I have faith in you."

Sniffling, I pulled myself together and gave him a soft smile. "I wish I had as much faith in myself. I just . . . don't know."

He offered me his handkerchief and then, as we headed toward the bar, he saluted us. "Be safe. Contact me within four days' time or I will send a search party." And then, before I could say a word, he leapt into the carriage and the horses clattered off down the cobblestone streets.

THE INSIDE OF the tavern was dour, filled with shadow and the scent of overly sweet wine and hops. I glanced around, and toward the back, sitting at a long table alone, with a pitcher of beer in front of him, sat the Great Winter Wolf Spirit. Oh, how he shone. The season had quickened him. His wolf pelts were shimmering white and he sat tall, his skin pale against the dark tones of the table.

I motioned for the others to follow me and we headed toward the table. Howl glanced up at me.

"And so you come, Lady Iris."

"And so I do. These are my friends, Smoky, Camille, and Rozurial."

He gazed at them silently for a moment, then bid us all sit down. "Dragon, Witch, Incubus. And all bound to shadow, as is the Lady Iris." He turned to Camille. "Though your shadows stem from another realm, far more terrifying than her own."

At Camille's startled look, he added, "I am an Elemental Lord. You expect anything less than my insight?" Before she could answer he drained his pint and stood. "You have struck the bargain, Iris. There is no turning back. Come, follow me. The sooner we leave, the sooner we can find out the truth of your past."

Howl led us to the door, then out into the snow-shrouded street. I glanced up at the shimmering flakes that softly drifted to the ground. The elfin cloaks were warm, and I was grateful that Trenyth had stopped us before we left. We'd brought packs and gear, but now we were much better prepared. Smoky and Roz were carrying most of the equipment on their backs, leaving just our packs to Camille and me.

Passersby gave us wide berth—Howl was well known in Elqaneve and Dahnsburg, though he seldom went south of either city. The Winter Wolf Spirit was known to be volatile. He'd tear out your throat for as little as looking at him wrong, and yet he might just as easily rescue your child caught in the rapids of a rushing stream. Most people—elves, Fae, and Cryptos alike—found it safest to avoid the Elemental Lord.

We followed him through the darkened streets until we were on the outskirts. He led us to one of the barrows where a seldom-used portal waited. The guard look mildly surprised.

"Not many folks pass through here. Are you sure you want to go? The mountains are fiercely cold and winter is deep—" But then Howl, the Winter Wolf Spirit, walked to the front of the line. The guard fell silent, bowing his head quickly. He readied the portal.

"Where will this take us?" I asked.

"Deep into the upper reaches of the Tygerian Mountains, miss." The guard glanced quietly at Howl, who did not speak. "From there, I assume you will be taking the portal to the Northlands. But you should rest for the night there—the village is safe for outsiders. Once you get into the heart of the Northlands, the accommodations are few and far between, and mostly to be found with private households."

"I know the Northlands well, elf." Smoky turned to him. "We won't have any problems, but thank you for your concern."

"The portal is ready. You may pass. May the Queen of Stars watch over you." The elf stood back and we faced the glistening portal. The energy between the two standing stones crackled and popped, blue and white bolts rebounding from one stone to the other and back again.

Howl nodded to Smoky. "You first, then the incubus. Then the women. I will come last." And so, without another word, we passed through to the Tygerian Mountains, where we did not tarry but instead crossed silently to the next portal and jumped all the way to the Northlands.

THE NORTHLANDS EXISTED in their own region, though they abutted Earthside, Otherworld, Valhalla, Kalevala, the Dragon Realms, and several other planes of existence. As we came through the portal, a blast of frigid air hit me—Elqaneve might have been chilly, but this was true cold. I pulled my cloak tighter around my shoulders as my breath puffed into white clouds in front of my face.

I stepped into a small room—it was a cavern actually, formed by hand, chipped out of the mountainside in the rough approximation of a square room. The man standing guard looked human, but I could tell he was one of the Northmen, a breed of humans who had sprung from the Norse and Finnish gods as they intermarried with humans.

Living between "heaven" and "earth," the Northmen stayed in the Northlands between Valhalla, Kalevala, and Earthside. They were as strong and quick as most Fae, but over the years the powers they'd inherited from the gods had diminished. Even so, they were still hardier than any human and could take chill temperatures without exhaustion. Some of the Northmen could see in the dark, and others were extremely adept at fighting and shield work. Their magic was in their singing voices and in their ability to charm the energy of metals and woods and weather.

"Welcome to the edge of the world," the guard said in the common tongue. He glanced at Smoky and let out a little cry, before giving the dragon a swift bow. "Lord Iampaatar, welcome back."

Smoky returned the nod. "Well met, Hanson. We need lodging for the night. Can you send word ahead to the inn? Three rooms—one for myself and my wife, one for Lady Iris, and one for Rozurial. The Winter Wolf Spirit will no doubt wish to make his own accommodations."

I gazed at Smoky. He was well known here, that much was

obvious. Hanson motioned to another man who had been standing nearby, and the man took off with a single nod.

Howl let out a low grunt. "I have a standing room at the inn. We stay one night. Tomorrow we begin the journey at daybreak. We cannot afford to be out in the mountains come evening. I would survive, and the dragon, but the women and incubus would freeze." He swept out of the stone room without another word and we followed him.

It had been cold inside, but outside, it was brilliant and icy. The darkness ate up every light except the glow from the crusted snow beneath our feet. The sky was clear—the stars twinkling over our heads.

Camille immediately pulled her cloak in front of her face and I did the same, although I was more adapted toward these temperatures than she. It felt a good fifteen degrees below zero, and we moved silently along the trail, which had been marked by ropes on both sides and eye catchers spaced evenly along the way. If we wandered off the path and got lost, we could die.

Howl led us along the trail, nimbly striding along the packed crust. As we skirted a snowbank to the right, then a thick copse of fir and cedar to the left, a faint light began to sparkle up ahead.

Rounding a curve in the path, we found ourselves facing an inn, just right of the path, about sixty yards ahead. Lit up like a Yule tree, with eye catchers all over the outside framing the three-story building, the inn had been carved out of stone. As I gazed at it, I suddenly remembered: I'd been here before. This inn had been witness to the end of my life in the Northlands.

THE JOURNEY DOWN from the temple had been achingly hard. There had been several blank spots in my memory, then the image of a sparkling woman in the mists who had carried me across a chasm. I'd struggled through the snows, not sure if I would survive even to reach the next morning.

They'd cast me out before I fully healed from their interrogations, and every joint in my body ached. The ishonar— magical flames of ice colder than anything in nature—had stripped my back with every lash, and while there were no open wounds, the weals that the whip had raised along my back ached. But the pain of my body was nothing compared to the pain in my head. Closing my eyes, I forced myself to take a deep breath, to keep it together.

Vikkommin, Vikkommin . . . his name echoed in my head.

Did you kill Vikkommin?

No, I don't know, I don't know anything.

The pain of a lash slashing across my back. *Did you bind his soul to a shadow?*

I don't know . . . I don't remember anything. I loved him—I loved him with all my heart. How could I have done anything that horrendous to him?

Another lash, another hellishly cold sting of ishonar, another scream that I slowly realized was emanating from the back of my own throat.

Tell us what happened.

I don't remember . . . There was a knock on my door. I answered to find a message from him. He had called me to his room. I went, and I remember him opening the door . . . then it's all blank, until you found me.

A pause, and then the lashes began to fall in earnest, as if all the pain in the world could break through the wall that had formed in my memory. And I began to scream, unable to stop, as I realized I had just lost everything dear to me in the world. And at that moment, I willed myself to die.

Later, when they had done all they could to me, but could prove nothing—no truth uncovered—I stood on the edge of the temple as they administered the final punishment: With one quick lop, the High Priestess sheared off my ankle-length hair at the nape of my neck. Now everyone would know I'd been banished from the temple—at least as long as it took to grow it out again. As she threw the golden strands into a fire pit, my nose wrinkled at the smell, and I hung my head, weeping silently.

My life was shattered. My head ached from the violation my mind had suffered. My back hurt beyond any pain I'd ever felt. But I understood that I wasn't going to die, as much as I'd prayed for it.

The doors slowly began to shut. I turned and screamed,

throwing myself to the ground. "Don't forsake me. I am called by the goddess! She is in my heart. Kill me, please."

The High Priestess stared down at me and a sorrowful look filled her eyes. "This is the last any of us will ever speak to you unless you can prove that you did not kill Vikkommin and bind his soul to the shadow. You have been stripped of your strongest powers and are no longer a threat. You have been stripped of the title of Ar'jant d'tel. You are excommunicated from the order. Go forth, back into the world. For your life here is over."

She turned away, slamming the giant doors against me.

I stayed prone for a long time, weeping until the tears froze on my face. Slowly, when the cold ate into my body, I stood and shouldered my pack and—as it rubbed against my wounds, setting off sparks of pain—began the harrowing journey down the mountain toward the portal that would take me out of the Northlands, back home to Finland where I would have to lie to my family to avoid the embarrassment my downfall would bring on them.

"IRIS, ARE YOU okay?" Camille poked me on the arm.

I shook out of my memories and blinked. "I just . . . it's been a long time since I've been here. I stayed at this inn a long, long, long time ago. It is very old yet still it stands against the ice and snow." *And so do I*, I thought.

We headed up the steep flight of steps—the entrance to the inn was a full story off the ground, to avoid being snowed in every winter. When we reached the door, Howl pushed it open and we followed him in.

The central dining hall was huge and jam-packed. Northmen, a few ogres, a large party of dwarves, and other mountain-hearty folk filled the room. Howl motioned for us to follow him to the bar.

"Jonah, you have the rooms ready?" he asked the barkeep.

Jonah, a dwarf, gave him a curt nod. "Aye, Master Howl. They are ready, indeed. Here are the keys." He pushed four keys across the counter. "Will you all be wanting dinner?"

"Yes, we'll eat over there." Howl nodded toward an empty table, then handed the keys around. "Stew, bread, solid food for traveling."

We made our way through the crowd to the table and slipped onto the benches. Smoky seemed unusually silent and I tapped the table in front of him.

"Is everything okay?"

He gave a quick shake of the head. "As far as I know, but I am uneasy. We need to keep watch. My father could be in this area and he would have the advantage here."

Smoky's father had a grudge against Camille, as well as his son, and had threatened to kill them just a few weeks prior. Now we were headed into territory that led to the Dragon Reaches and could easily meet Hyto or his friends.

"We'll keep our eyes open," I murmured.

Roz let out a long breath. "No matter how many times I come here, I am astounded by the strength and resilience of the inhabitants. I cannot imagine living here."

"It is beautiful, if you like your beauty sparse and cold," Smoky said. "The Dragon Reaches are snowy, but they are at the top of the world, where the mountains are craggy and overlook fields filled with mist and fog. During the summers, the North-men bring their goats and oxen to the fields to feed, and we have bounty. They always bring extra, as a tithe, for we allow them use of the fields. An ox cow can feed a dragon for well over a month."

He leaned back, draping one arm around the back of Camille's chair. "At some point, I will take you home to meet my mother, love."

She paled. "After meeting your father, I'm not sure how much I look forward to that."

"My mother is far more pleasant than Hyto." Smoky grinned at her, but then a scowl crossed his face. "If he comes near you, he will die." Hyto had threatened to rape and eat her when they'd met.

Just then Jonah appeared at the table with a cart covered in plates. Heaping bowls of beef stew, thick loaves of bread and a crock of butter, a wheel of cheese, an apple pie, and a pitcher of beer soon sat in front of us. The rising aroma made my stomach rumble. My last meal had been lunch.

Howl motioned for the bartender to pull up a chair. "Sit for a moment. We seek information for our journey."

Since nobody in their right mind refused an Elemental Lord, Jonah was only too willing to do so.

He glanced at the rest of us. "How do? I'm Jonah and I own this inn." He looked at us each in turn, and when his gaze fell on me he paused. "You look familiar. Have we met?"

STRUGGLING INTO THE inn, my pack was so heavy that I could no longer feel a thing in my legs or arms. Somehow, I'd made it down the mountain despite my pain and humiliation, although at one point I could swear I'd had help crossing a chasm from a beautiful spirit, and at another, I thought I'd fallen asleep in the snow.

But when I opened my eyes, I was sitting on the steps of the inn, so I must have walked in my sleep—or the pain was so bad that it had blanked my memory. I pushed myself up and in through the doors to find the room almost empty.

The barkeep, a dwarf, caught sight of me as I stumbled forward and fell. He rushed out, gathered me in his arms, and when I screamed, he gently carried me to a room and called for his wife. He left us alone while she removed my clothes and bathed and treated my wounds, all in silence.

When she was done fixing the last bandage in place, she held my hands and gazed into my eyes. "Ishonar leaves horrible welts, though it does not break the skin. Someone hurt you. Do you want to tell us who? There are remedies that can be taken . . ."

I knew the Northmen stuck together, dwarf, human, and Fae alike. But how could I ask them to go against a temple that was part of their culture? I shook my head. "No . . . no . . . there is nothing to be done. I'm lucky to have come away with my life."

"Are you sure?"

I held her hands, staring into her eyes. "I'm sure. I have to be sure. Please, ask me no more questions."

"Then we will let it rest. I'll bring you dinner and a drink. I assume you are headed toward the portal?"

"First thing come morning." As I fumbled for my purse, to pay her fee, she waved away the coin.

"You are a stranger in need. Rest now, and I will bring food."

And she did. I ate—stew and mince pie and fresh bread— and when I was done, I drained the pint dry. She must have put healing herbs in the beer because by the time I finished, I was falling asleep, and for the first time in several weeks, I slept without pain. Slept without dreams.

I GAZED INTO Jonah's eyes and gave him a slow smile. Should I say anything? Was I the same sprite who'd come down the mountain, still wanting to die? Would he and his wife even remember me?

"You and your wife paid me a great service six hundred years ago," I said quietly. "Your wife bathed my wounds, bandaged them, fed me, and helped me to sleep without pain for the first time in a long while. I wish you'd let me give you something—repay you for the kindness you showed me."

"My wife?" Jonah blinked. "Althea's been dead for nigh on two hundred years." He let out a long sigh and shook his head. "You look familiar, but anymore, I'm afraid I don't remember much that happened long ago. Thank you, though, for reminding me of what a gentle creature my wife was. The animals came to her for help when they were hurt. Came right up to eat out of her hands. She treated them and kept them in the stables until they were ready to head back into the wild again." He brushed his hand across his eyes. "I do miss her."

"What happened?" I asked softly.

"Werewolf got her. Tore her to shreds. I found her remains." He shuddered.

"I'm so sorry." I felt bad for bringing up the subject.

Camille noticed and jumped in. "This is incredible stew. What meat is it, might I ask?"

Jonah shook his head, inhaling deeply. "Oxen—the animal of choice around here. We add root vegetables: carrots and potatoes and turnips. Rich gravy and onions."

Howl set down his spoon. "We are traveling to the ice fields. You know the shadow that lurks on the Skirts of Hel?"

"Yes . . . Don't tell me you are headed up to challenge it. We've lost so many to that black shade of Hel. But then—you *are* an Elemental Lord," Jonah hastened to say.

"I am. And with me I have a dragon, a witch, an incubus, and your friend—the Talon-haltija. It is her fight, truly, but we come to give aid." Howl frowned. "Have you heard any reports lately of the shadow creature?"

Jonah was staring at me in earnest now. "Talon-haltija?" Blinking rapidly, he scooted his chair back. "There were reports, so many hundreds of years ago, of a powerful priestess, a sprite, who misused her powers, and the result . . . was the creation of the shadow creature. Are you she? Were you the Ar'jant d'tel who was disgraced and turned out of Undutar's temple?"

My cheeks flamed. "I do not know if I am responsible for the shadow—nothing could ever be proven and I have never been able to remember exactly what happened. But yes, I am Iris, and I was Ar'jant d'tel—Chosen of the Gods, the pariah of the temple."

I bit my lip, praying he wasn't regretting helping me all those years ago. "I come in search of the truth. To clear my name or to accept my punishment, whatever the case may be."

Smoky leaned across the table. "We need to sleep. Hold your questions till later, dwarf. Iris is an honored friend of mine, and I am dragon. Do not entertain thoughts I would not cotton to. Understand?"

Jonah's eyes grew wide. "Not a problem, Lord Iampaatar. I know who you are." He turned to Howl. "As far as your question, yes, the shadow has been active lately—in fact, he claimed a village girl from the Edanuwit people recently. They found her, her life force drained, her body mangled."

"How do they know it was the shadow?"

"It leaves a magical residue. If you go looking for it, you'll surely find it." And then Jonah bid us good evening and went back to the bar.

I finished my meal but felt terribly self-conscious. It was clear that our conversation had been overheard. The rest of the patrons skirted around us, which was probably just as well, but it made me feel like I had a big red bull's-eye painted on my back, or a scarlet A on my forehead.

As we headed upstairs to bed, I couldn't help but hope that when—if—I proved my innocence, every single person who had given me icy stares would hear about it. And in the pie-in-the-sky corner of my wishes, I wanted an apology from every one of them.

* * *

MORNING SAW US on the path at the break of dawn, after a hearty meal of eggs, bacon, bread, cheese, and soup. The network of trails joining the villages in the Northlands were a loose affair, opening and closing with the storms that raged down the mountains. We veered onto a fork that would take us to the Skirts of Hel, an ice field that buttressed up against Odin's Glacier. Apparently, Vikkommin had chosen to make this his home.

"Vikkommin has been following you for years?" Camille struggled to stay on her feet. The trail was hard going, with large patches of ice glazing the surface. In places, small boulders the size of my head were buried just deep enough in the snow to trip over.

"You saw him—that one time when we linked minds. He's been following me for hundreds of years, daring me to return. I think he believes I was the one who did it. He comes to me in my dreams, looking for revenge."

As we turned the corner, we found ourselves at a copse of trees. The forest was dark and old, but at least we wouldn't be pounded so badly by the elements.

Howl glanced at me. "Come. We must get through the woods with all haste." He ducked under the low-hanging cedar boughs, setting off a shower of snow from the upper reaches of the trees.

I glanced back at Camille, who gave me a brave smile. "I'm sorry I brought you—I asked too much. This can't be very pleasant."

"You're family, Iris. Smoky and I were happy to come."

"That we were," the dragon said, kissing the top of Camille's head. "We would have been worried sick with you out here by yourself."

"Ditto," Roz said.

And so, after a long breath, I followed Howl into the depths of the snow-covered wood, with the others behind me. Somewhere in the distance, the sound of wolves howling filled my ears. They were singing of danger, and I knew they were singing to me.

THREE

THE TREE BOUGHS WOVE A SNOW-COVERED lattice above our heads as we entered the White Forest. The path inclined, a steep grade. There would be no respite from now on as we climbed toward the Skirts of Hel.

During the summer, the birches shimmered, their brilliant green leaves shining against white trunks. But during winter, they were barren, lodged between cedar and fir, a reminder of the season long gone.

Creatures lived in the White Forest, twisted and ancient—Elder Fae like the White Woman and Jack-A-Johnny, Blue Manan and Swirling Devon. There were also plenty of Cryptos who made this wood their home: trolls and ogres and others even more terrifying.

We moved silently along the path. I noticed Camille was having a harder time of it—she might be half-Fae with plenty of endurance, but the going was tricky, and the path was already taking a toll on her. She used her yew walking stave for good purpose, keeping herself balanced as she skirted the worst patches of ice on our upward climb.

As we entered the heart of the forest, with the snowfield

behind us and the Skirts of Hel still far ahead, I began to notice the silence of the wood. Few birds were about during the season. Here and there a rustle in the wood warned of an animal. Twice, Howl stopped to let out a loud wolf-cry. His howls echoed through the forest, reverberating into the core of my heart.

"What are you telling them?"

"That their Master is here. That all who walk abroad with me are under my protection and not to be eaten." Howl smiled down at me. "The wolves will listen even though their hunger is keen, and they seek fresh meat. But the others—perhaps not. Do not count on my presence to offer protection against every creature who makes this woodland its home."

I blinked. "But you definitely help. As my granny used to say, 'When the wolves are at the door, best have their king sitting inside by the fire.' "

"Your grandmother was a wise woman." He seemed more comfortable now that we were in the forest, striding tall and strong, his pelts barely shielding his bare chest. The cold did not seem to bother him, the snow did not faze him. His feet were encased in thick fur boots, and his trousers were sewn of tanned leather. "So, Mistress Iris, tell me, will it be worth this journey, should you break the curse that lies so heavily on your shoulders?"

I shrugged. "In my culture, being a mother is the highest calling a woman can have. We are the ones who keep the race alive, we are the wellspring of history. Barren women are not ostracized, but those who have been struck barren by curse are pitied, and I am an outcast. When I went home after the temple excommunicated me, none in my family would speak to me. They gave me food and shelter, but they remained silent. They would not acknowledge me, so I left. I found a farm family who needed help, who didn't care about my past."

"The Kuusis?" Camille was walking close enough to overhear me.

I nodded. "The Kuusis. They were FBHs—full-blooded humans—and they did not care if my hair was cut short, they never asked about my past or my lack of a family. They took me in and gave me shelter and friendship."

"How did you happen to go to work for them?" She was using her stave to dig into the snow and propel herself along.

"I left home after an awkward stay and struck out on my own. When I got tired of walking, the first few weeks I slept in the open, and luckily nothing happened. But then I came to a farm. I snuck into their barn that night, and early morning Kustaa—the father—found me." I sighed softly, remembering that morning.

"What did he do?" Howl asked. "By the way, you do know that I am known by the name Aatu in Finland?"

It was my turn to smile at him. "Yes, I know, great and noble wolf. You are not just Aatu, but *the* Aatu. Anyway, when Kustaa found me, he asked who I was. I picked out a name, Iris—that was my favorite flower—and gave him that."

Camille stopped in her tracks. "Your name wasn't Iris all along?"

I shook my head, deciding I might as well tell her the truth. "No, my name was Pirkitta, but I was afraid that my reputation might have filtered down from the Northlands. News from the temples often did. So I picked my favorite flower, and then when I came over to the States, I used the Western form for it."

"So how did you go about working for the Kuusis after they caught you hiding in the barn?" Smoky paused by a tree that had fallen across the path and, with a nod from me, lifted me over it like he might lift a baby out of a crib. He did the same for Camille, then lightly leapt over the trunk.

Smoky had traded in his trademark ankle-length white trench for an ankle-length white fur cape that billowed around him. Rozurial was wearing a black fur cape, and beneath these they wore their elfin cloaks. I had my cloak over my parka, and Camille wore hers over her robe made out of the black unicorn hide.

When we were all on the other side of the deadfall, I answered. "I told Kustaa that I needed a job, that I had lost my family in a tragedy and was on my own. He recognized that I was a house sprite and offered me a place in his family, helping his wife with the children and gardens. He had such a kind demeanor . . ."

I closed my eyes, remembering his gentle voice that seemed so out of place against his gruff exterior. "I couldn't help but say yes. They had ten children, and his wife's parents were living with them, and a maiden sister and an unwed brother."

"That's a lot of work," Camille said.

"Oh, it was, but they treated me fairly and never raised a hand to me. Kustaa and the men would go hunting for weeks at a time, while the women watched the home fires. I was used to hard work from the temple—we had to shoulder our own weight there as well as learn all our magic, so it was no stretch to help out the Kuusis. And so I stayed."

"You became part of their family," Roz said, a gentle smile on his lips.

"Yes, and had I wed there and had children, we would be bound as a family to them. That's the way it works when you belong to one of the house sprite races. We love helping out, we're homey folk in general."

"You stayed for a long time, Mistress Iris." Howl glanced at me. I hadn't realized he'd been listening and felt slightly self-conscious.

"I did. As time wore on, the children grew. One of the daughters wed, and her husband moved into the house, and they raised their children there . . . and I stayed on after Kustaa and his wife died. I stayed for over four hundred years until the last of their line passed."

Camille bit her lip, looking like she wanted to cry. "When did you leave?"

"I left in 1875, after burying Kustaa's many-times-over great-granddaughter. She'd died unmarried, the last of her line who had stayed in the village. There are others of the family, no doubt, but long scattered. I buried her in the family plot, and then I took the money that she had left, and a few trea-sures, and I left the door unlocked for anyone who might need a home, and I walked away."

I remembered that day—I had felt both free, and sad. Sad to see a family come to the end. Sad to say good-bye to the sturdy house I'd lived in for four hundred years—a house I'd helped rebuild and renovate time and time again.

"From there I traveled to Spain and caught a boat to Lon-don, and from there I immigrated to Canada. I stayed in what's now British Columbia for over ninety years. In 1970, I began to feel a pull—as if I had to pick up and move again. And so I came to Seattle and settled in, living as one of the little people—the FBH little people. And then the portals opened and I was able to come out of the closet. And I met you."

I glanced up at Camille and smiled, my eyes teary. So many things had passed through the years, but I was barely entering the prime of my life as far as my people went. I was still young and considered pretty, even though so much had passed through my life. My hair had long ago grown back and I kept it ankle length, every night brushing the golden strands a hundred strokes and then braiding it up into long coils. I'd kept a good figure, and Bruce—my leprechaun boyfriend— wanted to marry me and have children.

Which is why I'm here, I thought. *Bruce needs to have children to continue his family name. I can't give him that until I break the curse.*

Camille dropped to her knees beside me and pulled me into her arms. "I wish you hadn't had such a hard life. I wish you'd been able to stay in the temple—but then I wouldn't know you and that would be my biggest regret."

"I know," I said, softly, patting her back. "But truly, the Kuusis were wonderful to me—oh, there were a few I'd rather not have known—but they always treated me as one of their kin. And I will never forget them. I honored them by taking their name."

"Come—we need to move. It's too cold to stay still and we have a long way to go." Howl nodded gruffly, but his eyes were kind.

We started up again, and as we trudged along, the snow began to fall in earnest. Delicate flakes, filling the air like a lacework crisscrossing the path. It fell through the lattice of branches, it fell through the open spots, it fell silently and softly, piling up in gentle layers.

As we walked, a faint whistle echoed through the woodland and then I could hear them—pipes echoing in the distance. A woman's voice called out, singing in a language I could not recognize, but it haunted me, her song, ricocheting off the trees. While I could not understand the words, I knew she sang of love lost, and trials left undone, and challenges failed.

The song began to work its way into my heart and I could only think, *Why go on? Why bother trying?* All things were lost in the end, death claimed us all, so why attempt to win?

All victory was shallow, and the victors' bones lay as bleached as the snow around us. Wouldn't it be easier just to sit here, to listen to the music forever? Wouldn't it be easier to let go of the past and forget about the future?

Stumbling to my knees, I found myself adrift in a snow-bank. Bleakly, I stared up as Camille leaned over me. "Iris? Iris! Shake out of it—you have to stand up. You'll freeze if you don't get moving."

"Loss, it's all loss," I told her, wanting to make her under-stand. The worm had eaten its way into my heart and I could see no more into the future. Everything felt tainted and rotten.

"Wake, wake and dance again, little sister," Howl said, kneeling beside me. He brushed his hand across my face and I blinked at the warmth. He was so warm, so vibrant.

"How can you be—you are one of the Elemental Lords of Winter . . . You can't be so warm and alive . . ."

"But I am. I am Aatu also known as Howl, Lord of the Pack, the Great Winter Wolf Spirit. My people live and love under the winter snows, they play and mate and feed and sing to the moon. They mourn the dead but they do not mourn the living. Come, sister, wake and remember your journey. The Singing Spirit has you in her grasp and you must push her away. Plug your ears if you have to, but do not let her seep into your heart and drag you away from us."

The warmth of his flesh began to pulse against my skin and I took a breath. Sharp, the cold was so sharp, but it jarred me and I shook the snow from my hair. Howl pulled me to my feet and spun me around, laughing. Dizzy, I begged him to stop, but he continued the dance.

As we spun, colors began to twist around us and they turned into a carnival of sight and sound. His laughter infected me and I couldn't help but return the mirth. And as I laughed, the shell of ice that had formed around my heart shattered and fell away.

When he stopped, holding me tight so I would not fall down, I tried to catch my breath. "Do you understand what happened, Lady Iris? Are you all right?"

I shook my head, unable to speak from the breathless dance.

"The Singing Spirit of the White Forest caught your atten-tion. She must have felt your sorrow and fear. She is a mournful thing, a powerful spirit who plays on emotion and leads travelers astray to their deaths. Hearkening them to give up all hope, they drop into a melancholy catatonia and die of hypothermia."

"These woods are truly cursed," Smoky said in a low voice. "Even dragon-folk tend to avoid them. Come, we have a long way to go and there are dangers ahead."

As I let out a long breath, shaking my head again to clear my thoughts, a low growl caught my attention. The others heard it, too, that much I could tell, and we immediately formed a circle with our backs to one another.

"Your people?" Camille asked Howl.

"No, not my people. They would never dare growl at my friends. No, I'm afraid we're going to be facing a bloodier pack than mine." He unsheathed a long knife with a bone fang for a blade.

"Trolls," I said. "I recognize the cadence. I'll bet you anything we've got troll blood following us."

"Oh fuck." Camille had fought trolls before.

She cleared her throat as Rozurial pulled out a blade and Smoky cracked his knuckles, his fingernails growing into long talons. I took out my Aqualine Crystal wand that I'd made, but then it hit me. My specialty was mist and snow magic, but that wasn't going to cut it here. The creatures who lived in these climes were used to snow and ice. My spells would be useless on them.

Slowly, I put the wand away and pulled out a dagger I'd had made for the journey. I'd asked Carter, the half-demon, half-Titan researcher we knew, to enchant it with fire, and he'd put a flame on it all right.

As we waited, the growls continued, and then out of the wood stepped dark shadows against the snow.

Trolls. Just as I thought. Two of them. The only saving grace we had was that they weren't dubba-trolls but mountain trolls instead. Dubba-trolls were two-headed and hard as hell to kill. Mountain trolls were still hard as hell to kill, but at least they only had one head per body.

"Trolls," I whispered. "May I suggest we make quick work of them? We've a long way to go and the sooner they're dead meat, the sooner we can move on." There was no question but that we'd have to kill them. Trolls weren't the type to respond if we asked, *Pretty please, could you not bother us.*

Camille began prepping what sounded suspiciously like one of her Moon magic spells and I took a healthy step away from her side. Camille's Moon magic often backfired and it wasn't a good idea to be too near when that happened.

Smoky let out a loud growl. "I don't have enough room here to shift into dragon form."

Howl shook his head. "There are only two. We can fight them. And remember: Fire will disrupt them faster than anything else." He raised his bone knife and pulled out a bottle, sprinkling the blade with some sort of oil that smelled suspiciously like oranges. The next moment, he lit the blade and it burned brightly with a steady flame.

The trolls took a step back, staring at the flaming blade. Then they began to come at us, one from the right, one from the left, attempting to avoid Howl and his crackling sword.

"Here, we'll see how they like my kind of toy," Roz said, reaching inside his duster. The man carried an armory in there, reminding me of nothing quite so much as a weapon-crazed flasher or Neo from *The Matrix*. Only with Rozurial, a good share of the weapons he carried were magical. He *did* have a miniature Uzi, but kept it for special times.

Roz pulled out a little round ball that was as red as Camille's lipstick. Oh hell, I knew what that was. *Firebomb!* I quickly backed up as he tugged on the wick and threw it.

The bomb landed near one of the trolls, who apparently had never seen one before and decided to pick it up. The troll, a seven-foot-tall warty gray skin-bag turned the ball over in his hand and promptly popped it in his mouth.

"Fire in the hole—literally!" Roz shouted and we all turned away to shield our eyes as an explosion rocked the area.

The troll stood there for a second, registering what happened, and then let out a scream of pain that ricocheted through woodland. It charged forward, unsteadily, arms waving like two giant sledgehammers.

"Watch out—it's wounded and dangerous!" As I shifted to one side, trying to figure out how I could get in on the battle, Smoky raced in and sliced across its belly, his long talons eviscerating the creature. A stench of entrails poured forth onto the ground, hissing on the snow like steaming slime. I covered my nose. The putrid scent was enough to make me lose breakfast as well as last night's dinner.

Howl let loose with a long swipe from his flaming blade and cut through the side of the troll, finishing the job. The monster began to fall and he was falling my way. I scrambled to the left, just as the troll hit the ground. If I'd been any slower, he'd have squashed me flatter than a hotcake. As it was, his innards came sloshing out before him and I managed to end up with troll slime on my cape. *Ewww.* That was going to leave a nasty stain. The second the creature hit the ground, he began to transform into stone. Mountain trolls *always* turned to stone when they died.

"Gah!" I let out a long sigh. Something told me that I wasn't about to emerge unscathed, but if troll guts were the worst of it, I'd be lucky.

His brother apparently decided that it was time to charge and he came rampaging into the fray. Camille let loose with a bolt from the Moon Mother and it bounced against the troll's head, leaving a smoldering patch of skin that sizzled like bacon on the grill. Troll #2 shrieked and slammed his fist down, hitting the ground right in front of her. The shock wave sent her flying back and she landed in a thick bank of snow.

Smoky lost it, going ballistic and raking his claws along the creature's arm as Howl flanked the other side with his flaming sword. Rozurial pulled out a vial and sent it flying onto the troll's clothing. A moment later, the furs the troll was wearing went up in a blaze, popping and hissing as the fire spread. The troll stumbled back but then wavered and suddenly headed my way.

I screamed and ran. If I jumped left, I'd end up jumping over the side of the trail into a deep gulch, and I wasn't sure just how far down it went. A jump to the right and I'd slam into a tree. I raced back down the mountain with the blazing troll lurching behind me, bellowing from the pain of his wounds as the flames fanned higher.

Smoky zipped ahead of the creature and caught me up in his arms. When we reached a part of the path with a turnout, he veered to the side until we were out of the troll's trajectory. The creature kept on track, downhill along the path, flailing against the flames and increasing their fury with every swipe.

Rozurial took aim with a handheld crossbow and the arrow flew true, piercing the behemoth's back. Within seconds, the troll dropped to his knees, then fell forward, dead.

I glanced at Roz. "What was on that arrow?"

"Fast-acting poison," he answered. "I don't often use it, but I always keep some around." He flashed me a soft smile and I understood: As dangerous as the trolls were, even though we'd had no choice but to fight, Roz didn't like seeing creatures in pain. He'd put the troll out of his misery as soon as possible.

He knelt beside the gigantic body, watching as it solidified into stone. "Good, now no creature will be tempted to eat the flesh. That poison travels through the body and can be absorbed through an open wound or by eating the dead meat."

He stood and, together with Smoky, we walked back to where Camille and Howl were standing. Howl doused his blade in the snow and then slid it back in the sheath again. Smoky's talons shortened back into nails. We all stood, staring at the stone bodies.

"Well, that was excitement we could do without," Camille said. She glanced at me. "You okay?"

I nodded. "Yeah, but it's not sitting very well that there wasn't much I could do to them, because all my magic is snow- and ice-based. Even my wand is focused on the northern energies and up here, so many creatures have a resistance against the magic of their environment. I have this dagger, it's got a touch of fire in it, but against trolls? Not so strong. I seriously need to expand my repertoire."

"Come," Howl said. "There's time enough for talking on the way. We must be out of this forest by nightfall or we risk bringing the glowing Skalla down on us. They journey through the White Forest at night seeking their victims."

"What are they?" Camille shivered. "The name alone sounds nasty."

"They are . . . skulls. But not actual skulls. They are the spirits of those murdered in the forest and they feed on travelers. They do not rest, nor can they be laid to rest as long as their remains lie hidden within this woodland." Howl gazed back at me. "You know the Skalla."

I nodded slowly. "They were well known in the temple. The wood here is old, it has absorbed the energy of many wars, and the energy from the Skirts of Hel filters down through the ground from the glacier on high. Some say a great mouth to the Netherworld exists in the heart of the forest."

"A mouth to the Netherworld . . . Do you think it might have something to do with Vikkommin?" Camille asked. "Since he lives in shadow now, could it be feeding him?"

I frowned. I'd never thought about that. "He didn't create it, if that's what you mean. The rip to the Netherworld was rumored to be there when I first came to the temple. Whenever a party traveled from the portals to the temple, there were always rumors of run-ins with the creatures if they crossed the forest at night. But that doesn't mean that it can't have played a part in what happened to him."

"Did the temple tell you exactly what happened to Vikkommin?" Roz hung toward the back, guarding our rear.

"They never really knew." I'd been over and over the story with Smoky and Camille, but maybe there was something I was missing. "His body was ripped to shreds—essentially turned inside out like I . . . I did with the guards at Stacia's first safe house. But his spirit was somehow embedded in a great shadow and the two merged. I know Vikkommin can't leave, not in body, for the shadow is corporeal and tied to this area, but he can travel on the astral."

"Camille, what do you know about shadow forms? Has Morio taught you anything?" Roz asked.

"Yes, actually." She frowned. "There are many forms of shadow, but most are created from astral entities rather than from spirits of Fae or mortals. There are some shadows, though, that have no consciousness. Maybe whatever happened to Vikkommin stuck him inside one of those?" Turning to me, she asked, "Have you ever gotten the sense that there's somebody else there with Vikkommin?"

Her breath came in little puffs. The temperature wasn't going to rise any higher, even though we were still at midmorning. I shivered and glanced at the sky. Snow was on the horizon—I could feel it in my bones and sure enough, before I could answer, a thin layer of flakes began to fall, drifting softly toward the ground.

I shook my head. "No, that I can say for certain. He's gone mad over the centuries, but it's him and him alone."

"Then I'd say that's what happened. Whatever ripped him out of his body, thrust him into one of the empty shadow forms. Sort of like a hermit crab, pulling on some other crab's shell."

"He didn't do this himself, did he?" Smoky spoke up.

"Why would he do something like that?" Camille gave him a shake of the head. "That makes no sense. But perhaps . . . were others among the Priestess-hood jealous of you? Maybe a woman in love with him herself? Or someone who wanted the position of High Priestess? Could this have been a frame-up so that you'd be, at best, kicked out of the temple? At worst, you'd be killed, and either way, their path would be clear?"

"The Elders thought of that. They queried everyone under truth spells. Once pledged to Undutar, if you tell a falsehood, it can be detected. We can see through illusion." As much as I wanted to hope for that, I knew it wasn't the answer. Not unless somebody had managed to pull off a deception against the entire Elder Council.

She paused to stare at the sky. "We're in for a storm. Even I can feel it. How much farther do we have to go till we come out of the forest?"

"This path will lead us out by early afternoon. We're on the narrow end of the woodland and will come to the Skirts of Hel by nightfall." Howl pushed ahead, walking faster. "We have to make haste, however. The snow threatens a thick fall and the going will be rough."

"Is there an inn on the other side? Or lodging of any sort? We'll be coming out near nightfall, and the weather is bound to be rough this evening." Roz pulled his fur cape tighter around his shoulders.

Howl smiled so softly I could barely see it in the flurry of flakes. "You'll be spending the night in one of my caves, with my Pack family." Falling silent, he once again took up the march.

FOUR

BY EARLY AFTERNOON, I WAS RIDING ON
Smoky's shoulders—the snow had begun falling so thick that
it piled up a good two feet in four hours. Camille was struggling, Roz helping her slog her way along, and Howl looked
nervous. We had another ninety minutes, by my reckoning,
before emerging from the forest, but the snow was growing
heavier and my weather sense was telling me it would get worse
before it got better.

"We haven't seen the worst of it yet," I said from atop
Smoky's shoulder.

"I fear you are right," he answered. "The winter storms
have started in earnest. The Northlands are a dangerous place
once autumn begins to depart. If need be, I can transform and
fly you out, but it would be difficult with the trees so thick
here."

The White Forest had gotten denser, conifers packing
together to create a picture-perfect snowscape, except for the
fact that we were in the middle of it and likely to be snowed in
by the time we found our way to the exit.

"Vikkommin used to come here a lot," I said softly. "He

spent a lot of time in the forest, working with the snow elementals that make their home here."

"He did, did he?" Camille's breath was ragged and even with her unicorn cloak and the elfin cape, her teeth were chattering. "And did the temple approve?"

I shook my head. "Not so much. They didn't like us spending much time away unless we were on a vision quest or an official mission." Closing my eyes against the pervasive snowflakes, I remembered back to the first vision quest I'd been on. And how it had led me to Vikkommin.

I WAS SO young. If I'd been human, I'd have barely passed sixteen. Many years before, the temple mothers had come to my family's house in Finland, shortly after I shed my first monthly blood.

"Your daughter is destined for the Order of Undutar. We've come to prepare you—she will come to the Northlands next year and live with us."

My mother had burst into tears. There was no refusal. When the gods called, you answered. If the gods wanted your children, you handed them over.

"Will we ever see her again?" Mother wrapped her arms around me, and, speechless, I leaned my head against her chest. I'd never expected anything like this to happen, although I'd been having dreams of snow and mist and storms for months on end now.

"You may come visit her in the temple once a year until she takes her oath of initiation. Then it's up to her whether you're welcome or not. Some of our Priestesses prefer to leave their old life behind for good. Others keep contact with family."

The Priestess, who was so old that I didn't even dare gauge her age, smiled softly at me. She was wrapped in a blue and white cloak, and her eyes were covered with the clouds of age. She traveled with assistants, as well as a younger priest, and they all sat in our cozy little house in the forest.

My father had gone hunting as soon as he let them in. He'd stared them down, silent, then left without saying a word. Everybody knew that if the Priests came to claim your children, all you could do was accede.

The thought of life in a temple, high in the Northlands, both terrified and intrigued me. I'd never had high aspirations, hoping only to marry and bear children and live as my mother had lived, and my grandmother.

Mother did the expected. Through her tears, she inclined her head to the Priestess. "It is an honor that one from our family be chosen. We have one year?"

"One year." The Priestess, who had once been human, rested her hand on a silver walking stick. "Spend it well and enjoy the time. Pirkitta will be well taken care of and she shall enjoy every luxury that comes with being one of Undutar's handmaids. You need never fear for her future as long as she belongs to our order."

And so the next year, I kissed my ma and da and brothers and sisters good-bye, and when the entourage arrived in our village to take me to the Northlands, the entire town turned out to bid me farewell.

I tried to numb myself as I climbed into the sleigh but as we journeyed toward the portals leading to the Northlands, slow tears etched down my cheeks as I watched everything I'd ever loved and known fall away behind me. Up ahead lay only the unknown. Everything was changing, and there was no turning back.

Long years were spent being schooled in both magic and history. But finally . . . our time came.

Fully a young woman now, it was time I underwent my vision quest. The Lady Undutar, in her infinite wisdom, would whisper to me and tell me the direction in which I would spend my life.

On Winter Solstice, I was taken out to the Skirts of Hel and left with only a thin blanket. Along with five other acolytes, I scrambled on the wide swath of ice, staring up at the cave that led into the underworld.

Hel's Mouth . . . Hel's purse . . . the Gates of Hel—the cavern was called by many names. Hel was not of our order, not of our pantheon, but we respected her and it was said that during the summer she and Undutar drank tea, and their ice cubes were the calves that broke off from the glaciers.

I looked for shelter—the night would be deadly unless I could forage for some sort of protection from the elements, and acolytes were not allowed to stay together. And then I saw it: a small cave opening, tucked away at the edge of a forest. The White Forest was filled with dangers, but a night on the glacier seemed even more dangerous.

I used the senses I'd been taught to heighten and reached out, examining the cave. It was small, big enough for one person, and empty. Nothing creeping within. Relieved, I scrambled down the glacial skirt—half sliding, half walking—and crawled into the opening against the side of the mountain.

The sense of earth was thick around me and I felt mildly claustrophobic. I'd been working with mist and fog and snow energy for so long that earth felt too solid. But it would protect me from the bitter wind.

As I calmed my thoughts and realized that, while chilly, I was no longer freezing, I decided to get it over with. No idea of what to expect, I pulled out the flask that my mentor had given me. She'd mixed the potion herself, spending three days in isolation to make it.

"Pirkitta, this will give you the ability to enter the Dream Time. It will call the Goddess Undutar into you, and she will show you the path of your life and give you your true name. I will be able to sense you while you are out in the Dream Time, but I won't be able to help. I will, however, be the one who records your true name into the historical ledger of the temple."

I sat in the dark, the smell of earth thick around me, sour and pungent, and held the potion to my chest. With a brief wonder at what my fellow acolytes were going through and whether they'd all be alive in the morning, I popped the top on the potion and drained the bottle.

At first, nothing seemed to be happening, but then I realized I was able to see inside the inky cave. The ground itself was giving off a faint yellow glow, and in wonder I picked up a handful and brought it to my nose, deeply inhaling its rich scent. The uncomfortable and frozen hideout had now become a warm, inviting womb, filled with the scent of fresh rain and windswept moors and hot soup simmering over a slow fire.

My fear draining out of me, I leaned back and closed my eyes. "What do you have to say to me, Lady? I feel you every morning when I wake, and I sense you watching over me every night when I fall asleep. Thank you, for bringing me into your Order. Thank you for choosing me."

And then, I was standing on a cliff, overlooking a steep valley below. All was crystalline frost and snow as far as I could see, clear and brilliant under a pale sky, and beside me stood a tall woman with hair as black as midnight, and eyes as piercing blue as my own. She stretched out her hand and the valley below came alive with deer and white hares, foxes and cardinals darting from tree to tree, their red a siren song in the endless vista of white.

"This is my realm, this is my land. And there walks my daughter."

A young woman, or she might have been ancient—I could not tell, but my senses cried out "youth"—walked across the field, the animals gathering at her feet as she silently glided through the snow. Her hair was long and silver, with hints of violet streaking it, and her dress was gossamer and sheer as lace. She glanced up at us and smiled, waving.

"The Lady of the Mists," I whispered, suddenly recognizing the girl. She was an Elemental Lord—or Lady, as the case might be. "She is your daughter? I did not know she was a goddess."

"Yes, she is my daughter, but she is not a goddess. Her father is the Holly King, and therefore she takes her place as one of the Immortals. Even the gods die, but the Immortals live on, forever, as long as the world beneath our feet lives." Undutar knelt by my side. "I chose you for a reason, Pirkitta. Your path will be neither easy nor comfortable, not for a long, long time to come. But you are mine, and all will play out in the end."

And then she kissed my forehead and her mark sang through me like the morning sun, warming me, blossoming out into my heart, and I knew I would forever love and cherish her.

"Do you accept me, child?"

"I do. I am yours, by heart and soul, by blood and bone, by breath and life." My breath caught in my chest. Whatever she asked of me, it was hers. If she commanded me to rip out my heart and hand it up to her on a platter, I would willingly do so.

"Then I name you my Ar'jant d'tel. You are Chosen of the Gods, and you will train for the position of High Priestess.

You will be my incarnation in the world and my voice. Remember me when times are bleak. I will always be at your side, regardless of what others say."

A silver buzz began to fill my head and I tried to focus, but it swept me under the layers of swirling fog. I rose into the air, arms outstretched, through layers of rock and stone and bone and ice, until all around me swirled the sparkling mist, a vortex of vapor, a whirlwind of whistling snow and my heart felt frozen through, as the ice clung to my body, melting through my flesh, sinking deep into my blood.

In my veins, the freezing rain took hold, blended into my very essence, singing its magic into the cells that made up my body and soul, and the world began to expand. I sucked in a deep breath as my Lady spun me round and round, a marionette on strings. Her laughter flowed like honey in my ears, her songs were siren's breath, and I knew that no matter what she would always be with me, because I was now a part of her.

At the core of my being, I was no longer alone. Undutar was with me.

Joy took hold, the snowflakes whirling in time to the music that raced by on the wind. I wanted to dance and sing. The Lady had chosen me, I was her handmaiden. I was Ar'jant d'tel—and I would someday be her voice.

Visions of leading her rituals in the temple, of walking in her glory through the rest of my days, of being the Priestess Incarnate washed over me and I dropped my head back and let out a slow, luxurious laugh.

At that moment, I noticed someone coming into view, through the astral fields of magic and mist, and he was glorious. He was not a sprite, but human, albeit quite short. His long dark hair tumbled to his shoulders, and his eyes were molten pools of chocolate. He was fair of face, though his jaw had a vaguely rugged look to it. He was slight of build, but the power in his walk—he was no acolyte.

He wore robes as blue as the summer morning, and when he saw me his eyes lit up with a warmth that immediately sucked me in.

"Vikkommin, my High Priest–to-be, meet Pirkitta, Ar'jant d'tel, who will one day take her place as my High Priestess. Together, as consorts, the two of you will be trained to take

over my temple and to lead my order. Get to know one another—
you will have a long lifetime together."

And so Vikkommin and I came together, on the astral in
front of our Lady, and began to explore each other's energy.
He leaned down, took me in his arms, and as his hungry lips
met mine, the world faded and I lost my heart to him.

I SHOOK MY head, surprised to see that we were almost at
the edge of the forest. I'd been wrapped in memories for some
time, and the snow had built up on my shoulders. I brushed it
off, letting out a long sigh.

*Vikkommin, what happened to you? What happened that
night?*

We walked in silence, Smoky and Howl striding through
the depths, Rozurial aiding Camille through the drifts. I
glanced down at the dragon on whose shoulder I sat, thinking
that we made for a strange little party of five. And how far I'd
come—how far I'd fallen—from the day Undutar named me
her Ar'jant d'tel.

And yet, I was not unhappy. Life as the High Priestess
would have been wonderful and strange and magical, but
when I looked over my life, except for the inability to have
children, I was content. I was helping out in a cause where I
was sorely needed. I had extended family and a new love. And
friends. I'd never expected anything spectacular before I was
first approached by Undutar's envoys—and though the land I
lived in now was far from the shores of my birth, it was a
beautiful and vibrant land.

Once I broke the curse and put Vikkommin to rest I'd be
content to return to Seattle and marry Bruce. *If you're innocent*, a little voice whispered inside. *If you're innocent.*

"There—up ahead. Just a little farther and we'll be on the
Skirts of Hel." Howl pointed, looking relieved in the growing
dusk. The snow was still swirling and we glided silently along
the path.

We were almost to the edge of the tree line when a swishing
sound slashed through the air, and Camille screamed. Smoky
turned, abruptly, catching me as I fell from his shoulder. He sat

me down behind Howl and I peered around from behind the Great Winter Wolf Spirit to see what was happening.

Camille was fighting against something—all I could see was a shine that flickered like strands of hair. And then Smoky was by her side, as well as Roz, and they were struggling to free her. Howl held me back by the shoulder.

"*Snow spiders*. Do not draw near them, Iris, for their venom is deadly and could kill you with one bite." He glanced around, pulling out his sword. "Where there is one, there will be others."

Smoky lashed out with his talons and Camille stumbled, as if freed from something. It was then that, glancing into the trees, I caught sight of her attackers. They were hanging down, a foot or so above her head, from the tops of the interlacing trees that crossed the path—a pair of wide, squat, joint-legged spiders. Almost alabaster, they shimmered in the late afternoon light, and it was then I noticed we'd been traveling under a layer of webs that spanned the treetops along the entire path.

"Why didn't you tell us?" I whispered.

Howl glanced down at me. "Would it have made the journey easier, to know?"

"No, no—I guess not." But the sight of the webs brought back thoughts of the web-laden forests of Darkynwyrd and of the hobo werespiders I'd fought with Camille and her sisters, and a chill raced up my spine as I saw a host of scuttling creatures racing along through the nets of silk.

Camille broke free from the snare line, thanks to Smoky, and leapt back, trying to shake off the webs. Roz pulled out a jagged dagger and began thrusting his Kris knife at the nearest spider.

Smoky leapt up and landed a blow on the other one, yanking his hand away as the creature struck at him with very visible fangs. The spiders were the size of a dinner plate, and a faint bluish glow emanated from their fangs. Magical.

Camille backed up, chanting something.

"Damn it, I suppose they're immune to ice and snow magic, too," I said, feeling useless.

Howl nodded. "I'm afraid so, Mistress Iris."

A wave of discontent raced through me, and I began to

stew. What good was I if I couldn't help my friends when they'd come along just for me? As my irritation grew, I found myself focusing on the spiders that were now scuttling down to the ground as Smoky and Roz sought to keep them from reaching Camille without getting bitten themselves in the process.

And just like that, I felt it well up—the same energy that had come rolling through when we'd faced the Tregarts who had killed Henry. The same energy that—

Before I could capture the memory, the rolling wave hit and I forced them into the stream of energy that poured forth from my outstretched hands.

With a little shriek, the spiders appeared to explode, but at second look, they were simply *reversed*. Turned inside out like a cast-off shirt. Torn to shreds.

I gasped. Once again, I hadn't realized what I'd been doing, although I knew I'd been driven to do something to protect my friends.

Smoky and Rozurial stared at the two bloody bodies, and then, together with Camille, they looked at me.

"Iris," Camille whispered. "You did it again. You . . . They're . . ."

"Yes, I can see," I said, not sure of what to think. "I thought once it might be a fluke, but twice . . ." I'd had this power when I was in training to be High Priestess and thought it stripped away from me, but now twice it had come flooding back, when I felt weak and angry and helpless.

I glanced up at them. "I was capable of much more than this when I was in my training. I could have so easily torn Vikkommin from his body and thrust him into shadow. So the question is, did I?"

"No," Howl said. "The question is, shall we remove ourselves from the White Forest before the rest of their eight-legged brethren come to capture us?" He nodded to the webs where the spiders looked to be amassing.

"Fuck! Run!" Camille said, grabbing my hand and struggling toward the entrance. "I have no desire to be lunch to a bunch of spiders."

Smoky grabbed the both of us up and, tossing us over his shoulders, ran with long leaping strides through the snow.

Five minutes and we stood on the edge of the Skirts of Hel. The edge of the world.

Howl and Roz joined us as we silently gazed up at the towering mountain of ice that stood before us. The White Forest marked the end of the tree line. Above here existed ice and snow and, for the brief summer, scattered fields of wildflowers and scrub brush that were as fleeting as a distant dream. The path, still compact snow, led ever upward, skirting the plains of ice, winding through the windswept trees that lay nearly sideways from the constant storms that buffeted the mountain peaks.

Camille gazed at the panorama of jagged peaks and frozen sheets of ice. "Where's your temple?" she whispered, as if afraid of setting off an avalanche.

"See the bend that winds to the left, near the stand of scrub there?" I pointed to a small thicket of scrub brush in the distance. "When you turn left, you pass behind a tall ridge and then curve back to the right. You can't see from here, but there's a fork in the road at that point. The path leads higher, the fork takes you on to the Order of Undutar. I haven't been this close to the temple in . . . six hundred years."

And then it hit me that I was on the way home—but to a home that had cast me out, that had branded me pariah. I'd spent so many centuries writing them out of my life, hiding behind half-truths and truths unknown. And now I had returned, to discover once and for all what the truth of my life was.

Would I like the answer when I found it? I didn't know, but whatever happened, I would know, forever, if I was a murderer.

FIVE

"WE'RE CLOSE TO SUNSET AND THE NIGHT winds will be howling down the mountain any moment. We have to reach my Pack." Howl motioned off the trail toward one of the nearest skirts of ice that stretched down from the glacial peak.

Most people didn't understand that glaciers weren't the mountains themselves but rather the ice that covered the mountain in large patches and sheets. Some glaciers melted during the summer—there were areas here that did, but unlike back in the Cascades near Seattle, the Northlands were not subject to global warming. During summers here, the temperature occasionally reached sixty degrees, but days like that were seldom and far between.

Bits of dried grass occasionally poked through the snow that blanketed the mountain. What rock we could see was dark and granite-hard, peeking out through the windswept snowbanks. We were reaching the highlands here, where the glaciers took hold and the alpine regions started in earnest.

The ice would be problematic in places, though most of it was rough and chunky. Not easy to navigate but easier than the smooth, hardened shell that streamed in long fingers down the mountain. The Skirts of Hel would be grueling to cross, even with our gear.

I thought over what we'd brought, but our mountaineering gear was limited. I'd assumed I'd be keeping on trail. I'd forgotten what harsh territory the craggy peaks around the temple really were.

Roz knelt beside me. "Take heart. I know what you're thinking," he said, staring at the expanse of ice before us. "We'll find a way across." He stood, turning to address Howl. "Where are we headed?"

"See that dark mouth against the rock, under the overcropping ledge up there?" Howl pointed to a barely visible splotch against the mountainside. If we could just hoof it without worry, we'd be there in ten minutes. But with the landscape reminiscent of a frozen lava field, it wasn't going to be so easy.

"I can see where it is. I can take Iris and Camille through the Ionyc Sea and meet you there." Smoky shrugged. "Easy enough."

"Sounds good to me," Camille said. "I don't fancy trying to work my way over that ice, and night is coming."

Howl gave him a nod. "That would be best. But let me go on ahead. My people would not welcome you kindly without my presence. Rozurial, how will you fare?"

"I can travel through the Ionyc Sea, too. It's easy with a visual marker."

And so it was settled.

Howl leapt forward and, in midair, became a huge white wolf, transforming in the blink of an eye. He stood shoulder high to Smoky, gigantic and fierce with red eyes and a swishing tail. He gave us a long look, then turned and bounded across the ice as if it were nothing. Within minutes, he was standing at the edge of the cave, waving to us.

Smoky wrapped his arms around Camille and me, and we flashed out of the snow, into the Ionyc Sea. The shift was abrupt, and if I had not experienced it before I might have been terribly frightened. It was like we were in a bubble, and the outer world had turned to smoke and fog around us. Before I could adjust my thoughts, though, we were standing near Howl, so quickly that Camille and I were both left breathless.

Howl nodded as Rozurial appeared beside us. "Handy travel, it is. Come, follow me and do or say nothing until I have introduced you. You are in my home now, and you will show respect for my people and my ways. They are leery of dragon folk," he added, looking at Smoky. "Dragons have been known to carry my wolves away and eat them."

"Wolves eat cattle, too, and sometimes people," Smoky said. "It is the way of the world."

"Aye, it is the way of the world, but here we will all eat venison stew." Howl smiled, then, ducking his head, led us into his world.

AS WE FOLLOWED him into the cavern, a strange glow took hold of the walls—faint like blue topaz, sparkling with a cold magical fire. The cavern extended far back into the mountain, with a high ceiling, and glistening stalagmites and stalactites shimmered their way to meet in the center, forming walls and chambers.

A rimstone pool sat in the center, but instead of being filled with hardened calcite, the water was clear and fresh, and warm—I could see the steam bubbling from it. Howl must have a way to heat it from below the floor.

Eye catchers floated lazily throughout the chamber, and everywhere we looked, wolves of all sorts sat, resting, watching us. Several men sat among them, strong and bare-chested, with six-pack abs, long, flowing black hair, and eyes that glowed topaz like Morio's—who was a youkai-kitsune. I looked for women but saw none. But scent on the wind told me they were here—females of the Pack. I had the feeling they were remaining in wolf form, protected from the sight of outsiders.

"This is your court," I said, suddenly understanding.

"You are observant, Lady Iris." Howl motioned to the men and they crossed their arms across their chests and knelt as the Great Winter Wolf Spirit passed by them. We followed in his wake, first me, then Smoky, then Camille and Roz behind her.

Howl stopped by a stone worn smooth into a throne. He slid off the heavy fur and, bare-chested but with a wolf pelt around his neck, took his place on the dais. With the headdress and pelts off, he reminded me a little of the Autumn Lord. His hair was jet-black streaked with silver, now that I could see it, and his eyes were the color of chocolate, dripping with gold flecks.

He was vivid in that unearthly way the Elemental Lords had, and as I gazed at him, surrounded by his people, I slowly dropped to the floor, kneeling. Beside me, Camille and Rozurial had done the same. Smoky stood tall but inclined his head.

Howl rose, then looked around at his people who gathered to watch—in both wolf and human form. He held up the staff that had been lying by his throne, with a handle made of wood, inlaid with bone.

"Listen well. These four are under my protection. Lord Iampaatar, Rozurial the incubus, Lady Camille, and Lady Iris walk under my cloak. Let no one who honors me lift paw or hand against them."

There was a collective shuffle, as if the Pack wasn't sure what to think, but then—as one body—the men standing by him went down on their knees, heads thrown back, exposing their throats. The wolves in the hall rolled over, all of them, onto their backs, again exposing their bellies and throats.

Howl took a long look around the chamber at every throat that had been presented. "On pain of death, you have submitted to my will. Remember well, my people."

He clapped and the wolves returned to attention. "Now, will my wife come forward? I wish to present you to our guests, my love."

Slowly, one of the largest, most beautiful white wolves rose and padded forward. In the blink of an eye, she shimmered, and a woman stood beside Howl. She was short—about five five—and sturdily built with visible muscle under an even layer of padding. Her eyes were glistening, pale blue, and her hair was as silver as Smoky's. She was dressed in a white pair of soft leather pants and matching tunic. A long white pelt draped down from her back and it was then I realized that these wolves weren't typical Weres.

They're like the selkie, I thought. Their pelts were worn as cloaks when they were in human form, around their necks. I decided to keep my mouth shut, though. The subject was personal and could be a secret that few mortals knew about.

And it didn't do to let the Immortals know you were in on their secrets.

"I present to you my wife, Kitää, Queen and Mother of the Katabas Wolf People."

She gave us a brief nod, taking us in with those brilliant blue eyes, her gaze stopping as she came to Smoky. "Iampaatar!" With a sharp laugh, she threw her arms around the dragon and gave him a hearty hug before stepping back. "What brings you to our lands? I'd heard you'd stomped out of the Dragon Reaches, vowing not to return."

Smoky sucked in a deep breath. He grinned and leaned forward in a deep bow, surprising all of us. "Lady Kitää, Queen of the Wind Wolves, I am honored to be in your presence. In the distant past, your people joined with mine to drive back the Northmen in the Rout of the Great Snow. I hearken back to that friendship on this journey and ask for a traveler's respite."

Kitää let out a low laugh. "My husband," she said, turning to Howl, "you have unleashed a dragon in our midst? What are you thinking, my Lord? But for a dragon, Iampaatar is one of the better ones. And he tells a feisty tale or two, at that." There was a shuffle and murmuring throughout the chamber, but she held up her hand and the room fell instantly silent. Stepping forward, she looked Smoky up and down, then gave a little shrug.

"You seem to be in fair enough health, Prince. Introduce your companions."

Prince? I glanced over at Smoky and saw Roz and Camille doing the same, but he gave us a short shake of the head, a warning in his eye.

"I left the name Iampaatar behind when I left the Dragon Reaches. I am known as Smoky by my friends," he said softly. "I present to you my wife, Camille. She is part Fae, part human. And our companions, Rozurial, an incubus, and the Lady Iris, one of the Ar'jant d'tel and a Talon-haltija." He slid his arm around Camille and stepped back a pace.

Kitää arched her eyebrows as she gave Camille a long look. "You must be exceptional to win the love and heart of a dragon prince and to make him rise up against his father.

I wish you luck, my girl. If you have not yet met your father-in-law, I quake for you when you do."

At Smoky's sharp glance, she merely said, "I have heard the rumors, Iampaatar—and do not think you can escape your Northlands name so easily. You cannot slip through without being recognized. I am not sure what you are doing here, but watch your back. There are those your father has driven into a frenzy with his treachery and lies. He was always a violent soul, and his ability to persuade others serves him well."

"We are not here because of my needs, Queen Kitää," Smoky said. "We are here as companions to the Lady Iris, who seeks to right a wrong some six hundred years old. Leave my concerns for another time."

She gracefully inclined her head. "As you will." Turning to me, she knelt and extended her hand. "One of the Ar'jant d'tel?"

"I was so named centuries ago," I said quietly. "The title was revoked and I was cast out of my temple for a crime about which I have no memory. I come to find the truth, either to free myself from a curse or to bear the punishment should it be proved I did this deed."

The Wolf Mother held my gaze for a moment, but then the hesitation slid away and she smiled at me, rich and full. "I see truth in your heart. I smell no lie, no hesitation. Lady Iris, you might be stripped of your title, but you wear it like a cloak in your aura. Mortals may give and take names, but they cannot remove the energy behind the title. Rest, and tell us what you need."

As she spoke, several of the other wolves shifted form, into stocky, lovely women with dark hair and eyes. Kitää clapped her hands and they hurried over to pull pelts and furs out from behind one of the columns and began to form a thick bed on the cavern floor.

One of the wolf men knelt and began to light a fire in the fire pit, rubbing two sticks together, but Smoky motioned for the warrior to hand him one of the sticks. He held it to his lips, blew on it softly, and the wood sparked to life. Handing the torch back to the man, Smoky leaned down and planted a kiss on the top of Camille's head.

Kitää led me over to the pile of furs and I gratefully sank

into the bedding. It was warm and cushioned, and I realized how bone-weary I was. Camille, Smoky, and Roz joined us.

"Food," Kitää said motioning to a couple of the women. "Make certain it's hot and hearty."

Howl sauntered over. "What think you of my home?"

"It's incredible," I said truthfully. The chamber led back into tunnels, and the eye catchers provided soft light all the way through. Even though the fire was limited in scope, the air in the chamber seemed warm compared to the outdoors and we shed our cloaks.

"You have a lovely home," Camille said, smiling at him. "Thank you for your hospitality."

"So what is your plan, Lady Iris? We stand on the edge of the Skirts of Hel. What do you need to do next? Go to the temple?" Howl motioned to Kitää and she curled in his arms as they sat back, resting against a stone column.

I shook my head. "They would not allow me entrance. No, I have to find Vikkommin's shadow and confront him. I need to break through his madness and discover what happened that night. Once I find out, then I can go to the temple and they can look into my mind and see the truth of the matter."

Memories of their inquisition ran through my thoughts and for a moment I felt fear. But then, what worse could they do to me than they'd already done? I was stronger now, tougher, and had already been through their torture.

Kitää reached out, ran her fingers up my arm. "You are a brave soul. Tell me what happened."

I glanced at Camille and she nodded. "Long ago, I was taken to the temple . . ." And I told them everything. This was the first Roz and Smoky had heard of the whole tale. Camille knew I'd been tortured, but I hadn't told the guys. I didn't want them playing hero before I needed them to.

"Let me see them," Kitää said. "Let me see your scars."

Camille looked at me. "It's up to you. Do you want to?"

I bit my lip. No one had seen my scars since I'd stopped at the inn on the way down the mountain. Not even Bruce, because I played it shy with him, keeping the lights off. He thought I was just demure, but really it was to prevent him from asking questions. They had healed without leaving raised bumps, but they were still there, across my back.

"Only the women." I glanced up at all of them.

Rozurial laid his hand gently on my arm. "Iris, my sweet. I know I've joked around, and tried to win you into bed, but trust me, I would never make light of your past or your need for privacy. Smoky, come on, let's go outside to stretch our legs and lose some drink."

Howl said nothing, but he followed Smoky and Roz. Kitää motioned and a ring of wolves—all female—surrounded us, their backs to us, keeping everyone at bay. I swallowed the lump forming in my throat. The moment of truth.

As I stood and dropped my cape to the floor, then unfastened my walking skirt and tunic and dropped them away, and finally my bra, the cold air hit me, chilling me through. Slowly I shifted my hair forward, letting it flow to the floor over my breasts, and turned so that Kitää and Camille could see my back.

"Oh, Great Mother," Camille said, her voice a low whisper. *"Ishonar."* She paused, then asked, "How many?"

"Thirty lashes," I whispered. And for the first time, my scars and my shame were fully exposed.

"PIRKITTA, TELL US now. Give us the truth and we won't have to do this." The Priestess-Mother begged me, but I shook my head, unable to do as she asked.

"I can't—I've told you everything I remember! Look into my mind, please, look into my thoughts and you will see."

I was naked down to my waist, my arms stretched between two posts, manacled with iron that was lined just enough so that pain seeped through from the metal but not the actual burns. My hair had been draped over my shoulder, spilling strands down to coil at my knees. I had never felt so vulnerable, so exposed or ashamed. I wanted to wrap my hands in front of my body, to cover myself, to curl in a ball weeping, but the manacles prevented all of those.

"Pirkitta, please. Tell us why you did this thing?"

"I don't know if I did! I have no memory. Please stop . . ."

The Priestess-Mother bit her lip and I saw blood swell, trickling down the side of her mouth. "My child. This is the way—there must be tradition. If you won't tell us the truth, then we have to administer punishment. And the punishment must fit the crime."

As she backed away, I gazed up into her eyes. She was old, old past counting, and I had been chosen to take her place. I knew now that would never happen. There would be no future for me here, if anywhere. I would die here, at the hands of those who believed I'd killed my sweet Vikkommin.

There was no tomorrow. No yesterday. Only today and the looming pain waiting to descend.

And then the lash fell, burning with white agony. I managed to keep from screaming the first time. The flames of ice licked at me, magical fire that hurt worse than the whip itself. Cold fire, the fire of deep ice, leaving marks but no wounds. Leaving no lasting damage but pain—and the memory of that pain—beyond what any normal lash could ever hope to achieve.

The second strike. The pain bit deeper, into my body and blood.

The third strike, and the pain wormed into my soul, jolting like lightning.

The fourth strike, and everything began to spin, the world falling away as the pain flayed apart my soul, opened me up, let every secret I had in the world come spilling out into the minds of my torturers. I could feel them poring over my innermost thoughts, my memories—everything I'd heard, seen, done, including my most private moments. Melting from the shame of exposure as well as the pain of the lash, I tried to sink to the floor, but the manacles held me fast in their iron grasp.

And on the fifth strike, the exquisite pain became all there was in the world, and I started to scream. And I went right on screaming until the lashes had counted to thirty.

"We could not find the truth," the Priestess-Mother said, staring down at my prone form on the floor. "It is cloaked so deeply in your psyche that we have no hope of ever knowing. We cannot allow you to stay in the temple, but neither can we punish you for his death if we don't know for certain you're guilty."

I sobbed, all my tears long shed but the pain unending. Ishonar would stay in my system for days, tearing at me every time I moved. "Please, don't send me away. I *loved* Vikkommin.

Just send me to him now if you're going to get rid of me. Please, please just kill me."

The Priestess-Mother ignored me. "You are excommunicated from the Temple of Undutar, turned away as pariah. You are stripped of your title, no more the Ar'jant d'tel. You are stripped of the mightiest of your powers."

And a new hell rushed through me, a great hand tearing power and spells out of me like it might rip weeds from a garden. The pain sent me into a convulsion, and next I knew, I was on the steps of the temple, and the Priestess-Mother stood there with shears and my hair in her hand.

"Pirkitta, as our last punishment, we take away your power to bear children and the symbol of your power as a woman. You shall never carry a child to term until you can find out what happened to Vikkommin and put to right what went wrong. You may grow your hair back, but it will never be the braid you were born with." Holding out the shears, she clipped off my hair at the nape of my neck.

I screamed, but she tossed the strands onto a fire and as the smell of burning hair filtered through my nostrils, the heavy doors swung shut and I lay sobbing for what seemed like hours.

Something inside took hold—an anger, a fury, a desire for revenge and to prove them wrong. I forced myself to my feet, and, still in agony from the ishonar and having my powers stripped, I trudged to the trail leading down to the portals. A voice calling my name on the wind led me forward, and I followed it until I could remember no more.

SIX

CAMILLE BURST INTO TEARS, AND KITÄÄ'S LIP was trembling, but I realized it wasn't out of pity. No, they were tears of sisterhood. After six hundred years of hiding my scars, of hiding my shame, it actually felt good to open up, to show someone else the reminders I carried on my back.

"You are going to face him? The shadow of your lost love?" Kitää asked.

I nodded. "I have to. There's no other way to break the curse than to find out what really happened. And I have to go alone. I asked my friends to come with me for support, but in the end I know I have to face him alone."

"When will you go? Shadows exist in the light more than in the dark, you know."

I thought about it. Waiting a day, two days, would do nothing for me. I'd no more be ready then than I was now. "I'll go out at daybreak tomorrow onto the Skirts of Hel and hunt him down. And then . . . I'll do whatever it takes to find out the truth and to help him rest. Vikkommin must know what happened. He's my only hope now, for the life that I want."

"Is there anything you need tonight? The Pack has trained

shamans and we would be glad to offer whatever help we can." She rested a hand on my arm. "Lady Iris, you are a brave woman, but don't look a gift horse—"

"In the mouth. I know. If you could provide me with a private place where I may pray, and if you have anything to strengthen me against the cold and ice tomorrow, I would not turn away the offer."

Facing the shadow of Vikkommin would be problematic and I had no clue as to what might happen. But tonight I knew I'd need to spend time in prayer. Even though I had been banished from the temple, Undutar still spoke to me and I needed to know she was with me when I confronted him. I needed to know that she cared.

Kitää motioned to one of the wolves. "We will prepare your quarters. I will oversee the preparation myself."

When Camille and I were alone, she turned to me and took my hands in hers. "Iris, why didn't you tell us all of this when we first met? Maybe we could have helped, come out here earlier. Are you sure you want to face him alone? You know I'll stand by your side if you need me."

"I know." And I did know. Camille would fight to the death for me if she had to. But that wouldn't help right now. "I had to be sure I could trust you first. And then, after I realized how happy I was with you and your sisters, I began to second-guess facing him down. But then I met Bruce, and he wants children, and the thought of telling him he had to choose between me and being a father . . . I couldn't do it."

"I think I understand," she said, helping me back into my shirt.

"I never thought I'd have the courage to face Vikkommin's shadow, but when he came to me on the astral this autumn—remember, you saw him, too—I realized he might somehow be able to hurt the people I love. Who I now call family. And I can't have that. I can't leave this undone. So here I am."

"What do you think might get through to him? You said he's mad."

"He is, stark raving mad. Wouldn't you be, lost in a shadow all those years? I don't know how I'll reason with him but I have to find something—some spark that still remembers

what we had. We were truly in love, or at least I thought so."
I stared at the floor, trying to remember.

"Why do you say it that way? Did he tell you otherwise?"

I thought back, but my mind was blank. "I don't know, but
I keep feeling I need to qualify it. I know how much I loved
him—from the first time our souls met, there was no one else.
The Lady showed me his heart and how could I not love him?
And . . . he did seem to love me. We spent most of our spare
time together—there was so much to learn, and we had to
learn how to work together."

"Did he ever tell you how he felt?" Camille let out a slow
breath. "Iris, could Vikkommin have been seeing someone
else? Someone who wanted you out of the way? Ever since you
told me about the whole situation, I keep thinking: Somebody
was jealous of you. Somebody wanted the life you were to
have."

I knew she meant to help, but it couldn't be that. It was too
simple.

"There was no one. Sure, Vikkommin attracted a lot of
attention and there were a few catty remarks about us—I also
attracted my share of male acolytes. But the temple Elders
questioned everyone. And it took years for another acolyte to
be named High Priestess—a century at least. Until then, the
Priestess-Mother stayed in charge. And the woman chosen
was new, brought in from another temple. If somebody had
wanted my position, why would they kill Vikkommin? They
would have killed me and tried to take my place."

I shook my head. "No, it wasn't one of my peers. That
much I know." I looked up at her. "I have been over and over
this, turning the puzzle in my thoughts for centuries. What
would I have to gain from killing Vikkommin? What would I
get out of it?"

"You say you loved him?"

"I did. I loved him and was looking forward to our wed-
ding. The only thing I used to get mad at him for was the time
he spent down in the White Forest. It was dangerous, but he
wouldn't listen to reason. He insisted on going down there
alone. I was so afraid he'd end up on the wrong end of one of
the snow spiders or a troll." I closed my eyes, remembering

our arguments over the subject. "We did fight, but he insisted he needed to hang out there for his magic. Something about the forest gave him strength."

Camille shook her head. "If the forest gave him strength, I wonder what it did to his magic. I've learned the hard way that working death magic has altered me—changed how I view the world."

Just then, Kitää returned. "I've arranged a private place for you. Follow Tezsa and she will take you there. I will wake you at daybreak with breakfast."

As I hugged Camille good night and followed the wolf to the private chamber, I wondered what tomorrow would bring me. If luck was with me, I'd resolve this matter—or even just go home no worse off than now. But there were so many other possibilities.

AS I KNELT on the soft pelts layered in the little cubbyhole, surrounded by the gentle glow of eye catchers, I took out my wand. Thanks to Camille and her sisters, it held an Aqualine Crystal—the stone sacred to my magic. Now I gently removed it from the silver that held it steady and set the wand aside. I held the crystal up so that the light of the eye catchers shone through, and I stared into the icy blue of the stone.

Aqualine Crystal, endemic to Otherworld, had a direct line into the magic of mist and fog and snow. And it was sacred to Undutar. I breathed softly onto the gem, cupping it in my hands. Closing my fingers around it, I let myself slip into a deep trance, my body becoming the mere vessel enclosing my spirit.

I slipped lower, and still lower, until I found my heartstone—the core of my being that no one could ever take away. It was this part of myself the temple Elders could never reach, and that I could never fully read. It was here, in the primal energy of myself, that the answers lay hidden and locked away.

I touched my heartstone and felt my spirit begin to rise on wings, to soar into the celestial realms, to sing with the stars. Slowly, I began the chant I'd been taught to summon Undutar, my Lady of the Frozen Wastes.

Lady of Mists, Lady of the Fog,
Lady of the Snow and Ice, hear me.
I, your Priestess, come before you.
I, your Priestess, do beseech you.
I, your Priestess, bow before you.
Listen to me, if you will.
Listen to my cries for help.
Listen to my sorrow-story.
Answer, Lady, if you will.
Answer to my cries for help.
Answer to my sorrow-story.

The crystal began to glow in my hand, and then slowly its luminescence spread until my fingers reflected the shimmering blue light. I gazed on its beauty and willed myself to flow into the stone, into the power of the gem as it slowly beat a cadence that was the flow and life of Undutar.

Pirkitta. And so you are back on the doorstep to my temple. I have been waiting for you. The voice was all around me, booming, and yet I knew no one else could hear her but me.

My Lady, I have returned to put this matter to rest. I have fought against this moment, but I had to come home. And I felt the tears beginning to come—the tears I had avoided for so many, many years.

There was a beat of silence, and then she said what I most feared to hear. *Tomorrow, you will face him. And you must destroy him. By your own hand, by yourself. You will find out the truth only in his death.*

Destroy him. Destroy the shadow that had been my Vik-kommin. I stared into the gem, tears streaming down my cheeks. *Lady, would you say anything but that, I would accept and obey. But you tell me to destroy the man who once was to be my love forever.*

He is no longer your love. And in some ways, he never was. Do as I order, my Ar'jant d'tel. You must, to break this curse and free yourself from the shackles of doubt. You will know the truth, and the truth will set you free to soar in my sight once again.

And then, the light faded, but not before my Lady said one last thing.

Pirkitta, remember: To counter shadow you must remove the light. Only in the darkness will shadow falter. Only in darkness can you destroy what is left of him. With that, she was gone and the crystal was, once again, merely a crystal.

I took a deep breath and sat back, staring at the stone. Remove the light. How was I to remove the light? If I went out in darkness, chances were I would not find Vikkommin to face him. If I went out in light, how could I remove the day? It was a riddle, one I decided I'd have to figure out as I went.

Fixing my Aqualine Crystal back in the wand, I set it to one side and burrowed deep in the pelts. The day had been long, and I was exhausted. And there was nowhere left but sleep for me to go without the memory of Vikkommin shadowing me.

WHEN I WOKE, Kitää had set a tray beside me. Hot broth, dense bread, and a soft creamy cheese. She had added an apple and a piece of jerky to the plate.

"Is it daybreak?" I had no clue as to what time it was. Surprisingly, I felt well rested and couldn't remember if I'd dreamed or not, but my body was relaxed and warm. "I slept well. Thank you for the chance to meditate and pray by myself."

"Aye, it is daybreak, nearly. Your friends still sleep. Should I wake them up? And yes, you would sleep well here. These caverns are protected by Aatu's magic, and Aatu watches over all of his children as they sleep."

That made sense. Being one of the Immortals, Howl would not need sleep. I gave her a soft smile. "No, let my friends rest. Wake them up after I am gone. I don't want them arguing and trying to go with me. They came for support, but they cannot face the shadow beside me. This is my battle, and mine alone."

I bit into the bread, and as it melted in my mouth I was struck by the thought that this might very well be my last meal, but I pushed it away. What would be, would be. What was destined to happen would, and I would live or I would die as my Lady willed it.

When I finished eating, Kitää helped me dress, gently zipping up my tunic and wrapping me with my cloaks. I grasped my wand and she stopped me.

"What is that ring?"

"Trenyth gave it to me. It's the ring of Shevah—an elfin gift from a wonderful friend." I held my hand out, gazing at the stone. I'd almost forgotten that I wore it—my hands had been buried in gloves since we'd arrived here.

"Do not forget you bear it. That gem will guide you to safety." She gazed at it, then reached out and stroked my hair back, brushing it for me with long, soft strokes. "Don't tie back your hair. I know it doesn't make sense, but let those golden strands be yet another cloak. Let your beauty and light shine forth, Ar'jant d'tel. You know you are still her chosen one—perhaps not for what originally was ordained, but she walks in your aura, she guides your tongue and heart. That is so easy to see."

I slipped into my boots, and Kitää arranged my hair so it streamed down my back, and I picked up my wand. "I'm ready," I said, looking up at her.

She flashed me a brave smile. "I have faith in you, my friend."

And so she led me to the mouth of the cavern where I slipped out into the early light of day.

THE SNOW WAS falling. I gazed across the expanse of mountainside. The sheets of ice were slick, glazing down over the rock. With a rock hammer, crampons on the bottom of my boots, and a length of rope over my shoulder, I was as ready as I'd ever be.

I slowly began to pick my way across the expanse of compact snow. It was so crusted over and I was so light that I only sank in to my ankles, but still, walking was slow going, and more than once I wished for snowshoes instead.

As the flurry blew flakes to stick on my hair, my eyelashes, my forehead, I wondered at the wisdom of letting my hair stay down. Ankle-length hair, when it didn't have a life of its own like Smoky's, could be dangerous in battle. And it was equally hard to manage in a storm like this. But Kitää had been so insistent that I decided she must have some sort of foresight on the subject.

Slowly, one step at a time, balancing myself with a walking stick I'd picked up before heading out of the cave, I worked my way across the expanse. I had one thing in my favor: Because of my small stature, my center of gravity was low and it was less likely I would fall than if I'd been of average size.

The wind blew something fierce, and I watched as the clouds raced across the sky, sending the snow into a sideways whirl. The flakes were small and they stung against the exposed flesh on my face, but the scarf I'd wound around my neck and over my mouth kept the worst of them at bay. I stopped for a moment and wiped my eyes against the glare of the snow as it threatened to blind me, then continued on.

Where would I find Vikkommin? Would he be hiding? Would I have to chase him out? The Skirts of Hel flanked an opening higher on the mountainside, a cavern in which I did not want to go because it was rumored to be an opening to the Underworld, and here, that very well might be right.

As the morning wore on, I looked back. Now the Pack's headquarters was a distant blur against the mountain, but I had the feeling someone was watching me—and it didn't feel like Vikkommin. Camille and the others would be awake by now, but I hoped they would heed my wishes and not come after me. Whatever I had to do, I didn't want them to interfere.

A little farther on, I stopped, gazing up the mountainside. Without even realizing it, I'd come to the center of the Skirts of Hel and was standing right below the cavern, which seemed to have a very small opening. But the energy from the cave blasted down the mountain to send me reeling, and I doubled over, my stomach wrenched in a thousand directions.

Truly, a gate to the Underworld. Truly, the Gates of Hel.

A single note inside began to quiver and ring through my body, forcing me higher on the slope. I began to crawl up the mountain on hands and knees, because the energy was impossible to deny and impossible to wade through while standing. One foot at a time, I headed toward the cavern, and now I could hear something calling my name.

Pirkitta . . . Pirkitta . . . Pirkitta . . . It's time for you to come back to me . . .

I froze. *Vikkommin.* That was Vikkommin's voice from down below. I whirled, turning as the shadow embraced me, rushing up the side of the mountain. Within seconds, he was around me, a thick cloud, his energy filling every pore in my body, and as I forced myself to my feet I realized that Vikkommin had been waiting for me, and he was *happy* to see me.

"VIKKOMMIN, WHAT ARE you doing? What do you want?" I tried to keep myself focused on the reason for my journey, but the feel of his life force was like heady wine. I realized just how much I'd missed him—so much more than I remembered. The meeting was like fire to a match, like magnets long parted.

Pirkitta, you've come back to me. You've come to join me.

"No, no, I can't join . . ." My voice drifted off. Could it be that Vikkommin still loved me? That he forgave me for what happened? Maybe I hadn't killed him. Maybe he was telling me in his own way . . .

Come with me. You don't know the power I have now, my sweet flower. My little concubine. You were my match. We can be matched again, in death as in life. And he surrounded me, a shadow taking form, his arms embracing me—his body made of smoke.

I dropped my head back, leaning into the billowing shadow that held me fast. His embrace felt so good and I remembered the nights we'd spent together, nights of passion and fire, nights of tasting love's delights, the nights where we'd made plans to rule the Order: wise, benevolent rulers, full of love and lust and magic to shake the mountains.

Remember . . . remember what we had . . .

Trying to shake my head clear, I brought my attention back. "Vikkommin, I need to know—I need to know what happened that night. I need to know if . . . if . . ."

If you killed me? If you turned me into what I am now, my sweet sprite?

"Yes. Please, tell me . . . I can't remember."

And then, Vikkommin pulled me back into his arms and he was kissing me, his shadow so strong I couldn't break away. I wasn't even sure if I wanted to. But then I saw a gleam—his shadow form had eyes as black as night and they were sparkling with the strength of a thousand dark suns.

Oh my sweet one, you most certainly did kill me. You tore me to shreds. You are most assuredly a murderess, and now you will spend the rest of your days with me, for I am going to do to you what you did to me. And we will be back together again, for eternity.

And then, he began filtering into my body, his shadow shifting through my pores, seeping in through the cells, and I started to scream.

SEVEN

—◆◆◆—

"NO! PLEASE, VIKKOMMIN, STOP!" I PUSHED against him but it was impossible to push against smoke and mirrors. And as he entered my body, his madness touched my soul and I screamed again, for I saw how far over the edge he'd gone. Enraged, he was, and angry and out to hurt me in any way possible. He didn't love me, he wanted to *punish* me for all time.

I struggled, fighting him, trying one spell after another. I *pushed*, but that had no effect, and I put up wards and barriers, but it was too late—the fox was already in the henhouse. Finally, in desperation, I screamed for a blast of ice lightning to aim itself directly at me—I could absorb the energy, I thought—but it bounced off of his shadow.

What the fuck was I going to do? I couldn't let him win. He'd be able to do exactly what he planned—turn my body inside out and absorb my soul into his—and I couldn't let that happen. I wasn't ready to die. I struggled, dragging myself along the ice, trying to keep focused. The feel of him inside my mind made me want to scream, to shake him off like ants at a picnic.

I have to stay calm, I have to figure out what to do. If I let him rattle me, he'll win.

I yanked the gloves off my hands, slamming my left palm down on a sharp chunk of ice. The pain broke through. I grabbed hold of the feel of torn flesh and hung on for everything I had and it cleared my thoughts for a moment.

Now what? I had only a few minutes to decide as he surrounded me, infiltrated my body more and more.

"The ring—the ring . . ."

I heard a faint voice on the wind and looked up the mountain. Standing on one of the rocky crags was Howl, watching but not interfering.

Of course! The ring of Shevah. I concentrated on it, begging for whatever help it might give me. A pulse rippling through my hand took me by surprise, and then another, and then a loud shriek ripped through the air and Vikkommin went sailing down the mountain in shadow form. As he picked himself up, I knew that I had to decide what to do next.

And then, Undutar's words rang in my ears. *Pirkitta, remember: To counter shadow, you must remove the light. Only in the darkness will shadow falter. Only in darkness can you destroy what is left of him.*

Darkness. The cave—the Gates of Hel! I scrambled to my feet, driving myself up the mountain, forcing myself on. I knew Vikkommin was gathering himself, aiming for me again, and I had to reach the cavern before he came. In darkness, he wouldn't have nearly the power he did out here in the light. All shadows need light to exist.

I struggled to catch my breath and, looking up, found Howl standing by me, in wolf form. He knelt down. I said nothing but leapt on his back and he raced for the cavern ahead, with me clinging to his back as if my life depended on it—for it did. We reached the cave and he knelt again so I could get off. Quickly, he turned back into his human form.

"I cannot go with you, little sister. I am proscribed from entering the Gates of Hel. But I will stand watch. Blessings, my Ar'jant d'tel."

I gave him a soft smile. "If something happens, tell . . ."

"I will bear the news to your friends, if need be. Go now. Your adversary is nearly on your heels." And he backed away.

With a glance over my shoulder at Vikkommin, who was almost within reach, I took a deep breath and plunged into the cavern, into the darkness, into what I hoped would be my salvation.

THE CAVERN WAS dark, so dark I couldn't even see my hands before my face. I quickly moved away from the opening, away from what little light emanated in from outside. I couldn't allow Vikkommin to have any form of power over me, and the less light there was, the less power he'd have.

As I moved ahead, using my walking stick to sweep the path, I began to realize there *was* a form of light in here—my hair; the strands were glowing with a soft gold light. Just enough so that I could see the rock forms on the wall, even though all around me was inky and black. How the hell . . . ? And then I realized that when she'd brushed my hair this morning, Kitää must have put something on it. But there was no time to figure it out now.

I hurried ahead, and finding an outcropping, I stopped behind it to catch my breath. He couldn't see me in here, but he could probably hear me.

Pirkitta . . . Pirkitta . . . Where did you go now? You're being a very naughty girl and I'm going to have to punish you for it. Come out now, back onto the ice, and I'll make it easy on you.

I forced my tongue still, even though I wanted to shout out a retort, a snide comeback. This was no time for pettiness. I had to destroy him, but more than that, I had to find out why I'd done this to him.

I headed toward the back of the cavern and found yet another passageway leading down. Since I had no idea if I was coming out of this alive, I decided I might as well follow and find out where it led. As it was, I had no clue as to how I was going to destroy Vikkommin. Undutar seemed convinced I could do it while in the darkness, but I wasn't so sure.

The passage led down a narrow ledge with steep ravines on either side. I glanced over the edge and quickly pulled back. I couldn't have seen what I thought I saw—no, it wasn't possible. But a second look and I knew I wasn't hallucinating.

There was a column in the center of the deep pit to my right. Along the column were row after row of faces—death masks and skulls, ornamenting the towering stalagmite that was a good eight feet thick. Holy Hel, no wonder they called this cavern the Gates of Hel. It truly was a death chamber.

I turned back to see the faint glimmer I knew was Vik-kommin. He was waiting at the top of the path and I sensed a hesitancy now—a pause in certainty.

"What's wrong? Are you afraid to come down here?"

Come up. You know eventually I'll have you. Or you'll starve to death, waiting for me to leave. Pirkitta, you don't know the power you'll have when you are with me. You can't imagine the beautiful strength that flows through my being now. You will have all that, once you're with me.

Power . . . power . . . Where had I heard that before? A fuzzy thought began to take shape in my mind.

"I don't think so. You're an abomination, Vikkommin. If I'm the one who turned you into this, I promise you, I will give myself over for punishment. But you cannot go on like this— you feed on the life of the Northmen and their families. You are no longer part of the cycle."

Oh, that's what you said long ago, that's what you pre-dicted would happen to me. But look—you are the reason for my existence in this form. You created the monster you feared I was becoming. How do you feel about that, my love? How do you feel now that you know you've fucked things up and birthed a fearsome shadow who is the terror of the northern wastes?

I glanced around, staring at the skulls on the central tower, trying to think. The pit over the edge was so vast that if I had to, I could throw myself in and he'd never be able to get me. Had I really done this to him? Was I, at the heart, responsible for all of this?

You're making a mistake, Vikkommin. You're going against the Order, Vikkommin. You're turning into a monster, Vikkommin . . .

His voice mocked mine, in perfect precision, and suddenly, the years began to slide away as the secrets I'd locked within my heart broke open . . . and I was standing back in his room that night, facing my love for the last time.

* * *

VIKKOMMIN HAD CALLED me to his room. Nothing unusual—we spent a great deal of time together, but tonight something was different. He had a look on his face that I didn't like. One I recognized all too often as of late.

"You've been in the White Forest, haven't you? What are you doing there, Vikkommin? You promised you'd curtail how often you go. You know I don't like it and neither would the Priestess-Mother."

Vikkommin, strikingly handsome and with a rogue look in his eye, swept me into his arms. "Kiss me before you scold me," he said, and I did. His lips pressed against mine, warm and like fine wine, and they sucked me in deep, into his love, into his passion, and I wanted nothing more than to strip off my clothes and climb into bed with him.

But there was something—something that struck me as odd . . . off-kilter. I pulled away, and catching my breath, I turned back to him.

"What are you doing, my love? What calls you to the forest? We have everything we could want here. Everything we could ask for."

A flame shot wild in his gaze and he shook his head. "You truly believe that? You don't understand, do you? I have to show you. If I show you, you won't object. You'll want to be part of this—and I want you to be. You're my love, my soul mate, my chosen one. Pirkitta, let me show you what I have discovered."

I sighed. He wouldn't be content until I said yes, and I decided that maybe this was the best way to keep him out of trouble. If I knew what I was fighting, I'd know how to engage it.

"All right, then. Show me what you've learned from the White Forest."

"Come here, then. Come and let me enter your thoughts. Let me show you what I've been learning. What I plan to teach you."

He held out his arms again and I moved into them, shivering as he wrapped them around me in an embrace so tight I could not break it. He began to turn me, to spin me—or at least it felt like it—and we whirled onto the astral, our souls joined together.

"Look—look what I've found how to do . . ."

And then I entered his mind. The brilliant flames were there, flames of ice, so violent they rocked his soul. I screamed, trying to avoid the wash of the burning ice as the spiraling flames took shape into dancers, who spun around us in a circle of madness. *Ishonar* . . . the most dangerous of elements— somehow Vikkommin had tapped into the elemental power of ishonar.

"No—ishonar is reserved for punishment only. It is the most powerful form of ice, and we are never to touch it unless it be in urgent need with approval of the Elders." I tried to break away, but the ishonar Elementals rushed at me and I stopped. "My gods, Vikkommin, you have control over them."

It couldn't be—no mortal could control this power. No sane mortal tried. It was like controlling dragons—it just wasn't done. In fact, the ability to tap into the icy fires of ishonar had been passed to the silver dragons, and they were the *only* creatures alive who could use the magic as they wished without losing themselves to it. For there was a madness in the extreme cold, a fury when unleashed, that could bring the worst of nature's wars—the ice ages—upon the world.

"You can't control this! You can't possibly hope to control this power."

Vikkommin laughed and held me tighter. "Oh, on the contrary—I can control it. I have *learned* how to use it, and I *will* use it. Once we are in control of the temple, we will wage holy wars upon our enemies. We will freeze our enemies in Pohjola to the core. We will eradicate the fire giants. We will raise ourselves to be at the side of Lady Undutar herself. *We will become gods with this power.*"

And then I felt her—the Lady herself—coming through me.

"This is madness," she whispered, and I spoke the words for her. "You dare to compare yourself to the gods? You will pay for this, and you will pay mightily."

Without a second thought, I reached out—or perhaps Undutar did, or the both of us—and we ripped Vikkommin's soul off the astral and thrust it into the nearest shadow form. To prevent him returning to his body, I leapt off the astral back into the room. And I gazed on my love one last time, before turning his body inside out. Everything faded, and the next thing I knew, I was screaming, and my world turned upside down from then on.

"OH, GREAT MOTHER. Vikkommin, how could you? How could you hope to ever . . ."

The memories kept flooding back. The sound of his body ripping as I tore him apart. The mad laughter of his soul as he nestled into the shadow. The scream caught in my throat as I killed the love of my life to prevent him from hurting others. He'd gone mad with power and there would be no stopping him.

In that brief glimpse of his soul, I'd recognized that he was even more powerful than the Priestess-Mother and he would rampage across the land and tear it asunder with the ishonar.

But how could I tell the Elders Council? How could I make the Elders believe, when even I was in shock and disbelief? And so the memories retreated, fading back into a little corner of my heart, and I locked them away.

Because I also knew there was danger to myself. For when Vikkommin had entered my mind to show me what he could do, he'd not only shown me how to use the ishonar myself.

Now, as the memories flooded back, I realized *I* also knew how to control the ishonar—I could make the ice burn and I could shift the weather in ways no mortal or Fae should be capable of. If the Elders had known what I could do, they would have instantly put me to death. Somewhere deep in my subconscious, I must have realized that and blocked off all memory.

Horrified that I was now far too powerful for my own—or anybody else's—good, my first thought was to throw myself over the edge of the pit, but then Vikkommin laughed, and his laughter stopped me.

You never could handle the concept of being a goddess, could you? I see you remember now. But you do not frighten me—you are terrified to use your strength and you won't use it for fear of setting off some chain reaction.

I stood my ground, staring at the glowing edges of his shadow form. He was less powerful down here. The darkness drained his strongest abilities, and what little light my hair gave off did him no good.

I had to make him come to me.

"You'll never win. You may kill me, but the Lady is out for your death and you'll never be anything but what you are now: a shadow of your former self. Because you can't do it now, can you? You can't control the weather. You can't control the ishonar, and it beckons you and drives you mad."

He let out a howl of rage and moved closer. *Pirkitta . . . I would have shared this with you. I would have brought us back together and we would have lived together in the shadow. But you mock me—and I will destroy you.*

I steeled myself. "I not only mock you, I spit in your path. I abjure what you have become. I deny you, Vikkommin. I deny your power and your shadow and the madness reeling within you."

You! You deny me! I can tear you to pieces, I can make you into what I am and you have the gall to deny my power?

And then he moved. He headed my way and I picked up my wand. I wasn't sure what I was going to do, but now that I had the power of the ishonar in me, I knew I could destroy him. I waited until he was within arm's reach, and then I raised my wand.

"To the Gates of the Underworld I send thee, to the depths of Tuonela I command thee, to the arms of Tuoni I direct thee. Thou creature of darkness and shadow, thou power-mad sorcerer—you are no longer Chosen of the Lady, you are a vile creature, an abomination, and I send thee to the arms of oblivion."

I focused and caught hold of one of the ishonar Elementals. She was dancing on the edge of my wand, and I thrust her forward, burning in all her frozen and brilliant glory. She rose up, growing larger, and her face, faceted in ice and bathed in purple fire, changed from sublime to monstrous as her mouth opened wide and she turned in Vikkommin's direction.

He lunged toward me, but she interceded, touching his shadow and sending shock waves of pain through the smoke. He screamed, loud and plaintive. But I held fast, dropping to my knees. This was it, this was the only way, to turn the power that he'd so craved back on him. I reached deep, sought for all

of the threads within myself that knew how to use the ishonar.
I gathered them up into one mass and ripped it out of myself,
toward him: a rolling, wheeling spiral of energy that flamed
so brightly it illuminated the chamber.

For one moment it seemed to strengthen him and then I
caught his thoughts as it touched the outer edges of his being.

*Pirkitta—what are you doing to me? No—how could you
do this? How could you do this to me?*

And then he began to scream, and his scream echoed in
the chamber, rising to a howl as his anguish grew. The wheel
of ishonar rolled on, encompassing him, surrounding him,
and he became the center of the wheel, spokes of fire radiating
out from his core, meeting to eat away at his soul and devour
and break him into shards.

I covered my eyes, not wanting to watch, not wanting to see
what I was wreaking on Vikkommin's soul, and yet I could not
help but lower my hands as the shriek rose to a crescendo.

Vikkommin was in the air now, caught in the currents of
wind that buffeted the chamber. He was being pulled apart,
scattered to the four corners, ripped asunder. The wheel of
ishonar moved on, rolling through him, and then it fell over the
edge of the footpath, taking what remained of my love with it,
down to the depths of Hel, where he would be washed clean
and returned to the universe as new matter. *Oblivion's son.*

I sat in the darkness, breathing heavily. Memories flooded
my thoughts, memories of that night. Yes, I had killed him at
the directive of my Lady. I'd set in motion all of these events
at her bequest. And she had left me to wander, to take punishment, because if I remembered what had happened, the
temple would have killed me.

But what now? What of the ishonar? What of my ability to
control it?

*Look inside, my Ar'jant d'tel. Look inside yourself. Don't
be afraid.*

And there in the darkness, I went deep into my soul, let
myself sink to the depths of my core. When I came to where
the power of the ishonar had dwelt, I realized that I'd ripped
out my knowledge of how to use it when I killed Vikkommin's
shadow. I'd used the knowledge this one time, to end his life—
for it was the only hope I had of destroying him.

My ability to use the ishonar had died with him.

I slowly picked myself up, dusted off my cloak, and gathered my wand and everything I needed. I took one last look at the depths of the cavern, and using my walking staff, I made my way back toward the entrance.

As I emerged from the cavern, Howl leapt off of the craggy ledge. He stared at me. "Oh my Lady, what happened to you?"

"What do you mean?" I asked.

"Your face. Look at your face."

I pulled out a small mirror from my pack and gazed into the glass. Along the sides of my forehead were intricate spirals and loops, beautiful designs in deep indigo, like water flowing down my cheeks in rivers and streams. I reached up and touched them. They did not hurt, but they were permanent—that much seemed clear.

"I don't know," I whispered. "I don't know what to think."

And then, Howl turned to wolf form, offered his back, and I crawled on and we began loping across the Skirts of Hel, back to the cave, back to my life.

EIGHT

CAMILLE, SMOKY, AND ROZURIAL WERE WAIT-
ing for me when I returned. I gave them a silent nod and they
withdrew. Kitää motioned to one of her women, and within
fifteen minutes a hot bath was waiting for me.

Camille and Kitää attended me, helping me remove my
clothing. As they peeled off my tunic, Camille gasped.

"What?" I asked.

"The scars—they are different."

I struggled to see, so Kitää brought a small mirror in for
me and held it while I glanced over my shoulder, into the mirror. The scars, the lash marks from the ishonar, had shifted
and changed. They now covered my back in an intricate set of
coiling waterfalls—beautiful and strange and matching the
tattoos on the sides of my forehead.

"You have been marked by your goddess," Camille whispered. "I recognize the energy—it's the same when the Moon
Mother claimed me and branded me with her symbols."

"But what could she be thinking?"

"We visit the temple tomorrow. Perhaps you'll have your
answer then?"

I nodded and stepped into the steaming tub of water, sinking gratefully into the soothing warmth. I had to visit the temple, to ask them remove the curse. To tell them of what really happened and set the record straight.

"Will you take your old name again once you are cleared?" Camille handed me a soft cloth for washing, and some soapwort.

I shook my head. "No. I have been Iris for so long . . . and truly, I am not Pirkitta anymore. It would no more fit my nature than . . . than returning to the temple for good would. I realized today, on that mountain, that part of my life is over. It was what it was, and the Lady needed me to stop Vikkommin from becoming a terrifying sorcerer who would have used our religion as a battering ram against the world."

Camille let out a soft sigh. "Power is so easily abused."

She still hadn't asked me what happened, only if I had resolved things. Now, waiting for her question, I realized she wasn't going to, not until I was ready to talk about it.

I leaned back and closed my eyes. "I will tell you after I've bathed and eaten. Right now, it's still too fresh. But tomorrow will you go to the temple with me when I make my stand and demand they break the curse?"

Camille laughed then. "Iris, I would think that by now you'd know we'd go to the ends of the earth—and beyond—for you. You're family, babe. And not just because you take care of the house. You are as much family to me as Delilah and Menolly are."

Considering that Camille's sisters were her world, that was a great compliment and one I would not forget. Content with my place in the world, I let the water draw the chill out from my bones and tried to forget the sound of Vikkommin's screams echoing in my head.

HOWL AND KITÄÄ, along with a contingent of their people, led us to the doors of the temple. "We will wait out here until you are done. We will not leave you here."

I turned to all of them. "If you are sure, then I will try to make it brief. Camille, Smoky, and Roz will have to wait out here, but you may go with me." I lifted the heavy knocker and let it fall against the door. I'd sent word to the temple the night before and they seemed to know that Vikkommin was gone, because I'd received a summons to attend the next morning.

The door opened, and for the first time in six hundred years I was allowed to enter the temple of my goddess. As we stepped into the elaborate hall, carved from the solid mountain rock and inlaid with marble and silver and alabaster, my heart broke. I'd been ostracized for so long that it physically hurt to enter these halls where I'd spent my youth, where I'd fallen in love, where I'd been tortured.

The temple was as I'd remembered it. The main hall was so tall a whisper would echo on the currents, get caught, and rebound from wall to wall. Benches wrought in silver and marble were scattered around the hall. The floor was an elaborate stone mosaic depicting Undutar fighting one of the fire giants.

"My gods, this is beautiful," Camille whispered. "Our temples to the Moon Mother are more wild and feral, as is her nature."

"It is lovely, isn't it? I don't know how many centuries it took to build this hall—look, someone's coming."

I watched as the woman I immediately recognized as the Priestess-Mother slowly walked across the hall, flanked by two Elders. Her station was evident by the ornamentation on her robes. And I recognized the Elders with her, even after all these years. They had been present at my torture and denial.

Starting to kneel, I found myself unwilling to show them respect. I had to force myself through the proper genuflections. I stood again, as quickly as I could while still paying homage.

"I have destroyed Vikkommin and released his soul. I also found out the truth of that night. I come to offer you proof of what happened and to demand that you remove your curse." Of course, technically I had killed him, but it had been at the bequest of the Lady. Surely they couldn't fault me for that.

"Follow us, Pirkitta." And for the first time in six hundred years, my name had been uttered in the halls of Undutar.

We followed them through the long corridor that led to one of the examination rooms. I stared at the chamber—it was very much like the one in which they'd tortured me.

The Priestess-Mother motioned for us to sit down. "Pirkitta, while in my prayers last night, Undutar came to me. She told me that Vikkommin no longer lived and that this had been a test for you. That you were innocent of all wrongdoing toward him."

Test? What the fuck was she talking about? Undutar had said nothing about a test. And I most certainly *had* killed Vikkommin, even if at the Lady's bidding. I wasn't really innocent, although I'd had good reason for what I'd done. But I decided to keep my mouth shut and find out more.

"She came to several of the Elders in their dreams, in fact, and told us all the same thing. We are to immediately remove your curse and give you back your robes. You are welcome to rejoin the temple if you like—she did not indicate whether you would do so or not, but we talked about it among ourselves this morning. We would welcome you back with open arms."

She smiled widely.

Struck dumb and rather confused, I simply nodded. Camille gave me a sideways glance, but I shook my head just enough for her to see and she kept her silence. I'd told her—told all of them—during dinner just what had happened.

I let out a long sigh. Stay in the temple . . . The thought had crossed my mind more than once but I knew—even before I came to the Northlands—that I would never be able to do so. So much had changed. I was not the same woman, not the same Talon-haltija I'd been.

"I welcome my robes but will not stay in the temple. I will not be visiting here again, in fact. I've done what I needed to do, and if you would remove the curse from me, I'll return to my life as it is and darken your door no more."

The Priestess-Mother motioned for me to enter the ring of Elders, and they joined hands, working in silence. I felt a chill run through me, then a quickening—as if my blood jumped and danced—and then they dropped their hands and that appeared to be that.

"Is that *it*?"

"Yes, the curse is lifted. You are free once more to bear children, and you are definitely young enough to do so."

I blinked. I'd expected something far more intricate, but apparently the lifting of curses called for a lot less formality than the bestowing of them. Then again, considering the pain that went into receiving the curse, I decided that short and sweet was good enough for me.

As I gathered the bag containing my robes, I noticed there was something else inside the sack, but once again instinct told me not to look until we were long gone from the temple.

I made my good-byes and, gazing one last time at the intricately carved walls and the magnificent mosaics, took my leave of the temple as quietly as I'd arrived. We'd been inside about an hour, and it was the last hour I intended to ever spend in the Northlands. Howl's Pack was waiting, and with Camille and me riding the backs of two of the biggest warriors in wolf form, we headed back down the mountain.

When we were far enough away, I rooted around in the sack and withdrew what had caught my eye. It was a crystal statue of Undutar, but there was something magical about it. Something I couldn't quite pick up on. I also noticed my robes were different, and as I gazed at them, trying to figure out what that difference was, it struck me. They were embellished with the same embroidery as were those of the Priestess-Mother's.

"What is it?" Camille asked.

"I don't know," I said, but inside I had a glimmering suspicion. I just didn't want to say what yet.

WE STAYED YET a third night with Howl's Pack. I headed outside before supper, wearing my new robes, carrying the statue. There were yetis and trolls to contend with, yes, but Howl had guards on duty and with Vikkommin's shadow long gone, I wasn't terribly afraid.

I stopped on the edge of the ice field, staring out at the Skirts of Hel. The cold still made me shiver, but I was also warmed by the knowledge that I'd done what I set out to do. Now I could return home, marry Bruce, and have the children I longed to have. Visions of motherhood danced in my head, and I wondered just what characteristics they'd inherit from me . . . from him.

As a flurry of flakes fluttered around me, I knelt in the snow and placed the statue before me. I lowered my head to the ground, then sat back on my knees, closing my eyes, willing the words of a prayer to my lips. But no prayer came, only a deep feeling of peace and vindication.

I have plans for you yet, my Ar'jant d'tel. You are Chosen of the Gods, all right, but not to become Priestess-Mother of the temple here.

Jumping, I looked around. There, up ahead, was the shimmering form of my Lady, her long dark hair flowing in the wind. Her cloak was of the whitest fur and her eyes swirled with frost and mist.

"What is your will, my Lady? I am yours, forever and always, marked in body and soul." I realized that I bore no ill will to her for using me to combat Vikkommin. A priestess was the hand of her goddess, the extension of her Lady's will. I had been the best tool to stop him. That I'd accidentally learned his abilities, setting my own self at risk, had been collateral damage.

You will return home, and you shall set up a small shrine to me. You will run this shrine and be the Priestess-Mother to all who seek me out. My power is needed now, as the Earth warms and the glaciers lose their strength.

I nodded silently, realizing that Undutar meant to be more of a force in the world. Her cooling ways were needed; her mist and snow and fog were vital to the survival of so many creatures. And I would be, as forever and always, her handmaid.

With a sudden laugh, I realized how far I'd come. I'd crossed worlds to stand at her side, only to find myself her priestess in a suburb of Seattle. I'd trained for years of silent contemplation, yet now I was fighting demons with the D'Artigo sisters and their friends. I'd destroyed my lover to prevent him from misusing his power and had nearly turned myself into a carbon copy. I'd returned to the temple, only to be told to set up another temple on my own.

Life was filled with one ironic turn after another. But that which mattered most to me: my friends and their fight . . . my goddess and the fact that she loved me . . . that I could marry the man I loved and bear his children—those were the only things that would, in the end, make up the true story of my life.

DOUBLE HEXED

A STORMWALKER NOVELLA

———◆———

ALLYSON JAMES

ONE

◆━◆◆━◆

IT STARTED, INNOCENTLY ENOUGH, WITH A leaky faucet.

I called my hotel's plumber, Fremont Hansen, who agreed to come right away, and asked the guests in room 6 to go out for a while. Fremont had a balding head and gentle hazel eyes and believed he had magical powers. His true power lay in fixing the plumbing, but today, after nearly two hours, he crawled out from under the sink, still baffled.

"Don't know about this one, Janet," he said, pushing back his cap to rub his high forehead. "I've taken everything apart and replaced the faucets and resoldered the pipes. I've used plenty of plumber's enchantment, but nothing is working."

"Plumber's enchantment?"

Fremont wriggled his fingers. "You know what I mean."

"Oh brother," came a drag-queen drawl from the mirror above him.

Fremont did have a touch of magic in his aura, but I'd never had the heart to tell him how minor it was. The magic mirror, on the other hand, had no such compassion. The true magic mirror hung downstairs in the saloon, but it had learned to project itself through every mundane mirror in the hotel, kind of like a magical CCTV. Fremont couldn't hear it, because only those with very powerful magic could—lucky us.

"Honey," the mirror said, "he's got as much magic in his fingers as a shriveled-up transvestite has in his—"

"Stop!" I said.

My one maid, Juana, who was bringing in clean towels, thought I was talking to her and halted in the doorway.

Fremont leaned to peer at the bathroom mirror. "I swear something is buzzing behind there."

I'd told the guests they could return by six, and it was five forty-five now. "Anything?" I cut in.

Fremont heaved a sigh. "Let me try something." He got back down on his hands and knees while Juana went out for more towels. By the time she returned, Fremont scrambled up again, looking triumphant. "I think that's it." He grabbed the faucet's handles and cranked them wide open. "Here we go!"

The faucet exploded in blood.

Hot, red gore fountained over the bathroom, soaking us, the floor, walls, ceiling, shower, and Juana's clean towels in scarlet horror. It was blood all right, with its metallic tang, and warm, as though it had just erupted from a human body.

"Shut it off!" I yelled.

Fremont dove under the sink again. "Damn it, damn it, damn it . . ."

The aura that radiated from the blood was horrific—black, sticky, evil. Juana kept shrieking as the rain continued and so did the mirror.

"Shut up!" I shouted at both of them.

Juana's eyes blazed through the blood running down her face. "I go home! I don't work for you no more, you crazy Indian!"

She flung the blood-soaked towels at me, turned, and high-tailed it out the door. Fremont's wrench clanked against pipe, and the shower of blood abruptly ceased.

Fremont pulled off his cap to reveal that only the top of his balding head had escaped the red rain. "I don't know what the hell happened, Janet. Or what's making the water that color. Corrosion?"

"It's not corrosion. It's blood. The real thing."

"Plumbing don't bleed, not even in Magellan—"

Fremont broke off when he saw me staring not at him but at the mirror. He turned around, and his face drained of color.

The mirror now bore words, washed across it in red blood. *You are doomed.*

THE GUESTS OF room 6 chose that moment to walk back in. They were well-groomed, well dressed, and pale white from northern climes, the kind of people whose money I needed to keep my little hotel in the hot Southwest open. They took one look at the mirror, at me and Fremont spattered with blood—not to mention the walls, mirror, and part of the bedroom carpet—and walked back out again.

I grabbed the cleanest of the towels and rubbed at my face as I chased them down the stairs.

Cassandra, my neat and efficient hotel manager, didn't betray any surprise when the couple approached reception and demanded to check out, me covered in blood and panting apologies behind them. My offer to move them to another room was declined.

Without asking questions, Cassandra calmly told them we'd charge them only half the fee for the night they'd spent and give them vouchers for the restaurants in town. I let her. She suggested the restored railroad hotel in Winslow as an alternative and offered to have their bags delivered there if they liked. They accepted.

Cassandra disarmed the guests with her cool charm, but they still left.

Once they were gone, I beckoned to Cassandra with a stiff finger. She followed me upstairs, her fair hair perfect in its French braid, her silk suit crisp. A far cry from me with my black hair, jeans, cropped top, and motorcycle boots now coated with blood. I probably looked like a murder victim, except that I was still up and running around.

Fremont stood in the bathroom where I'd left him. His arms were folded, his eyes closed, and he rocked back and forth.

"Fremont," I said in alarm.

He opened his eyes but kept rocking, his face drawn in terror.

"Stop it," I said. "It's just a little blood projection. Some witch is messing with us, that's all. Or maybe Sheriff Jones hired a sorcerer to drive me out of town. I wouldn't put it past him."

Fremont drew a shaking breath. "You shouldn't joke about dire portents, Janet."

I grabbed the glass cleaner and paper towels Juana had left in her cart. "*This* is how I deal with dire portents."

Fortunately for me, the cleaner cut right through the blood. I wiped away the words, the paper towels squeaking against the glass.

"Mirror, mirror, on the wall," I whispered to it. "Who the hell did this?"

"Beats me, honey bun. That was *scary.*"

So helpful. I finished with the mirror and started on the rest of the bathroom. The other two wandered out to the bedroom, tracking blood on the carpet. Fremont sat on the bed, dazed, his bloodstained coveralls planted on the quilt one of my aunts had made. Cassandra gazed out the window at the distant mountains in silence.

"Cassandra?" I asked, continuing to spray and wipe. I at least was one hell of a bathroom cleaner. My grandmother, who'd raised me, had been a stickler for cleanliness, and she'd trained me how to scrub at an early age.

Cassandra turned to me, and I stopped in mid-swipe. Her face was pale with fear, my always cool, always contained manager-receptionist looking like she wanted to be sick.

"You all right?" I asked her.

Cassandra shook her head. "I'm sorry, Janet." She gave me another look of anguish and ran out of the room.

I HANDED FREMONT the rags and told him to keep wiping. I caught up to Cassandra on the stairs, but she wouldn't look at me, wouldn't talk.

I'd never seen her like this, my unflappable manager who'd managed luxury hotels in California and who ran this place better than I ever could. I ordered her to accompany me into the saloon, which wasn't open yet, and tell me what she knew.

We entered the saloon to see a broad-shouldered biker

with black hair leaning over the bar to help himself to a beer. He took one look at me covered in blood, slammed down the mug, and rushed me. I found myself lifted in arms like hard steel, and I gazed into the blue eyes that had looked back at me the night I'd first lain with a man.

"What the hell happened?" he demanded.

Mick's fire magic tingled through me, searching for injuries and ready to heal them. Because I was unhurt, my body started to respond the way it wanted to, with desire.

"I'm fine," I said swiftly. "The blood isn't mine."

Would Mick set me on my feet and let me go? No, he slid his big hands along my back and pulled me closer. "I felt it in the wards. Something got in."

He wanted to shift, to fight. Mick was a dragon, a giant black beast with black and silver eyes and a wingspan that rivaled a 747's. As a human, his dragon essence was contained in the dragon tattoos that wound down his bare arms and in the fire tattoo that stretched across the small of his back.

"I was about to ask Cassandra all about it," I said.

Cassandra had seated herself dejectedly at one of the empty tables. I'd restored the saloon to its original Wild West glory, complete with tin ceiling, varnished bar, and wide mirror on the wall. The magic mirror had shattered in its frame one night, the product of one of my harrowing adventures, but the fact that it was broken hadn't dimmed either its magic or, unfortunately, its personality.

"I'm sensing a wicked imbalance in the force, sweet cheeks," it said. "Micky, maybe you should get naked in case you have to shift."

I envied the way Mick could utterly ignore the thing. To Mick, the mirror was simply a powerful talisman, good to have on hand, and the fact that it kept up nonstop sexual suggestions rarely bothered him. Mick and I had awakened it from dormancy one night while working some Tantric magic, which meant that the mirror now belonged to us. It never let us forget *how* we'd awakened it, and its ongoing innuendo drove me insane. But I'd never throw it away. Magic mirrors were rare and powerful, and the mage who owned one could work amazing magic.

I took a seat next to Cassandra. I badly needed a shower,

and a beer wouldn't hurt, but more than that I wanted to know why Cassandra had been so spooked by the blood. I'd never seen anything frighten my ultra-efficient hotel manager.

Cassandra studied her bunched fists that rested on the table. "I'm sorry, Janet. I never should have come here in the first place."

"Yes, you should have. I can't run this hotel without you. Why do you think the message was for you, anyway? It appeared when Fremont and I were up there alone."

Cassandra looked straight into my eyes. "Because I used to work for John Christianson."

She obviously expected me to clutch my chest and fall over in shock. I blinked. "Who is John Christianson?"

Mick answered for her. "He's a filthy rich hotelier and real estate magnate. Owns half of Southern California—commercial real estate, hotels, anything high-dollar in Los Angeles and down the coast to San Diego. Prominent in social circles, contributes to more charities than anyone in the state."

I spread my hands. Big business, especially big business in other states, was far away and unimportant to my day-to-day existence.

"He's a first-class bastard," Cassandra said with venom. "I worked at one of Christianson's hotels, the 'C' in Los Angeles."

All right, so even I'd heard of the "C," which featured in Fremont's favorite television shows about the rich and famous. The "C" was a boutique hotel in Beverly Hills that attracted celebrities, high-profile politicians, and the ultra-rich. They could check in for the weekend and have every need met and every decadent wish granted, without ever having to leave the building.

"What has the 'C' got to do with messages on my bathroom mirror?"

"Because the secret of Christianson's success is deep, dark magic," Cassandra said. "He can't work magic himself, but he's hired some of the best in the business—mages into the blackest arts. At first, when Christianson asked me to manage the 'C,' the top of his chain, I was thrilled. It would be a huge step forward in my career."

"But . . ." With a setup like that, there was always a "but."

Cassandra shivered. "Please don't ask me what really goes

on at the 'C'—what you get with the most secret and expensive of packages. Let's just say there are people out there who will do anything—*anything*—and pay any price, for pleasure. And please don't ask me what Christianson expected me to do, with my magic, with . . . myself. One day, I'd had enough, and I left. Escaped is more like it. I didn't tell anyone, didn't plan anything. I just walked away."

"And came to Magellan," I finished, finally understanding why she'd turned up on my doorstep, looking for a job. "Interesting choice. Why here and not half the world away?"

"The first place they'd look is half the world away," Cassandra said. "I thought I'd give a small town in the middle of nowhere a try. I changed my name and got you to hire me."

"So you're not really Cassandra Bryson?" I'd taken her information for tax purposes, and it had all checked out, but I conceded that a competent witch could have taken care of such trivialities.

I'd read Cassandra's aura when she'd first arrived and saw what I saw now: a powerful witch who liked things clean and tidy, but without a taint of true evil. I'd liked her, she'd had experience running hotels, and I'd been out of my depth with this place and knew it.

"If you don't mind, I won't tell you what my real name is," Cassandra said. "They can hear names, and use them."

Mick gave her an understanding nod. He'd explained to me once that his name—the full version of it unpronounceable to me—wasn't his true name, which would sound more like musical notes. Only a dragon and its dam knew its true name, because knowledge of a dragon's name—and Cassandra had told me this part—could enslave it.

I also had a true name, a spirit name, one my father had given me the day he'd brought me home, which was between me, him, and the gods. Names were powerful things.

"I came to Magellan because of the vortexes around it," Cassandra said. "What better place to hide my magic than in a place permeated with it? When I drove by your hotel and saw the wards all over it, I knew I'd struck lucky. Even if you hadn't been looking for a manager, I'd have washed dishes for you, anything for a chance to live here. Plus your aura held so much innocence, Janet, I knew I could trust you."

"*My* aura?" I stared. "Held innocence?" This was the first time in my life I'd heard someone refer to Janet Begay as innocent. Janet, the Stormwalker with the goddess-from-hell mother and magic she was just beginning to understand, was a long way from innocent. Most people called me "trouble-maker," "pain in the ass," or "oh-my-god-it's-her-let's-run."

Cassandra smiled at me. "Trust me, Janet, after knowing the people I knew, your honesty was refreshing." Her face fell. "But I've put you—and Mick and everyone here—in the worst danger."

"You think the blood message in the bathroom means Christianson has found you?" I asked.

She nodded. "And I can't risk that he won't kill everyone in this building to get to me. I have to go."

Cassandra started to rise, but I pulled her back down. "Don't be stupid. If they've found you, the safest place for you is here. We have Mick, and I'll call Coyote—if I can find him—and we'll get Pamela up here. There's some damn strong magic within these walls. We'll defend you. It's what friends do."

Cassandra looked pathetically grateful. Mick and Coyote were the strongest magical beings I knew, but my magic is plenty damn powerful as well. Mine is a mixture of earth magic—Stormwalker power that I inherited from my Navajo grandmother—and the crazy, white-hot goddess magic from Beneath.

Beneath is the shell world below this one, where the evilest of the gods got stuck when Coyote and others sealed the cracks between that world and this one. The vortexes around Magellan held gateways to that world, and one of the evil goddesses stuck down there was my mother. I'd inherited the nasty, unpredict-able, insanely powerful Beneath magic from her.

I'd recently learned to twine my Diné-inherited storm magic and my Beneath magic to temper both, but earth magic and Beneath magic mix like oil and water. It's like having a blender inside you all the time. An angry blender.

Cassandra flinched. "No, I don't want Pamela here. I don't want her hurt. If they don't know about her, they can't use her to get to me."

Pamela was a Changer, a shape-shifter who could take the form of a wolf. She and Cassandra shared a small apartment in town, and Cassandra had met her here, in my hotel, the day Pamela had tried to choke the life out of me.

"Pamela will be pissed as hell if you keep her out of it," I said.

"Yes, but that means she'll be alive."

"Good point." I got up. "But I'm calling Coyote. It never hurts to have a god on your side."

"I'll reinforce the wards," Mick offered. "Janet is right; this is the best place you can stay. Plus I can have a phalanx of dragons here anytime I need them. I don't care how powerful a mage Christianson sends—he can't work magic if he's being fried to a crisp."

Cassandra got to her feet at the same time we did, the emotion in her eyes touching. "Thank you, Janet. Mick. You are good people. I should have told you right away."

I shrugged. "We all have our secrets."

Mick, who had more secrets than most, returned my look blandly and said he'd head to the roof to work the wards.

Cassandra and I returned to the lobby, she to reception and I to my office to hunt down my cell phone. I never could remember to carry the damn thing, so anytime the cell rang, I had to race to find it before it went to voice mail. I've never made it yet.

I didn't make it this time, either. Finally locating the thing stuck in the big potted plant that Juana had obviously watered before our adventure upstairs, I was brushing dirt from it when Coyote himself waltzed through the hotel's front entrance, followed by Maya Medina, my on-call electrician and pretty much my best friend.

Coyote was a tall, broad-shouldered Native American with a long black braid and intense dark eyes. He didn't come from any specific tribe that I knew of, because he was Coyote—trickster god, being of raw power, and a royal pain in the ass. He wore his usual jeans and jeans jacket, cowboy boots, a button-down shirt, and a big belt buckle studded with turquoise. Maya, on the other hand, wasn't in her electrician gear; she was dressed to kill in a tight black dress, red lipstick, and stiletto heels.

Coyote halted in the center of the lobby. He threw his head back to study the gallery that ringed the second story, then he laughed, a big, booming laugh.

"I smell a curse," he said. "A big, *bad* curse. What are you still doing in here, Janet?"

As soon as the words left his mouth, the front door slammed shut behind him. A hurricane-like blast blew through the lobby, ripping papers into the air, shoving pictures off the walls, and shattering glass. Every open window banged shut.

The wind died abruptly, followed by a heavy clanking as the big lock on the front door fastened itself. Then all the lights went out.

As the four of us stood in twilight gloom, the magic mirror's voice rolled from the saloon.

"Uh-oh, kids. I think it's showtime."

TWO

MAYA RAN TO THE FRONT DOOR, TRIED TO unlock it, failed, and started pounding on the wood. "Hey, let me out of here!"

Cassandra checked the saloon. "Everything's locked down tight in there."

Coyote, damn him, kept laughing. He flicked magic at the windows in the front room, his amusement dying when they stayed firmly shut.

"Come on, Janet," Maya snapped. "Open the door. There's somewhere I need to be."

I shrugged, trying to remain calm. "If you can figure out how to get out, you let me know."

Maya gave me a disgusted look and marched past me and into the kitchen, where we heard her start beating on the back door.

"So, little witch," Coyote said to Cassandra, his eyes gleaming in a way I didn't like. "What have you been up to?"

"Leave her alone," I said. "What exactly did you mean by a curse, Coyote? I thought this was just a warning spell."

"Nope," Coyote said, almost joyfully. "A curse, a hex, very

bad juju. You can't smell it? It stinks like shit, all over this hotel. I'd say you're in for one hell of a night."

"So break it," I said.

Coyote grinned. "Wouldn't it be more fun to see what happens?"

"No," Cassandra and I said at the same time.

Coyote just chuckled. I was glad he thought this was so damn funny.

He looked Cassandra up and down, and his laughter died. "I don't see the connection, though. This might be tough."

"What connection?" I asked.

"The one between Cassandra and the hex. Could be a general hex, on anyone and everyone near her. Or a blanket hex, on the place she happens to be."

"Whatever it is, just fix it." I headed for the kitchen. "We need lights."

Coyote called after me, "The best spells might need a little sex magic. You game?"

I gave him a signal he'd understand and went on into the kitchen.

Maya at least had stopped banging on the back door. She leaned against it to face me, her slender arms folded, her dark eyes full of rage.

"What the hell, Janet? Every time I come near you, I get battered, taken hostage, held at gunpoint, buried in rubble, or all of the above. And I always, *always* ruin my clothes. What is it with you?"

"Would you believe me if I said that this time it's not my fault?"

"No." Maya uncrossed her arms, gave the door one final thump, and stalked back into the middle of the big kitchen.

It was eerily quiet in here without the appliances humming. My temperamental cook, Elena, hadn't shown up today. Elena Williams was an Apache from Whiteriver, a culinary genius but given to fits of sullenness. Some days she never came to work at all.

"Whether you believe me or not, can you fix the electricity?" I asked Maya.

"In this dress?"

"You can wear something of mine."

"You're two sizes smaller than me, and you only have biker-chick clothes." Her voice went sad. "I was going to meet Nash."

"Oh." Maya's so-called relationship with Nash Jones, the sheriff of Hopi County, was drama with a capital *D*. I'd seen them a couple of times together lately, eating sedate meals in the local diner, looking like two people afraid to talk to each other.

"Call him," I said. "Tell him you're stuck because of me. He'll believe that." My run-ins with Sheriff Jones were volatile and memorable. He blamed me for anything weird that went on in his county, and the trouble was, he was usually right.

"I tried." Maya's face went even more glum. "My cell phone won't work." She fixed me with an accusing stare. "What did you do this time?"

I started rummaging in a drawer. "Why is everyone assuming that *I* did something?"

"Because you usually do."

She had a point. I pulled out a screwdriver. "Here."

Maya sighed, but she yanked the screwdriver out of my hand and headed for the back of the kitchen, where the junction boxes were. I knew that if anyone could bring the lights back, it was Maya. She was the only one currently in the hotel who wasn't magical, but when it came to electricity, she had talent to burn.

I returned to the lobby to find Cassandra trying to get a signal from her cell phone. I couldn't get one on mine, either, and my landline was out as well. A good curse would take care of pesky things like phones.

But I had a couple of secret weapons at my disposal. I poked my head into the saloon and looked at one of them. "Mick still on the roof?" I asked the mirror.

"Yes." It sounded as glum as Maya. "There's some bad things stirring, sugar."

"That's why I want Mick."

"I mean, *really* bad, sweetie. I'm having a bet with myself how fast you'll replace me if I die."

"Don't be so melodramatic. You're a magic mirror. You can't die."

It sighed. "I can be melted into slag, ground to powder. And then I'd never see your beautiful ass again."

I ignored it. Besides, even a melted magic mirror could be re-formed with no loss to its power. "Are you still tied in with the mirrors at the compound in Santa Fe?"

"The place with Bancroft and Drake and their hottie houseboy? I might be."

I had the feeling my mirror had been training his magic eye on the twenty-two-year-old human who did errands for Bancroft, a member of the dragon council. The houseboy's name was Todd, and his job was to make sure that the needs of the dragons' guests were met. Each and every need.

"Drake owes me one, he and Bancroft both," I said. "Stand by to contact them if we need help. *If* we need it, that is. I don't want Drake out here giving Mick hell if it's not necessary." Drake worked for the dragon council, and he was more arrogant than the three council members put together. But I couldn't ignore his potential as an ally.

"I'll stand ready, sweet cakes." The mirror paused. "Could you show me your beautiful bod, one more time? Just in case . . ."

I made a disgusted noise and left the room. I was surrounded by perverts, but they were powerful perverts, and I couldn't afford to do without them.

I ascended to the second floor, took the back stairs to the third, and opened the door out onto the roof. Mick was there, gazing out over the desert beyond the Crossroads—what the locals called the T-intersection of two highways. My hotel and the Crossroads Bar sat on desert east of the T, but the Crossroads was also a mystical crossroads, I'd learned, where magic and reality could blur. A railroad had been built here once but had gone bust nearly a century ago, the empty railroad bed and a derelict hotel the only reminders of its aspirations to glory.

I paused on the roof a moment to appreciate the fineness of my boyfriend. Mick's body was broad, hard, and strong, the muscle shirt and jeans he wore, despite the chill, showing it off in a good way. Wind tugged at his wild black hair, which he usually tamed into a short ponytail. Tonight he'd left it loose, and it was all over the place. I wasn't sure why Mick had hair at all, or why it was always that length, but he never changed it. I didn't mind, because his hair was wonderful to run my fingers through.

Mick had been my first lover—my only lover—though we'd spent five years apart before we'd both ended up in Magellan. He was the only being who could tame my Stormwalker magic when it threatened to overwhelm me. Thoughts of *how* he did it started wicked fantasies bubbling inside me.

The dirt parking lot I shared with the Crossroads Bar was filling with motorcycles as the sun set in splendid glory to the west, silhouetting the distant San Francisco Peaks.

Mick turned as my boot scraped on the roof, but he'd known I was there. Mick always knew where I was.

He gave me the smile that turned my heart inside out. "Hey, baby."

I silently damned whatever mage had tracked down Cassandra. Stupid curses. Mick and I should be making love up here under the blaring sunset, the red light touching our skin, not discussing malevolent magic.

"Coyote says it's a hex, not a spell," I said as I approached him. "All doors and windows are locked downstairs." I looked around. "So why doesn't it apply to the roof?"

"Who says it doesn't?" Mick picked up a pebble and tossed it upward as hard as he could. About fifteen feet above our heads, the pebbled exploded into dust.

"Shit," I whispered.

"Funny, that's what I said." Mick dusted his hand on his pants. "If I change to dragon up here, and my body expands . . . *zap.*"

Terrific. There went my hope that Mick could spread his dragon wings and fly away, maybe go for help or find whatever mage was chanting the curse and fry him.

"How did this get by you?" I asked. "This is the best-warded building I've ever been in. You must have felt someone trying to cast a spell. How did it get by *me*?"

"Like Coyote says, it's a curse, not a spell," Mick said. "Different thing."

"Oh, right." Wiccan magic isn't really my thing. Mick had taught me to work minor spells such as those for healing or protection, but my true power is more raw and basic. Instinctive. Mick was the one with the encyclopedic knowledge of magics.

"Hexes can fasten themselves like leeches or barnacles to a person or a place and then spread," Mick explained. "They can be cast on one target, like a building, a car, or even a whole town if the caster is strong enough. An expert witch can slide the curse onto protective wards and use the wards themselves to sink the curse into the building, kind of like an infection."

Great. A magical bacteria.

I hooked my thumbs into the waistband of my jeans. "So how do we get rid of it? Can we infuse the wards with defensive magic, kind of like sending in antibiotics?"

"Possibly. Or we could take down the wards altogether, but that might be exactly what the mage wants. Hexes are tricky. Let me think about it. In the meantime, we need to minimize casualties."

Minimize casualties. Just what I wanted to hear.

I raised my gaze to the mountains in the west that were quickly fading into the dusk and said a prayer. The gods of my people lived in those mountains, and so did the kachinas, the Hopi spirits who were watching me, not always in a friendly way.

"This was not how I envisioned spending my evening," I said.

"No?" Mick's smile heated my blood. "And how did you envision spending it?"

I traced the reddish dust on the rooftop with my boot. "Since I haven't seen you in a couple of days, how did you think?"

"I can guess." His smile widened. "I have a couple of new things I want to try."

"New things?" I gave him a mock-innocent look. "You mean there's more?"

"So much more." Mick came to me and drew the knuckle of his forefinger down my cheek. "I want to teach you everything, Janet."

Believe me, I wanted to learn. I turned my head and pressed a kiss to his palm. "Maybe a little Tantric magic would loosen up the curse?"

Mick's growl wasn't human. "I wish, but we can't trust the hex. It might make some seriously bad shit happen."

Like things falling off, maybe? Figures. I had the feeling the hex wasn't going to let us have any fun.

Mick brushed his thumb over the corner of my mouth.

"It would be a hell of a way to go, but I'm not ready to lose you yet."

I wasn't ready to lose Mick, either, especially when I still wasn't really sure I had him. I raised on my tiptoes and kissed his lips.

"Let's go minimize casualties," I said before I could turn the kiss into something more satisfying. "But when this is done . . ."

Mick slanted me his bad-boy smile. "When this is done, I won't hold back."

I returned the grin. "Good. I'm looking forward to it."

WE WALKED INSIDE together, hand in hand. "Who's in?" Mick asked as we started down the stairs.

I considered. "Maya, Coyote, Cassandra, me, and you. Fremont. Juana walked off the job, and Elena never showed up. I only had three rooms filled, and one couple left after the curse played the little trick with the blood. I don't know whether the other guests have come back for the night . . ." I stopped in my tracks. "Crap."

Mick and I looked at each other, realizing at the same time. "Ansel," we said together, and we took the stairs at a run.

THREE

JUST THE QUESTION TO MAKE MY DAY
bright—what effects will a very powerful mage's curse have
on a Nightwalker who's trying to stay on the wagon?

The door of room 2, where Ansel had taken up lodgings a
few weeks ago, was firmly closed, and no sound came from
behind it. Usually I wouldn't have let a Nightwalker into my
hotel, but Ansel had seemed so alone and morose the night
he'd arrived that I couldn't turn him down.

He'd so far kept to himself and been far less trouble than
some of my human guests. I'd learned to have cow's blood on
order for him, but I wasn't certain of our supply. I'd left a note
for Elena the cook to check, but of course she'd decided to not
come in today.

I grabbed a flashlight from my office and headed to the
kitchen while Mick stayed in the lobby to both check the
wards and keep an eye on room 2.

When I reached the kitchen, I could just make out Maya in
the back, her long legs a pale smudge in the darkness. The
occasional curse in Spanish floated to me.

I yanked open the walk-in refrigerator and quickly splayed

my flashlight over the shelves. The refrigerator was depressingly bare, but I relaxed a little when I spotted a plastic gallon bottle full to the top with blood. Good. One of those usually kept Ansel going for a couple of days, so he would be all right. The rest of us might get a little hungry if the doors stayed locked for too long, but at least we wouldn't be Nightwalker food.

Out in the lobby, Mick was hugging the wall by the front door, cheek pressed to it, palm moving over the plaster as though he caressed a lover's skin. I envied the wall. I knew what he was doing, though, feeling the essence of the building, connecting with his own magic in it.

Coyote sprawled in a chair with his feet up, watching Mick with interest. Cassandra sat on one of the leather sofas, arms pressed over her stomach, staring at the floor. I plopped down next to her.

"Cassandra, you are the most amazing witch I've ever met," I said. "Your power could light a city."

Cassandra didn't look up at me. "Is there a point to this little pep talk?"

Her acid tone surprised me, but I let it go. We were all a little nervous. "I mean that if anyone can defeat a curse it's you. I'm here to help you, and so is Mick, and we have Coyote. The four of us are damned powerful. We can break this, especially if we work on it together."

"And me." Fremont came down the stairs, minus his toolbox, his overalls, face, and cap still spattered with blood.

"And Fremont." I knew Fremont's magic was minimal, but even a minor mage can contribute to a group spell. "Thanks, Fremont. We'd welcome your help."

He gave me a pleased look, but Cassandra raised her head, her eyes red-rimmed and moist. "Janet, will you quit with the team-leader attitude? This is serious."

"I know, which is why I'm trying to come up with answers."

Cassandra wiped her eyes as Fremont went back upstairs, probably to check the plumbing. "Do you know what an *ununculous* is?"

"An unun . . . a what?" I asked.

"It's a sorcerer who is a master of the blackest arts," Cassandra said. "And when I say *master*, I mean the best sorcerer in the world, practitioner of the darkest magics. There are mages out there who summon demons to enhance their power, but an ununculous has more power than any demon ever could. Demons fear *him*. If he summons a demon, it's to steal all its power and then try out a new way to kill the demon. The Nazis used an ununculous during the war—there was a branch that tried dark sorcery."

"Oh, nice. But you keep saying 'he.' Are there no female ununculouses?" I paused as my tongue twisted. "Or is the plural of ununculous *ununculi*?"

"There is no plural, because there's never more than one at a time." Cassandra's voice weakened as she spoke. "When he reaches the highest stage of his power, he fights the current ununculous, and only one survives. An ununculous never trains any other mage, because he knows he'd be teaching his own killer. They do their best to murder any mage who shows inclination to study the black arts too deeply. An aspiring ununculous trains in utmost secret, or he or she doesn't survive."

I blew out my breath and scrubbed my hand through my still-blood-caked hair. "And that's what's after you?"

Cassandra nodded. "I won't name him, in case that calls him. But John Christianson employed the ununculous from time to time, paying him millions, to do things for him and for the 'C.' The ununculous took the money and did the deeds because he likes money; he's the ultimate hedonist. I met him a couple of times." She shuddered. "He knows me; he must have tracked me here."

I smiled grimly. "But can this ununculous stand against a god, a dragon, a Stormwalker, and one hell of a witch?"

Cassandra gave me a deprecating glance. "Oh, yes. It's likely he'll welcome the challenge. He'll enjoy experimenting until he figures out the most satisfying way of killing us, one at a time."

I gestured to Coyote, who was still watching Mick fondle the walls.

"Coyote's a *god*. Your ununculous, whatever he might aspire to be, is still mortal. Coyote can unmake him anytime he wants to."

Coyote shrugged. "Maybe."

I was tired of playing team leader. I got off the couch and headed for the hall that led to my private bedroom and bath. "You three figure something out. I need a shower, even if the water heater is out."

"No can do, Janet," Fremont called to me, coming down the stairs again. "Water's out completely."

I swung around. "What do you mean? Are the faucets still spraying blood?"

"No, I mean nothing's coming out. I opened up all the faucets, but they're bone-dry. That's all right, though. I can work on the pipes better if the water's gone."

"That does it." I didn't discount Cassandra's worry, but damn it, I wanted a shower. "Coyote, blast the curse and get rid of it. We'll deal with Cassandra's ununculous when he shows up to finish the job."

Coyote yawned. "As Fremont says, no can do."

I marched to the all-powerful god and stuck my finger at his face. "Don't you dare give me any crap about not interfering in the lives of mortals, because you do it all the time. I'm filthy, it's getting cold, and there's a Nightwalker about to rise upstairs while the blood I bought for him slowly spoils in the non-working refrigerator. Just get rid of the curse. If you are holding out to see how we deal with it, I'll . . . I'll tell my grandmother."

Coyote's eyes flickered. "Oh, hey, that's not fair."

My grandmother, from whom I'd inherited my Storm-walker magic, often hung around my hotel parking lot in the form of a crow, watching over me (or watching to see what I did wrong). She didn't like Coyote. Once upon a time, she'd run him off our place in Many Farms, he in his coyote form, she with a broom. Grandmother had no fear of trickster gods.

Coyote looked troubled. "I really mean I can't do it, Janet, sweetie. I seem to have lost my mojo." He opened his hand and made a throwing motion at the windows, but again, nothing happened. The panes didn't even rattle.

My heart squeezed. "You're a god. Your magic can't disappear."

"Apparently, it can."

"You're tricking me, right? Pretending to be powerless so you'll see what I'll do? Some god thing about observing the human condition?"

Coyote leaned to me until we were face-to-face. His nose had been broken at some time in his human form and hadn't healed in the best way. Why he hadn't fixed that, I had no idea. "No, Janet. I truly can't work any magic."

I went cold. If this ununculous was so powerful that his curse could render a god helpless, what could we do against him?

Fear and rage awoke in me, and that, in turn, stirred the all-powerful, goddess-from-hell magic I fought every day to control. I'd been teaching myself, with the help of my friends, to twine it with my Stormwalker magic, to form a warm and strong power without the side effect of chaotic destruction, but it was tough going.

There was no storm in the sky right now, and if I chose, I could let the Beneath magic untwine itself and become as hot and crazy and devastating as ever. Coyote didn't want me doing that—a mortal with god magic was a dangerous thing, he'd told me—but I considered this an emergency.

"To hell with it," I said. "Get out of the way, Mick. I'm breaking the curse."

Mick stood up, his hand still pressed to the wall. His eyes had gone coal black all the way through, no more trace of blue. "The hex runs pretty deep. If you rip it away from the wards, you might destroy the walls."

"I don't care if I bring down the whole damned hotel. I can rebuild it—I've done it before. *After* I take a shower."

Coyote rose, his height and bulk a formidable barrier. "Janet, you know I can't let you use the Beneath magic."

"Make an exception. *You* can't do shit right now. You just said that."

"But if you use that magic to break the curse, my first order of business will be to kill you."

At the moment, I didn't care. I was angry, grungy, and not a little worried about what Cassandra had told me. And for some reason, I was convinced I couldn't fight this ununculous until I'd scrubbed myself clean. I was obsessing, yes, but I didn't care.

I looked up at Coyote, unafraid. I knew by the expression on his face that my eyes had gone ice green, the color of my mother's eyes. "Get out of my way," I said calmly. "Or I'll do this through you."

Coyote lunged for me. I stared in shock, not really believing he meant to kill me, but at the last minute, when his hands were wrapping my throat, I realized—yes, he did.

And then Mick was there. Mick ripped Coyote away from me and took the big man down. Coyote's god power outweighed Mick's dragon magic any day, but with them both in human form, neither using magic, they were well matched in strength.

While the two of them fought it out on my earth-colored tile floor, I raised my hands, willing the worst of the Beneath magic to come out and play. White-hot light roared from my fingers and hit the door full force. The hotel shuddered, glass tinkling in the windows.

I threw back my head and laughed. I hadn't felt power like this in months. I'd forgotten how much I loved it.

"Feel that, sorcerer," I said, my entire body crackling with magic. "Fucking feel it."

There was a sizzling noise, and sparkling electricity danced across every wall. A high-pitched scream shrilled from the kitchen.

Maya.

I snapped off the Beneath magic—or tried to. A glowing nimbus clung to my hands as I turned and sprinted for the kitchen, Fremont and Cassandra right behind me.

FOUR

—◆◆◆—

WE FOUND MAYA SITTING ON THE FLOOR
against the wall, cradling one arm, her black dress hiked up to
her hips. When she saw me charge in with my hands glowing
white and my eyes bright green, she screamed again.

"Are you all right?" I yelled at her. "What happened?"

Maya's face was streaked with mascara and tears. "What
do you think happened? I shocked myself. What the hell are
you doing?"

Fremont crouched next to her. "Didn't you switch off the
power?"

"Of course I switched it off. I threw the main. I'm not stupid. A big arc jumped out of the generator and wrapped
around my arm. Damn, and I'd almost gotten it working."

Had I done this? With my wave of Beneath power, had I
sent electricity through the building to electrocute Maya? Or
was it the curse simply not wanting Maya—or me—to get the
lights back on?

"Don't worry about the electricity, Maya," I said, trying to
bring myself under control. "We have plenty of candles, and

we're going to break this spell. Let Cassandra look at your arm."

"She's a medic?" Maya asked.

"No, but she's good with a healing spell."

"A magic medic." Fremont grinned.

Cassandra tented her hands over her mouth, tears trickling from her eyes. "I'd better not. If the ununculous behind the hex is after me, using magic will draw him here faster."

"Cassandra," I said, my jaw tight. "You need to hold it together and help us."

"I can't." Cassandra started to sob, crumpling to her knees. "I can't. Don't make me."

"What's wrong with her?" Fremont asked, wide-eyed.

I wished I knew. I'd never seen Cassandra lose her cool, no matter how desperate the situation. "Either the hex is making her a little nuts, or the ununculous really is that terrifying." I sighed. "So, that's one powerful Wicca and one god down for the count."

"You still have me," Fremont said quickly.

"Yes," I said, giving him a grateful look. "And me. And Mick."

And the mirror, I added silently. Time to have it send messages. Dragons knew everything about everyone, even though they mostly sat back and observed. I had no doubt that Bancroft of the dragon council would have heard of the ununculous and know who he was. Time to call in my favor.

I dug in drawers for emergency candles, happy we had so many. In the desert, storms summer and winter could easily knock out electricity, and even though we had our own generator, it didn't always work—like now. Fremont started helping me set the candles into holders and lit them with a butane lighter.

"Fremont, can you and Cassandra fix some food for all of us? Something simple, even chips and dip would work. Maya, come out front with me, and Mick will take a look at your arm. He has healing magic, too. We'll have our little meal and figure out how to beat this."

"She's being team leader again," Fremont said.

"It's better than sitting on our asses waiting to be picked off. Now do it."

Cassandra looked up from her huddle on the floor. "Sorry, Janet."

Fremont helped Cassandra to her feet and gave me a salute. "Aye-aye, ma'am. We're on it."

I put my arm around Maya's waist and guided her to the lobby. Mick was back at the walls, the fight over. Coyote sat on the stairs to the second floor, near the statue of the coyote my friend Jamison Kee had made for me. Blood stained Coyote's face where it had run from his nose and a cut on his lip, but Mick looked whole and unscathed.

I gave Maya to Mick's capable healing—for a man his size, he could be incredibly gentle—and strode into the saloon.

Through the saloon windows I could see the Crossroads Bar, now teeming with life. Floodlights glared to illuminate the motorcycles parked in front, and I saw movement inside the open door. Oh, to be there sipping beer provided by the taciturn Barry Dicks, fending off unwanted passes from drunk bikers. Paradise compared to being stuck in a curse-ridden hotel.

As I turned away from the windows and moved to the mirror, Maya wandered in. She still cradled her arm, but less tenderly now. Mick's magic would have easily fixed whatever burn or damage she'd sustained.

Maya walked to the window in her high heels and looked out at the bar with the same wistfulness I'd had. "Mick and Coyote are growling at each other again. I never thought I'd say this, but *you* are acting the least weird of anybody, Janet."

She flattered me. I went behind the bar, unfolded the stepstool I kept back there, and stepped up to look into the mirror.

"I think it's time to get Drake," I murmured to it. "And while you're at it, tell him to call the Hopi County Sheriff's Department." I couldn't have the mirror contact Nash directly, because Nash was unable to hear it, but Drake knew who Nash was and would find him.

Silence met me.

"Hello?" I tapped on the mirror. "Is this thing on?"

"Janet?" Maya said from the window.

I stood on tiptoe and shook the mirror in its frame. "Wake up, damn you."

A piece of glass fell out and shattered on the floor. The

mirror made no sound, and my breath stopped. It hated pieces of itself breaking, would scream in melodramatic terror when it happened. Simple breakage couldn't hurt it, but the mirror always acted as though it was on death's door when a piece broke.

"Hey." I shook it again. "Talk to me, or I pulverize you."

Nothing. No *Oh, sugar-pie, don't hurt me, I'll be good.* Or *Only if you promise to wear a leather bustier and thigh-high boots.*

"Janet, who are you talking to?" Maya asked. "I take it back about you not being weird."

"Damn it all to hell." I jumped down from the stool and fetched the broken pieces of mirror, cutting myself on one. I put the pieces into an ashtray, selecting one of the smoother ones to shove into my pocket.

I'd been arrogant, thinking that while the ununculous might be a big, bad sorcerer, we stood a chance to defeat him because we had a magic mirror. Even a minor witch can face the strongest mage if she has a magic mirror behind her.

If the hex had rendered the mirror dormant, we could be seriously screwed.

"Hey," Maya said, rushing to the window. "There's Carlos."

Carlos was my bartender. At the moment, he was staring in confusion at the outside door while he rattled the handle, trying to get in to work his shift.

"Janet?" he called. "Anyone home?"

"Carlos!" Maya banged on the window, but Carlos didn't hear her. Maya started beating on the window so hard I feared she'd break the glass. "Hey, we're here! Carlos!"

Carlos obviously didn't see her either. He kept trying the door, and then he attempted to pry open the window right next to Maya. He backed away from the building, frowning. Maya shouted at him, calling him names in both English and Spanish, but Carlos wandered away toward the front of the hotel.

"Idiota," Maya screamed at him as he walked away.

"Give him a break, Maya. He can't hear you."

"Why not?"

"It's a curse. A hex. Magic badness. Cassandra's enemies want her trapped in this hotel, and they don't want her to get help."

Thinking about that, I wondered why the ultra-bad sorcerer hadn't waited until Cassandra was alone to confront and kill her. I could understand a sadistic man making Cassandra watch her friends die first, but why would he allow her the potential help of a dragon and the god Coyote? Why risk that?

Something was wrong here, and I needed to know what. But even if Cassandra had neglected to tell us everything, it didn't really matter. We were cut off and in trouble, and now we were without the magic mirror's communication ability. We needed help.

"We need Nash," I said. If dragons were out, Nash Jones was the next best thing.

"Don't you think I've been trying to call him?" Maya demanded. "I told you, all the cell phones are out and so is your landline."

She went silent as we both watched Carlos circle back to the saloon, frown in puzzlement at the door again, then drift to his car and get in it. He started up, his taillights flashing as he pulled away from the parking lot. Maya muttered under her breath, calling Carlos more names.

"Let him go," I said. "And let's concentrate on contacting Nash."

"How?" Maya asked sourly. "Smoke signals?"

"Maybe. I'll think of something."

I left the saloon a lot less confident than when I'd gone in. I made for Coyote, who still lounged by the coyote statue as though drawing comfort from the stone. He'd at least wiped the blood off his face.

Mick was touching the walls again. He was becoming obsessed. Maya thumped down on a couch, folded her arms, and pretended to ignore us.

"Tell me you really do have your god powers," I said, sitting on the steps next to Coyote.

"Sorry, Stormwalker. Tell me you're not going to try the Beneath magic again, when we can't predict what the hex will do to it."

"I will use it to defend my friends if I have to. I'll not stand by and let the sorcerer, whoever he is, kill us or get to Cassandra." When the ununculous attacked, I planned to kill him. Quickly. End of problem.

"When he comes," Coyote said, as though he'd read my mind, "Mick fights him, not you. Mick's the only one who can."

"Like hell I'm letting Mick face an over-the-top powerful sorcerer on his own. If I can take this guy down, I'm doing it."

Coyote gave me a stern look. "You need to stop and think about what kind of forces you'd be unleashing if you use your Beneath magic, Janet. Undampened, on something like that sorcerer, with everything complicated by his hex. There's no way of knowing what kind of magic *he'll* be drawing on. The two of you could rip open the vortexes and release who the hell knows what, including your bitch-queen goddess mother. I will *not* let you do that."

My blood chilled. The desert to the east of my hotel was riddled with vortexes, confluences of mystical energy. New Agers liked them, thinking that they enhanced their *chi* or whatever, but I knew what vortexes really were—gateways to the world Beneath. If my mother got out, she wouldn't be looking to have a happy family reunion. She'd destroy every single person she could get her hands on, beginning with those most special to me. What she'd do with me, I had no idea, but it wouldn't be anything good.

I was about to concede that Coyote had a point when Mick rushed across the room, yanked Coyote up by the shirt, and slammed him against the statue.

"Mick!" I protested.

I was more worried about the sculpture than Coyote, but Mick's eyes were black with fury. "I told you what I'd do if you threatened my mate again," Mick snarled.

"He wasn't threatening," I tried. "He was explaining."

Coyote might be out of magic, but Mick wasn't. His eyes were still black dark, and fire flared from his fingers. Flame magic licked up the arms of Coyote's jeans jacket, threatening to burn him alive.

Coyote solved the problem by turning into a coyote. Mick suddenly had his hands full of a hundred or so pounds of enraged beast while Coyote's clothes fell from him in smoking shreds. Mick's eyes filled with fire, and his tattoos began to glow red.

"Don't turn into a dragon!" I shouted at him. "Don't you dare turn into a dragon!"

Coyote kept snarling, fighting, clawing, and Mick fought him. Maya drew her legs up under her on the sofa and watched. The commotion brought Fremont and Cassandra from the kitchen, but they only stopped and watched in alarm.

Coyote bit Mick on the shoulder, and blood blossomed on Mick's shirt. Mick's hands filled with fire, and Coyote's fur began to smolder.

No way should I shove myself between the ripping, clawing, and fire-striking males, and Coyote had just scared the shit out of me about using my Beneath magic. But I didn't see that I had any choice. I couldn't let Coyote kill Mick, the man I loved, and if Mick killed Coyote, I didn't want to imagine the consequences.

I drew on my Beneath magic, finding it scarily close to the surface. Just a little bit, I thought, nothing like what I'd done when I'd tried to break the wards. The tiniest amount was all I needed. I would separate the two wrestling alpha males and then shut it off.

What rushed up from inside me was a huge blast of otherworldly power that made me gasp with its intensity. I desperately held on to the magic, sweat pouring from me, knowing that if I let the magic go, it would blow off the roof.

"I can't," I babbled, the sweat freezing on my face. My breath fogged out. "I can't."

I didn't have to. A pair of thin, but incredibly strong, arms locked around Mick's waist, tore him from Coyote, and tossed Mick aside. Coyote, still in his fighting frenzy, went for Mick's assailant, but I leapt between them and yelled at Coyote, "Stop!"

Coyote skidded to a halt, his eyes yellow with rage. The tall, slender man stepped beside me and fixed Coyote with a steady gaze.

"Hey, Ansel," I said. "Thank you."

"Mind telling me what is going on?"

Ansel's voice was calm and matter-of-fact, and that made me edgy. Ansel, an Englishman who'd been turned Nightwalker at age twenty-three when he'd been a prisoner during World War II, was quiet, soft-spoken, and a little nervous. He collected stamps, watched lots of television, and generally kept to himself.

What he was unlikely to do was throw Mick across a

room—he was afraid of Mick—and then calmly ask me what was the matter.

"Hex," I told him. "You all right?"

The night-dark eyes Ansel turned on me smoldered with a deep hunger. Once you've been given the once-over by a ravenous Nightwalker, you don't forget it. Or you die.

"I *am* a little peckish, my dear," he said.

And Ansel *never* called me "my dear."

"There's blood for you in the refrigerator. But the electricity's out, so please keep the door closed."

Ansel reached out and traced my cheek with an ice-cold fingertip. "Anything you say, darling."

Mick started for him. I got myself between Ansel and Mick's headlong rush, a frightening place to be. "Mick, *no!*"

"Let him come," Ansel almost purred. "I'm hungry, and dragon blood would be delicious."

"Mick," I said in warning.

Mick stopped, but his eyes flashed fire. "Touch Janet again, Nightwalker, and I tear your head off."

Ansel gave him a derisive look and turned away, only to have his attention arrested by Maya. Maya self-consciously tugged the hem of her skirt down her thighs.

"Ansel," she said, not sounding pleased to see him.

"Maya." Ansel gave her a smile full of teeth. "Want to raid the fridge with me?"

"No." Maya looked away, a woman's universal signal for "Get lost."

"You go alone," I said to Ansel. "Drink at least half that gallon jug of blood, and then come back in here and help us figure out how to break this hex."

Ansel turned the smile on me. "Anything you say, *mistress.*"

Gods, he sounded like the mirror. Ansel finally went off to the kitchen. Fremont and Cassandra got out of his way as he went by, and no one followed him.

Coyote, still a coyote, growled at Mick. I planted myself in front of Coyote and raised my hand, palm out.

"Sit!" I commanded. "Stay!"

Coyote gave me a look that said "Fuck you" and then sauntered over to the sofa, climbed up next to Maya, and lay down.

I drew a long breath. "All right. It looks like the hex is

working to bring out the worst in us—or at least release that part of us we try hardest to control. Ansel, bloodlust; me, my Beneath magic; Mick, his dragon instincts; Cassandra, it's messing with her emotional control. Coyote—I don't know what's going on with Coyote."

Coyote growled again. I was aware of Mick at my back, right *against* my back, pressed all the way along me. His arm stole around my waist, strong and possessive.

"It hasn't affected me, Janet," Fremont said. "I'm being strong for you. And I'm coming up with all kinds of ideas to enhance your plumbing."

I had to love him. "I can honestly say, Fremont, that so far you are the only *male* here I haven't wanted to strangle."

Fremont winked at me. "I've got your back."

"Janet." Cassandra's voice was weary. "I can't keep letting this happen. I can try a summoning spell, bring the ununculous to me, and let him kill me. He won't have orders to do anything to the rest of you."

"Screw that," I said. "You can't know what this guy has in mind—he might decide that Mick, Coyote, Ansel, and I are a threat to him. Or he might kill us for the fun of it."

Cassandra's face crumpled as her tears came again. "I promise you that if I need to be sacrificed to save the rest of you, I'm willing. I'm the one who got you into this in the first place."

"No one's getting sacrificed." Except maybe Coyote or Mick, if they continued to piss me off. "Besides, I have a few ideas up my sleeve—"

My words were cut off by a gut-wrenching moan from the kitchen, which wound quickly into a wail of anguish. I rushed past Cassandra and Fremont and into the kitchen, Mick hard on my heels.

Ansel was bent over the big stainless steel sink on the other side of the room, vomiting his guts out. The gallon jug of blood lay on its side on the floor, the remaining liquid spilling across the tiles. As we piled into the kitchen, Ansel looked at us over his shoulder, blood all over his mouth.

"It's bad," he snarled. "The blood is bad. Are you fucking trying to poison me?"

"No," I said in surprise. "It was fresh yesterday, never out of the fridge."

"It's tainted, and it's cow."

"You always drink cow."

Ansel dug his fingers into his mouth and scraped out more blood, which he flung into the sink. "Not tonight, I don't. I need to feed, and I need to feed *now*. Either one of you volunteers, or I simply start biting."

FIVE

MICK STEPPED IN FRONT OF ME, AND FOR
once his overprotectiveness didn't irritate me. "You touch anyone here, and I'll kill you," Mick said. His words were quiet,
deep, and unshakable.

"Come on and have a go, then," Ansel said. "I'd like some
dragon blood."

Fremont gaped. "Is he a *vampire*?"

Cassandra started to answer, then snatched paper towels
from the counter and pressed them to her overflowing eyes.
"Damn it, why can't I stop crying?"

"Ansel is a Nightwalker," I said crisply. "Much like a vampire, but a little different from ones in the movies. For one
thing, he's real."

Ansel's lip curled. "He's real *hungry*."

"I'm killing him," Mick said. "Sorry, Janet, I know he's
your friend, but no one here should be a Nightwalker snack,
and I'm certainly not letting him get his fangs into you."

"It's not his fault," I countered. "I'm betting that the cow's
blood would have been perfectly fine if not for the curse."

"It's also not a demon's fault it likes to devour human flesh," Mick said. "That doesn't mean I'd let one feast on you."

"Ansel," I said, trying to ignore Mick. "If I can give you fresh cow's blood, will you drink it? It would take the edge off at least, right?"

Ansel gave me a grudging nod. "Possibly." He wet his lips, then grimaced when his tongue touched a drying drop of the tainted blood. "I really need a human vein."

"For me, Ansel." I held his gaze with my own. Nightwalkers could mesmerize with their gazes, but none had ever been able to do that to me. "There's another jug in the back of the refrigerator. Go get it, and drink it. If you don't, and Mick tries to kill you, I won't be able to stop him."

Not without killing Mick in the process. If I had to choose between Mick and a Nightwalker ready to go on a rampage, sorry, Mick won.

Ansel sneered, fangs still long and nasty, but he headed for the fridge. I could tell he was trying to control himself, but he nearly ripped the handle off the refrigerator door when he opened it.

As soon as he stepped inside, I rushed the door. Mick caught on and got there first. He slammed the door just as Ansel realized what we were doing and turned around. Ansel hit the door from the inside, the *boom* rattling the kitchen windows. Mick fused the latch with a lance of dragon fire.

Ansel screeched, an unearthly, ear-shattering sound. He pounded on the door, and Mick stepped away from it, breathing hard.

"That should hold him," Mick said. "For a while."

"A while is all we need." I wiped my brow. "The air in there is still cold enough to make him a little sluggish. By the time he breaks out, hopefully we'll have this curse thing resolved."

"Breaks out?" Fremont asked, his eyes wide. "What happens if he breaks out?"

Cassandra answered from behind her tear-dampened paper towels. "Then he'll want more than a snack."

Maya put one hand on her hip. "You do know that most of our food is in there." Aside from the little pile of half-made sandwiches on the counter, dangerously close to spattered cow blood, she was right.

I gestured to the refrigerator, where Ansel was already denting the door from the inside. "Go on in, if you really want to. Pick something out for me, too. In the meantime, there's something I need to do on the roof."

"IS THIS SOME crazy Indian thing?" Maya asked me as she walked out onto the roof with me.

"No," I answered. "Just some crazy desperation thing."

Mick followed us, but Cassandra, Fremont, and Coyote remained below to make sure Ansel didn't get out. Or at least Coyote and Fremont did. Cassandra had curled into a ball on a sofa, still weeping.

I was pleased to see, as we walked outside, that the emerging stars were being swallowed by thick clouds to the north and west. My skin prickled. A storm was coming, a big one, and my Stormwalker magic wanted to lick it all over.

Once the storm grew big enough, I'd suck it inside me, bind it to my Beneath magic, and let it rip.

Mick laced his fingers through mine, and I knew he sensed my storm magic awakening. The aftermath of storms usually involved him calming me down from the overwhelming magic, and *that* involved our grappling bodies and plenty of sweat.

Maya shivered as the approaching wind cut through her thin dress. "You think Nash will see your smoke signals from twenty miles away and come running? Nash never even looks out the window."

"No." I crouched down and set out the supplies I'd grabbed: a brazier, sage, charcoal, and towels from the linen supply closet. I piled charcoal and sage in the brazier and looked at Mick. The butane lighters had stopped working, and I hadn't been able to find any matches.

Mick's eyes were still black, without a hint of blue. He pointed at the brazier, a fireball streaked out of his forefinger, and the brazier exploded into flames. Maya and I jumped away.

"I only needed a spark," I said as I grabbed a towel and beat the flames in the bowl back to manageable size.

Mick balled his hand. "Sorry, I was trying for a spark. That just came out."

Terrific. If Mick lost control of his Firewalker fire, he could burn the hotel down around us. The hex might burn with it, but we, trapped inside, would still be dead.

Was that what the hex meant to do, I wondered, bring out the worst in us so that we were the means of our own destruction? The wind turned suddenly icy.

"So, what happens now?" Maya asked.

I got to my feet and fed the towel I'd been using into the fire. The cloth sputtered and caught, then started to smolder, sending up a wisp of stinking smoke.

"I'm hoping that someone will see smoke coming from the top of the Crossroads Hotel and report it. A 9-1-1 call will bring firefighters, the police, and Nash."

"Carlos couldn't see me or hear me through the window," Maya said. "What makes you think the smoke will be visible?"

I had no idea. Mick had demonstrated that the bubble of the hex extended fifteen feet upward. Possibly the smoke would simply collect in the bubble and not disperse, but wouldn't that look weird enough to attract attention? A glowing ball of smoke on top of the Crossroads Hotel?

"If Nash hears about it, he won't be able to stay away," I said. "He'll have to know what trouble I'm getting myself into this time, so he can gloat if no other reason. Besides, he and you were supposed to meet tonight, right? He'll get worried when you don't show up."

"He won't." Maya folded her bare arms. "Our last date didn't exactly end well."

I grew curious. "What happened?"

"Do you know what he talked about during our nice dinner out? Nonstop? You."

"Me?"

I felt Mick at my shoulder, his breath hot on my skin. "Why?" he asked, his voice taking a dangerous edge.

"Because he and Janet had just had another run-in," Maya said. "He was angry at her, and he told me all about it at the fancy restaurant he took me to—through the appetizers and the wine, and all through dinner. Couldn't shut his stupid mouth about you, Janet."

"Sorry." It was hardly my fault that Sheriff Jones was clueless when it came to women, but I felt bad that his choice of conversation had hurt Maya. "What did you do?"

"Poured my wine in his lap and walked out."

Mick snorted with laughter. "Good for you."

"This was supposed to be our makeup date. If I don't show, he'll assume I'm still mad at him. Which I am."

Mick put his arms around me from behind while I dropped another towel into the smoking mess. His dragon tattoos glowed eerily in the light from the brazier. "Tell Jones to back off Janet, or he'll answer to me."

I suppose some women would be thrilled by a gorgeous man leaping to her defense for every little thing, but his tight protectiveness was starting to worry me. Mick was possessive, yes, but he usually was more sensible about it.

"Nash is immune to your fire," I pointed out.

"I can't hurt him magically, no," Mick said. "But I can break things, like his neck."

"Let him, Janet," Maya said. "I wouldn't mind seeing Nash beaten up a little. But don't hurt him too much. I want a turn at him, too."

"Enough with the bloodthirstiness, both of you." I coughed from the thickening smoke. "Right now, we need Nash whole, and we need him here. Mick, you spent lots of time feeling up the wards. Were you able to strengthen them? Can we fight the hex through them?"

Mick let me go, but he remained standing against me. "I don't think so. It was a stealthy spell, latching onto the wards themselves. From there it spread through the building like a net, affecting everyone within its drag. If we could find its key, we could unlock it, but the hex itself makes anything we try to do against it or every attempt to decipher it go wrong. I'm lucky I could find out as much as I did."

"So what do we do? How long will a spell like that last?"

He shrugged. "No way to say. It's growing in intensity. I'm watching everyone become a little crazier as the night goes on."

"Including you," I said.

Mick looked surprised. "It's not affecting me. I feel a bit of demon in the spell, but Cassandra said the ununculous could steal demon powers. And here's one more interesting thing about it: The caster had to be very close, as in within the building."

Mick dropped that bombshell and closed his mouth.

Maya's eyes widened. "You mean, like he's hiding in the basement? *Dios mío*, why don't we go get him, then?"

"I don't mean that the ununculous is here," Mick said. "I'd know. So would Janet. I meant that someone brought the trigger for the spell in with them and set it off. One of us."

SIX

———❧❧———

"DON'T LOOK AT ME," MAYA SAID QUICKLY. "I didn't set off any curse. I think you two are nuts."

"We know it wasn't you," Mick said, voice soothing. "Of all of us, you are the only one untouched by magic. You'd have to be at least a minor mage to bring it in."

"A minor mage," I said in dismay. "Like Fremont?"

Maya snorted. "Fremont? You don't mean all that crap he says about being magical is true?"

There was nothing like a good, old-fashioned curse to bring out the paranoia. "He wouldn't do that," I said. "Fremont's a nice person who would never hurt anyone."

"He could be wholly innocent of the fact that he brought in the curse," Mick said. "He might have carried it like a mosquito carries a disease. This all started when he came to fix your leaky faucet, right?"

"Right," I said glumly. "Let's go talk to Fremont."

I glanced at the brazier. My fire was smoking merrily, sending a heavy gray-white plume into the darkening sky. As I'd suspected, it stopped about fifteen feet up and simply vanished. But that might be enough. "Maya, can you stay here and make sure that the fire doesn't go out?" I asked.

"Fine with me." Maya hunkered against the stone wall, out of the smoke. "I don't want to go back down into Hotel Crazy."

"Thank you."

"But go easy on Fremont," she said as we passed her. "He can be an idiot, but he's not a bad person, you know?"

"I know," I said, and I followed Mick inside.

"I SWEAR TO you, Janet, I never met the guy!" Fremont, white-faced, stared at the tribunal of me, Mick, and Coyote. We were in the kitchen again, where the others had decided to at least nibble on the sandwiches. Cassandra leaned against the wall, her arms folded, her face pale, and her eyes sunken into dark sockets.

Coyote remained a coyote, his yellow eyes a study in irritation. The fact that he'd chosen a form in which he could neither berate me nor give sexual suggestions worried me a bit.

As for Ansel—he was still banging on the door of the refrigerator from the inside. He'd slowed from frantic pounding, settling for a bang every thirty seconds or so.

"You wouldn't have realized who he was," Mick said, keeping his voice mild. "Someone you talked to at the diner, a tourist passing through, someone you saw at the gas station . . ."

Fremont shook his head vehemently. "I know everyone in Magellan and Flat Mesa, have for years. I know when someone's new, and I remember every single person I talk to. I didn't talk to a nasty sorcerer who wants to kill Cassandra. I'd have noticed his aura, wouldn't I?"

Bang.

"Not necessarily." I was amazingly good at reading auras, and I could see Fremont's magic one now, like pale smoke in sunshine. But Fremont's magic ability was small, and I doubted he could see them all that well. "If Cassandra's sorcerer is as good as she says, he'd be able to hide his aura. Very powerful people can do that." I knew this from personal, and frightening, experience.

"What does he look like, Cassandra?" Mick asked.

Cassandra gave a listless shrug. "Ordinary. So ordinary you wouldn't look twice."

"Can you be more specific?" I asked, trying to be patient. Her apathy was grating on me.

"About five foot seven. Dark brown hair. Receding hairline. He looks like any other suit-wearing forty-year-old man in an office."

Bang.

"Well, I haven't seen any men in suits in Magellan," Fremont said. "They'd stand out. I haven't talked to any man looks like that who I didn't already know. All right?"

"Can the ununculous change his appearance?" I asked. "If he's tracking you, he might use a glamour or even a simple disguise."

Cassandra gave me a watery smile. "Him? He's the most arrogant man I've ever met. What does it matter to him if one of us identifies him? He'll crush us and not care."

Bang.

"All right," I said, drawing a breath. "Could he have seeded the curse in Fremont without Fremont seeing him or noticing? Maybe by brushing by him in a store, something like that?"

Mick answered, "Eye contact is better. If the sorcerer greets you, shakes your hand, he can make sure you received the spark. It's more emotionally satisfying for him as well. But I suppose it could happen with a brush-by. Like a pickpocket in reverse."

Fremont waved his hands. "What you're not getting is that I haven't seen *anyone* like who you describe. Not brushing by me in the diner, not even passing me in a car on the road. *I would have noticed.*"

"I believe you," I said. He was right, he would have. Fremont loved to watch, and then talk about, his fellow man.

"Thank you." Fremont let out a sigh and rubbed his hand over what was left of his hair.

"Mick?" I asked. "Have you seen anyone like Cassandra describes?"

"No."

Bang.

"Okay, then. Neither have I."

Fremont glared. "Wait, you believe him without grilling him like you did me?"

"Sorry, Fremont. I'm on edge. Mick's a dragon—if someone seeded a curse on him, he'd notice right away." I glanced at Mick. "Right?"

Mick affirmed. I'd like to think I would have noticed right away, too. A spark like that would sting both my magics, wouldn't it? Then again, if this sorcerer was as powerful as advertised . . .

"It was probably me," Cassandra said.

Fremont looked at her in surprise. "You saw him? Why didn't you say so?"

"I mean the last time I met him. Christianson might have had the ununculous seed a hex on me, so that if I double-crossed him, it would activate, like a time-release pill. It would wait until I felt safe and then go off. The ununculous would feel it, and come for me. Revenge served cold."

A bolt of lightning slammed to the ground not a mile away, followed by a boom of thunder that rolled on, and on, and on. Before its rumbles died, another bolt cracked not far from the first one. My body pulsed with electricity, my Stormwalker magic reaching to suck it in before I could stop it.

Wind struck the hotel with such force that the building creaked. It howled through the eaves and every crack in the edifice, and I felt a breeze cross my face.

"Janet," Fremont said, staring at me. "Your eyes."

"What about them?" Sparks laced my fingers as I raised my hands. "Are they green?"

"No. Black. All black. Like nothing's there."

I could see out of them fine, no change there, but Mick was watching me in concern. I snatched out the piece of magic mirror I'd shoved into my pocket and stared into it. Sure enough, my eyeballs had gone all black, no pupils or irises. I looked into the black void that was me, until lightning struck again, and white electricity encircled my face.

"I see," I whispered in a voice that didn't sound like mine. "I see so much. Darkness. Pain. Terror. The end of all things."

"Janet," Fremont said, worried. "What the hell are you talking about?"

I wrenched my gaze from the mirror and looked up. I had their attention now, even Cassandra's.

"I don't know why I said that." Or did I? I had seen it, deep in the mirror, flashes of terror, darkness, fire, white light rising from the ground. Everyone I loved in torturous pain. And then, nothing . . .

Lightning struck again, its white flare rendering the candle flames ineffectual pinpricks. Electricity crawled up my arms, and I bunched my hands to keep from blasting the table, floor, my friends, everything in sight.

I wasn't certain how I was pulling in the storm magic when the hex wasn't letting anything physically in or out, but maybe it was because magic isn't physical. It's the coupling of the mage and the elements that mage uses for power—Mick and his dragon nature, Cassandra and her spell accoutrements, me and a storm. A psychic connection no one understands. I don't actually direct the storms themselves—I absorb their elemental might and use it to fuel my own magic.

Or the hex might be letting me use my storm magic so it could busily fuck it up.

I couldn't control the power. I'd felt this before—at age eleven, when I'd first called a storm's power, not on purpose. I remembered flailing my hands, trying to get rid of the lightning that clung to them. I'd succeeded only in blasting a tree and burning down a shed. I'd run off into the desert in terror, the storm following me.

This storm was big and close, and I was locked inside my hotel by a curse. No running away to keep my loved ones safe.

"Janet," Cassandra said, watching me with a hint of her usual witchy focus. "What did you see?"

"I don't remember now." The visions were fading, dying as fast as they'd come. "Fire, darkness. The vortexes. Nothing."

Bang.

Cassandra didn't answer, but she held on to the back of a kitchen chair, her knuckles white.

More lightning struck, and electric arcs crawled all over my body. I moved my hand, and a tail of lightning caught the end of the counter and blew it into pieces.

"Whoa." Fremont threw up his arms to shield himself

from the rain of wood and tile. Coyote, still a coyote, grabbed Cassandra by the skirt and towed her back out of my way.

Only Mick stood his ground. Mick, whose eyes had gone as black as mine, watched me with a predatory stare.

"Mick," I whispered.

He moved to me and took my hands. His body jolted as the lightning jerked into him, but he smiled a wide, bestial smile. "Want me to draw it off?"

"This is a full storm. The last time you were with me in a full storm, I nearly killed you."

"That was different." Mick leaned down and bit my cheek, and the heat of his mouth awoke every need I'd ever had. "That was battle. This is me, drawing off your power so you can function. Give me your lightning, Janet."

Bang.

I turned to Mick and kissed him.

The kiss canceled out every worry I had, every terror of the night. This was me and Mick, and this was raw. His lips bruised mine as he drew me up into him and explored my mouth with deep, hot strokes. I clung to his shoulders, and my lightning flowed straight into him.

Mick cupped my breast, his palm rough through my shirt, and I wound my leg around his thigh. I wanted him; gods, I wanted him. The lightning was driving me crazy, the storm outside was escalating, and I craved Mick.

I wrapped my arms around his neck and melted against him, finding him hard for me. Sex with Mick could be fast, brutal, and exciting, and then he could turn around and be so incredibly tender it made me cry.

Tonight, I wanted him with everything I had. If the others hadn't been in the kitchen with us, Mick would have had laid me across the stainless steel table and taken me then and there.

Bang.

"Um," Fremont said. "I appreciate that you guys are in love, but . . . a time and a place?"

"He's toning down her storm magic," Cassandra said, sounding weary. "He's afraid she'll kill us with it. Dragons can imbibe storm magic. It won't hurt him, I don't think."

"Yeah, but . . ."

I was aware of Coyote watching us closely, a far-too-interested look in his yellow eyes. As if in answer, Mick lifted me into his arms and strode with me out of the kitchen. I clung to him, my mouth still seeking his, blue crackles of electricity crawling over both of us.

Maya came charging down the stairs as Mick carried me toward the back hall. "I'm not staying up there to get struck by lightning," she said. "Anyway, it's raining now, so the fire's out." She stopped. "Janet, what the hell?"

"Go to the kitchen," I said breathlessly. "Talk to you later."

Maya rolled her eyes as Mick whisked me into the hall that led to my bedroom. Before we hit the threshold, I shouted back, "Keep Coyote away from us."

Mick kicked closed the bedroom door, cutting off Maya's deprecations directed at me in Spanish.

MICK DUMPED ME onto the bed and started pulling off his clothes. Even while my bedcovers started to smolder from the lightning in my hands, I didn't mind sitting back and watching my boyfriend strip.

His body was delicious. I remembered the night I'd first seen it, in a hotel room in Las Vegas. I remember sitting on the bed, nervous as hell, while he pulled off his shirt to reveal a chest and six-pack abs a bodybuilder would kill for. As he'd turned around to toss the shirt somewhere, his jeans had dipped to reveal the jagged fire tattoo riding across his lower back. Plus the fact that he wasn't wearing any underwear. By the time he'd turned back around, I'd had my shirt off, too. Mick had smiled at me, his eyes so damned blue. He'd put his knee on the bed, touched my face with his big hand, and said, "Gods, Janet, do you know how beautiful you are?"

His eyes were black tonight, but my heart still pounded as hard as it had then.

Mick threw his shirt on the dresser. "What are you smiling at?"

"Memories," I said.

Lightning struck right outside, and Mick stripped me, not slowly, not gently, but with the skill of long practice. He jerked out of his own jeans and laid me down on the mattress, his mouth all over me. My lightning fired into him as he covered my skin with openmouthed kisses, his breath hot when he kissed the stud in my navel.

He looked up, my lightning sizzling around him and sparking in his eyes. "More," he whispered. "Give it to me good."

The power in me wanted to dive into him, like the best sex, but I worried I'd hurt him. Mick never touched me when the storm was at its peak; it would be too much.

Mick pulled me up until we were kneeling together, naked, sweat slicking our bodies. "Don't hold back," he growled. "I want it. All of it. As much as you can give me."

"Mick, I don't want to hurt you."

"You won't. I want it, Janet. I want you."

When I still hesitated, Mick grabbed me, opened my lips with his, and sucked the power out of me.

I screamed against his mouth. Mick imbibed my lightning as though it were the best wine, his body hard, his whispered groans driving me crazy.

Gods, I love him.

The fire tattoo on his back was hot under my touch, his body sizzling with my lightning. We risked blasting a hole in the floor and tumbling into the basement, and it was the most erotic thing I'd ever experienced. Mick laid me back down on the bed, his eyes devouring me, and he entered me in one swift thrust.

He pinned me down, my Mick who liked to play the master with me, made even more exciting because I knew he'd never, ever hurt me. He'd taught me that first night to trust him with everything I had, and the reward was pleasure I'd never dreamed existed.

Tonight bore the wild edge of danger because of the hex. Mick had been reluctant to try sex-enhanced spells, but now we tossed away caution like a used tissue and gave in to the ecstasy. This was different from spell casting—this was Mick simply driving into me, and me giving him every bit of power I had.

I met his thrusts with my body, my nails raking down his back, my cries ringing to the ceiling. Outside the storm wound up, and inside we did the same.

Mick's eyes shone with fire. "Love you," he grated. "Love you so much."

The snakes and whorls of electricity slowly dimmed, Mick's dragon magic absorbing them all. But Mick was a long way from being finished. He pinned my wrists over my head and kept going, this lovemaking session growing ever more crazy.

I think we would have gone on until we died, if the magic mirror hadn't chosen that moment to let out a high-pitched keen. The sound spiraled up until it knifed through my head, and even Mick cursed and jammed a hand over his ear.

"What the fuck?" he snarled.

I rolled out from under Mick, and Mick landed next to me, panting, while I leaned from the bed and scrabbled for the piece of mirror in my pocket. "Hey!" I yelled at it.

The keening wound all the way down and flattened out into a word. *Summertiiime.*

"Hey, you moronic piece of glass. Call Drake. Get him over here."

The mirror kept on belting out the song from *Porgy and Bess.* I shook it and yelled at it, but my mirror ignored me.

"I don't think it can hear you," Mick said breathlessly.

"Damn it!" I flung the mirror into the wall. The voice dimmed somewhat but didn't stop. I didn't know which was worse, having the mirror dark or stuck singing show tunes.

"If he starts singing to the dragons, Drake will be out here fast enough," Mick said. He ran a firm hand down my body. "Right now I need more." He kissed my back. "So much more."

It would be stupid to stay in here and have sex while Cassandra's enemy waited for us to be at our weakest. But I willingly rolled over and drew him into my arms.

Mick had started kissing me again with hungry strokes when someone beat on the bedroom door.

"Janet," Maya called through the wood, her agitation strong. "If you're done screwing in there, Nash is out front. He's with Pamela, and they're trying to get in."

SEVEN

I YANKED ON MY CLOTHES AND WAS ABOUT
to hurry out after Maya, but Mick put his arm across the door,
blocking my way. He was a big man and made a formidable
barrier.

"Wait," he said. "Let me check it out first."

Impatiently I buttoned my jeans. "It's Nash, Maya said.
Exactly who we need."

"*Maybe* it's Nash. I want you to stay in here and lock the
door behind me."

This was getting annoying. "Staying in my room won't
save me from the hex," I said.

"Even so, wait for me to clear it before you come out."

I wasn't about to obey. I knew I couldn't fight Mick, but I
was small enough and swift enough to duck under him before
he could grab me. I heard him growling in anger as he came
after me, but this was my hotel, and I was more than ready for
Mick's alpha-dragon instincts to recede.

Someone was pounding on the front door. "Janet!" Nash
called. "Open up. It's Jones."

As though that weren't obvious. The blue lights of the Hopi County Sheriff's Department SUV flared behind him, and his sheriff's badge winked on the uniform coat he wore against the cold. Pamela, a Native American Changer in black leather pants and jacket, stood next to him in tall fury.

"Let me break it down," we heard her say with impatience.

Cassandra pressed her hands to the window. "No, Pamela, get out of here! I don't want you here!"

Pamela didn't hear, and neither did Nash, nor did they see the rest of us at the windows like lizards against glass. Nash kept pounding and then trying the door handle, which wasn't budging.

"Come on, Nash," I whispered. "Open it."

Nash took a step back, drew out his nine-millimeter, and shot the lock. I cringed, thinking of the Native American artisan who'd crafted the door handle and lock for me up in Santa Fe. His exquisite work was now slag with a bullet in it.

Nash and Pamela slammed against the door in unison, and the wood bulged inward. Another blow and the door splintered from the hinges. I felt the wards around the entrance crumble and die, reacting to the magic void that was Nash Jones. The curse magic that had piggybacked on them faded to nothing.

The wards in the walls were still intact, and so was the hex, but Nash was able to burst in and swing his pistol around the lobby.

He took us in: Maya, Fremont, Cassandra, me, Mick. I had no idea where Coyote had got to.

When Nash realized there was no immediate threat, he pointed the pistol at the floor. "Janet, what is this?"

Pamela rushed past him and caught Cassandra in a crushing hug, lifting her off her feet. "Are you all right, baby?"

Nash pinned me with an ice gray stare. "Ms. Grant charged into my office, insisting there was something wrong at your hotel. So what are you up to?"

Bang! Bang! Bang!

Nash looked past me to the kitchen door. "You have someone back there?"

"Nash," I said. "Touch the walls. Hurry. Please."

Nash completely ignored me to listen, his gun held ready.

"That's just Ansel," Maya told him. "He started going crazy, so we locked him in the refrigerator."

"Nash, the walls. Please!"

Nash started for the kitchen. Mick was on him before he'd gone three strides, but Nash, combat-trained, knew how to fight. He had himself out of Mick's grip in a flash, the pistol now pointed at Mick's head.

"I suggest you start explaining, Burns, before you spend the night in my lockup."

"Fine by me," I said cheerfully. "Let's go." Get out of cursed hotel now, finish breaking the hex later.

Coyote came bounding out of the kitchen. In his coyote form, he was the size of a large wolf, and he sprang full force onto Nash. The momentum, with an assist by Mick, carried Nash the five feet needed to land him against the lobby's brightly painted wall.

The hotel shuddered. I screamed as I felt my wards, as infected as they were, stream from the brick and plaster into Nash's body. I was deeply connected to the wards, and through them, to the hotel, and so was Mick.

Mick doubled over in pain, but this purging was necessary. All the wards had to go, no matter how much it hurt us. Then Mick and I would reset them, clean and free of the hex.

It was hurting Nash, too. Nash clenched his fists, the pistol still in one, eyes shut in silent agony.

"What are you doing?" Maya shouted. "Nash!"

"He's negating the curse," Cassandra said from within the protective circle of Pamela's arm.

"*Nash* is?"

"He's a magic null." Cassandra sounded tired. "His touch renders anything magical harmless. Spells don't work on him, and he can pull in even the strongest magic and dissipate it."

I yelled again, my voice breaking as I collapsed to the floor. Mick tried to get to me, to help me, but his knees buckled as soon as he took a step.

Fremont crouched down and touched my shoulder, but Mick snarled at him. "Get away from her!"

Fremont raised his hands and backed away. "Easy there, big fella. Easy now."

There was something wrong. Nash continued to suck in

the wards, and I felt the last of them rush into him and vanish. But whatever was inside Nash didn't stop at the wards. It reached out to me and then to Mick and began to drain us dry.

My Beneath magic flared up to stop him, but Nash sucked that in, too. The white-hot aura of it streamed into Nash's body, and the agony of that had me falling flat to the tile. I saw Mick's fire being pulled from him while Mick fought a losing battle to keep it.

"Ow!" Fremont said, slapping his hands to his head.

A tiny stream of yellow light—Fremont's magic—yanked from him to Nash's body. Cassandra was on the floor now, Pamela with her, as Nash drained their magical essences as well. A scream so high-pitched it was on the edge of human hearing streamed from the saloon, the magic mirror singing no longer.

Coyote shimmered and became the man Coyote, lying naked, facedown on the floor. Ansel stopped banging in the kitchen, and I wondered if he were dead, the magic that kept him alive stolen by Nash's magic suction. Ansel might be nothing but decaying blood and bone on my refrigerator floor.

"Nash, stop," I gasped.

He didn't, and I had the feeling he had no idea how to. Mick lay next to me where he'd crawled in an effort to protect me. His tattoos faded to thin lines of ink, and then those shrank and disappeared. Cassandra struggled to breathe, and Pamela lay limply next to her. Coyote didn't move.

Maya wasn't affected, being the only non-magical one among us. She stared at us as we slowly died, the magic that had been part of us all our lives draining away.

Then she looked at Nash. I watched Maya draw a breath for courage, and then she stalked across the floor in her mile-high heels, grabbed Nash, and jerked away him from the wall.

Nash turned on her with eyes as white as twenty suns. Maya let him go in surprise, and Nash moved that awful gaze to the rest of us.

He'd absorbed everything. He shouldn't have been able to do that—Nash only affected magic within a certain radius, or only if touched by it directly. He'd never simply stood in one place and sucked in all magic around him.

"Maya, get away from me," Nash said, voice harsh. "Get out of here."

I wanted to encourage her to go, to run, but I had no strength for speech. Fremont climbed to his feet, looking the least sick of the rest of us, but still not looking good.

"I'm not going anywhere," Maya said. This from the woman who'd been the first to beat on the door when the curse locked us in. "Nash, what is happening to you?"

"I can't." Nash dragged in a harsh breath. "I can't contain it."

He'd just absorbed the power of a dragon, a major witch, a Changer, a Stormwalker with goddess magic, and a magic mirror, not to mention Coyote's god magic and the super-charged wards of the hotel. And Nash seemed surprised he couldn't contain it.

Nash's eyes became incandescent. He threw back his head, opened his arms, and roared as the magic came pouring back out of him.

The Beneath and Stormwalker magic slammed into me simultaneously. The impact lifted me several feet and threw me across the room, and I landed hard against the reception counter. Cassandra started retching. Fremont sat down on the floor, his hands to his head. Mick shouted, his body on fire, and I saw his flesh crackle and expand, the dragon in him trying to get out.

All I could do was fold up into myself, my body a ball of pain. I heard animal snarls coming from Pamela and knew she was now a wolf. The magic mirror's high-pitched keening returned.

I felt the wards burst out of Nash and flow back into the walls, all of them, doubled in strength. And with them the curse, twice as strong as before, clinging to our wards and permeating the building. The candles we'd lit died at the same time, leaving us in absolute darkness.

"Damn." Cassandra's voice came as a weak whisper, but it held a hint of awe. "It's a double hex."

"AND A DOUBLE hex is . . . ?" I asked irritably about a half hour later.

We couldn't get the candles lit again. The eight of us huddled in the dark in the lobby while rain beat down outside. Our only light was what filtered through the front windows from the floodlights on the Crossroads Bar.

Ansel hadn't made any noise in the kitchen since Nash sucked out the wards, but the magic mirror had returned to singing. It finished *Porgy and Bess* and began *Cabaret*.

"A double hex is exactly what it sounds like," Cassandra said. In spite of what had happened, she sounded as apathetic as ever. "Most hexes eventually wear off or weaken enough to be broken by the victim, if it doesn't kill them soon enough. Therefore, some sorcerers take the precaution of making it a double hex—if the curse gets broken, it casts itself again, this time twice as strong. It's tricky, and only the best sorcerers can do it."

"Or gods," Coyote put in. He'd remained in his human form, lying flat on the floor. He'd refused Mick's offer of clothes, so he was stark naked. At least it was dark.

"And one of the best sorcerers is after you," Fremont said.

Cassandra looked at me. "I told you, let me summon him and get this over with. It's me he's been sent to kill."

"No summoning," I said firmly. "We aren't in any shape to defend ourselves, and like I said, there's nothing to say the ununculous won't try to kill the rest of us for the hell of it."

"What do we do, then?" Fremont asked. "Sit here and wait for him?"

"No, we keep trying to break the hex," I said. "Every sorcerer has a weakness. We need to find his."

"Sage words, Stormwalker." Pamela's voice was bestial and odd.

She'd gotten stuck in the form between wolf and human and looked like something from a horror movie. Pamela's face was wolf. She had the limbs of a human covered in wolf fur, a tail, and two complete sets of breasts, human and wolf. She sat with her back against the couch and held Cassandra, who didn't seem to mind that her girlfriend was now a nightmare beast.

I'd made Mick sit close to Nash, hoping Nash's strange canceling effect would keep Mick's need to become dragon at bay. I also needed Nash's now-increased dampening field to keep my own magic quiet. The storm magic was at least calming as the lightning moved off, though I still had urges to grab the rain and sweep it in through the windows. The Beneath magic, though, kept wanting to come out and play. If I lost control of that, everyone here could die.

I actually did have a plan, one I didn't bother mentioning, especially not to Mick. If Mick knew what I had in mind, he'd simply lock me in the basement and secure the door with dragon fire. But once I had everyone busy working out the ununculous's weakness, I would sneak away, call the ununculous myself, and face him alone. The way my Beneath magic was raging, I could kill the bastard with one blow, and I would.

I felt Coyote looking at me. Hard at me, his eyes glittering in the darkness.

Damn it, he wasn't telepathic. And yet Coyote always did seem to know what I was thinking. I remembered what he'd said about me ripping open vortexes if I tried to fight the curse or the sorcerer, but I saw no other way. Anyway, I didn't plan to *fight*, I planned to kill quickly and get it over with.

I returned Coyote's stare with a determined one of my own before asking Pamela, "How did you know something was wrong here? Did you see my fire?"

"No." Pamela's voice was thick. "Cassandra didn't come home, and then I saw your bartender at the gas station. He told me the hotel was shut down and dark, and he didn't know why. I came up here, but I couldn't get the door open and couldn't see through the windows, so I rode up and got the sheriff."

We must have been busy with Ansel in the kitchen when Pamela arrived, because none of us had seen or heard her.

"What was the sheriff doing at his office?" Maya studied her polished nails. "Did he forget something, like, I don't know, our date?"

Nash's voice went cold. "I didn't forget. I assumed you found something better to do, so I went back to work."

"You thought I stood you *up*?" Maya's screech rang to the rafters. "I spent two hours getting ready for you. Why would I stand you up?"

The mirror's voice cut through her shout with something about life being a cabaret.

"And you look great," Coyote said from his supine position.

"*You*, shut up," Maya snapped. "If I hadn't agreed to give you a ride up here, I would have been in Flat Mesa in plenty of time. But no, I had to be nice. Look what it got me. Stranded here all night with the freak show."

"Coyote's right, though," Fremont said. "You do look great, Maya. That part was worth it."

"Thank you, Fremont." Maya gave him a big smile. "Forget you, Nash. I'm going out with Fremont."

"Hold on . . ." Fremont started.

"Fremont already has a girlfriend," I said. "In Holbrook."

"Not anymore." Fremont sounded sad. "She went back East. She asked me to go with her, but what the hell would I do back East? So, she's gone."

"I'm sorry." I really was sorry. Fremont was a nice guy, and he deserved someone who appreciated that.

"Her loss," Maya said. "Take me to the movies."

"Maya . . ."

We were spared further argument about Maya's love life by a huge bang in the kitchen. This time, not only did Ansel strike the door of the walk-in fridge, he tore it from its hinges. We were on our feet, sprinting for the kitchen, when the door landed on the floor with a second *bang* and a clatter.

Ansel was alive, awake, and free.

EIGHT

I'VE DONE SOME FRIGHTENING THINGS IN MY life, but I think stumbling into a pitch-black kitchen, knowing that somewhere in there lurked a blood-starved, very angry Nightwalker, rates as one of the scariest.

Nightwalkers don't breathe, so we couldn't listen for his breath, and Ansel had chosen to go into silent mode. The fire in Mick's hands was our only light, but even by that Ansel was nowhere to be seen.

"He couldn't have gotten out, could he?" Fremont's nervous voice was right behind me.

He and Maya were staying as close to me as they could. I'm not sure why they thought I'd keep them safe, because my fingers kept drawing the pounding rain, and my Beneath magic was going to flare out of control any second. I had contained the magic relatively well in the living room, but fear of the Nightwalker was bringing it out of me.

A check of the back door proved it was still solidly shut, as though it had been fused. Ansel couldn't have escaped that way. He was as trapped as the rest of us.

We found him when he whispered, right behind Maya, *"Hola, señorita."*

Maya's scream took me a few inches off the ground. Mick's fire roared high at the same time Nash yanked Maya from Ansel and shoved his gun into Ansel's face.

Ansel laughed and ignored the pistol. "I'm *hungry*, Janet. What do I have to do to get some service in this hotel?"

I knew then that the double hex had doubled Ansel's strength and need for blood. Unless his appetite were slaked, and slaked soon, he'd simply rip into us. A Nightwalker in a blood frenzy was not a pretty sight—I'd seen the aftermath of one on a rampage before. I never wanted to see that again.

We could knock him out—if we could—or find another place to lock him up, but Ansel would break out of whatever prison we devised sooner or later, hungrier than ever. We still had six or seven hours to go before daylight would force him to find a dark place to sleep.

"We need to let him feed," I said.

Pamela had Cassandra safely behind her, her werewolf lips curled. "And who would be the fool to volunteer for that?"

Ansel wrinkled his nose. "Not you, wolf-girl. Changer blood is disgusting. I want the Spanish lass." He licked his teeth. "Mmm, the dark-eyed beauty of Maya Medina."

Nash's pistol was back, the barrel digging into Ansel's cheek. "Touch her, and I blow your face off."

"Or maybe Sheriff Jones," Ansel purred. "What does the blood of a man who lives to harass my friends taste like?"

"No," I said.

Nash exchanged a glance with me. "Janet."

We'd both, once upon a time, seen the effect of Nash's blood on a Nightwalker. "What's happening is not Ansel's fault," I said firmly. "He stays alive."

"What about the rest of us?" Pamela asked in her thick Changer voice.

Ansel looked us over. "I don't trust the witch. The coyote? Hmm, the blood of a god?"

"Would be bad for you," Coyote rumbled. "And Janet wants you to live. She's such a sweetie."

"I see." Ansel turned away. "I don't want the plumber. He probably tastes like a sewer. But Janet." Ansel touched my neck, his fingers ice cold. "Pretty Navajo girl. Fine blood of a Stormwalker."

Mick was beside me in a heartbeat, lifting Ansel by the throat. Mick's eyes were black with rage, and his hand burst into flame as he pinned Ansel against the wall.

"Mick, no!" I shouted. As frightening as Ansel was, I knew that, at heart, he was a shy man who'd be horrified when he remembered that he'd tried to hurt anyone. I also knew that if we couldn't subdue him, Ansel would have to die before he killed us all.

Mick let his fire fade. "You don't touch Janet. If you need to feed, you feed on me."

Ansel didn't trust Mick, for good reason. "No, give me the *señorita*. I'll make it good for her."

Mick's barely contained dragon frenzy made him as strong as Ansel. He grabbed the back of Ansel's neck and yanked the man's mouth down to his jugular. "Drink me, damn you."

Ansel's eyes went bright red as the bloodlust took him. His mouth opened—the narrow, catlike mouth of a Nightwalker—and he plunged his fangs into Mick's neck.

Fremont gasped in horror, and I wanted to scream. Ansel might drain Mick dry before we could pull him off. Nightwalkers hung on like leeches even after their victims were dead.

I lunged for them, but Mick put out one arm to stop me, fire flaring from his palm. His muscles bulged as he held Ansel in place, the other man's mouth working, sucking, pulling at Mick's neck. Mick grunted, his face creased in pain, but still he held me off.

The rain continued to pour outside, building to a deluge. Water slid between my fingers, starting to patter on the floor. As much as I felt sorry for the real Ansel, I wanted to kill the Nightwalker for hurting Mick. When Mick gasped for breath, blood running in rivulets down his neck, Ansel still drinking, I almost did it.

"No." Mick lifted his hand again, the fire keeping me back. "Let him. I'll heal."

"Mick, damn it."

I was aware of the others, in a semicircle, tense, watching, waiting to see what would happen next. Mick started to sag, but so did Ansel, Ansel's frantic, moist sucking noises slowing.

When Ansel fell from Mick like a full tick, a smile on his face, Mick folded to the floor next to him. I got to Mick's side, but Mick raised his head and gave me a weak nod. "I'm all right."

"That was stupid."

"No." Mick caressed my thigh, his fire gone. "I couldn't let him touch you, baby. I'd die before I let him do that. I'd do it again even if it killed me."

Part of me was pleased with the sentiment, part of me furious he'd even consider dying for me. I dragged myself away from Mick, past the others, and sat on a stool at the stainless steel work table. I put my head in my hands, finding my fingers wet with rainwater.

I had to stop this. I'd begun the evening believing this a simple hex that Mick and I could handle. Now Mick's dragon nature was taking over, the one that took unbelievable risks without fear of death. Cassandra had lost all emotional control, and Coyote's power was down.

It was up to me. The light from the parking lot touched my hands, which were sopping with water, my storm magic taking over. My body ran with water, my clothes began to soak, and a faint spark of lightning danced on my skin just before we heard the rumble of distant thunder.

I would stop the ununculous. I would carry out my plan to pull the sorcerer to us and kill him, but I no longer felt the need to be secretive about it. Coyote wouldn't like it, but Coyote could kill me later.

My Beneath magic agreed. It rose to twine the storm magic, its incredible power squeezing through my body.

The visions returned. More distinct now—fire, the town burning, the desert itself on fire. White light of the vortexes, a darkness rising: behind it, the dragons, and Hopi and Navajo gods fighting for their lives. Terror, destruction, and in the center, one lone figure. I didn't know who it was.

Maya gasped. "Look at Janet."

I sensed them turn my way, all of them, even Ansel, and with a precise flash of vision, I saw what they saw. I sat at the table, my body rigid, fists clenched on the metal. Water flowed out of me, across the table, and to the floor. My black hair hung in sodden clumps around my face, which had turned almost sheet white, my eyes burning black within it.

"Go," I told them in a booming voice. "Leave this place, while I cleanse it."

Coyote got to me first, though I know Mick would have if he hadn't been weakened by Ansel's feeding. Nash was right behind Coyote, and Mick made it a staggering second later.

"Look at me, Janet," Coyote said.

I turned my gaze to him, the vision of myself through his eyes fading. I saw only Coyote, his stern face and dark god eyes that no longer held any power.

"You can't fix it," I said. "So I will."

Nash's ice gray eyes were a cold contrast to Coyote's dark ones. "What the hell are you talking about?"

I smiled at him. "Hello, Sheriff. Do you remember what fun we had out by the vortexes? Want to do it again?"

Nash recoiled, and so he should. The encounter had been violent and nasty, mostly with me doing all the violence. Nash hadn't known what was going on at the time, but Mick and I had filled him in since then.

The real me, the Diné woman screaming deep inside myself, begged me to stop, but the new me, the Stormwalker-Beneath goddess, was angry. I loved the men in this room, but they had their places in my life, and when it came down to it, they were pretty useless. The goddess in me had to fix everything, even if those men had to be sacrificed to do it.

I stood up. "I will cleanse this place," I repeated.

"Stop her," Mick said.

"No, don't." Cassandra had been crying again. "Let her. What choice do we have? We can't win, and if she can destroy the curse and the ununculous, I say, so be it."

Mick hemmed me in with Coyote and Nash. Coyote said, "If she unleashes what's inside her, you're going to wish you were facing the ununculous. We'll all die."

"What does it matter? Either Janet kills us or the sorcerer does. I'd rather it be Janet, who can take him down with her."

"Glad you feel that way," Fremont said. "I don't particularly want to die at all."

"Or me," Maya agreed in a hard voice. "Sit the hell down, Janet."

I laughed. After all this time, after everything I'd done for them, they still didn't trust me. They deserved to die, my so-called friends who belittled me and bothered me, whined at me to solve their problems, and then tried to stop me when I wanted to go after the evil in the world.

I turned my smile on Coyote. "You can't stop me, powerless god. Or you." I swung on Mick. "Dragon sacrificing his blood that others might live. So noble is the dragon. The one who wants to drag me to his Pacific island and trap me there."

"Hey, I'd go with him," Maya said. "I'd love some beach time."

"He'd pen me up in his lair," I said, my voice dripping scorn. "His mate, he calls me. More like his *pet*."

I smacked the man I loved with a wave of water that washed him off his feet. Mick responded with fire that slammed me back onto my ass. A dragon after being drained by a Nightwalker is still five times more powerful than an ordinary human being.

I was on my feet again, my magic—both Stormwalker and Beneath—gathered in my hands. My mind's eye found all the wards in the walls and over the windows and in the doors, the hex clinging to them like a sticky black infection.

All I had to do was burn away the infection, every atom of it, and the wards would be clean. The hex had doubled in strength, and the task would take all my power, but I could do it. I knew the walls would melt into rubble under such forces, and we'd be buried alive by three stories of hotel, but at least the magic of the sorcerer, who'd dared to penetrate my realm, would be gone.

I raised my hands. Water and white light streamed out of me, and I opened my mouth to cry the words of power that would begin the cleansing.

And found myself falling over the stool and to the floor, crushed by a blanket of blackness that sucked out every bit of my power and left me helpless.

Nash Jones, the walking magic void, had tackled me. He pinned me to the floor in the perfect law-enforcement technique for subduing a suspect, his magic-null field absorbing storm power and goddess power alike.

I screamed and screamed as my magic drained. It was like having my soul ripped out. I beat on the floor, but Nash was a big guy, and I couldn't dislodge him.

Mick crawled to me. "Back off, Jones. I think she'll be all right now."

If being weak, magic-less, aching, exhausted, and for some reason, hungry, was "all right," then sure, I was. I lay limply on the floor as Nash got off me and to his feet, our mighty sheriff none the worse for wear.

Mick lifted me into his lap. "You okay, baby?"

"Sorry," I croaked.

He kissed my forehead and cuddled me close. That was my Mick. Forgiving me for turning into a crazy, murderous, insulting bitch who'd just tried to kill him. Times like these kept our relationship strong.

Dear gods.

WITH ME DOWN for the count, my head pounding with the worst magic hangover I'd had in months, and Mick still weak from the blood draining, Nash took charge. Back in the lobby, he grilled us all for possible answers to the predicament.

Ansel wasn't there—fairly sated, he'd gone back to the relative coolness of the refrigerator, which he said would keep his blood thick and his hunger down for a while. But the blood-frenzy still danced in his eyes, and I knew it was only a matter of time before he'd need to feed again.

As Nash stood like a drill sergeant grilling his troops, my gaze strayed to Maya. She huddled in one corner of a sofa, her elegant legs pulled up under her, her beautiful eyes riveted to Nash. She loved the idiot, and one day, I was going to smack him upside the head and make him understand that.

"The best thing to do is the summoning," Cassandra repeated stubbornly. "I will give myself up, John Christianson will have his revenge, end of problem."

"Like hell you will," Pamela growled. "I'm not letting that asshole kill you."

"But this all-powerful sorcerer is the cause of this hex thing, right?" Nash asked. "And if he's dead, no more spell?"

Nash didn't have much knowledge of magic—only what he'd learned, reluctantly, from me and Mick—but he was good at grasping essentials.

"I think so," Cassandra said. "Some hexes can outlast their

creator, but this one is so intense, it needs big magic to keep it up. If the ununculous dies, I'm sure this hex would go or at least weaken enough for someone like Mick to break it."

"Then we kill him," Pamela said. "Simple as that."

Cassandra wiped her nose with the back of her hand. "If it were that simple, someone would have killed him a long time ago." The Cassandra I knew would never wipe her runny nose with anything but an antibacterial tissue. She looked awful, her hair dangling loose from its French braid, her eyes red-rimmed in her sallow face. "No one here is strong enough to best him, except maybe Coyote, and the hex has made sure that Coyote can't fight."

"Could we conjure something else, then?" Fremont asked. "Someone bigger and stronger to kill the ununculous for us?"

"With this hex in place?" I rasped. "Who knows what would go wrong if we tried that? Besides, if Cassandra is right about how powerful the sorcerer is, we'd have to summon something with enormous power, like a god or one of the demon deities."

"And then we'd be left dealing with the god or demon deity," Mick said. "No thanks."

Nash nodded. "It would be like asking the leader of the strongest gang to take out the leader of a weaker one. Then we'd just be in debt to the top gang leader. Not a good idea."

"I was thinking something more like an angel," Fremont said.

Coyote, sitting, still naked, against the wall, finally contributed to the discussion. "You start calling gods, and you risk messing with the vortexes. Gods come when they want to. They don't like being summoned."

"No kidding," I muttered. "Sometimes they won't even answer their cell phones."

"I heard that."

"I've conjured angels," Fremont said. "Well, one. Once. Sort of."

I had my doubts about that—I wasn't sure Fremont had enough magic to summon anything, but even if he had, lesser beings could pretend to be angels.

"Maybe we don't have to kill the sorcerer," Nash was saying. "Couldn't we contain him? Force him to remove the spell?"

I couldn't help laughing, sounding a bit drunk. "What are you going to do Nash, arrest him?"

"Not a bad idea," Fremont said, animated. "Do a binding spell—I can help with that—and then Mick threatens to burn the man's balls off if he doesn't drop the hex."

"True," Maya said. "Men are very attached to their gonads."

"Unless they have ice in their veins," Cassandra said. "Like this ununculous."

Nash cast his gaze on Mick. "Could you do it? Could you restrain him with magic?"

"Possibly. Cassandra can help."

Cassandra pressed her lips in a tight line and shook her head. "We won't be able to. But it doesn't matter. Summon him, and I'll die. I'm ready."

"Cass—" Pamela began, and I joined in the protest. Coyote cut us off.

"Before you all go getting excited," he said, "what Cassandra's not telling you is that calling a dark sorcerer doesn't simply involve drawing a pentagram, lighting incense, and doing a little chant. A summoning like this one, strong enough to keep the hex from interfering, will take a sacrifice. A blood sacrifice. A death. And I'm not talking about a chicken you later make into stew."

My mouth went dry, and Fremont's eyes widened. "You mean a *human* sacrifice?"

"You got it."

I hadn't known that. I thought of my crazed plan to slip off on my own and summon the sorcerer myself and felt cold. No wonder Coyote had given me the evil eye.

"I know," Cassandra said, resigned. "I figured the sacrifice would be me."

NINE

————◆————

THE ROOM ERUPTED IN NOISE. MAYA'S VOICE rose above the others, first in English, then in Spanish. Inside the saloon, the mirror kept on singing. We'd graduated to *Oklahoma!* and "The Surrey with the Fringe on Top."

Pamela leapt away from Cassandra in fury, her fearsome mouth in a bloodred snarl. "Is what we have that bad, Cassandra? That you'd walk away from it and *die*?"

"I'd be dying for you, sweetheart," Cassandra said. Her calling the seven-foot walking nightmare "sweetheart" made me want to giggle hysterically, even with my headache.

"I vote we sacrifice the Nightwalker," Pamela said. "Get rid of two threats at once. What's Ansel doing but waiting to drain us dry?"

"Typical," Ansel's voice came from the kitchen doorway. He leaned on the doorframe, his stance unthreatening, but I saw the red shine to his eyes. "Changers. Half animal, half human, not one thing or the other. You think like animals. Rut like them. You must be fun in bed."

"She has a point, though, Janet," Fremont whispered to me. "He is the most dangerous of us."

"Ansel is not being sacrificed," I said in a loud voice. Ansel would have heard Fremont anyway—Nightwalkers had terrific hearing. "It's not Ansel's fault he's blood frenzied. When the hex is broken, he'll revert to normal."

"Sure about that?" Fremont asked worriedly.

No, I wasn't sure. Nightwalkers were unstable by nature. Ansel might decide he liked the taste of living blood and be unable to give it up again.

"Don't anyone look at me," Maya said irritably. "I know I'm the only one here without so-called magical abilities, but the fuck I came here to have someone stick a knife in me."

"Yeah, me either," Fremont said.

I sat up. "No one's getting sacrificed, because we're not calling the sorcerer. We'll think of another way."

Coyote huffed a breath. "Like you blowing up the building? Forget that. *I'll* be the sacrifice, ladies and gentlemen. You can stick the knife into my heart."

Everyone stared at him in silence. I opened my mouth to object, but Mick beat me to it. "No, they'll need you once the hex is broken. The logical choice is me. As long as I become dragon after I get stabbed, I can heal from it."

His words worried me. Mick was so far into his dragon bad-ass I'll-do-anything-to-nobly-save-you mode he might just let himself be killed—permanently. "Too risky," I said. "What happens if there's too much time between the knife thrust and the sorcerer removing the hex, or us killing him? I'm pretty sure you'd have to shift right away, and you can't do it while we're locked in here."

"There's not much choice," Mick said.

"There is," Coyote said. "Me."

"Stand down," Nash began, but Maya cut him off.

"Don't you dare volunteer, Nash Jones. You do, and I'll kill you myself."

"Listen to Maya," I said to Nash. "Magic won't kill you, but I guarantee a foot-long blade to the heart would."

Coyote raised his voice over ours. "There's no more argument. I'm doing it."

"But your powers are gone," I said in alarm. "You might die for real."

Coyote's smile became genuine. "Aw, Janet. You mean you'd

miss me? I'm touched. But I'm a god, sweetheart. Sacrifice, life and death—it's all part of the job."

"He's right," Cassandra said in a choked voice. "His blood would boost the spell through the hex."

"No!" I tried.

Coyote stood up, walked to the middle of the room, and lay down flat on the floor. "Sorry, Janet. It's got to be done, and it's got to be done now. Mick, grab the knife and the incense. Let's get chanting."

I COULDN'T STOP them. Cassandra made us sit in a circle—Ansel included—with Coyote at the center. Because Cassandra didn't trust herself on her emotional jag to work the necessary magic for the summoning, Mick conducted the ceremony.

He stripped off his shirt and knelt, his sculpted muscles gleaming with sweat. His dragon tattoos glowed with fiery light, and the bite marks where Ansel had fed were black against Mick's neck.

Coyote was the calmest, lying flat on his back, arms at his sides, eyeing the knife blade without fear. I had no idea whether Coyote was working some ploy—he couldn't really die, could he? He must be planning some trickster god thing behind his unruffled expression. He'd let Mick stab him and then spring to his feet as soon as the sorcerer showed up, rip the guy's head off, and laugh at us for being afraid.

Wouldn't he?

Sage burned in a bowl, its sweet smoke dulling my senses. I was drained from the magic I'd tried to work in the kitchen, and with Mick's warm voice intoning the spell, plus the smoke, I wanted to drift to sleep in spite of my fears.

Mick spoke phrases in Latin, a language I'd never bothered to learn. He raised the knife, clasped in both hands, and called the ununculous by name, which, Cassandra had finally revealed, was Emmett Smith.

I'd started laughing when she said it. I'd expected something grandiose like Lucifer or Ezekiel or Damien, and she gave us Emmett Smith.

Maya sat next to me, folded in on herself, her face on her

knees. She rocked back and forth a little, miserable, and I didn't have the strength to comfort her. Nash at least had seated himself protectively beside her, his gun in his lap. Fremont sat on my other side, wedging himself against me to seek *my* protection, because Ansel was beyond him. Then Cassandra, then Pamela, and around again to Nash.

Mick's face ran with sweat. His voice wound louder and louder, until finally he shouted the mage's name and slammed the knife into Coyote's chest.

The blade entered with a wet, meaty sound, and blood washed out to coat Mick's hands.

"Holy shit," Fremont whispered. Maya whimpered and turned her face to my shoulder.

Coyote's body arched as it fought to live, but Mick held the knife hard in the wound against Coyote's struggles. Ansel's nostrils flared at the sharp stench of Coyote's blood, and he lunged forward, unable to stop himself. Pamela and Nash silently grabbed him and hauled him back.

I saw Coyote's blue aura start to fade, a darkness rising from the chalk marks in the circle to suck the aura into it. The darkness swallowed Coyote's aura and became palpable, clinging to Mick's hands like ink. Mick kept chanting, tears mingling with his sweat and the blood that splashed his body. Under him, Coyote's struggles weakened. Then his eyes went blank, his breath released in one gurgling gasp, and Coyote went still.

I held my breath, certain that any minute Coyote would sit up again, laugh, and ask whether the spell had worked.

Any minute. Any minute now.

I didn't realize I'd whispered the words out loud until Maya lifted her head and glared at me. "What is the matter with you? Mick killed him. I'm going to be sick."

I thought I would be, too. Coyote didn't move. He was a human body, dead on my Saltillo tile, eyes staring, unseeing, at the ceiling. My boyfriend had just killed him.

"So where is this big, bad sorcerer?" Fremont demanded in a shaky voice. "Shouldn't there be a flash and a bang or something? And smoke? Where is he?"

Nowhere. The room was empty. Mick peeled his hands from the knife as though he had to force himself to, the look on his face one of anguish and self-loathing. I wanted to go to him, to comfort him, but I couldn't move.

"Nice," a voice said above us.

Cassandra scrambled to her feet. I shot up as well, adrenaline propelling me out of my stupor.

A man stood above us on the second-floor gallery. He wore a business suit, his tie dangling as he leaned on the rail to look at us. His balding head gleamed in the faint light from the windows, as did his wire-rimmed glasses.

"What was he?" he went on in a dry, emotionless voice. "A god minus his powers? Powerless gods are always so pathetic."

Cassandra stood as one stricken, and Emmett Smith looked her over with interest. Ansel had quieted, although Nash still stood between him and Coyote's bloody body. Even the magic mirror had gone silent.

"You touch Cassandra, and you die," Pamela said thickly.

"She's calling herself *Cassandra* now, is she?" the sorcerer asked. "Fitting choice." He started down the stairs, his glasses glinting as he studied us. "With a Changer woman stuck in the between stage. Interesting. What else do we have? A dragon barely containing his power, a minor mage with an inferiority complex, and a Nightwalker in a blood frenzy." He drew to a halt in front of Maya. "But this one is human. Poor thing. This must be hard on you. I'm surprised they didn't use you as the sacrifice."

"Screw that," Maya said, her head up. "This is a new dress."

Emmett chuckled. "Now I understand." He stopped laughing and peered at Nash, who had moved himself protectively in front of Maya.

"But I don't know what *you* are," Emmett said. "I'd have guessed just human, but . . ." He shook his head and turned away, as though determined to solve the mystery when he had more time. "And you." Emmett pointed at me almost joyfully. "You, young woman, are something extraordinary."

"Stormwalker," I said. "This is my hotel. But you knew that."

"No, I had no idea. And Stormwalker is not all you are. Your aura is amazing." He sniffed. "You've got goddess in you. Goddess and something else . . . I can't quite . . . Oh, damn, hang on."

Emmett pulled a handkerchief from his breast pocket and dabbed his nose. He looked at the handkerchief in surprise. "Nosebleed. I never get those unless . . ."

He looked at us—no, at me—and his aura suddenly flared blacker than that of the most evil Nightwalker I'd ever encountered. "What the hell is this?" he demanded.

Mick answered him. "This is us, breaking a curse."

"Curse? Cassandra, explain. Did one of your hexes go wrong?"

"One of *my* hexes?" Cassandra said. "We're breaking *your* hex. These people haven't done anything to you. If Christianson wants me, fine. Janet and her friends have done nothing but take me in when I needed somewhere to go." Her voice broke.

Emmett pressed his handkerchief to his nose. "Christianson? What makes you think I'd waste a good hex for someone like Christianson? The man is a selfish, grasping, weak little bastard."

"How about for the millions he pays you?" I suggested.

"Yes, I take his money. That doesn't mean I live at his beck and call. I was surprised when you started working for him, Cassandra. You're too good a witch for that walking cesspit."

"I didn't know what he was like," Cassandra said. "When I found out, I left."

"Good for you." Emmett glanced around the lobby. "I can't say much for where you ended up, but I admire your moxie." His gaze came back to me. "But then there's *her*. You might be smarter than I think."

I raised my hands for attention. "I hate to break up this little reunion, but what are you saying? That Christianson *didn't* hire you to kill Cassandra?"

"I wouldn't have taken the job if he had. Cassandra's a damn good witch, and I don't waste power like that. I might need her someday."

"I don't understand." Cassandra looked at Coyote, lying dead at our feet. He wasn't coming back to life, not a move, not a peep. "This was for nothing?"

"Nice gesture, the sacrifice, but unnecessary. Next time you want to summon me, just text me."

I looked up into Emmett's face. He wasn't even as tall as Fremont, who was a few inches shy of six feet, but Emmett's lean body made him look taller than he really was. The sorcerer's suit was finely tailored, and he wore a silk shirt and tie. His glasses weren't off-the-rack from a discount optical shop; they were designer, with tiny diamonds winking in the corners. I didn't waste time wondering why such a powerful mage would need glasses. Likely he wore them for effect.

Emmett looked like an ordinary but successful businessman from a big city, the kind you'd find all over Los Angeles or New York. That is, until I looked behind the glasses and into his eyes.

I saw there a cold, hard ruthlessness, with all the warmth of frozen metal. In the darkness, I couldn't tell the color of his irises, but it didn't matter. There was power in those eyes, uncaring power that would take and take and have no remorse about who it had to destroy to keep on taking. Power and no conscience, the most dangerous combination in the world.

"You didn't cast the hex?" I asked him.

"No. Nice one, though."

"Can you tell us who did?"

Emmett dabbed his nose as he tried to stare me down. Lucky for me, I'd grown up staring down my grandmother, a small Diné woman who would have had this man crumpling at her feet.

He shrugged and turned away, implying he'd let *me* go, though I knew better. He strolled to a wall and put his hand on it.

"Ah, a double hex. Very clever. And it used your own wards to ride in and infect the place. This took power. Precision. Planning. I can see why you thought I'd done this." He sniffed the wall, then brought his fingers to his mouth and tasted them. "There's demon in this. Succubus, I'd say. But more than that. A demon-goddess, who enjoys playing succubus for her own reasons . . ." His voice died, and his dark aura suddenly constricted. "Oh, no. Oh, you didn't."

"What?" I demanded, marching to him. "Oh, we didn't, what?"

Emmett looked at his handkerchief again, his voice rising. "Damn it to hell. You brought me here. You summoned me to lock me in her trap." He raised his hand, darkness surrounding it. "You stupid bitch, you brought me here!"

He let the darkness fly, not at me but at Cassandra. Pamela

jerked Cassandra out of the way, but the arrow of darkness followed her like a heat-seeking missile. But Nash was there. He shoved himself in front of Cassandra, and the spear of darkness—so black it shone with its own light—shoved itself right into Nash's chest.

Nash flinched the slightest bit, his mouth firming as the magic met the void inside him. Emmett watched, open-mouthed, as his magic was sucked into nothingness. Without so much as a flicker, the magic vanished, gone as though it had never existed.

Nash straightened up, eyeing Emmett coldly, none the worse for wear.

"How the hell did you do that?" Emmett asked, dazed.

Nash didn't answer, because of course, he had no idea.

Emmett slowly turned his ruthless gaze on me. "What is this, Stormwalker? What did I ever do to you that you've brought me to my death?"

"She didn't do anything." Cassandra's hysterical tears returned. "I'm the victim here."

"Janet." Mick was at my side. I didn't look at his hands, still covered in Coyote's blood. "Something is terribly wrong."

"No kidding."

Mick's voice was hot as he whispered into my ear. "If he didn't cast this hex, if a demon-goddess did it, then how the hell did she? We're back to whoever brought in the seed." His eyes were black, fire dancing in them.

"Don't look at *me*," I said. "I haven't been anywhere near the vortexes lately, and if my mother had touched me in any way, I'd know. She's sealed in. I promise you."

"Then if it wasn't you, who?"

We exchanged a long glance, and then both of us turned to look at the man hovering at my shoulder. Not Emmett Smith.

"Fremont," I said carefully. "About this 'angel' you conjured . . ."

Fremont's brown eyes widened. "You believe me?"

"Yes. I do. Why don't you sit down and tell me about it?"

TEN

"SHE WAS BEAUTIFUL." FREMONT RUBBED HIS forehead, his eyes taking on a faraway glow. "I found this spell in a book I bought at Paradox. That's our local New Age store," he said for Emmett's benefit. "I just wanted someone to talk to. It didn't seem dangerous or like dark magic. It's not at all what we did here with . . ." He broke off, looking at Coyote's body covered with congealing blood.

"And she had sex with you," Emmett said. "Didn't she?"

Fremont looked embarrassed. "She was an angel. I was going to say no?"

"She wasn't an angel, you stupid little fool," Emmett snapped. "She's one of the most powerful demon-goddesses of the earth. She heard your little conjuring spell, took her succubus self to you, and seeded you with the hex. You trotted in here and leaked the curse into the wards. She must have guessed that Cassandra would believe the hex was all about *her*, because Cassandra always did think herself the most important witch in the room. In the end, Cassandra, or one of you, would summon *me*, and now the demon-goddess has me trapped. I hope you're happy."

I folded my arms across my chest. "And why should we think this is all about *you*?"

"Because it is. The demon-goddess has been after me for decades, has used every wile she's had to trap me. All because I killed her son. I needed his magic, and his blood, and he was a fucking crazy demon, for the gods' sakes. Why shouldn't I kill him?"

"I can't imagine why that would upset her," I said.

"And now she traps me with such a simple ploy. The spell of an incompetent wannabe mage that I'd never notice in a million years. Damn it!" Emmett jammed his handkerchief to his nose again.

I walked to him, stood under his stupid bloody nose. "First," I said, "lay off Fremont. He's my friend, and I get annoyed when people yell at my friends. Second, a man died to bring you here, so you need to make yourself useful, to not let his death be in vain. Who is this demon-goddess slash succubus, how do we break the hex, and what is it with your nosebleed?"

"I used to get nosebleeds when I first started using big magic," Emmett said, irritated. "I couldn't handle the pressures. Looks like the hex has taken me back to that happy time. Weakening my magic—I should sue you."

I could see that going over well in court. "Just tell us how to break the hex, oh powerful mage."

"Fuck if I know. Hexes like this are unique to the caster. You'll have to ask her yourself. Once I'm far, far away, if you don't mind."

"We're locked in, shit-brain," Maya said hotly. "*We* can't get out, and I'm willing to bet you can't walk out either."

Emmett glared at her, his eyes almost glowing with his rage. "How dare you—"

"What's her name?" I interrupted him.

Emmett's handkerchief was firmly against his nose now, but he took his awful gaze from Maya and focused it on me. "No, you don't. You're not strong enough to face her, and neither am I. Not yet."

I wondered what he meant by "not yet," but I didn't really want to know. I didn't plan to wait long enough to find out what he had in mind for getting out of this, and I had the feeling it wouldn't involve saving any of us.

"Fremont," I said. "Show me how you conjured the angel."

"That won't work," Emmett said.

"It might," Cassandra broke in. "She'll come for Emmett sooner or later, but if she likes Fremont, she might come to his call."

"Don't be an idiot," Emmett said frantically. "You can't fight her while you're under her hex."

"I don't plan to fight her," I said in a hard voice. "None of us will. We'll give her what she wants—you—and then she'll lift the hex. End of problem."

"You think you're so smart, do you, little Stormwalker? If she can best *me*, then she'll turn around and feast on you. She's always hungry, worse than the bloodsucker here. She devours everything. I don't care how much goddess magic you have in you; you won't be able to stop her."

That didn't sound promising. Coyote stared lifelessly at the ceiling, his skin gray with death. Maya had taken up a throw and tucked it gently around him. Coyote wasn't waking up or coming back to life. He was gone, my friends were hurt and scared, and this entire adventure had come about because of Emmett Smith's search for power. Emmett was going to pay for that.

"Janet isn't alone," Mick said, quiet in his anger. "And the succubus wants you, not us."

"Why don't we just kill *him*?" Pamela asked, pointing at Emmett. "He's human, in spite of all his sorcerer magic. Sheriff Jones can shoot him, and then we can give this demon woman his dead body."

"Don't think that isn't tempting," I said. "But the demon-goddess wants her revenge, and if I know goddesses, she'll want to kill Emmett herself. Fremont?"

Fremont shrugged. "It just took a crystal, a candle, and a verse."

I put my arm around his shoulders. "I love you, Fremont. Let's do this."

I WASN'T CERTAIN the simple spell would work, but I wasn't about to let Emmett know that. Cassandra fetched a clear quartz crystal from her desk behind reception, and I had Mick light another sage stick, because we couldn't get a candle going for some reason. The curse didn't want us to have light.

The verse Fremont used was a simple rhyme, straight out of any "witchcraft for beginners" book. But Mick had taught me that chants and candles or sage and crystals are only vehicles for the witch's focus. The intent of the spell mattered, as did the mage's concentration and strength, not whether the candle was red or yellow, whether the witch used sage or myrrh, or whether they spoke complicated Latin verses or a few simple phrases. Those choices could help, but the whole spell was so much more than the sum of its parts.

Fremont, though he had only a touch of magical ability, had focus and sincerity. I imagined that the demon-goddess had heard that sincerity, Fremont's need to connect, loud and clear, and had homed in on him.

She homed in on him now. In a burst of hellfire tinged with sulfur—which is a cheap effect and not necessary—the succubus-demon-goddess was upon us.

Her aura nearly knocked me over. Fremont must not have been able to see it—to him she'd appear as the black-haired woman who stood before us. No red-clawed siren in black leather, she was draped in modest robes and had a pretty, rather soft face. She looked almost nice.

Except for her aura. That was sticky, gray-black, and foul. I didn't sense Beneath magic from her, which must mean she was an earth entity—born solidly in this world, not the one Beneath. But she was old. Ancient. I read that in her eyes, an ancientness that had allowed her evil to build, that had knocked out any compassion she might ever have possessed. That and her son being murdered to feed a sorcerer's power guaranteed she wouldn't be friendly.

"Hello, Emmett," she said. "Remember me?"

Blood ran in rivulets from Emmett's nose and down his silk shirt as he raised his hand. "Die, whore."

The demon-goddess watched his dark magic come, a little smile on her face. She lifted her hand, and the darkness harmlessly dispersed.

"Don't be an idiot." She moved her gaze from Emmett and fixed it on Coyote. "What have we here? Aw, poor dead little Indian god. They always think they're better than anyone."

"He died to bring the ununculous here for you," I said. "In return, you can lift the hex."

"Now, why would I want to do that?" the demon-goddess asked me. "Much more entertaining to watch you play it out until your own natures kill you. A few of you I might keep alive with me for the fun of it. Like you, Stormwalker. And that one."

She was looking at Nash, giving him an interested once-over, much as Emmett had.

"A magic null," she said as she neared him. "I've heard the theory but never seen one."

She touched Nash's face. Nash didn't like being touched, but he flinched and took it. I wondered what would happen if she tried to hurt him with magic—would her power be absorbed into Nash's doubly enhanced magic void? Would Nash be strong enough to contain it? Probably. That was worth a second thought.

The demon-goddess traced his cheek. "What couldn't I do with you, Mr. Magic Null?"

Maya growled at her. "Take your hands off my boyfriend, you bitch."

In response, the succubus picked Nash up by the neck and threw him across the room. Nash crashed into the reception counter, toppled over it, and landed on the floor beyond. Maya gave a cry of anguish and ran to him.

"A magic null who is still human," the demon-goddess said. "Which means he can die."

I didn't dare go check whether Nash was still alive. I didn't hear Maya wailing in grief, so I hoped for the best. Nash was pretty tough.

"We'll give you Emmett Smith," I said. "He hasn't done much to make us like him, so he's all yours. Take him and lift the hex. I have things to do."

"Don't bargain with me, girl. I'll take Emmett and anyone else I choose. I haven't eaten a Nightwalker in a long time, and I see he fed off the dragon. Doubly delicious."

"Stop it!" Fremont charged to us, anger giving him courage.

"Just stop it! This is all my fault. I brought you here. Not them, not Janet. They have nothing to do with this."

The succubus turned to Fremont, but she didn't try to touch him. Good thing; I'd have broken her fingers if she had, and who knows what she would have done then? "Aren't you sweet? I really like this one, Stormwalker. He's got stamina in the sack, believe me. I might let him live so he can please me again."

I couldn't tell whether Fremont found her declaration terrifying, flattering, or embarrassing. "Can't you do something, Janet?" he pleaded.

I wanted to. I thought about what Coyote had said about the Beneath magic in me tearing open the vortexes. I thought about how I'd felt when I'd drawn on it, ready to blast out the wards and bury us alive, and Nash having to smother me to stop me. I might be just as dangerous as the demon-goddess. Which was the lesser of two evils? Her or me?

The best thing would be for us to let her and Emmett fight it out. Whoever survived such a battle would be weakened, and then Mick, Ansel, Pamela, and Nash could clean up. I and my reality-ripping magic could stay out of it.

The demon-goddess turned to me as though she read my thoughts. "It's difficult, isn't it? Watching those you love die? I know exactly how you feel, because my own son was torn apart by this monster." She flicked her fingers, and Emmett's nose started streaming even more blood. "But I despise you at the same time, Stormwalker. It's such a human thing, to throw someone to the wolves in order to save yourself."

If she were trying to make me feel guilty for my choices, she was wasting her time. Coyote was dead, and the grief in me would know no bounds. He'd died for us, and had known he'd truly die—*Sacrifice, life and death—it's all part of the job,* he'd said.

This entire situation was about the demon-goddess and Emmett, and if one or both of them had to perish to solve the problem, I really didn't care. The world would be minus one demon-goddess and a nasty sorcerer. Good.

"You cast the hex so you could get Emmett here to punish him," I said. "So punish him, already. I'm getting bored, and I want a shower."

The demon-goddess smiled at me, and the similarities between her and my mother unnerved me not a little. "Don't you understand? This is no longer your show, Stormwalker. It's mine. Torturing and killing is what demons do. It's fun for us, and I plan to have fun." She focused on Mick, who had his fire in his blood-caked hands. "Him first. He's the strongest. And I'm at my peak."

My heart went cold. She could easily kill Mick, and there wouldn't be any debate about whether I should stop her.

With one flick of the demon-goddess's slender finger, Mick's fire died. Mick looked at me with fire-streaked black eyes, while the dragons came to life on his arms. "Run, Janet," he said in his soft voice. "Just go."

He was going to turn dragon. He was going to let the huge beast in him erupt in my lobby and take care of this the dragon way. *Chomp.*

"Down!" I screamed. "Everybody get down!"

I felt the succubus reach into the hex and let it flare. A Murphy's Law spell—everything that could go wrong with us, would.

Mick wouldn't be able to contain his dragon, and he'd kill us all, maybe himself, too. Emmett Smith, mighty sorcerer, was cursing as nose blood gushed all over his pristine suit. He desperately held his handkerchief to his face, gasping for breath. No help there.

Cassandra was flat on the floor, Pamela over her. Her half-wolf body contorted, flashing in and out of wolf and wolf-human. Claws raked against Cassandra's back, and Cassandra cried weakly. Ansel, fangs gleaming, eyes molten red, launched himself at Coyote's body. There was no one left to hold him back.

My Beneath magic, which had been waiting below my surface, now gleefully sprang forth, knowing I wouldn't be able to control it.

The demon-goddess sensed my building power and smiled at me. Our battle would be the death of us all—whether or not we opened the vortexes, there would be a smoking crater where my hotel had once stood.

"Bring it, girl," the succubus said.

I forced my hand down to my side, the incandescent ball of light in it fighting to get free. "No," I said.

"No? You want to, sweetie. You want to see who'd win this fight."

"Maybe. But they'd all die," I said.

"What do you care? They're far weaker than you, even that pathetic ununculous who killed my son."

"Coyote died to help us. *Sacrifice*, he said. If you let the rest of them go, I'll stay and fight you. Give you a chance to kill me."

The succubus's gaze moved to Emmett. "I want the sorcerer."

"Fine. Whoever wins, gets him."

"Damn you," Emmett burbled. "I'm not a prize."

"You are today," I said. "Shut up. Your hunger for power has resulted in the death of my friend, and you get to pay for that." The ball of light flared in my palm, its incandescence making everyone cringe, even the big, bad Emmett. My headache vanished, and I felt whole, healed, and unstoppable.

The demon-goddess's lip curled. "Do you challenge me, Stormwalker?"

I drew a breath to answer, but before I could, someone rushed past me. Fremont, the least affected by the hex, snatched up the knife Mick had dropped on the floor and hurtled himself toward the succubus.

"Fremont!" I yelled. "No!"

Fremont ignored me. I had to banish my Beneath magic again before I could grab for him, and then it was too late.

"I thought you were an angel," Fremont sobbed, his voice harsh with betrayal. He plunged the knife straight into the succubus.

It didn't kill her. She was a demon-goddess, immune to the weapons of man. Coyote had died because his god powers had been somehow stripped away, rendering him mortal.

The succubus was immortal and could only be defeated by magic. Collective magic, maybe. If I could get Cassandra and Mick functioning, maybe Emmett as well . . . If I could make the hex work against her somehow . . .

Without stopping to think, I charged. She smacked Fremont

away, and raised her hand to knock me aside. I grabbed the forces of the storm outside and filled the hotel with wind.

The hex made certain it turned into a tornado. Wind ripped through the lobby, tearing the remaining pictures from the walls, overturning furniture. It lifted the coyote statue and sent it flying through the air. The statue smashed through a window, tumbling end over end to land in the parking lot outside. The window immediately sealed itself once again, the hex not wanting the living inside to escape.

The succubus laughed at me. She seemed to stand in a bubble of protection, and the wind didn't touch her. The knife still stuck out of her chest, and she put her hands on her hips and laughed.

I couldn't reach her. Screw Coyote's warnings about the vortexes. I had to end this.

I lifted my hand again, my Beneath magic thrilled to come out. I hefted the white ball of magic. "Hey, succubus," I said.

The succubus's eyes widened, but not at my magic. Her chest had started to smoke. She grabbed the hilt of the knife and tried to pull it from between her breasts, but the blade stayed inside her as though welded in place.

I snuffed out my ball of Beneath magic and watched, open-mouthed.

Sacrifice. Life and death. Coyote insisting on giving his life so that the rest of us might survive.

Coyote's blood coated the knife. Fremont had shoved the blade into her heart, or whatever passed for a demon-goddess's heart.

The blood of a god wasn't the blood of a mortal. Coyote's blood held his essence, and now that essence wound itself through the demon-goddess.

That crafty little trickster god. It wasn't his death that would save us, but the knife that had killed him.

The succubus's sticky gray aura exploded and splattered all over the room. The aura stuck to the walls and worked its way inside, trying desperately to draw strength from the hex.

Forget Beneath magic. I reached for wind still whipping through the room, drawing the cyclone to me and making it mine. I laughed as I sent it at her dying body.

I ripped her apart. As the succubus fell, a misshapen creature ten feet tall, mottled green and blue, and ugly as hell rose from the wreckage of her body. The demon, in its true form, the succubus's glamour gone. It screamed at me through a fang-laden mouth as it clutched at the knife.

Mick dragged himself up, his tattoos still going crazy, his eyes flickering red. He blasted the demon with a white-hot stream of fire, and I followed with a burst pure from the storm. The demon succubus fought with renewed fury, its chest smoking, but it couldn't withstand the two of us, Stormwalker and Firewalker, assisted by Coyote's blood sacrifice.

The demon screamed once more before it fell to my tile floor in an explosion of goo.

"The wards!" Mick shouted. He redirected his magic to the hotel's walls, and I followed. The black aura of the dead succubus resisted us, but our poor, battered wards burned with renewed brightness.

Our wards twined happily around our magic like pets welcoming home long-absent humans. The hex crumbled and dissolved, our magic rushing through the walls like a river of fresh blood through shriveled veins. The demon-goddess's aura dissipated with the hex, until both died with a little shriek on the wind.

Mick's fire went out. The gale swirled around me once, embracing me, then rushed away, leaving the hotel lobby in silence.

The lights sprang to life, followed by a soft hum as the central heating clicked on. Outside, thunder boomed, and then the storm drifted away on a gentle rain.

I turned to Mick, wiping dead demon gore from my face, but before I could reach his open arms, all strength left my limbs, and the floor rushed up to meet me.

ELEVEN

I WOKE IN ONE OF MY FAVORITE POSITIONS, my head in Mick's lap. His eyes had returned to the dark blue I loved, but the look in them was bleak.

"What the hell happened?" Pamela demanded. She'd reverted to her human form, and she glowered down at me, tall and naked, a Changer woman in all her glory.

"Coyote's blood," I croaked.

We all craned to look at Coyote—and found him gone. Vanished, not a trace of him, not even a coyote hair left behind.

"His heart's blood." I moved my tongue inside my parched mouth. "Coyote had to die to release it. I guess he figured that whoever we faced would be so powerful we'd need that formidable weapon."

"So he's really dead?" Fremont asked.

Who the hell knew? Coyote might have gone back to whatever sacred place gods went to when they left the world, maybe never to return in the form we knew. My heart ached.

"But Ansel tasted his blood," Pamela said. "I couldn't stop him."

I sat up in alarm, clutching my aching head. "Ansel? Is he all right?"

I spotted Ansel on a sofa, cringing against the arm as though trying to make himself as inconspicuous as possible. The red in his eyes had gone, and dried blood caked his lips.

"I'm fine," he said in a shamed voice.

"So why isn't he dead?" Fremont demanded. Fremont looked tired, blood all over his hands, but there was a satisfied look in his eyes. The succubus had screwed him over, but he'd gotten even. Fremont might have inadvertently invited the problem into our lives, but he'd also been instrumental in solving it.

I slumped back against Mick, liking the feel of the strong arms that wound around me. "Because Ansel isn't inherently evil," I said. "He's a human being who got turned into a Nightwalker. It's a different thing."

Ansel said nothing as he rose and silently faded up the stairs. Nightwalkers could move without sound, and Ansel vanished quickly into the gloom. He'd be punishing himself for a while, poor guy.

Someone stopped next to me. I looked from pristine leather wing tips up cashmere pant legs to Emmett Smith, his nosebleed gone, his dignity restored.

"All this compassion is making me ill," he said. He gave me a sharp look. "That demon was an ancient one, Stormwalker, born in the brimstone of the earth, created even before the dragons. Yet your storm magic tore her apart as though she were a paper doll. Even with the trickster's magic and the dragon helping, you shouldn't have been able to do that."

I shrugged. "I was provoked."

Mick's voice held a hint of steel. "And I suggest you leave before she gets provoked again."

Emmett straightened his tie. "Yes, all right, I take the hint. One day I'll meet you again, Stormwalker—or whatever you are. That, I think, will be an interesting day."

"Yes, it will be," I said, pretending I wasn't as weak as I felt. "By the way, if you happen to see John Christianson, tell him you have no idea where Cassandra is."

Emmett snorted. "Christianson is an idiot. If he can't find

Cassandra himself, then he doesn't deserve to." He gave Cassandra a mocking bow. "I applaud you, witch. I'll meet you again one day, too." As he spoke, his body shimmered, and then he was gone.

"Is everyone all right?" I asked wearily. I wasn't certain I was. I was so damned tired.

No one answered. Pamela and Cassandra were holding each other, and Nash pulled himself up from behind the reception counter. I felt better. If a building in Iraq falling on him couldn't defeat Nash Jones, a little tumble behind my reception desk wouldn't be able to either.

Nash hauled Maya to her feet beside him. "What were you thinking?" he demanded. "Calling a dangerous person names makes them more dangerous. She could have killed you."

"Just kiss her, Nash," I said.

"What?"

Maya squirmed out of Nash's grasp and marched away, grabbing her purse from the table where she'd left it. "Fuck you, Nash. I am so out of here." She banged the front door on the way, and we heard her truck roar to life.

A voice came out of the saloon. "*She's* a feisty beeyotch. Gotta love that Maya."

The magic mirror. I heaved a sigh of relief. "Where the hell have *you* been?"

Nash answered, thinking I was talking to him. "Behind your reception desk. I was thrown here, remember?"

The mirror nearly sobbed. "I was trying and trying and trying to talk to you. But all that came out were those songs. Not even when I *screamed*. And I couldn't focus *anywhere* but on the saloon. Good thing I love show tunes, but I missed all the sex."

Mick started to smile. "Hey, maybe there were a few good things about that curse."

I shared a grin with him, but I for one was damn happy to hear the mirror again. "But you shut up entirely when Emmett arrived, even stayed quiet after the hex broke. I can't believe you did that by choice."

"Janet, who the hell are you talking to?" Nash was in front of me now. There were actual wrinkles in his uniform shirt. Two of them.

"But I did shut up by choice," the mirror called. "That nasty ununculous was here, and he's got a lot of magic. I thought maybe you wouldn't want him to know you have a magic mirror."

That was smart, I had to admit. "Thank you."

"Oh, you can thank me in many ways." It snickered. "Ununculous. Sounds like a flower. Or do I mean ranunculus? Do think he'd mind if I called him Flower-Power?"

"Do what you want," I said.

Nash slid on his jacket. "What I want is to get out of here. Things seem back to normal—that is, as insane as ever." His shoulders slumped a little. "I can't believe I condoned a murder, even encouraged it."

"Coyote's a god, Nash," I said. "He's probably fine." I believed that, didn't I? "Go see Maya."

"In the mood she's in, I doubt she wants to see me."

"Go find her, help her, and go to bed with her, for all our sakes. She loves you. Damn it, Nash, you have to *try*."

Nash gave me a long stare from his ice gray eyes. Then he gave me a nod and departed. Whether he went after Maya, I wasn't to know.

Mick drew me back against him. "Good advice. Damn, I love you, Janet. Crazy magic, weird prophecies, and all. Bed?"

"Please."

He lifted me as he rose, my dragon boyfriend as strong as ever. As Mick started with me down the hall, all the faucets Fremont had opened during the hex suddenly exploded with water.

"Fremont!" I yelled.

"I'm on it!" Fremont grabbed his toolbox.

"Oh, and Fremont," I said from the safety of Mick's arms. "Next time you want to sleep with a woman—check with me first?"

"Right." I could tell he had no interest in discussing his choice of girlfriends right now. The plumbing called. He charged into the kitchen, and Mick carried me down the hall.

"Oh, yes," came through my bathroom mirror. "I get to see some action now. This will make up for my downtime." The magic mirror's gleeful chuckles died off into protests as Mick shut off the water in there and firmly closed the bathroom door.

* * *

MICK MADE ME leave the hotel for a few days and take vacation. Ansel, remorseful and guzzling cow blood by the gallon, offered to stand guard over it for me, and Cassandra, her cool efficiency restored, assured me she had everything under control. Elena showed up to work the morning after the hex, surveyed the wreck of her kitchen, and started an hours-long rant. I was happy I didn't understand much Apache. We left her to her kitchen, her diatribe, and her knives.

I went with Mick to a place outside of Santa Fe that we loved, where the air was frigid, the snow was high, and beauty existed in every breath. We basked in the joy of time alone, especially snuggled up in bed at night, but I was still uneasy.

Mick hadn't quite come to terms with his choice of killing Coyote, even though his act had ultimately saved us. I'd tried to find out what had happened to Coyote's body, but of course, I couldn't. Plus, I was a bit worried about those flashes of visions I'd had while under the hex. Something coming, they implied. Something not good.

On the third night, I slid into warm slumber after wild lovemaking with Mick and found myself standing outside under the tall pine trees, stark naked in a gently falling snow.

I blew out my breath, which fogged, even though I knew I was asleep and dreaming.

Tracks of a large wolf dented the snow. I followed the tracks deeper into the woods, and there he was, a huge coyote standing in a clearing, moonlight in his yellow eyes.

I stopped myself from rushing to him and throwing my arms around him. I was naked, and he'd like that too much. "Are you alive? Or is this all I'll ever see?"

Of course I'm alive. I'm a god. The *god.*

As he spoke, the coyote shimmered and morphed into the man Coyote—tall, broad-chested, black-haired, and as naked as I was.

"Damn you!" My voice rang to the stars. "It's been days. Why haven't you told us you were all right? Mick's eaten up with guilt."

Coyote winced. "Keep it down, Janet. Little animals are

trying to sleep. I didn't tell you right away because I needed to heal. I had a knife in my heart. Give me a break."

"You should have told us you wouldn't really die."

"But I *did* die. I had to die. Sacrifice. Death and rebirth. I told you; I'm a god. It's kind of in my job description." He shrugged. "Besides, don't you know your Coyote legends? I can only die if the tip of my tail is destroyed. I wasn't letting anyone near *that*."

"Did you know about the demon-goddess? Did you know that Emmett wasn't the hexor?"

Coyote shook his head. "I still can't believe his name is *Emmett*. And no, I didn't know. As soon as he showed up, though, everything made sense."

"Now explain why you didn't tell me that your blood would help. I was grieving for you, damn it."

"Aw, that's sweet. But think about it. Whoever sent the hex could have been listening to us the whole time. Plus, if you'd known, you all wouldn't have viewed it as a sacrifice. You had to believe I truly faced death—and I did. The attitude of the spell caster is as important as the ritual. More."

I remembered thinking much the same thing when we chanted Fremont's spell for his demon.

Coyote touched his chest, which bore no scars. Not one. "And don't think it didn't hurt. Mick's damn strong."

"Wait. You said that everything made sense once Emmett showed up. But you were dead. So how could you know what happened if you were lying there dead?"

"I was kind of in transition. I heard everything, saw everything, I just couldn't do anything. I told Fremont to get her with the knife."

"You *told* him? How . . ."

"He didn't realize I told him. I planted the suggestion in his head, and he thinks he acted on his own. That's fine with me. He needs to feel like a hero."

"Why didn't you plant things in *my* head? I was grieving, you idiot. You couldn't at least have let me know you'd be all right?"

"Because you needed to figure out the rest of it on your own. I can't always be there to fix all your problems, Janet. But you smacked that demon down without using any of your

Beneath magic. You did good, Stormwalker. I'm proud of you."

That did it. I ran at him, screaming. My fists met flesh, thudded on muscle.

"Ow." Coyote caught my hands. "Easy. Still healing."

I tried to jerk away, but he kept hold of my fists. "Just because it worked is no justification!" I shouted. "What if I hadn't known what to do, and we'd all died? What if even one of us had? You'd have let Maya or Fremont die so I'd learn a lesson? For your principles?"

"Not principles." Coyote's voice went stern, even harsh. "Life or death. The lesser or the greater evil. It's the kind of choice I have to make every day." He fixed me with his god stare, the one that terrified me. "It's the kind of choice *you* will have to make."

I shook my head, kept shaking it. "No. I would never decide that one of my friends had to die."

"And yet you did. You chose me."

"Because I thought you would come back to life, you ass-hole! And I was right. You did."

"Because I chose to," Coyote said. "Because you need me."

He finally let me go, and I backed away, jamming my arms over my cold chest. "I would never, ever sacrifice those I love for any reason. Ever. Do you hear me?"

"Yes, I hear you." His look was somber. "And yes, you will."

I unfolded my arms. "Bite me," I said, and I turned and walked away.

"Go on back to your lover," Coyote said behind me, voice gentling. "Comfort each other the way you do." A pause. "Hey, mind if I watch?"

"In your dreams," I called over my shoulder.

"Or in yours. Whichever." He chuckled. "You know, Janet, you do have the sweetest ass."

I flipped him off and kept walking.

The dream faded and I woke in Mick's arms, his blue eyes half open, his drowsy smile welcoming me.

I could still hear Coyote's laughter in the night. It dissolved into high-pitched coyote yips and then faded on the wind.

BLOOD DEBT

JEANNE C. STEIN

ONE

"I'VE GOT HIM."

I'm off like a bullet across the dark parking lot. The guy I'm chasing, a skip wanted in L.A. for drug trafficking, runs like he's used to it. Head up, long strides, hands pumping. And he's fast.

Trouble is, he doesn't know what's chasing him.

I hear my partners, David and Tracey, fall behind. Good. I can kick in with the vampire speed and—

A car door opens right in front of me. Smacks me square in the chest and I go down like I've been shot.

Shit.

I jump up and shake my head clear. David and Tracey pound past me.

"You okay?" David says over his shoulder.

I'm looking at the guy who coldcocked me. "Yeah. Get Smith."

That guy is looking at the guy still running. "I'll call the cops," he yells, brandishing a cell phone.

"What the hell are you doing?" I've grabbed his wrist,

yanking the phone out of his hand. A car door can't kill a vampire, but getting whacked by one can sure as hell cause pain. Right now my ribs are screaming like a son of a bitch.

"Stopping a mugging," he says, trying to free himself from my grip.

He can't. For the first time, a glimmer of uncertainty shadows his face. "You're strong."

"Yeah, I know." I release him, toss the phone into the lot. When I turn back, he's eyeing me and I return the favor. Late thirties, good suit, good shoes, good haircut. Looks like he might be a salesman at Men's Wearhouse.

"We weren't mugging that guy. We were trying to arrest him."

His eyes narrow. "You guys are cops?"

"Not exactly."

He takes a step backward. "Not exactly? You're either cops or you're not."

I'm looking for David and Tracey. As a vampire, I have excellent night vision. But I can't see through buildings, and from the echo of running feet they're around the corner of a building in the far end of the lot.

"Shit. I've got to go."

"I don't think so."

I turn and find myself staring into the barrel of a nice little .22. The guy has it pointed at my chest. I release a breath of exasperation. "Look. I told you I'm not a mugger. I'm a fugitive apprehension officer. A bounty hunter. And my partners may be in trouble. Now point that gun somewhere else, or I'll take it from you and stick it up your ass so far, you'll be shitting bullets."

"Big talk," he says. But I notice his hand is not quite so steady. "No, you and I are going to—"

He doesn't get a chance to finish. I have the gun out of his hand so fast his brain can't process what happened. He's still staring at where the gun used to be. His eyes flick back and forth from his empty hand to mine—and the gun now pointing at *his* chest.

"How'd you do that?"

"Just get in your car and get out of here."

He doesn't wait for me to say it twice. He slips behind the

wheel and cranks over the engine. I step away and slam the door.

But like most pain-in-the-ass bystanders, he has to get the last word. "I'm still going to call the police," he yells back, gunning the car out of the parking lot with a squeal of rubber.

I see David and Tracey at the far end of the lot walking back toward me. Just the two of them.

"You do that," I say quietly to the departing car.

Fucking-A.

The skip got away.

I stick the gun I took from the now-fleeing driver into the pocket of my jacket.

Over my shoulder, a sound.

A laugh? Or a growl?

I whirl around.

Vampire senses spring to alert. Nothing. Nothing moving, nothing breathing. No supernatural blips on my internal radar screen. Was it my imagination?

But the echo hangs in the air before the sound fades away like fog in the sun.

TRACEY AND DAVID beat me into the office the next day. The mood is glum. I walk straight over to our gun safe in the corner of the office and work the combination. Stick the .22 inside and twirl the lock.

"Where'd that come from?" David asks.

"Took it off our good Samaritan last night. So, what's up?"

David slaps the flat of his hand on a folded newspaper. "The cops picked Smith up. Fucking civilian cost us a bounty."

"And I'm fine, by the way," I say with mild amusement. "Thanks for asking."

David blows out a breath. "You're tough. The minute I saw you on your feet, I knew you were okay."

He's a big guy, a former pro–football player who has some experience with on-the-job accidents. His philosophy is if you can get up on your own after being hit, you're still in the game.

Tracey isn't so sure.

"Did you get yourself checked out?" she asks. "That door clocked you pretty good."

She's a tough one, too. An ex-cop who's tall and willowy as a whippet but with the staying power of a pit bull. She signed on as a partner a little over three months ago. Her concern makes me smile. Neither of them knows that I'm a vampire. Nothing short of a stake in the heart or a well-aimed ax to the head can put me down permanently.

"I'm fine. Really." I pick up a pile of flyers hot off the fax and fan them. "Anything promising here?"

"Maybe one." David takes the flyers from me and pulls out a single sheet. "Not as big a payday as the one we lost last night but better than nothing."

He hands it over. An arson suspect skipped bond and was last seen in Phoenix. He's got a ten-thousand-dollar bounty on his head. I look up. "Phoenix? In August?"

"Yeah." David frowns. "I know. That's why I think we should flip to see which one of us accompanies Tracey—"

"*Accompanies* Tracey?" Her voice croaks a protest. "Why don't I get a shot at that coin toss?"

"Because you're the rookie." David fishes a coin out of his pocket, flips it with one hand, slaps it down on the back of his other. He looks at me. "Call it."

"Heads."

He peeks. "Shit. Okay, Tracey. Go pack an overnight case. We leave in thirty minutes."

TWO

—▶◀—

AN HOUR LATER, DAVID AND TRACEY ARE ON the road, and I'm alone enjoying my little victory. I pick up the newspaper and take it out to the deck that spans the back length of our office. It's Saturday so most of the other offices on our block are closed. We're situated on Pacific Highway a stone's throw from Seaport Village. Traffic noise and the chatter of tourists mingle with the shrill, sharp squawk of scavenging seagulls. The deck hangs over San Diego Bay. It's noon and the sun is high in the sky, bouncing off bobbing sailboats and turning speedboat wakes into bright silver froth. The kind of day San Diego is famous for. Mild. Sunny. Beautiful to behold.

A thousand times better than the desert hell David and Tracey are headed for.

I plop into a chair, congratulating myself on my good luck. All I have to do is mind the office for an hour or two and then I'll take the afternoon off. I shake open the newspaper. Read the article about the one that got away. Smith was picked up two hours after we lost him, in a bar, recognized by someone who saw his picture on the news. No mention of our run-in with him or of any indignant citizen complaining that three "muggers" had assaulted him in a parking lot.

The chase replays in my head. I rub at my ribs—reflex really, now there's not even a mark left to show that I got whacked by that car door. Wonder what the guy in the car was doing there at 2 A.M.? The mall stores had been closed for hours, no bars or restaurants in the area. He took a chance insinuating himself in a situation he knew nothing about. There's no way he could have missed the fact that there were three of us.

And he had a gun.

Curiouser and curiouser.

And what about that creepy sound I heard? Or thought I heard. It could have been the wind. Or . . . what?

I've been a vampire for a little over a year and I've come across so many strange things I've lost count. I'm no longer surprised or startled by anything that I see or hear. I can't explain most things, I don't try anymore. But the guy in the parking lot was no supernatural being. I could get some answers from him. At least I can find out why he was hanging around in a deserted parking lot and why he had a gun.

I go back inside, open the safe, examine the .22. The serial number is easily distinguishable. A call to a friend at SDPD and he agrees to check the gun registry and get back to me.

Nothing to do now but wait.

THE CALL COMES in a long hour and a half later. I jot the information down on a notepad, thank my buddy, and ring off with the promise that I owe him one. Then I sit back in my chair and look at the name.

Alex Hampton.

I power up my laptop and do a directory search—of both legal and illegal sites. In the bounty-hunting business you cultivate certain talents. Knowing how to get information is one of them. In less than ten minutes, I have an address and phone number. Should I call first? No. Alex surprised me last night. It's my turn to return the favor. I eject each bullet out of the cylinder on his .22 and drop them into a desk drawer. The gun itself I stick in my jacket.

Hampton's address is on Hilltop Drive in Chula Vista, a manicured street of upper-middle-class houses. Hampton has one of the nicer ones. He lives on the west side of the street with a view in back that stretches along the coastline. There are children's toys in front, a trike, a two-wheeler with training wheels. He has at least two young kids.

I ring the bell. The door opens a crack, the length allowed by the chain at the top. One round, blue eye peeks out. A cacophony of sound from a Saturday morning cartoon show spills out, too. I kneel down so I'm eye level.

"Hey. Is your daddy home?"

The door slams shut. I hear the thud of little feet and the yell of "Daddy" as the kid runs to find his father.

When the door opens next, I'm greeted by a disheveled, pajama-clad man who rubs the sleep from his eyes as he asks, "Yes?"

This guy is about forty, overweight, balding.

Not the man I met last night.

"Sorry. I must have the wrong address. I'm looking for Alex Hampton."

"You found him, lady. What do you want?"

I have two choices now. Retreat or barge ahead. I pull the gun from my jacket. If he acts frightened and slams the door in my face, I know I have the wrong guy and I'd better get the hell out of here.

He doesn't.

He steps outside, closing the door behind him. "Where did you find it?"

He's reaching to take it, but I pull it back. "Where did you lose it?"

He tilts his head, studying me. "Are you from the police?"

"No."

He looks back at the door, as if to assure himself it's still closed, but lowers his voice anyway. "I lent it to somebody. He called early this morning and said he lost it."

"Who did you lend it to?"

"I can't tell you."

"Did he tell you how he lost it?"

A shake of the head.

"Look, I'm not a cop," I say. "But I am an officer of the

court." Sort of, anyway. "If you don't tell me who had the gun last, any crime committed with it will be laid on your doorstep."

I have no idea whether or not a crime has been committed, but a pint of bluff is worth a pound of fact.

His face reveals the inner battle. Should he rat out the friend or risk his own well-being? A no-brainer, in my experience. The only question is how long will he take to decide to give up his "friend."

Not very long.

His expression clears. He breathes out a shaky breath. "Stephen Powers." Then he waits, as if I should recognize the name.

It does sound familiar. But no face pops to mind. "Did he say why he needed a gun?"

"No. And I didn't ask."

"Okay. I'm going to keep the gun for a while. You'll get it back when we've had a chance to check out your story."

"'We'?" The cloud descends once more. "I thought you said you weren't a cop."

I smile and hold out my hand. He takes it. We shake. "I'll be in touch, Mr. Hampton. Best to keep all this to yourself for now."

I leave him before he can think about it too long or hard. I figure I have at least a day before he contacts the real cops. Time enough to locate Stephen Powers and find out why he needed a gun.

THREE

I DRIVE BACK TO THE OFFICE ACTUALLY EX-
cited at the prospect of doing a little sleuthing. Too much of
my life this last year has been taken up with fighting supernatural battles. I like the idea of tackling a human puzzle.
Though there may be no puzzle at all. For all I know, this Stephen Powers may have a perfectly logical reason for sitting
alone in a car in a deserted parking lot at 2 A.M. with a gun.

Maybe I can help this guy. Maybe he's been threatened in
some way. Maybe someone in his family is in trouble.

Right.

My inner cynic raises her ugly head—more likely Stephen
Powers is an addict and he was there waiting for his dealer.

I've been dealing with scumbags too long.

No. I prefer to think positively. When I pull into the parking lot, I've convinced myself once more that I'm going to find
this Stephen Powers and solve his earthly problem for him.
Even if it means using unearthly methods.

I'm already ticking off ways to track him down as I unlock
the door and step inside. The telephone is ringing. In the spirit

of my new, optimistic brain set, I answer, "Angel Investigations. We help the helpless."

There's a moment of silence. Followed by a click.

Doesn't even faze me. As I suspected it would, the phone rings again. This time, I use my professional voice. "Anna Strong."

A pause, but much shorter this time. "Anna?"

I don't recognize the voice. "Yes?"

"This is Susan. I need to talk to you. Can we come to your office?"

Recognition floods back. Susan is one of the witches from the Watcher Organization. The "we" can only be her sister witches, Min Liu and Ariela Acosta. "What's this about?"

"I'd prefer to talk to you in person. Do you mind if we come over now?"

It takes only a second to decide. "No. Do you need directions?"

A short burst of nervous laughter. "Witches, remember? We'll use a locator spell. See you in twenty minutes." She disconnects.

My brain buzzes with possible reasons—mostly negative—the three witches would want to see me. I'm so busy guessing, it takes ten minutes for something else to percolate through the bog.

Susan's last name is Powers.

Coincidence?

Spidey senses start to tingle.

No need to start a search when my gut tells me Stephen Powers will soon be a puzzle no longer.

I'm at the door to wave them in the minute I hear footsteps approaching from the sidewalk.

Susan says, "Anna, we need your help."

They file in silently: a petite Chinese woman of indeterminate age with black eyes and waist-length raven hair; a middle-aged soccer mom with a neat highlighted bob that curls at her chin and frames her face; a twenty-something Latina with long, straight hair drawn back in a ponytail from a pretty, even-featured face. I motion them to take seats across the desk from me.

They are uneasy. I didn't need vampire senses to pick that up. The glances they exchange as they perch themselves on the edges of the chairs, the restless way their eyes dart around the office lighting on everything but me, the foot tapping and finger drumming—all dead giveaways.

Since they came to me, I decide to wait them out, even though my curiosity is quickly nearing the boiling point.

I've reached the impatient finger tapping on the desktop when Ariela clears her throat. She glances at her sister witches and begins to speak.

"Anna, we come to you for help."

"You already said that."

Breaking the silence loosens the tongues of the others.

"We wouldn't if it weren't so important." This from Min Liu.

"It's a matter of life and death." From Susan Powers.

No longer avoiding me, their attention becomes focused with the intense fierceness of cats watching a moth on a windowsill. An internal alarm buzzes and flutters. "What can I do for you?"

Ariela seems to be the spokesperson. She draws a shallow, shaky breath and folds her hands in her lap, her fingers clenched so tightly that her knuckles turn white.

"It's a friend of ours. He's been kidnapped. We need you to find him for us. We need you to bring him back."

Something in the way she says "bring him back" raises that alarm from buzz to scream and makes the question that springs to my lips rhetorical. "Kidnapped? Shouldn't you be going to the police?"

A brisk shake of her head sends the ponytail dancing. "No. The police can't help."

Why does that not surprise me? The three sitting in front of me are part of the supernatural force called the Watchers. They maintain order among the otherworldly members of the local population. They are powerful witches who have powerful friends. Much more powerful than the mortal police force. I ask the obvious. "Why are you coming to me? I am not a Watcher anymore. There must be many among you who could help."

Another exchange of glances. More anxious frowns. I'm not aware that witches can communicate telepathically, but at this moment I wouldn't have bet on it. *Something* passed between them.

"No one else can help," Ariela says.

"And why is that?"

"Because you're the reason he's been taken," she replies. "And only you can get him back."

"I'm the reason?"

A collective nod.

A spurt of anxiety quickens my blood. I take mental inventory. I know where David and Tracey are. I spoke to my parents early this morning. As dismal as it sounds, the only other friends I have are shapeshifters and they can take care of themselves. I can't think of anyone else who is close enough to me to warrant kidnapping. Or a reason why anyone would be. I haven't been vampire long enough for the miracle of compound interest to make me financially independent. I still have a day job.

Skepticism replaces concern.

"It's someone I know?"

"We didn't say that."

I lean forward. I'm getting impatient. Again. "No more riddles. How can I be responsible for the kidnapping of someone I don't know?"

"Because you committed a crime and you must answer for it." Ariela holds up a hand, whether to stop me from interrupting or to stem the torrent of words that spill out of her mouth, I can't tell. "You didn't know you had committed a crime. We didn't know, either. But we helped you and, in doing so, are being held responsible. Our friend—Susan's brother—has been taken hostage. If you don't agree to go back, he will be killed. A life for a life."

Tears spill down Susan's cheeks, tears she either doesn't notice or is too preoccupied to wipe away.

I reach into a desk drawer for a tissue. I've done my share of killing—I can justify every life I've taken. "I don't know what you're talking about. I haven't committed any crime. I haven't killed anyone who didn't try to kill me first. I think—"

"It's Belinda Burke's life you have to atone for." Ariela says it quietly.

Her words stay my hand and stir the hair at the back of my neck.

She leans toward me. "You killed her and you killed her in a sacred place. Now you have to go back."

FOUR

ASTONISHMENT DOESN'T BEGIN TO DESCRIBE the reaction evoked in hearing Belinda Burke's name in the same sentence as "life you have to atone for." Belinda Burke was a powerful black-magic witch who almost caused the death of two close friends of mine and threatened to kill me and her own sister for helping rescue them. She was an evil bitch who among other things bled young female vampires to death to use their blood in an anti-aging cream. A cosmetic, for fuck's sake.

"Atone for what?" I'm speaking through clenched teeth, fighting to keep my tone civil. "She was evil. You know that. You all know that. It's why you helped me."

Sadness pulls at the corners of Susan's mouth. "We know," she replies softly. "What we didn't know was that Belinda Burke had gone to a place of sanctuary to recover from her wounds. She was under the protection of a powerful tribunal and we never should have allowed you to penetrate their defenses. We shouldn't have been *able* to penetrate their defenses. It's part of what's made them so angry."

"Them?" I repeat. "Who are you talking about?"

"The powers that rule the astral universe," Min Liu replies.

"Who or what they are is not entirely clear. They contacted each of us in a dream last night. The message was the same. They would hold Stephen until you appear for judgment. Sanctuary has been violated and that cannot go unpunished."

"Unpunished?" The vampire stirs and bares her teeth. "They plan to punish me for killing a monster like Belinda Burke? If they offer sanctuary to creatures like that, they need to rethink the concept."

Susan wipes at her eyes, takes a breath. "I know. It's not fair. But Stephen is an innocent and shouldn't have to suffer for our"—she makes a sweeping motion to encompass us all—"mistake."

She digs into a purse she'd tucked in the chair beside her when she sat down and pulls out a picture. She thrusts it toward me. "This is Stephen."

I take it from her outstretched hands, but do I even have to look at it? Stephen Powers. Last night. I drop my eyes and look at the picture.

It's a studio shot. Professionally lit, professionally staged. The man is handsome, square-jawed, blue-eyed, looks to be in his thirties. He's facing the camera, gaze clear and direct, a blue button-down deepening the color of his eyes. His hair is a golden blond, touched at the temples with silver. His demeanor projects confidence. And a comfortable familiarity with the spotlight.

Different from last night, when he wasn't in his element.

But definitely the same man.

Seeing the picture, I finally connect name and face.

I glance up at Susan. "Is he a reporter?"

She nods. "For the local CBS affiliate."

So he might have been in that parking lot to meet a source? Smith, maybe?

I must have taken too long, or been staring too hard at the picture because Susan says, "What is it, Anna? Do you know Stephen?"

Know him? Not yet, anyway. I shake my head. "I've seen him. Recently."

Susan skewers me with her gaze. "You've seen him? Where? On television."

Thank you. No sense adding to her concern by mentioning

her brother was in a deserted parking lot last night waving a gun. "Yes." I'm sure I have seen him on television at one time or another. I start to hand the picture back to her but she waves toward me. "Keep it."

I laid it on the desk. "When did you say he went missing?"

"I'm not sure. Must have been late last night or early this morning. He was supposed to meet me for breakfast. He never showed."

"Why do you think they took *him*?"

Ariela answers. "Because he is well known. And he knows about our community. I think they realize his absence would be missed and should we not cooperate, his death will cause ripples in both the mortal and otherworldly planes. A warning to others not to make the same mistake we did."

Suspecting that Stephen, a reporter, was in that lot to meet somebody he didn't trust explains the gun. What isn't so clear is why whoever is after us didn't take us both when he had the chance. I see no point is sharing this with the witches. These questions will be better answered once I get wherever it is I'm going.

"You said he knows about our community. Is he a witch, too?"

Susan shakes her head. "No. He inherited no supernatural powers. But he grew up in the household of a powerful witch, our mother. He watched as my abilities grew. He knows that there are other supernatural creatures sharing this world and he pledged to keep that secret always. To this day, he has."

Min takes Susan's trembling hand in her own. "Anna, none of us is to blame for what happened. No. That's not quite right." She looks at her sister witches. "We take responsibility for not knowing enough about what we did for you that day. But our excitement at penetrating the astral plane and our belief that you were doing the right thing in following Belinda Burke there blinded us to everything else. It's up to us to make things right and get Stephen back."

I look from one anxious face to another. I can't bring myself to tell them that I'll never regret killing Belinda Burke, sanctuary or no. But I won't let an innocent take the rap for something I did.

What did Ariela say? The powers are demanding a life for a life?

Do they expect me to give up my life for a stranger? Not fucking likely. Not without a fight.

I made it back from that "place of sanctuary" once before. I figure I can do it again.

"What do we do now?"

Susan's shoulders drop in relief. "You'll help Stephen?"

I nod.

She stands up. "We have to go to the park."

I stand up, too, and step from around the desk. "Let's go."

FIVE

‹—➤●◄—›

THE PARK IS BALBOA PARK AND IT'S ALIVE
with people this clear, sunny summer afternoon. But still the
magic works. As if invisible, the four of us separate from the
crowd heading into the Natural History Museum and melt
into the bushes across the way. We pass through a magical
barrier, a touch of damp against our skin, and without drawing a glance from people on the sidewalk, we are at a door
hidden behind a mystical waterfall. Min Liu pulls a big brass
key from her purse. The door opens at her touch and we step
inside.

This is the entryway into the hub of San Diego's supernatural community and yet it looks like a nondescript reception
room—a desk with a computer, a rack of magazines, a couple
of chairs. Min Liu punches a few keys into the computer and
with a whir of machinery, the entire room descends. On the
ride into the bowels of the building, I think of the many times
I've taken this trip and how different it feels now.

It's been months since I've been here. Months since my
enemy turned mentor turned tormentor, Warren Williams, was
killed and my link with the Watcher community was broken.

The emotions I feel when the door slides open and I step into the room tumble over themselves like pebbles in a stream. It's at once familiar and threatening, foreign and natural. This should be where I belong.

But it's not anymore. I believe now it never was.

Everything looks the same. The central core of the large square room is filled with cubicles—this is the financial heart of the Watcher organization. Psychics—real psychics—man a bank of telephones to dispense advice to fee-paying clients. But the clients here are not looking for hints about their love life or seeking contact with newly departed love ones. These clients are world leaders seeking advice on matters that affect us all.

I let my gaze sweep the room, irony burning like acid at the back of my throat. From the state of the world, I'm not sure how much good they're doing—or whose side they're really on.

Susan's hand on my arm yanks me from the bitter reverie.

"This way, Anna."

I follow the three toward the back of the room. My presence causes a ripple among the psychics. Most know who I am, recognize me from previous visits. The ones who don't catch the hostile vibrations emanating from their comrades. Almost all hold me responsible for the death of Warren Williams. They know I didn't kill him myself, but a deluded vampire who thought I was a reincarnated goddess killed him because of me. His soul mate destined to rule the world by his side.

My lips tilt up reflexively in a tight smile. That monster is dead. I *did* kill him.

No consolation to those here who are still in search of a leader to replace Williams. I've kept away from this place and haven't a clue who heads things now. Neither do I want to know. I don't belong here anymore. The feeling that I never did floods back stronger than ever.

I try to shake off the gloom settling over my shoulders like a shroud. All the negative energy being directed my way brings the vampire inside close to the surface. I'm relieved when Susan opens a door and we're shut off from the hostility.

Another familiar room. This one where the witches sent me, at my bidding, to the astral plane to deal with an enemy.

I don't see any of the trappings they used then—no candles or goblets or amulets to speed me on my way. The room is empty except for a circle drawn in the center.

I remember something else.

"I needed blood to make the spell work last time. An innocent's blood." The blood of someone who is no longer my friend. Another repercussion of that fateful trip.

Susan casts an uneasy glance at her sister witches. "This time will be different," she says.

I don't like her tone. It rings with apprehension and uncertainty.

"How?"

Her eyes flutter closed for an instant, but then she squares her shoulders and looks directly at me. "They are sending an escort for you."

"An escort?"

A bob of the head. "Yes." She touches my hand. "But some things will remain the same. You will not be vampire on the ghostly plane. You will be human. You will have no power except mortal strength and cunning."

Ah, yes. I remember that, too. "I suppose taking a weapon with me is out of the question." I let a sigh escape my lips as three pairs of troubled eyes flash in reply. "When is this escort supposed to arrive?"

"Before he does," Susan says, "there's something—"

Her words are choked off by a blaze of white light, brilliant, blinding. A sound like the furious beating of wings. Instinct says I should close my eyes. Curiosity keeps them wide open. At first, it's like looking into sun reflected on snow. Disorienting and too bright. Then gradually a shadow forms—like a negative film image. Dark is light, light, dark. Finally, my vision clears. Wings. Outstretched. There one second, gone the next. All that's left then is the figure of man. He looks up at me and my breath catches in my throat.

He's the most beautiful man I have ever seen.

An angel.

SIX

⟶⟣✦⟢⟵

I'M NOT EASILY IMPRESSED BY HANDSOME
men—my last boyfriend was a model who looked like Adonis
but had the soul of Judas. Nevertheless, this creature is strik-
ing. With his blue-green eyes and close-cropped head of tight
curls, he looks like another Greek god—marble turned flesh
and blood. I know the witches beside me are thinking the
same thing. I heard their gasps when he materialized out of
the light. Now we all stand here with our mouths hanging
open in astonishment, too stunned by his beauty to do more
than stare.

But he's looking just at me, and he has an expression on his
face that seems to reflect surprise. Did he think I wouldn't be
here, that I'd refuse to cooperate? Did he think me a coward?
Then he's smiling, his gaze taking us all in.

His smile is benevolent, but there's something darker lurk-
ing under the surface. I recognize it even if the others don't.

And they obviously don't. They are spellbound by his
beauty.

He's dressed in jeans. Tight jeans. And a form-hugging
T-shirt of white cotton. His clothes suggest he's comfortable

with modern attire while the vibe he's sending off is ageless and old. He drinks in the appreciation and wonder with the casual acceptance of one who is used to this reaction. Who welcomes it.

Who expects nothing less.

Which brings the vampire to her senses even if, like the witches, the human Anna wants nothing more than to run her fingers along those bulging biceps.

It takes effort, but I douse the flame of carnal desire and focus on the reason he's here.

"What kind of creature are you?" I ask.

"What kind of creature do you think I am?"

"An angel?" Ariela's voice is a whisper beside me.

He laughs, a sound as pure as the ring of silver on crystal.

"A deity?" From Min Liu, breathless.

"A cupid?" Susan takes a step forward.

I put out a hand and hold her back though I understand the impulse to want to *touch* him. "Why don't you tell us what you are?"

His smile sends off dizzying waves of pleasure, warm, like the effects of the sun bursting through clouds on a cold day. I fight the urge to close my eyes and bask in it.

He's gauging my restraint. A little of the warmth seeps away.

"You are a tough one," he says with a sigh that could be of disappointment or chagrin. "I am your escort to the tribunal."

"That I guessed. What I'm asking is what kind of creature are you?"

His eyes narrow a little and in that instant, he doesn't seem as harmless as he's pretending. But the impression is gone just as quickly. The beatific smile is back. He spreads his arms. "I am Samual, a simple messenger of the powers that be. I mean no harm. I am here to ensure your safe passage to the tribunal. What happens there is of no concern to me." He looks around. "I do the same thing you do, Anna Strong. I return those who have fled justice to face their accusers. Nothing more."

He does the same thing I do? So he knows I'm a bounty hunter. It's the last part, though, that gets my attention.

Fled justice, huh? I'm tempted to wipe that smile from his face with a scalding reply. But he's right. As a bounty hunter, his mission is the same as mine. The guilt or innocence of a fugitive has never been my concern.

"A supernatural bounty hunter, huh? That I understand. Shall we get on with it?"

I feel the three witches behind me stir uneasily. I turn to face them. "Don't worry. I will bring Stephen back to you."

Susan steps forward. I think she's going to hug me, but instead she holds out her hand. "Go with the goddess," she says.

I press my palm into hers. At first, I feel just her hand. Then a small charm materializes. It's round and warm and wet, as if conjured from flesh and blood. Her eyes hold mine with an intensity that burns. She wants to speak, but her eyes dart to the creature behind me.

I acknowledge her gift with a small nod and close my fingers around it. It moves through the skin of my palm with a tingle and when I glance down, there's nothing left to show for its passing but a faint flush.

When I turn back to the creature, he's studying me. Did he see what passed between Susan and me? Did he sense the magic?

SEVEN

<hr/>

SAMUAL HAS AN ODD EXPRESSION ON HIS face. A mixture of humor and pity. I think he knew Susan passed something to me in that handshake, but he's not about to let on that he knows. Not about to acknowledge a simple human trick.

Condescending bastard. His attitude infuriates me. Well, I can be infuriating, too.

I get right in his face. "Okay, Sammy, let's get this show on the road. The sooner I clear myself of these ridiculous charges, the sooner Stephen and I can come home."

I think he actually winced at "Sammy." His eyes certainly narrowed.

Then the spark of irritation is gone. He's smiling again, opening his arms. I take it to mean I'm supposed to step close to him. Reluctantly, I do. He folds his arms around me. The heat and scent of his body envelopes me in a cocoon that's unnervingly arousing. Testosterone exudes from his pores, making me press myself against him as if drawn by a magnet. I feel my body respond to his masculinity just as I feel his body respond to me.

I experience no sensation of movement. What I feel I think

at first is my imagination. My body hums with sexual tension. Then it's being touched by a hundred fingers—skilled fingers that roam, probe, manipulate. I am powerless to do anything. I can't move. Can't escape.

I am powerless to do anything but surrender. Truth is, I'm not sure I'd stop it if I could. I'm trapped inside a pleasure cocoon being transported to what might be my doom. I should be outraged.

Instead, I'm loving it.

If this is teleporting, no wonder Captain Kirk always had a smile on his face. The climax, when it comes, is purely a physical reaction. The release is there, but that's all.

Makes "flying United" take on a whole new meaning.

When my feet touch ground, I have no idea if the encounter took two minutes or two days. I draw a head-clearing breath. I look up at Samual, see the smirk, and all illusion of pleasantness evaporates. He has the self-satisfied leer of a man showing a woman that he is the one in control.

I begin to wonder if he's an incubus. If he is, I'd better be on my guard. We know what those bastards intend.

I square my shoulders. "Is that how you get your jollies, Sammy? Was it as good for you as it was for me? Can I expect to be entertained the same on the way back?"

His eyes darken, smoldering with suppressed anger. "Do not speak my name with such disrespect. You are out of your element here, Anna Strong. You will be wise to remember that."

I look around. The room is stark, bare, blindingly white. "So, what happens now?"

He takes a step back from me, folds his arms in front of his chest. "Now you wait."

He fades away like a whisper, leaving only a wisp of smoke and a faint odor that tickles my nose. It smells like sex.

How could I have ever thought him an angel?

This was not exactly the way I imagined my reentry to the astral plane would take place. I suppose arriving on the wings of an orgasm is better than arriving in shackles. Should I feel embarrassed or ashamed? I feel neither.

What I feel is confusion.

I let my gaze sweep over the flat, unbroken surfaces all around. I can't tell how big the room is. Or even if it is a room.

It encircles me, front and back, above and below. An unbroken sweep of colorless, formless—what?

I squat down to touch the floor under my feet. My hand touches . . . nothing. Yet whatever I'm surrounded by supports my weight. At least I think it does. Maybe I'm actually in a state of suspended animation.

I don't like it.

"Hey, Sammy. Where is everybody?"

My voice bounces and echoes and comes right back at me.

This isn't at all like the first time when I arrived to be instantly guided to my objective.

Which, in hindsight, was a mistake on someone's part, now, wasn't it?

I hunker down to wait.

I *FEEL* THEIR eyes on me.

Someone or something watching. For what? For me to make a break for it?

Christ. I don't know where I am. I don't even know if there's a *break* to make for. As far as I can see, I'm surrounded by a great barren sea of nothingness.

I straighten, stretch, release a deep, impatient breath. The waiting is getting old.

When I glance at my watch, I see it has stopped. Since it's a Rolex and works on the principle of perpetual motion, something in this universe must affect time. At least, time as we know it on earth. Stop it or slow it down.

Interesting.

My right palm begins to itch. I glance down, not wanting to be obvious to prying eyes. Susan's charm glows softly just below the surface of the skin. I wish she could have told me what it does.

I rub both hands against my thighs, the rough denim fabric of my jeans offering a little relief.

A sound. I straighten with a jerk. Look around, though I have no idea where the sound originated or what exactly it was. I strain to listen. The silence is deafening. This is like being in a sensory deprivation chamber.

"Anna Strong?"

At the sound of the voice so close behind me, I swing around, fists clenched, every muscle taut as an arrow in a bow, ready to spring. I square off, actually draw back a fist before I realize who I'm looking at.

"You're Stephen."

He clearly hasn't recognized me yet. He nods, standing his ground, not flinching or cringing away from my offensive reaction to his appearance.

Earns him a few points.

My shoulders drop about six inches. I let my hands fall, my muscles relax, my fists unclench. I blow out a breath and look him over.

He's as handsome as his picture—more so, really, without the stage makeup and carefully coiffed hair. He's tall, over six feet, looks well muscled under a loose-fitting polo shirt and not-so-loose-fitting khakis. He has a strong face, straight nose, wide-set eyes, full mouth. Details I didn't notice last night. His hair is longer than in the picture, too, brushed back, touching the collar of his shirt.

"You look all right. Are you?"

He smiles. It's a good smile.

"If you can call being kidnapped and brought to"—he waves a hand—"wherever the hell this is and told I'm being held until some murderer shows up to face justice, and if he doesn't, my life is forfeit—" He pauses to catch his breath. "Well, if that's what you mean by all right, I guess I am."

He stops, narrows his eyes. "Wait a minute."

It's about time. "Yeah. It's me. Last night in the parking lot."

"*You're* Anna Strong? The one Susan said would come to take me back?"

"One and the same."

"Shit. You cost me a story. A guy named Smith said he had some information for me that would blow the ring off a local drug gang."

"You cost me a payday, so I guess we're even."

"What do you mean?"

"I'm a bounty hunter. Your *source* skipped on a hefty bail."

He pauses, crossing his arms over his chest. "So we were both in that parking lot at the same time, and now we're both here. Huge cosmic coincidence, wouldn't you say?"

"Coincidence? I doubt it." I wave a hand to take in our surroundings. "But right now, don't you think we have bigger problems?"

He still looks chagrined, like a kid who had his favorite toy yanked away. I want to shake him but instead I glom on to something he said. "You talked to Susan? When?"

"Right after I arrived . . . Where are we, anyway? Do you know? Can we get out of here now? If you're here, whoever they've been waiting for must be, too."

No way I can answer that without bursting his optimistic bubble. Besides, I'm more interested in his communication with his sister than answering his questions. My palm is itching again. If he's in contact with her, she can explain how this charm works. "How did you get in touch with her?"

He takes a step closer, lowers his voice. "You'll think this sounds crazy, but we can communicate telepathically sometimes."

I have to choke back a laugh. Sound crazy? Vampires do it all the time. But clearly Stephen doesn't know that. Or he doesn't know I'm a vampire. I think I'll keep that information private. "Can you reach her now?" I ask.

He shakes his head. "I haven't been able to reach her since that first time. She must be frantic. But obviously if you're here, everything has been resolved. They must have caught who they were looking for."

"I wish it were that easy. We can't leave quite yet."

"Why not?" A flash of anger sparks behind those blue-green eyes. "This is beginning to piss me off. I have no clue why I've been drawn into this. I'm not part of the magical world. I have no business being here. You were sent to bring me back. Well, do it."

"I will. But not yet."

"Are you messing with me? I want to leave. Now."

His "me Tarzan" act has him all but beating his chest. Still, I understand his frustration. Whatever Susan communicated with him, she either didn't have time or didn't want to burden him with all the facts.

"There's one problem. I have to do something first, before we can leave."

"Oh Jesus. What is it?"

"I have to defend myself. Defend you, too, really."

"Defend yourself against what?"

"Against those murder charges you mentioned before. I'm the reason you're here."

EIGHT

✦━◆━✦

STEPHEN'S EXPRESSION SHIFTS, SIZING ME UP. There's a little skepticism mingled with a great big blob of uncertainty. He did see me in action last night.

"Who'd you kill?" he asks at last. "And what does it have to do with this place?"

I meet his eyes squarely. "I killed a black-magic witch. I did it here where she'd come to recover from the effects of a spell turned bad. I didn't know this was a place of sanctuary. It wouldn't have made a difference if I had."

"At least you're honest. I still don't understand what it has to do with me, though. Why am I here?"

I don't get a chance to answer. The room shifts under our feet, knocking us off balance. I feel Stephen take a step closer to me and we stand back to back as forms materialize around us. Two spectral desks separated by a podium. A ghostly ring of chairs—thrones, really—suspended above us.

A voice from everywhere and nowhere. "All your questions will be answered," it says. "Let the trial begin."

Stephen's back is pressed against mine. His touch is somehow reassuring. We lean against each other for comfort as well as support as form becomes substance. It's like watching a cartoon where lines are first drawn, then filled in with color to bring realism from the abstract. The wood grain of the desks shimmers and hardens. Two high-back chairs appear behind one, one chair appears behind the other.

"You may sit." That same eerie voice that told Stephen his questions would be answered echoes again from above. When I look up, the ring of thrones still looks to be empty. Yet there's something alive, a sentient consciousness permeates the room.

"Show yourselves," I call out.

"You do not address the tribunal." Samual's voice roars out the command. "You are not worthy. You address only me."

He's materialized next to the second desk, standing ram-rod straight behind it. Now he's dressed in a white robe with a scarlet rope around his neck. A gold filigree charm hangs from the rope.

So much for having no interest in what happens with the tribunal. "You're my prosecutor?"

"Among other things," he replies, smug-voiced and self-assured. He may as well be twirling the ends of a black mustache. "And you will speak only when spoken to—and you will speak only to me."

"Fuck you. I will talk to whomever the hell I please. I am here to defend my life. I have a right to face my accusers."

"I am your accuser."

"No. You are a liar. You said you were a supernatural bounty hunter. A simple messenger."

Samual remains silent. He may be playing a bigger part than he said, and yet instinctively I know where the power lies.

I wave a hand upward. "They are my accusers. They are the power. I demand they face me."

Stephen leans hard into me. "Maybe you should tone it down a little," he whispers.

His words are all but drowned out by Samual's howl of outrage. "How dare you! I could smite you where you stand. Flay the skin from your bones inch by inch. Make you beg for death."

"Enough!"

Stephen whirls around, clapping his hands over his ears. "What the fuck was that?"

If I thought Samual's bellowing was loud, it's a sigh compared to the earsplitting thunderclap that shocks all three of us into stunned silence.

Something stirs above us. Samual spreads his hands, face turned upward. "You see what I mean about these mortals, Elder? They have no respect. No reverence for their betters. It's a travesty to have admitted them into your presence. Let us be done with this. Let me have them."

Silence greets his request. Too much silence. I start to think maybe whoever is up there is actually considering turning us over to him. I glance at Stephen. I could probably put up a pretty good fight against Samual, but what about Stephen?

"Wait," I hear myself saying. "I'm sorry. If I offended you, I apologize. But I thought this was to be a trial. A trial signifies you have some kind of judicial system, which in turn means you have laws. Evidently I broke one of those laws. I think I can justify my actions." I wave a hand toward Stephen. "What can't be justified is holding this man. It's me you want. Send him back."

Stephen shifts beside me, grabs my left hand. "I won't go without you."

"Don't be ridiculous. You can't—"

"How noble," Samual interrupts, baring his teeth. "But he stays."

"Why? He had nothing to do with what happened."

"Maybe. But you took two lives that day. Remember?"

God. Burke's bodyguard. "You can't be serious. He attacked me. I had no choice—"

Samual turns on that thousand-watt angelic smile. "No matter. Two lives were lost. Two lives must be accounted for."

A terrible awareness stirs the hair on the back of my neck. "You had no intention of sending this man back, did you? You *are* a liar."

Before Samual can reply, the rustling voice from above speaks. "If you are found guilty, both your lives are forfeit. It is the law."

Samual looms over us. "And you will be found guilty."

I look at Stephen. "I'm sorry."

He grimaces and says through a tight-lipped smile, "I knew it was too easy. Just don't be found guilty, okay?"

Suddenly the Elder interrupts. "I understand your outrage. Evidently, you were brought here under false pretenses."

Is it my imagination or does Samual cringe a little at that? But I don't have time to gloat. The Elder continues speaking.

"Our laws are based on concepts of justice tempered with mercy. One must be cognizant of all the facts if one is to make a just decision. You will be heard. As to facing your accusers, we have hidden our physical form from you because we are not like you and thought you might be disturbed by the difference. However, if you insist on facing us, as is your right, we will comply with your request."

I'm not sure if I should be relieved or nervous that I've won this first little skirmish. One look at Samual, though, and the uneasiness fades. He's furious. I must be doing something right.

"Please be seated," the disembodied voice says. This time the tone is conversational, polite.

Stephen and I take seats behind the desk nearest us and look up to watch.

The thrones sparkle as if made of diamonds. First they appear empty, then gradually robes of gossamer, shaped like the human body, fill the spaces. Ghostly hands materialize from the sleeves, bare feet from the hems. Just when I begin to wonder what could be "disturbing" about their forms, the apparitions solidify and the differences become apparent.

Where the head should be, faceless skulls peer down at us through eyeless sockets. Jaws open and close continually as if of their own will. No sound emanates except a rasp, like rusted locks on a broken gate.

Explains the wind-in-the-willows sound of the voices we heard.

The seven appear identical, though the throne in the center is a bit larger than the rest and set a little above the others.

Stephen prods me with his elbow, jerking a thumb in Samual's direction. "Think he looks like that, too, without the glamour?"

Samual casts us a poisonous glare, obviously having heard Stephen's remark. His expression changes, though, when he addresses the tribunal. "Shall we proceed, Elder?" he asks. His tone loses its sarcastic bite.

I flinch, thinking of the joy ride that brought me here. Yikes. But as the one in the middle is nodding, his constantly moving jaw snapping closed for an instant at the motion, I put that disgusting thought out of my mind. Better concentrate on the one who seems to be in charge.

Is this Elder Samual shows so much deference to the chief justice in this astral Supreme Court?

Samual takes his place at the podium. He addresses himself to the hovering beings above us, but his eyes are on me.

"If it please your honors," he begins. "We are here to right a terrible wrong. Our universe has always been a place of sanctuary. A place where all otherworldly creatures can come to seek shelter from whatever demons or angels hunt them. The only such place in all the dimensions, established by the ancients and sanctified by succeeding generations because it is important to create balance. Good and evil alike know they can seek refuge here. It is not our duty to judge. It is our duty to protect."

He points a finger at me. "This woman—this vampire—violated that sacred duty. She allowed herself to be transported here with the aid of three ignorant witches, and with malice, struck down a woman recovering from life-threatening wounds. Wounds inflicted by the vampire herself. This violation was compounded when she killed the woman's human bodyguard—an innocent not here of his own volition.

"But we can make things right. Here. Now. Restore faith in this sacred place. The man, a mortal, seated beside the murderess is the brother of one of the offending witches. Find them guilty and both will be punished according to the law. A life for a life."

I feel Stephen's startled reaction to Samual's words. Up until this moment, if he had any doubt his fate was entwined with my own, he does no longer. I touch his arm in an effort to offer consolation.

He's looking at me, eyebrows raised. "You're a vampire?"

That's what got his attention? I raise an eyebrow of my own.

He shakes his head. "Interesting. Well, remember what I said before? Don't be found guilty? Goes double now."

I nod and since Samual has taken his seat and is staring at

me, I assume it's my turn to offer opening arguments. With a final pat on Stephen's arm, I take my place behind the podium.

Okay, time to channel my inner Jack McCoy. I just don't know where to begin. Should I fill in the backstory? Do they already know it? Will they care?

Since who Belinda Burke was has everything to do with what happened, I take the plunge.

"It's true. I killed the black-magic witch Belinda Burke. We had a long history. I met her first when she was raising a demon to do her bidding on Earth. Her offerings to the demon were to have been a young girl and my friend Culebra. I stopped her. But not before the innocent was sacrificed. In retribution, she turned me over to a Mexican drug lord who tried to kill me. I escaped."

Samual rises to his feet. "Is this really necessary?" he asks the tribunal. "Does it matter what brought her here? Do we intend to temper our decision with emotion or look at the facts? And the only fact we need to consider is whether or not she killed someone under our protection. Since she admitted it, what else do we need to know?"

"It's important you understand," I argue. "Your laws are based on justice tempered with mercy. Isn't that what you said? How can you determine what is right if you do not have all the facts?"

There is a rustling from above; faceless forms lean in toward one another as the tribunal confers. No sound reaches us except the continual rasping of the jaws. I tap my foot nervously awaiting their decision. If they refuse to allow me to continue, this will be the shortest trial in history. I look around for an escape route. A stupid thing to do since I have no fucking clue where we are.

Finally, the Elder raises his hand as if signaling the end of the discussion, the others resume their positions, and the grating voice issues his edict. "Speak. Whether or not we will take what you say into consideration at the time of judgment is undecided. But you have the right to proceed."

A subtle but irritated sigh escapes Samual's lips as he sits back down.

I refocus. "I next met Belinda Burke when she set up a

cosmetics firm offering an anti-aging cream that promised miraculous results. The miracle was attributed to a key ingredient—vampire blood. Harvested from young, newly turned vampires bled like slaughtered cattle. When she found out that I was on to her, she cast a spell that once more put my friend Culebra in mortal danger. To save him, I enlisted the help of her sister. We managed to reverse the spell and send the curse back into her. That the curse was powerful was proven by the extent of her injuries. She sought refuge here to recover."

I draw a breath. Now comes the tricky part. "I followed her to this place. When I confronted her, she vowed to come after me, my family, her sister, all who had worked against her. I couldn't let that happen. It was then I did what I knew I had to. I killed her."

NINE

SAMUAL IS ON HIS FEET THE MOMENT MY voice runs down.

"You admit it. You killed both Belinda Burke and her bodyguard."

"I had to."

"But there's more, isn't there?" he asks. "How did you determine how to find Belinda Burke?"

I turn to face him. "Her sister told me."

"What else did her sister tell you?"

"Not that this place offered sanctuary, if that's what you're asking. I knew nothing of that."

"But she did tell you that her sister's wounds were serious, didn't she?"

"Yes."

"In fact, didn't she tell you her sister was no threat to you? That it would be months, maybe years, before she would be well enough to return to your dimension?" He raises his face to the Elder. "Belinda Burke spoke to me when she first arrived. Warned me to be on the lookout for a vampire out for revenge—a vampire who was in league with her own sister."

I'm tempted to ask why he didn't take her warning seriously. The only reason I don't is my reluctance to focus any more attention on the witches who got me here the first time. I have a feeling Samual will want to pursue that after he rids himself of me—or tries to.

Instead, I look to see how this is affecting Stephen. He face reflects a little surprise, a little confusion. He's been hit with a lot. The fact I'm a vampire, the fact I killed a grievously wounded witch. I can only hope he knows the damage a black-magic witch can inflict and why I felt I had to do it.

But Samual isn't through with me yet. My skin crawls at the smug look on his face. How could he know that Sophie had told me how serious Burke's injuries were? Does he also know that she had begged me not to go after her sister?

Samual barks out the question again. "Did she or did she not tell you it would be months, maybe years, before Burke would be strong enough to be a threat to you or anyone?"

"Yes. She told me."

"And you came after her anyway. Why? Because you knew in her weakened state she would be an easy target? Do you always prey on the weak, Anna Strong? Oh. Wait. You are a vampire. Of course you do."

Anger ignites in my blood like flame in dry tinder. "I protect the weak. On Earth, I am called the Chosen One. If you have any knowledge at all of what that means, you know I've made it my mission to defend the mortal world from evil."

"So this was an anomaly? Just this once you plunged a blade into a defenseless old woman's chest and held it there until the last beat of her heart?"

I swallow down a quick, heated retort, knowing what I say next may make the difference in the outcome of this "trial." When my blood has cooled a little, I reply.

"Belinda Burke was capable of unimaginable evil. She killed indiscriminately. Even her sister feared her power. I knew when she recovered she would wreak her vengeance on all who crossed her. I have a family to protect and friends. She had already proven she could get to anyone close to me. I couldn't take the chance she'd slip back without my knowing. I couldn't risk losing anyone I loved."

I pause, sucking in a breath. "When I first arrived at this

place, I battled her bodyguard. You know I have no vampiric powers here. I fought him mortal to mortal and won. Even then, Burke showed no remorse. Neither did she ask for mercy. Instead, she vowed to come after me and all I knew, including her sister, and to kill every one of us. She used the fact that she was bedridden to taunt me. She believed I wouldn't harm her because *I* was weak and incapable of doing what I needed to. She was wrong."

I press fingers against my eyes. "I took no joy in killing her. But there was a greater good to consider. There is always a greater good. I think you may have forgotten that. Some creatures do not deserve sanctuary."

Samual is on his feet again, outraged. "And you are the one to make that determination? You, who have been on Earth a mere thirty years? What do you know of good and evil? Are the lines so clearly drawn in your world?"

"Of course not." I drop my hands and face him. "My existence is an example of how blurred the lines can get. I am vampire. I should be a predator, existing merely to feed on the mortals beneath me. And yet, I have been given the gift of choice. I choose to live as a mortal. To be a friend. But I see evil everyday. I battle it as I can. I have a duty to perform and I take it seriously."

"As do we," the Elder interrupts, motioning with a robed hand. "We will adjourn for the present. There is much we need to consider before proceeding. We will summon you when we are ready to reconvene. The prisoners may take their rest."

And so fast it roils my stomach, Stephen and I find ourselves in a space that looks like the dining room in a well-appointed hotel suite. There is a table set with a meal that has to be for Stephen and a wineglass filled with what looks suspiciously like blood.

Stephen picks up the wineglass gingerly and hands it to me. "This has got to be yours," he says dryly.

TEN

STEPHEN AND I TAKE SEATS AT THE TABLE. IT'S
set with china and silver and a bowl of flowers as a centerpiece.

Nice touch, that. Very civilized.

I watch Stephen dig into his meal—steak, a baked potato,
a green salad. He eats with gusto. "Glad to see our little predicament hasn't affected your appetite."

He grins. "Isn't a condemned man always given a last
meal?" He motions to the wineglass, sitting untouched on the
table. "What about you? Aren't you hungry?"

I nudge it away. "No. I ate before I left." A lie. But the idea
of downing a glass of blood in front of him makes me uneasy.
It can't be a pleasant sight for the uninitiated. And who knows
what kind of blood is in that glass? Or where it came from.

Stephen pauses, his knife and fork suspended. "What do
you think they're *considering* up there?"

Besides whether we live or die? I shrug. "Maybe they're
checking my story."

Stephen continues to chew, cutting the steak into bite-sized
pieces with a butter knife. Must be tender. Even after a year,
the sight of real food can kick-start my salivary glands. The

temptation to reach over and grab a piece of that steak is strong but while I have no vampiric powers on this plain, I *feel* no different. I can't trust my physiology is changed. Something the Elders must know or they wouldn't have left the blood.

To distract myself, I stand up and take a walk around the room. Is this real? Or something fabricated from the human collective memory? Unlike the room I found myself in when I first arrived with Samual, the floors and walls in this one are solid, the furniture physically exists. I run a finger along the back of a chair.

When I turn around, Stephen is watching. "What are you thinking?" he asks.

"I'm wondering how they conjured this up. If any of it is real."

"You think it may be a figment of our imaginations?" He takes another bite. "Who cares? The steak is delicious."

I return to my place at the table. "You're taking this very well."

"Is that a problem? Should I be curled up in a corner bemoaning my fate? I'm a realist, Anna. I was in Manhattan on 9/11. I've been a war correspondent in Afghanistan, spent time with the troops in Iraq. I'm a survivor. I have a feeling you are, too." He scoops a forkful of potato. "Besides, who knows when we'll eat again."

He turns his attention back to his meal while I watch him. I've only known this man for what—I can't even tell since time has all but stopped for us. I like him. He's strong and brave. Self-sufficient. Practical. Maybe when we get back home . . .

"What's it like being a vampire?"

This time it's my pleasant little fantasy that gets popped like a pricked balloon. We're both mortals here, but once we get home . . . I shake my head. "Like being anything else— good days and bad."

"That can't be true," he argues. "You said you were 'the Chosen One.' What does that mean?"

I close my eyes for the length of a heartbeat. It's hard enough to explain it to other supernaturals, how can I make a mortal understand? When I open my eyes again, Stephen is studying my reaction.

"You think I won't understand, don't you? Try me."

"It's not an easy story to tell."

"The best ones never are. Give it a shot."

I rest my elbows on the table, eyes downcast. Who knows what lies ahead for us? For this moment and in this place, we are merely two humans. I have no more power than he does over our fate. I look up at him. His expression is quiet, contemplative. His interest seems genuine enough. "Okay. Where would you like me to start?"

I expect him to say with my turning, but he surprises me. "Tell me about yourself. Before you became vampire. Has it been a long time?"

"No. I've only been a vampire for a year. And yes. It's been a lifetime."

He smiles at me again, waving his knife. "See? I knew it would be a good story."

I can't help but return the smile. "You sure you want to spend what may be your last moments hearing the story of my life?"

The smile becomes a grin, eyes twinkling. He places his knife and fork down on his plate and takes my hand. "You have a better idea?"

Wow. He works faster than I do. His expression makes my blood quicken.

"Maybe. But I'd rather save that until you hear the story. You may not feel the same way after."

"Okay." He takes up the utensils and resumes eating. "You have my full attention. Tell me your story, Anna Strong."

ELEVEN

I FEEL STEPHEN'S EYES ON ME AS I COLLECT myself to begin. I'm wondering if I should back off, laugh the offer away as a joke. I've never done this before—spill my guts to a complete stranger. Is it because he's a reporter? Does he work some kind of mojo to get subjects to open up? To *want* to open up?

Or is it because if something happens to me and he survives, there will be someone who can bear witness to my existence?

God. This place is making me sappy.

Stephen reaches out, touching my hand. "Tell me."

His hand is warm. His interest seems genuine enough. What do I have to lose?

I tell the story simply, unfold it in the order that makes the most sense. Start at the beginning.

Typical childhood. Raised in a loving family—two parents, both working professionals, an older brother. I was a tomboy, preferring my brother's friends and their games of flag football and basketball to more girly pursuits.

Stephen smiles at that.

"What?"

"I can see it. You racing across a field with a football tucked under your arm or on the court in a game of horse. I bet you won more than you lost, too."

"Damn straight."

But I feel the smile fade from my face. I know what comes next.

Stephen sees it, too. He says, "Go on," in a quiet voice.

"Everything changed when I was seventeen. My brother was killed in a hit-and-run accident."

Stephen pushes his plate aside and leans toward me. "I'm sorry about your brother."

I believe he means it. I acknowledge his words with a nod and go on.

"My parents never fully recovered. I doubt any parent ever does. They became overprotective of me, and because I understood what they were going through, I put aside my own career aspirations, to become a cop, maybe, or a private detective, and chose a safe career—teaching—to please them.

"It was a safe choice, not the right one. It only took a couple of tedious years in a classroom for me to realize it."

"You didn't like teaching?"

"It's not something I'm particularly proud of. Teaching is not a career for one who has no interest in her students. When I realized I was probably doing them more harm than good, I took a hard look at my life—and my brother's death. He played it safe and a drunken driver killed him. Something completely out of his control. I thought again about becoming a cop. But when my brother's killer was finally caught and arrested, he spent only a year in prison. I couldn't see myself part of a system that served more to protect the rights of the criminals than secure justice for the victims."

I realize how bitter I sound. "You sure you want me to continue? You probably never expected the rant."

"But I think you're getting to the good part, right? How you became a bounty hunter?"

I nod. "That's when I met David."

"The big guy? He's your partner?"

"Yes. We met in a kickboxing class. He was a former football player and one day, he mentioned what he did. I'd never met a bounty hunter before. I suppose at first I was attracted to the romantic idea—bringing lawbreakers back to face their day in court. I invited him to coffee and peppered him with questions. When he said that business was so good he needed to take on a partner, I pestered him until he agreed to give me a shot. I proved I could handle myself. I loved the action. It was a perfect fit."

"The action. Yeah. I saw you in action last night." There's just the briefest of pauses. "Are you more than business partners?"

"Why would you ask that?"

He looks down and away and then back at me. "Something in your voice when you talk about him."

I can't help it. A snicker escapes my lips. "Does it matter if we are?"

His expression shifts, smoothes. "No. Sorry. It's the nosy reporter side of my personality rearing its ugly head. Ignore me."

Is it? Or do I feel his spark of jealousy? Do I like it?

"David and I are just friends. Good friends, but nothing more. He's a love-'em-and-leave-'em kind of guy."

Stephen shows no reaction to the reply.

"What? You don't believe me?"

Again, no reaction. Then he asks, "Were you a vampire then? Does David know what you are?"

A nice change of subject. "I wasn't, and no, he doesn't know. No human I'm close to does."

Finally a change in his expression, a look that says he gets why I'd keep that secret. Since I know he was raised in a magical household himself, it makes sense. He motions for me to continue.

"David and I are good at what we do. I've never regretted taking that leap—except for one thing. It changed my relationship with my parents. There was nothing I could say to make them understand let alone accept the choice. To them it was foolhardy and irresponsible. I was taking unnecessary risks to satisfy some deluded need for adventure. Worse, I was selfish for disregarding their fears."

I stop, suddenly overcome with the memories of how we fought. The two people who were my only family. The two people I loved most.

This time, Stephen doesn't press for me to go on. He lets me take my time, recompose myself. Are my emotions really this close to the surface or is it this place? I shrug away the sadness, concentrate on what happened next.

"I've distanced myself from them since then," I say.

"Because you know you'll eventually have to disappear when they realize you're not aging?"

His grasp of the situation startles me. "Are you an empath?"

He laughs. "Hardly. I just know a little about vampires. Eternal life has its drawbacks. Watching living relatives grow old and die would be a big one."

My insides grow still. Stephen understands so much. I meet his eyes. Will he understand the rest?

"I was turned against my will. Raped and beaten by a monster who thought he'd killed me. He hadn't. During the fight, I bit him. That was the exchange of blood. When I woke in the hospital, a doctor, a vampire, took me under his wing, explained what had happened. It took time, but eventually I came to accept it, to learn to control the hunger, to make loyal friends."

"But you are not just a vampire, are you? What does it mean to be the Chosen One?"

I expected the question, but it's not an easy one to answer. It took me a year to discover the ramifications of a title I neither sought nor wanted. How do I explain it in one hundred words or less? I guess without bullshit. And quickly.

"My fate is to lead the vampire world, to determine what the relationship between mortals and vampires is to be. I don't know why I'm the one. I don't know how it's determined, and so far no one can tell me who's behind the decision. I just know there is a faction in the vampire world that wants vampires to assume what they see as their rightful place in the world—masters of the human race. For now, I have the power to stop them. That could all change, though, if my leadership is challenged."

"Or if you and I are not freed to return to Earth." Stephen says it softly.

He releases a breath, comes over to stand beside my chair. He kneels down, takes my hands. "I grew up in a household where consorting with supernaturals was the norm. I can't believe how well you've adjusted to life as a vampire when you had no similar background. Before today, I'd never met a vampire, but I knew they existed, which was more than you knew before you were turned. We'll get out of here. After all you've been through, there's no way a bunch of walking skeletons can hold you."

I feel color flood my cheeks. I have to force my words through a throat clogged up with embarrassment. "Did I just make a complete ass of myself?"

He shakes his head, pulls me to my feet. "Are you kidding? Wait until we get home and I tell you the story of my life. You think growing up with normal parents was a challenge? Try being the youngest in a family of witches. I can't tell you the number of times I was turned into a frog."

"You are so full of shit," I say. "But thank you, anyway."

We're standing close—too close. I'm tempted to say the hell with it and wrap my arms around his neck and pull him even closer. His expression says he'd like to do the same thing.

Then I'm struck with a thought. I drop his hand and make myself step back. "Whoa. Stephen. I think Samual may be doing this."

He looks around. "Samual is doing what?"

"This." I waggle a finger between us. "Making us feel like—"

"Samual is making me want to kiss you? How exactly would he be doing that?"

"I think he's an incubus."

"An incubus." His eyebrows ratchet upward. "An incubus? Why would you think that?"

No way I'm going to answer that. At least I don't have to explain what an incubus is to Stephen. "Look at us. We've known each other, what? A few hours? And there's this attraction. It's unnatural."

He smiles. "Unnatural? Why would two people being attracted to each other be unnatural?"

"You have to ask that? Look at where we are."

The voice of reason takes this moment to thump me on the side of my head. Strategy, idiot. You need to talk strategy.

I take another step back. "We need to talk strategy," mimicking the little voice that pulled me back from a delicious opportunity to taste those lips.

Stephen frowns. Now he looks confused. And disappointed. "Strategy?"

"They're going to call us back soon and we need a plan. I can't help feeling we're missing something."

I start to pace, as much to distance myself from Stephen as to jump-start the brain cells. Stephen still stands in the same place, his expression puzzled, his brow furrowed. I think he's trying to process the last few minutes and having trouble sorting it out.

I don't blame him. But I don't know how much time we have before we're pulled back, either.

"Listen, Samual is making what happened between Belinda Burke and me personal. Why would that be? She was an evil bitch. Even if there is some sort of sanctuary agreement, a system that has laws must recognize her threats constituted danger to innocents. Unless they're completely without conscience, that can't be acceptable."

Stephen's eyes focus again, narrow. He's back with me. "You're right. Maybe Samual has more at stake in the outcome of the trial than we know. The trick is finding what it is. Let's start at the beginning. When you got here the first time."

I feel a flush of excitement "No. Let's start before that. How did I manage to slip undetected into what is supposed to be a protected environment? Who fucked up and let the barriers down?"

Stephen and I look at each other and smile.

It had to be.

Samual.

TWELVE

I CAN'T BELIEVE I DIDN'T THINK OF THIS before. Is Samual pursuing me with such vigor because he's the one being held accountable for my breaching sanctuary?

Stephen is standing close again. My body likes it, though I'm still self-conscious. I can't believe I just told him the story of my life.

I can't believe how easy he is to talk to . . . and that he didn't react to my story by shrieking in horror or laughing at the idiocy. I've been tempted to do both myself.

We're standing face-to-face, grinning like idiots. I can tell if I moved just an inch closer, I'd be in his arms.

Damn it.

Get a grip. His presence makes my skin tingle and thinking more difficult than it should be. Is this more of Samual's doing?

"It's too early to be congratulating ourselves." I make myself move away. Again. "I agree Samual is a little too eager to nail me but turning things around on him is not going to be easy."

He follows me. "Might be easier than we think. I'm

assuming you'll get a chance to question him. Why not just ask him how he thinks you were able to get in, get close enough to kill Belinda Burke, and get out without anyone stopping you. See how he reacts."

Stephen may be right. Samual is a slippery bugger, but he's not the power. Those seven ghastly specters are the power. Especially the one Samual calls the Elder. If I can get them to . . .

Shit. One instant Stephen and I are considering our options, the next we're back behind the desk in our astral courtroom. It happens in an eyeblink. If this keeps up, I'm going to ask for Dramamine.

Samual ignores us, no smirk, no snarky remark. He doesn't even look our way. I'm not sure how to take his sudden ambivalence. Is he worried that we may have won a few points with his bosses or confident that his case is so strong it makes no difference?

I don't like it either way. I much prefer the blustering asshole to the enigmatic demon.

The Elder waves a robed arm. "Proceed."

Proceed? That's it? I thought the whole idea of the break was for them to consider the things I said. I didn't expect a resolution, but I was hoping for a hint, some indication that they might have understood why I felt justified killing Belinda Burke.

Samual rises. He spreads his hands, a frown of concern pulling at the corners of his mouth. "Your Honors, I am baffled. We have heard the accused admit to breaking sanctuary, admit to killing not one but two charges under our protection, admit to knowing the victim was powerless to defend herself. What more evidence do you need? I ask that you bring this proceeding to a close. Now. Return the rightful verdict of guilty and let us get this regrettable incident behind us. Make this once more a place of safe refuge for those seeking our protection."

I rise, too. "I have explained what brought me here. Are there no provisions for considering extenuating circumstances in your rule of law? You speak of safe refuge. My family and friends would have had no safe refuge on Earth had Belinda Burke come after them."

Samual scoffs. "You have a human police force. She broke human laws. They could have dealt with her."

"Really? A witch as powerful as Belinda Burke, who could and did change her appearance at will? What human force could deal with that?"

"You have yourself. You could have handled her when she reappeared. You have the resources, to say nothing of your own strength and power. You proved it when you broke the spell that sent her here."

"And would I have been given notice that she had returned? Or would I have found out when the bodies of my loved ones started showing up?"

"What takes place on Earth is of no concern to us."

Stephen must feel the way my body tensed at that because he puts a restraining hand on my arm. He doesn't know me. Screw restraint. And screw these arrogant assholes. I'm trembling with outrage and my voice shatters the silence like a rock through glass.

"Damn you. You speak of manipulating people's lives with no regard for the consequences. You are despots. You are as evil as the witch you allowed refuge."

Samual's eyes flash fire. "Do you hear what she says? She calls us evil. We who seek only peace. She is the one who committed murder. Two murders. Killing with her bare hands. And we are the evil ones."

No reaction from above. Not even the grinding of those gaunt jaws breaks the pall that settles over the room.

I glance at Stephen. His eyes are glued to the figures hovering over us like vultures on a tree branch. For the first time, his expression reflects a shadow of fear. I want to say I'm sorry. Not for what I said, but that it put him in danger. I should have thought of him before I started yelling. Meeting him was the only bright spot in this ridiculous situation. I think we could have been friends under different circumstances.

What the fuck am I thinking?

It sounds like bullshit even to me. How the hell did we get here?

How are we getting out?

Which leads to the question Stephen and I asked a few minutes ago. How did I get in the first time?

The gloom lifts from my thoughts. I have nothing to lose. May as well go on the offensive.

"If I'm to be found guilty in this kangaroo court, I have a question or two of my own."

Samual glances upward, the Elder lifts a finger, Samual nods for me to go ahead.

"You speak of sanctuary. How is it granted?"

"There is protocol."

Samual's eyes are on the thrones, and he answers as if bored.

"Protocol? Like an application that has to be filled out? An admissions office?"

Now he shoots me a venomous look. "You are applying earthly concepts to an otherworldly universe."

"Than explain it. Please."

A sigh. "The supplicant or his advocate appears before the tribunal. The case is heard. A decision made."

"Is anyone ever turned away?"

"Only if it is determined the supplicant's presence here may be a danger to others. There are some creatures who cannot control their primitive urges. Even wounded or near death, they are predators capable of inflicting grievous harm to those around them. We cannot allow such creatures in." He points at me. "Creatures like you. Who kill indiscriminately."

"Indiscriminately? I thought I explained that. But it doesn't matter. So how do you keep such creatures out?"

"There are spells and barriers. Set in place by the ancients."

"And who works the spells? Erects the barriers? Do you have a team of witches? Is there an army of supernatural guards who patrol?"

"That is unnecessary."

"Why?"

"Because no one has ever breached sanctuary."

I raise an eyebrow. "Oh? Have you forgotten why *I'm* here?"

Looks like Samual's composure is beginning to slip. A finger taps restlessly against the desktop. "You are not being charged with how you managed to get in," he snaps. "But with what you did after you got here."

I cast a glance upward. "I would think breaching security

would be equally important. What's to stop someone from doing it again?"

"You." Samual's voice is tight with rage. "It won't happen again because your death will serve as an example to anyone who dares try."

"Ah. So it's not so much what I did but that I was able to do it." I raise my voice to those above. "If that's the case, maybe I'm not the only one who should be on trial."

THIRTEEN

"YOU MAKE AN INTERESTING POINT, ANNA Strong." The voice of the Elder interrupts the cheerful banter between Samual and me—as I hoped it would.

"Samual, just how did this vampire breach security? You have never given us a satisfactory explanation."

Samual's hand twitches on the podium, but he smoothes his contempt for me from his face when he looks upward.

"It was the work of the three witches. They accessed a forbidden power, the domain of the beast, to gain access. In truth, they should be made to pay for this transgression along with Anna Strong. Bringing forth the beast is a threat to all living creatures."

The reaction of the tribunal to his remarks is immediate and disturbing. As one, they recoil, skulls bobbing at one another on bony necks like birds startled by a snake. Invoking this beast must be the most grievous of offenses.

Samual smiles at me. A smile that says, *Get out of that one, bitch.*

I stare at Samual. What the hell is the beast? There was no *beast* when the witches cast their spell.

He's worked the tribunal into an apoplectic state. "Wait a minute." I have to raise my voice again to be heard over the clacking and snapping of bone on bone. "What is the beast?"

The Elder quiets the others with a raised hand. "The beast controls the underworld. He is no longer allowed to rise above the crust of Earth because he is the carrier of plague and death. Invoking the help of the beast is an act forbidden in every quadrant of the universe. The arrival of the beast unleashes terrible evil. All know this and yet somehow you were able to convince the witches who helped you to disregard the consequences. Was pursuing your selfish ends worth such a price?"

"What price?" I shove my chair back out of the way to stride to the front. "There was no beast at the ritual that brought me here. It was a spell wrought with an amulet and chanting by three good witches who are protectors of the world, not destroyers. Samual is lying."

Samual raises his hands, palms up. "And we are to believe this murderer? She speaks now to save her worthless life."

"I speak now to tell the truth. If this beast unleashes such horror, what new catastrophe has been inflicted? As far as I can tell, it's business as usual on Earth. No more war, famine, or plague than before my trip."

This quiets the tribunal. For all I know they have an internal monitoring system and they're scanning the Earth to see if what I've said is true. Let's just hope man hasn't inflicted any more than the typical quota of suffering on his fellow man in the last few days.

The Elder points at Samual. "She is speaking the truth. Earth is a troublesome place, its people always embroiled in conflict. Yet there are no new disturbances of the magnitude that would signify the beast's influence. Therefore, you were either in error or lying. You will want to consider your response carefully."

I glance at Stephen, and when our eyes meet he smiles.

Got him, he mouths.

Samual is drawing himself up, eyes hard, mouth pinched tight. "We should discuss this among ourselves," he says. "If I was in error of the way the breach took place, I promise you I will investigate until I root out the problem. I must reiterate, though, that *how* she got here is not what you're here to consider. It is her actions *after* that you are bound by law to judge."

"We are well aware of our duty."

The Elder's voice is even more grating than usual, as if he's forcing the words through those yellow rotted teeth. I'd say he's displeased. Which pleases me. I shoot Samual a look.

I'm not the only one in trouble.

Samual addresses the Elder. "I ask for a recess. To find out how such an error could have been made. My resources were obviously guessing when they put forth their theory that the beast had been invoked. I will get to the bottom of this, I vow."

"We are confident that you will."

Smooth. Oily. Even I hear the threat behind the words.

FOURTEEN

FOR THE FIRST TIME, I FEEL LIKE SMILING.
Really smiling. Samual's expression is downright anxious.
Does my heart good.

Stephen and I are transported back to our holding cell
without warning or explanation. Not that either is needed. It's
obvious the tribunal has had its focus shifted from me to
Samual. It may be a temporary shift, but I'll take it.

Stephen is grinning and shaking his head. "I was worried
there for a minute. You don't always think before speaking, do
you?"

"You mean when I called the judges evil?"

"Not the best choice of words. Those things take themselves seriously."

"So do I. But I don't intend to let them walk all over me.
They are arrogant bastards. I wonder if they've ever been
challenged before?"

The dining room has been replaced with a sitting room—
couch, chairs, coffee table. On the coffee table a fan of magazines invites perusing. I pick up the top one, the newest *People*
magazine.

"Well, at least they're current." I toss it back on the pile.

"How long do you think we'll have to wait?" Stephen asks.

I plop myself down on the couch. "I have no idea. May as well make ourselves comfortable."

He takes a chair across from me. I hope the flush of disappointment that he chose to sit there instead of beside me doesn't show on my face.

Jesus. There it is again. What is happening to me?

I clear my throat. "So. I told you my story. Want to tell me yours?"

Stephen waves a hand. "Not after hearing your story. Mine is downright dull."

"Manhattan on 9/11? War correspondent? I hardly call those things dull."

"Anna, I won't say the things I've experienced haven't impacted me. But I'm still basically the same man I was before I became a reporter. You, on the other hand, had your entire reality altered. I'm amazed at your courage."

"Courage? If you mean the courage to continue living, what choice do I have? I don't want to die any more than the next person does."

"It's not just choosing to live—it's choosing to live the way you do. With regard for the mortal world. On Earth, you could be the way these creatures are here—all-powerful."

"And we see how that's worked out for them, haven't we?" I blow out a breath. "I've also seen what power does to vampires who feel they're above the mortals they depend on for sustenance. The old ones forget what it's like to be human. They see humans as merely a food source. They forget that it's mortals who create and that we vampires merely consume. Destroy the human spirit and the world they love would fall into ruin."

Stephen's expression is so intent it makes me roll my eyes. "Shit. I really sound like a pretentious idiot, don't I? The vampire philosopher. I can't believe you're not laughing your ass off."

Stephen's expression darkens. "Don't do that. Don't hide your feelings behind sarcasm. You spoke from your heart. That's never wrong—or easy. I'm glad you feel you can open up with me."

Open up? I wish these couch cushions would open up and swallow me. Being stripped of my vampiric powers must be affecting my brain. Subjecting me to human emotions I've kept buried the last year. Why is he so damned easy to talk to?

Am I that hungry for human contact? The part of my brain still working sounds the alarm. Relationships with mortals have not worked out so well for me in the past.

Stephen's eyes bore into me like a laser. Not very subtle. He's trying to assess what he sees on my face and hears in my voice. I don't think he's buying my theory that Samual may be behind how we're feeling.

I'd better set him straight. "Stephen, I—"

It happens again. Stephen and I are back in "court." I never get the chance to tell him that even if Samual isn't manipulating us, it's hopeless to think we might have a future.

No matter how I might want it.

FIFTEEN

◆━━◆◆◆━━◆

SAMUAL DOESN'T LOOK TOO GOOD. HIS FACE
is drawn, his shoulders slumped. Whatever happened during
that recess, it doesn't appear to have been to his advantage or
liking.

As much as I'm tempted to gloat, I know I'd better reserve
that reaction until I hear what *my* fate is to be. However it turns
out, I'm going to make sure Stephen gets out of here safely.

Even if I have to take out Samual and one of those bone
bags to do it.

The Elder rises, he appears to float in space, but there's
nothing ethereal in his expression. Even without facial features, his dark anger comes through. He points a finger at
Samual.

"Our servant has betrayed us. He has been dealt with." The
finger sweeps in my direction. "You will be returned to Earth,
vampire. Along with the man. Do not suppose you have won a
victory here. If the circumstances of your actions had been
different, you would have suffered the consequences. As it is,
if your presence is detected here again, you will be executed
without benefit of trial."

And he is gone. Along with his skeletal sidekicks. Vanished into air without so much as a clatter of bone to mark their departure.

Stephen and I look at each other. And wait. Will we be transported back the way we've been moved from one place to the other? Should I ask Scotty to beam us up?

Suddenly we both become aware of another presence. Samual is still here, too. The look he skewers us with is no longer the cowed, unsettled expression he wore for the tribunal, but is instead malevolent and calculating. "Well, shall we get on with it?" he asks smugly.

"You've got to be kidding. You aren't the one who's supposed to take us back. You can't be."

He raises his eyebrows in mock surprise. "Why not? It seems my punishment is banishment. To Earth. And if along the way, we should have an accident, if one or both of you should slip from my grasp, what can anyone do about it?"

He looks downright giddy. "I should have thought of it sooner. When I brought you meat puppets up here. I could have snatched you both in that night in the parking lot. Disposed of you along the way."

Ah. That sound—the laugh. "You were there."

"That I was. Too bad I was having such a good time watching the human dump the big bad vampire on her ass. I lost track of my purpose. Well, that won't happen again."

"Looks like nothing worked out the way you planned it, did it? Did you suppose it would be easy? That I'd cower, beg for my life? You underestimated me."

He shrugs. "No matter. I can make you two disappear and no one will be the wiser. My sentence is indefinite. By the time I'm allowed back, this entire incident will have been forgotten. And while I'm on Earth, who knows what mischief I can get into? I needed a break. I should really thank you for the opportunity."

I stare at him. He has to be stopped. Should I call out for the Elders? Tell them of Samual's plan? Would they care? Judging from the cavalier way they had been willing to throw Earth to the wolves with Belinda Burke, I doubt it.

Stephen is beside me. "What should we do?"

I don't know. If I attack Samual, what would happen? Would

the Elders take that as an attack on them all? And even if I beat Samual and it went unnoticed, how would we get out of here? I can't risk Stephen's life.

My brain is buzzing, my palm itching again. I glance down at it. The skin is flushed. I turn to Stephen. "When you communicated with Susan, did she say anything more than I would be coming for you?"

He shakes his head. "Just to stay close to you. That you would bring me back."

It couldn't be that easy. Could it? "Take my hand."

He raises his eyebrows. "You want to hold hands now?"

I grab his left hand in my right. "Don't let go."

At the touch of his palm, the charm embedded in my hand begins to grow hot. He feels it and his first instinct is to pull away. I don't let him. The charm is working its way back through my flesh and materializes between our hands. "Hold on," I whisper.

Stephen's grip tightens. He's beginning to understand. "Susan?"

But understanding blooms in Samual's mind, too. "What are you doing?" He takes a lunge toward us.

The charm is hot and wet between us. Its purpose is clear now. Susan implanted a way to bring us back. Together.

There is a dizzying cyclone of air and we're swept up. I glance down to see Samual, his hands clutching at air.

The last thing we hear is Samual's howl of rage.

SIXTEEN

STEPHEN'S HAND GRIPS MINE LIKE A VISE.
Then his free arm finds its away around my waist, pulling me
closer. Wind whips at us, forcing us to keep our heads bowed,
our backs bent. We're clinging to each other with the desperation I imagine passengers on a plummeting aircraft must feel—
helpless on a headlong plunge to Earth.

I only hope Susan is ready on the other end with a safety net.

It's over in a matter of moments—moments that last an
eternity. Stephen and I are tossed around but land on our feet,
winded and confused.

I look around, Stephen's hand still clutching mine.

At first I don't recognize the barren landscape. Sand and
scrub cactus. There's a bright full moon that flings shadows
like clawed hands out to touch us. We're in the desert?

But there's a sound in the distance—like the rumble of the
ocean. I cock my head to listen—my powers are back. To the
ears of the predator, the vampire, the rumble of the ocean
becomes the hum of freeway traffic.

"Balboa Park," I announce to a startled and skeptical Stephen. "We're in the cactus garden."

"Are you sure? I didn't even know this existed."

"Behind the rose garden."

Stephen glances at his watch, which makes me glance at mine. The hands are spinning like the spokes of a wheel. When they stop, it's 11:55 P.M. The date has not changed.

I've been gone less than twelve hours.

"Can you communicate with Susan now?" I ask Stephen. "Tell her we landed."

He nods and closes his eyes. After a moment, a slow, sweet smile touches his lips. When he opens his eyes again, the smile becomes a grin. "She'll be waiting for us. By the fountain."

Our fingers are still entwined. I don't feel the charm anymore and when I start to draw my hand away to look, Stephen's grip tightens. "Don't," he says.

A simple request. Why not go along with it? The cynical side of my nature knows full well I should let go. The adventure is over. We're back on Earth, and for all I know Stephen has a wife and kids somewhere. Then there's Samual.

"Stephen. We have to get out of here. Samual may be right behind us."

"He's not here now, though, is he?"

There's something in his eyes. He startles me by bending close to brush his lips against mine. I can't help myself. I lean into him. The feather touch becomes a kiss.

A good kiss. The kind of kiss that could lead to—

"Well, isn't this something."

Samual's voice rumbles in the still night air like thunder heralding the threat of a storm.

Stephen and I jump apart. I whirl around. Samual is dressed the way he was when he first appeared—jeans and a T-shirt. Two things are different. He no longer hides his true nature. The dark anger spots his complexion, hardens the lines around his eyes and mouth. His hatred is palpable. His desire obvious.

And the second—a dagger he carries in a leather sling at his waist. He fondles it when he catches my gaze.

He's here for revenge.

"Did you think you could get away from me so easily? Was that another parlor trick courtesy of those meddlesome witches? You can be sure I plan to pay them a visit, too. When I'm through with you."

He's actually rubbing his hands together. "Finding you two in an embrace was an unexpected pleasure. Obviously, in the time you spent together, a bond was forged. It will make killing you all the more delicious." Then he peers at me. And at Stephen. "What? You think I'm working some kind of glamour on you? Stupid humans. You need no glamour to give in to lustful urges. I should have waited a moment longer. Probably could have caught you rutting like the animals you are. Killed you both in the act."

He stops, tilts his head. I can see in his eyes what he's considering.

"You'd better go after me first," I say. "Because unless you kill me, you'll never get a chance to hurt anyone else."

I move in front of Stephen, shielding him.

Stephen nudges me out of the way, to stand beside me.

His eyes are hard. "We're in this together. He's threatening my sister, too."

Nice sentiment. But when the attack comes, the vampire inside of me will do the fighting. She'll have to. I don't know what powers Samual has on Earth, but I know what powers she possesses. And she's here. At the surface, raging to be set loose. I feel her spring forth.

Samual shifts, draws the dagger from its sheath. He stands feet wide apart, eyes bright as he studies me.

A glance at Stephen. "Stay behind me."

He opens his mouth to protest, but when he looks at me, he's not looking at Anna.

He's looking at the vampire.

My heart turns leaden in my chest as his eyes widen. Even expecting it, the reaction hurts.

No matter. I snap my attention back to Samual. He doesn't look startled or surprised. Why should he? He knew what I was.

The vampire springs with a snarl. Samual leaps to meet me. We fall in a tangle of teeth and fists.

Samual is strong. His instinct is that of most predators: Go for the throat. He clasps his hands around mine and squeezes.

But I have instincts, too. Samual is a man, after all. And I suspect an incubus. I bring a knee up and deliver a kick to the groin that forces Samual back with a groan and a sharp intake of air. He stumbles, howling.

Stephen rushes in before I can stop him. He pushes Samual, sending him sprawling on the ground.

But Samual is on his feet faster than Stephen's human reflexes can register the movement.

I see the flash of the blade before Stephen. I fling him away just before the blade finds it mark. It slices into me instead. A white-hot eruption of blinding pain scorches flesh and scrapes bone just below my shoulder. I twist away as my arm goes numb, the blade still lodged deep.

The numbness lasts no more than an instant.

I shake off the pain. Flex my fingers to bring back feeling.

Samual's eyes narrow. Does he finally realize I may not be so easy to kill?

"Vampire, remember?" I hear my voice rumble from a dark place, taunting him. "You can't kill me with a knife. Shall I see if I can kill you with one?"

I reach up and pull the blade from my shoulder. It's warm and wet with my blood. I fight the urge to lick it clean. Instead, I steady it on my palm. The heft is just right, the blade and handle a perfect counterbalance.

Samual steps back and away, circling. He's moving toward Stephen. Does he think I will allow him to use the mortal as a shield?

Before he takes another step, I am on him. Faster than a rattlesnake strike, I have him on the ground, arms pinned to his sides with my thighs. The knife is between my teeth, then in my hand. His legs flail as he tries to buck me off. My eyes are on his throat. What does his blood taste of? Is it sweet or bitter?

I could throw away the knife. Tear out his throat.

I see Stephen from the corner of my eye. He's coming closer, his face reflects shock. If I feed from Samual, will that shock turn to disgust?

Do I care?

The vampire is hungry. Samual is gaining strength beneath

me. He's reading my hesitation as weakness. He prepares to do battle once more.

"Burke was right," he hisses in my ear. "Your human frailties will be your downfall. After I kill you, I kill the man, then the witches."

Stephen hears. "No." He meets my eyes, reads the question, turns unflinchingly toward Samual. "We kill him together."

I glance at the human. His expression is no longer shocked. It's determined. He's at my side. Reaches to take the knife from my hand and nods.

I let him take it.

Samual stares in confusion. "No. You can't."

Stephen strikes the first blow. He plunges the knife into Samual's chest. No hesitation. No faltering. A mortal blow. He pulls it out and steps back.

The blood spreads like a stain. I look up at Stephen. He dips his head. "Feed," he says.

Teeth tear at the throat. Find the jugular. Drink.

And I have my answer.

Demon or no, Samual's blood is sweet.

SEVENTEEN

———•◆•———

SAMUAL'S HEARTBEAT FLUTTERS AND STILLS under my palm. I continue to drink until the taste of salt replaces the sweetness of blood.

I don't know what to expect. Will he shrivel like a drained vampire? Or will his body remain intact? Is he really dead?

I sit back, the flush of feeding spreading warmth through my body, and wait.

Stephen is standing away.

I don't blame him. I could tell him that it's safe. That the vampire is satisfied and the human Anna once more in control.

Would he believe me? It won't be easy to forget what he's witnessed.

And yet he struck the first blow.

I steal a glance at him. His eyes are on Samual's corpse, too.

He's waiting as well. In a moment of clarity I realize why Samual didn't take us both when he had the chance in that parking lot. Human weapons are effective against him on our plain and Stephen had a gun.

As to the both of us being in the parking lot at the same time? I guess there are cosmic coincidences, after all. Samual may have been as surprised to see us as Stephen and I are at the way things worked out.

After a moment, I push myself to my feet.

"Do you think he's really dead?" Stephen asks when I join him.

He isn't moving away from me. A good sign. "I don't know. He's not like any creature—"

The sky above us grows darker, a bank of clouds billowing up to obscure stars and moon.

"I think we're going to get our answer." I turn to Stephen. "If they try to pull us back, run. Find Susan. She'll protect you."

He answers by grabbing my hand. "We'll both run or I'm staying. I won't leave you."

Stubborn. A trait I recognize. No chance to answer.

Samual's body is rising.

A familiar voice. The Elder. "It is done. The trial by combat complete."

Trial by combat?

Anger sparks when I realize what he's saying. I raise my voice to the heavens. "You son of a bitch. You planned for this to happen?"

"A resolution had to be reached. Both you and Samual committed transgressions that could not go unpunished. Samual shirked his sworn duty and you violated sanctuary."

"What if I had lost? You would have allowed this creature to walk the Earth unchecked?"

"He didn't win. It is done."

The body disappears into a turbulent bank of black clouds. The clouds disperse like smoke in the wind, leaving only wisps to mark their passing.

I watch the clouds dissipate, the bright moon once more claiming its spot in the sky.

A feeling of restlessness, of a task not yet completed, dims the satisfaction of whatever victory Stephen and I won here tonight. We sent one monster to his death. How many others have come back to Earth to wreak havoc from that place of "sanctuary"?

Stephen's grip tightens, drawing me back. His eyes are on the sky, too. "Damn," he says. "This is the best story I'll never get to write."

He doesn't fully understand. No reason why he should. He hasn't seen the things I have. He doesn't carry the burden that I do.

I look into his face and a tremor passes through my body. Why do I feel this is a story whose final act is yet to come?

EIGHTEEN

◆━◆◆◆━◆

SUSAN IS WAITING FOR US AT THE FOUNTAIN. If she's surprised to see her brother and me appear hand in hand, she doesn't show it. She rushes up and only then does Stephen drop my hand to embrace his sister.

"Are you all right?" she asks.

Stephen nods. "Thanks to Anna."

Susan touches a stain on his shirt. "You're sure you're not hurt?"

"It's not my blood," he answers. "Anna and I had quite an adventure."

I drag my eyes off Stephen long enough to smile my thanks at Susan. "That was a nice piece of magic, that charm."

"I wish I could have told you how it worked," she says. "I intended to, but Samual showed up too soon." She casts an uneasy glance around. "Is it over? Will he come back?"

"No. He's gone." Stephen's tone is grim and final.

Samual is gone. But—

Susan releases a breath. "Thank you, Anna. For bringing my brother back. I—we—owe you."

Do they? Stephen's warmth as he stands close makes me think I may be the one who owes a debt.

That is if what we seem to be feeling—Stephen and I—is more than a simple reaction to having survived a harrowing experience. Or the result of Samual's influence. I still can't shake the idea that watching Stephen and I dance around each other, feeling the attraction, fighting it, would have been his idea of a joke.

Still, when Stephen reaches again for my hand, I let him take it.

It may be the last time. When the adrenaline rush subsides, things may change. My skin feels human now, the result of feeding, but soon it will not. It will become cold. Only feeding and sex warm a vampire's blood. And then only temporarily.

Stephen doesn't let go of my hand as we walk back into the park. He gives Susan a brief recap of what happened both with the tribunal and back on Earth. It's a good summary, told in the style of a three-minute sound bite. A reporter to the core.

When we reach headquarters, Susan asks if we want to come inside. Ariela and Min are anxious to hear details.

Stephen shakes his head. "You fill them in. I'd like to go home."

She opens her purse. "You can take my car. Ariela can give me a lift."

"I can give him a ride," I hear myself blurting. Then, holding my breath to await his reaction, I add, "My car is in the parking lot."

My heart is thudding against my ribs. What if he says no?

And yet his grip on my hand remains firm and he's smiling. "I was hoping you'd offer," he says.

He scoops Susan into a hug. "See you tomorrow?"

Susan says yes. She looks happy when she leaves us on the sidewalk to disappear from sight through the magical doorway.

"My car is just at the end of the Prado," I say.

We're both quiet as we make our way down the shadow-strewn walkway toward the parking lot. Once, I glance at Stephen and he is grinning.

"What's that all about?" I ask.

"Susan says we make a nice-looking couple," he says.

I smile, too. "This psychic thing. Is the connection always open between you two?"

"Most of the time. Why?"

I pull him to a stop. If I don't do this now, the opportunity may never come again. "Can she tell when you're, um, *not* open to chat?"

He pulls me close. "You mean when I'm otherwise engaged?"

"Yes."

I stand on tiptoe, the better to reach his lips with my own. "You know this is crazy, don't you?"

His mouth is so close I feel the softness of his lips against mine. "Crazier than what just happened to us?"

"But you know what I am. You saw what I can do."

"And I'm still here. And Samual isn't, by the way. Doesn't that tell you something?"

Yes. Maybe. Oh hell. I let my reservations slip away. This time when he kisses me, I kiss him back.

This time when he kisses me, I let my passion match his own.

And this time when he kisses me, there are no interruptions. I lose myself in the kiss, blood races, skin becomes hot. Every cell in my body wants to throw Stephen down right here in the parking lot and satisfy what the kiss stirs up. It's been too long since I've had sex. Too long since I've experienced *wanting*. I feel like I'm about to explode with desire.

A sound from behind us. Another couple approaching from the Prado. It snaps me back to reality. I give Stephen a gentle push. "Let's go to my house. It's not far from here."

"It better not be." His voice is hoarse. I feel his heart thudding against my palm.

I grab his hand. "Come on."

NINETEEN

——◆◆◆——

ONCE INSIDE, WE DON'T MAKE IT TO THE bedroom. As soon as the front door closes behind us, we're in each other's arms.

Stephen's desire matches my own. He pushes me back onto the couch. His hands pull at my blouse, yank it free. I'm ripping at his shirt, too, tugging it over his head, hearing a rip of material as it comes free. Then I'm fumbling with his zipper as he fumbles with mine. After an interminable amount of time, we're finally free of our clothes.

No foreplay. No whispered terms of endearment. We don't need it. I'm so wet I want him inside me now. He's hard and ready, too, more than ready. He leans over me.

Then pulls back abruptly.

"Anna," he whispers, his voice hoarse. "I don't have a—"

If I weren't so aroused, I'd laugh. Instead I rasp, "Condom? Vampire, remember?" And raise my hips to meet him.

When he enters me, the same moan escapes both our lips. A moan of relief, of joy. He grinds into me, filling me, driving me. I respond with equal intensity, wrapping my legs around his hips to bring him closer, deeper. I don't know this man, know nothing about him. Yet at this moment, I know everything I need to know. And more important, he knows me. What I am. What I'm capable of.

He didn't flinch and he didn't turn away.

I hear Stephen's breath catch, feel the force of his thrusts intensify as he nears climax. He groans. "I don't think I can—"

I place a finger over his lips. "Don't hold back."

I'm not there yet, but it doesn't matter. I coax him on with the rhythm of my own body. Maybe being more interested in his pleasure than my own frees me to notice things I've never noticed before during sex. The way his muscles bunch and release, the touch of his hands holding me, the way his body presses urgently against mine. Sensations I've experienced only through the prism of my own needs.

His very smell is an aphrodisiac. Testosterone and aftershave. Shampoo and deodorant.

Suddenly he tenses and cries out.

I bury my head in his shoulder and hold him until the last tremor of release passes.

It's a shock to me. That a man's pleasure can be more satisfying to me than an orgasm.

Who would have thought?

I LIE STILL and unmoving under Stephen. His hands are tangled in my hair, his body rigid, his breath unsteady. It's as if he's reluctant to relax, to look at me.

"Stephen? Is something wrong?"

He raises himself on his elbows, traces my lips with his fingers. His expression is somber, concerned. "You didn't . . . It wasn't . . ." He takes a breath. "Can vampires . . . ?"

I realize what he's asking. And it makes me smile. "Can we orgasm? Yes."

"Did I do something wrong?"

"You did everything right. You were wonderful."

"Because if you need to—I don't know—bite me when we're having sex, it's all right. I trust you."

I think that's the nicest thing a human male has ever said to me. A male who wasn't a blood host and thought sex should automatically be part of the package. "It's not necessary, but I appreciate the offer."

He moves off me and gathers me close. He still seems troubled. I roll toward him and rest my head on his shoulder. "Tonight was a new experience for me. Thinking more of your pleasure than my own. I liked it."

He sighs. "I don't believe that. You're not a selfish person."

"It's nice you feel that way. I hope you always do."

He hikes himself up on one elbow, scooping me up with him. "I want you to tell me what pleasures you. The next time we make love, I want it to be the best sex you've ever had."

He doesn't understand. Hell, I don't understand. If I tell him what I'm thinking, that *this* was the best sex I've ever had, he won't believe it.

So I just smile and reach my hand around his neck and pull his head closer. "Kiss me."

I don't have to say it twice.

FROM *NEW YORK TIMES* BESTSELLING AUTHOR

Ilona Andrews

MAGIC SLAYS

➤ A KATE DANIELS NOVEL ➤

Kate Daniels may have quit the Order of Knights of
Merciful Aid, but she's still knee-deep in paranormal
problems. Or she would be if she could get someone
to hire her. Starting her own business has been more
challenging than she thought it would be—now that
the Order is disparaging her good name. Plus, many
potential clients are afraid of getting on the bad side
of the Beast Lord, who just happens to be Kate's mate.

So when Atlanta's premier Master of the Dead calls
to ask for help with a vampire on the loose, Kate leaps
at the chance of some paying work. But it turns out
that this is not an isolated incident, and Kate needs to
get to the bottom of it—fast, or the city and everyone
dear to her may pay the ultimate price.

AVAILABLE FROM ACE
penguin.com

M828T0111

ALLYSON JAMES

SHADOW WALKER

Racing her motorcycle down a lonely winter highway, Stormwalker Janet Begay feels the ground collapse beneath her. After tumbling two hundred feet into an underground cavern, she manages to escape with help from her sexy dragon-shifter boyfriend, Mick—but not before they disturb some dark forces.

As Janet contends with a hotel inspector intent on putting her out of business, as well as her grandmother, who's taken up residence, Mick's behavior becomes strange and erratic, until he is a clear danger to Janet and her friends. Janet's attitude-ridden magic mirror insists that Mick has been touched by shadows, and the Stormwalker realizes that someone is out to enslave her dragon. Now she must free Mick before he kills her . . .

It's been almost a year since bounty hunter
Anna Strong became a vampire, but as she's
about to discover, her greatest powers have
yet to be unleashed. . . .

From

JEANNE C. STEIN

Author of *Retribution*

CHOSEN

An Anna Strong, Vampire Novel

Though Anna has become accustomed to the fact that
she's now a vampire, she still enjoys the illusion of being
human. So when she suddenly notices that her primitive
urges are getting harder to control, she's worried. Then
she's attacked, narrowly escaping with her life. The only
person with enough motive to want her dead is her old
foe—Warren Williams. But another, more dangerous
enemy lies in wait.

What Anna doesn't know is that she's far too valuable to kill. For she's been chosen to shape the destiny of
the vampire race—and all of mankind. . . .

AVAILABLE FROM ACE

penguin.com